"... I'LL SEE YOU DEAD FIRST."

Gaining momentum, the car raced toward the boulevard at the foot of the hill. Gripping the wheel, her eyes wide with fear, Stephanie remembered words Zane hurled at her weeks ago. "You'll never leave me. I'll see you dead first." All of her careful plans were for nothing. He'd beaten her again.

Peripherally, she saw someone on the sidewalk, but she dared not turn to look. She braced herself as the car sped across the intersection and lurched up over the curb. It was a miracle there'd been no cross-traffic. In a blur, she passed a tree, then tore down the grassy embankment.

She was going to die. Her heart thumped frantically as the front wheels hit the water. No! This wasn't the way it was supposed to happen. Oh, God!

Then there was only darkness.

THE BEST IN CONTEMPORARY SUSPENSE

WHERE'S MOMMY NOW?   (366, $4.50)
by Rochelle Majer Krich

Kate Bauers couldn't be a Superwoman any more. Her job, her demanding husband, and her two children were too much to manage on her own. Kate did what she swore she'd never do: let a stranger into her home to care for her children. *Enter Janine.*

Suddenly Kate's world began to fall apart. Her energy and health were slipping away, and the pills her husband gave her and the cocoa Janine gave her made her feel worse. Kate was so sleepy she couldn't concentrate on the little things—like a missing photo, a pair of broken glasses, a nightgown that smelled of a perfume she never wore. Nobody could blame Janine. Everyone loved her. Who could suspect a loving, generous, jewel of a mother's helper?

COME NIGHTFALL   (340, $3.95)
by Gary Amo

Kathryn liked her life as a successful prosecuting attorney. She was a perfect professional and never got personally involved with her cases. Until now. As she viewed the bloody devastation at a rape victim's home, Kathryn swore to the victim to put the rapist behind bars. But she faced an agonizing decision: insist her client testify or to allow her to forget the shattering nightmare.

Soon it was too late for decisions: one of the killers was out on bail, and he knew where Kathryn lived. . . .

FAMILY REUNION   (375, $3.95)
by Nicholas Sarazen

Investigative reporter Stephanie Kenyon loved her job, her apartment, her career. Then she met a homeless drifter with a story to tell. Suddenly, Stephanie knew more than she should, but she was determined to get this story on the front page. She ignored her editor's misgivings, her lover's concerns, even her own sense of danger, and began to piece together a hideous crime that had been committed twenty years ago.

Then the chilling phone calls began. And the threatening letters were delivered. And the box of red roses . . . dyed black. Stephanie began to fear that she would not live to see her story in print.

Available wherever paperbacks are sold, or order direct from the Publisher. Send cover price plus 50¢ per copy for mailing and handling to Pinnacle Books, Dept. 585, 475 Park Avenue South, New York, N.Y. 10016. Residents of New York and Tennessee must include sales tax. DO NOT SEND CASH. For a free Zebra/Pinnacle catalog please write to the above address.

'TIL DEATH DO US PART

PAT WARREN

PINNACLE BOOKS
WINDSOR PUBLISHING CORP.

For Frank — for yesterday, today,
and all my tomorrows

PINNACLE BOOKS

are published by

Windsor Publishing Corp.
475 Park Avenue South
New York, NY 10016

First printing: February, 1992

Printed in the United States of America

Prologue

It was raining, a light summer drizzle, but Stephanie Westover scarcely noticed as she hurried to the red BMW parked in front of her home. Closing the door, she started the engine, then sat back and took in a long breath. As she lowered the window, her eyes automatically shifted for a last, lingering look at the house where she'd lived for nearly two years. The house that after today she probably would not see again for a very long time, if ever.

It was lovely, English Tudor, large and sprawling, with two wings and double front doors leading to a gently rolling lawn lush and green now in early June. From high atop a winding, hilly street, the house looked down on the short expanse of Windmill Road that ended at Lakeshore Drive, which bordered the Detroit River, and beyond, into Canada about a mile across. She'd moved in with the expectant joy of a new bride. Surrounded by the familiar, close-knit community of Grosse Pointe where she had grown up, the house should have been a source of pride and a haven. It had been neither.

Sighing, Stephanie shoved back two years of memories, more bad than good. Zane had left early this morning, reminding her that he'd be out of town on business until late tomorrow afternoon. She'd endured his husbandly kiss goodbye, telling herself it would be the last. Still, she'd had to fight to hide from his shrewd gaze a wave of revulsion at his touch.

Through the dining-room window, Stephanie watched their maid, Eula Johnson, move about, finishing her dusting before leaving for the day. Squirrels scurried up the trunk of the old maple tree in the yard, and a robin, taking shelter under a broad leaf, cocked his head at her curiously. An inviting and peaceful picture. Only nothing had been peaceful or inviting here for a long while.

The quiet hum of the engine purred on, and still Stephanie was reluctant to leave. Despite the recent pain, she would miss her life here in Michigan. She would miss Marjo and her friends at the Grosse Pointe Little Theater, where she was now heading for a final rehearsal of their current play. She would miss the symphony committee and the women at the shelter. Mostly she would miss her father, Stephen Sanders, who would be devastated by her disappearance. He would be hurt, but he would adjust. She couldn't let him pay the price for her mistake. If Stephen knew nothing, then Zane couldn't hurt him.

Her hands gripped the wheel so tightly her knuckles had turned white. With some effort, she made herself relax. She'd had over two months to perfect her plan, to go over every possibility. The arrangements were made, the clothes hidden, the airline tickets purchased and strategically placed. Everything was set to go tonight, after her usual Thursday evening dinner with Marjo. The rain had been a stroke of luck since it would enable her to maneuver the car into the river more easily. Nothing would go wrong. Please, God, nothing.

Stephanie pressed a hand to her stomach to ease the fluttering, then pushed the button, the window sliding up and sealing her in a silent world. Her heart hammered with fear, with anticipation. She had only a few more hours to get through before she'd be on her way. Until then, it was important that she follow her normal routine and not arouse suspicion. If something went wrong, if she'd made a miscalculation, someone could die. No! She couldn't think along those lines. Her plan *had* to work. There is no other way out, she thought as she brushed her hair back with shaky fingers. She had more than herself to think of.

With a last glance at the house, she shifted into drive. Immediately the powerful car drifted forward, quickly picking up speed. Her mind still on her troubled thoughts, Stephanie tapped the brakes to slow her descent down the steep hill. Suddenly, her heart lurched as she realized the brakes weren't responding. Perhaps they were wet from the rain. Her foot trembling, she pressed harder, all the way to the floor. Nothing.

Gaining momentum, the car raced toward the boulevard at the foot of the hill. Gripping the wheel, her eyes wide with fear, Stephanie remembered Zane's words, hurled at her weeks ago. "You'll never leave me. I'll see you dead first." All of her careful plans were for nothing. He'd beaten her again.

Peripherally, she saw someone on the sidewalk, but she dared not turn to look. She braced herself as the car sped across the intersection and lurched up over the curb. It was a miracle there'd been no cross-traffic. In a blur, she passed a tree, then tore down the grassy embankment.

She was going to die. Her heart thumped frantically as the front wheels hit the water. No! This wasn't the way it was supposed to happen. Oh, God!

Then, there was only darkness.

Zane Westover sat at the head of the long conference table, his attention focused on the speaker seated at the far end. The business meeting, taking place in Cleveland, had been under way since early afternoon, and they'd opted to continue through the dinner hour so every one of the twelve members could have his say. Zane's face was expressionless, his eyes never wavering

7

from the current speaker.

A hand touched his shoulder, and he looked up.

"Mr. Westover, a phone call for you, sir."

A mild frown passed over his handsome features. "I'm in the middle of a meeting, Bruce. Can you take a message?"

The young man looked uncomfortable. "It's a Detroit police officer, sir. He says it's important."

His frown deepening, Zane got to his feet. "Gentlemen, excuse me a moment, please." He walked to the credenza by the door and picked up the phone. "Zane Westover."

Facing the wall, he listened attentively. "What? . . . Oh, my God! . . . Where did it happen? . . . No, that can't be."

He breathed hoarsely into the phone. "I see. . . . Of course. I'll catch the next plane back. Thank you, Officer Crawford."

With a steady hand, Zane replaced the receiver. Just before turning around, he allowed himself a small smile.

Bessie Norton was tired. Rubbing her sore knee, the one with the touch of arthritis, she braced herself against the cleaning cart and yawned expansively. Another half an hour and she'd be through for the day, and it wouldn't be a minute too soon. Giving in to a sigh, she straightened her black uniform over her ample hips. She really must go on a diet next week.

She waited impatiently until the teenage girl at the sink finished washing her hands and hurried out of the restroom. Through the swinging doors, she could hear the smooth voice of the announcer paging a traveler to return to the ticket counter. An airport never slept, even during the late evening hours. Bessie sprinkled cleanser into the sink and went to work.

It wasn't a bad job, all in all, especially on nights like this when the last restroom she was responsible for wasn't being heavily used. One more cubicle to clean and she'd be on her way. A woman wearing a drab raincoat and carrying a shopping bag had entered the far stall some time ago, and she still hadn't come out. Angling her head, Bessie heard the unmistakable sounds of . . . The woman was obviously being sick in there. Bessie hoped she wasn't making a mess for her to clean up.

Finishing the sink, she walked over to the bin of used paper towels and emptied it into the trash compartment of her cart. She bent to pick up a few stray wads of paper just as the stall door opened. Grabbing her brush, Bessie turned, then stopped.

That was odd. At the sink washing her hands stood a tall redhead wearing a fashionable green dress. Frowning, Bessie studied the woman, who gave her a quick smile in the mirror. What had happened to the dowdy one who'd walked with a shuffle, stringy hair sticking out from under her wet scarf? Bessie could have sworn that woman had been the last to enter. Shaking her head, she went to work.

She was getting old, she decided as she checked the paper supply. So many people slipped across her vision every day that she lost track. The redhead must have plenty of money. Didn't have to work for it either, by the looks of those long red fingernails. That dress had to be pure silk. Bessie had always wished she could wear clothes like that. But even if she could afford silk, she was too short for that long, lean look. Sighing again in acceptance of her fate, she came out and dropped her supplies in the cart.

The room was momentarily empty, and Bessie was glad. She didn't feel like smiling or talking. Quickly she sprayed air freshener all around and was about to leave when she noticed more trash in the bin she'd just emptied. Her supervisor was a stickler for details and might be checking tonight. She pulled out the bin. One used towel and a large rolled-up paper sack were in it. About to stuff them into the trash compartment,

9

her curiosity stopped her.

It wasn't every day someone discarded a bag from Saks Fifth Avenue. Unrolling it, she peeked inside just as a woman with a small child entered noisily and headed for one of the stalls. Bessie pulled out the contents. The wrinkled raincoat, a damp scarf, muddy tennis shoes, and wet underwear.

Bessie frowned at the door through which the redhead had disappeared minutes before. So she hadn't been mistaken. The woman had changed her looks completely. Shrugging, she stuffed the items back into the bag. It was none of her business if that woman wanted to disguise herself. Watching passengers come and go for nearly twenty years on the job, she'd seen it before. People had their reasons — a married woman meeting an equally married man, a teenager running away, a wife trying to shake a jealous husband. All kinds of problems in this world.

Adding the bag to the rest of her trash, Bessie pushed her cart out the restroom door. The loudspeaker urged several people to pick up white paging phones. Moving somewhat wearily, Bessie made her way to the airport utility room.

Chapter One

Stephen Sanders moved from the heat and sunshine of a June afternoon into the cool dimness of the sedate old church on Lakeshore Boulevard. Rich mahogany pews, velvet-cushioned benches, the raised pulpit off to the side, and a huge hanging transparent cross through which could be seen the magnificent mosaic depicting a joyful sunrise.

Standing at the rear, Stephen patted his damp forehead with an immaculate white handkerchief. He needed this moment, this quiet moment, before the others arrived. Drawing a deep breath, he looked around the church of his youth. He'd been married here, had held the funeral service for his wife here twenty years ago. And now he was attending a memorial service for his only child.

He wasn't a religious man in the true sense, he supposed. He believed in a Supreme Being certainly, but had little patience with rituals; therefore his attendance had been sporadic. Still, there was comfort here, if vague and fleeting. And, God knows, he could use some comfort, though he doubted if he could find enough to dispel the rage he'd felt building inside him during the past week.

Only one week since he'd received that devastating phone call. A terrible accident. Stephanie's car careening out of control, plunging into the rushing De-

11

troit River. Stephanie missing, presumed drowned. Stephanie gone.

Stephanie Sanders Westover, his bright and lovely daughter, only twenty-seven. Slender, almost willowy, with blue eyes so like his own and long hair the color of wheat blowing in a Kansas breeze. So alive, so sweet, so caring. Stephanie with her warm laugh, her quick wit, her quiet charm—gone. All gone.

No! He would not—could not—believe it. Stephen smoothed his thick white hair with a trembling hand. She wasn't dead. She couldn't be. There was no body, no casket up there in front of the altar. There was only a perfunctory police report, one of her shoes and her purse found several miles downstream from the submerged BMW. And there was Zane Westover, with his smooth and practiced presence, entering from the side door. A chilling reminder that he'd warned his daughter not to marry the man.

Zane had been the one to call him, sounding properly mournful. Disbelief had been Stephen's first reaction, then fury, and finally a growing suspicion. Stephanie was a cautious driver, not given to daydreaming or impulsive moves. The police report on her car wasn't available yet, but he was most anxious to see it. There'd been trouble in his daughter's marriage for some time, he was certain, though she'd taken great care to hide the signs from him. Even as a child, Stephanie had hated confrontations. Maybe she'd run from Zane rather than face their differences. But then, where was she?

The room was suddenly too warm, the smell of flowers too cloying, and Stephen longed to step outside and breathe deeply of fresher air. Shoving his hands deep in his pants pockets, however, he decided he wanted to watch Zane's performance more than he wanted to escape. He had to hand it to him—the man was good. Zane's chiseled profile, tanned to perfection, showed just the right traces of sadness, confusion, and disbelief. His tailored suit—black, of

12

course—immaculate white shirt, gray silk tie, and Italian leather loafers were the best money could buy. His handshake as he greeted friends and neighbors was firm, his eyes clear yet reflecting flashes of pain.

Zane had moved into Grosse Pointe a mere four years ago after purchasing an import business on Jefferson Avenue known as The Antique Connection. Next he'd completely renovated and refurnished one of the large old mansions on a quiet street off Lakeshore Drive. Then he'd set about meeting the right people, being sponsored for membership in the best clubs, and getting himself invited to dine with the oldest and wealthiest families. And he'd charmed his neighbors into thinking he was just like them—a decent, honest citizen and a true gentleman. Yes, he'd managed to fool them all, but not Stephen.

Watching his son-in-law approach, Stephen felt his hands curl into fists and he had to force himself to unclench his fingers. There was an arrogant confidence about Zane that always made Stephen's blood boil. Maintaining his role as chief mourner, Zane had a somber expression, but his eyes were sharp and vigilant.

"Thank you for coming, Stephen," Zane said in his slightly high-pitched voice. "This is difficult for both of us."

He noticed Zane hadn't offered to shake hands. From the beginning, the man had been astute enough to realize that Stephen didn't like him and probably hadn't wanted to chance a rebuff. "It's been only a week since the accident," Stephen answered, his own voice curt despite his best efforts. "What was the big hurry in scheduling this service?"

Zane's dark eyes narrowed slightly, his dislike at being questioned obvious. "What would be the point in waiting? She's gone, isn't she?"

If Zane was hoping to get a rise out of him, he had miscalculated. Through the years, Stephen had all but perfected the art of cloaking his feelings in business

13

dealings. The ability carried over into his personal life. Yes, she was gone—but maybe not dead. For now, he thought it best to keep his suspicions to himself. "We could have used a day or two more to get used to the idea."

"I'll never get used to the idea," Zane said smoothly. "There'll never be anyone but Stephanie for me." He waved a manicured hand adorned with a dull gold and diamond pinkie ring in the direction of the altar. "I've reserved a seat up front for you, alongside me."

"Thank you, but I prefer to stand back here for now."

Zane's displeasure at Stephen's refusal flashed across his features for an instant, then was gone. "As you choose." Turning, he moved up the aisle to greet recent arrivals and accept their condolences.

Stephen watched a bulky figure unobtrusively follow Zane, the man's small eyes alert and watchful. Chester Thomas, a former boxer and Zane's constant shadow, rarely joined in conversations, yet always hovered nearby. Quite some time ago, Stephen had asked Zane why he seemed to think he needed a bodyguard in this quiet, affluent neighborhood. Zane had calmly explained that Chester was his chauffeur, since he hated to drive. A chauffeur, Stephen mused as he watched the broad-shouldered man with small, mean eyes swing about and check out the crowd. About as deliberately misleading as the rest of Zane's odd explanations.

Stepping up to Zane was Bob Triner. A bookish man with a slight build and thick glasses, Bob was Zane's attorney, accountant, and adviser. Stephen assumed Bob to be a professional hired to keep his boss out of legal hot water. Still, Bob was more likable, more genuine, than the other two. Why, Stephen wondered, and not for the first time, did Zane not go anywhere without one or both of those men close behind?

14

At the sound of a door opening Stephen glanced toward the back, then smiled as he watched a striking brunette in a white linen suit enter. She removed her sunglasses to reveal dark eyes slightly swollen from recent tears. Marjo Collins, Stephanie's college roommate and closest friend, turned toward him. He walked over to meet her, extending both hands.

"Stephen. Damn, I can't believe this is happening." With effort, she blinked back a fresh rush of tears.

"I know, Marjo. I'm having trouble accepting it myself." He allowed her a moment to compose herself. "Have the police been in touch with you?"

"Hell, yes, they have—twice. I couldn't tell them much, but they kept on asking." She looked longingly toward the door. "God, I need a cigarette. I don't suppose I can smoke in here?"

Stephen shook his head, her irreverence oddly lifting his spirits. Marjo was brash and outspoken, and he'd always loved her for it. Her comments had undoubtedly shocked even the seasoned officers. "Can you tell me what you said to the police?"

"Just that I'd talked with Stephanie that morning. She told me she planned to leave around four, run some errands, then come straight to the theater and join me. After the rehearsal, we were to have a late dinner, which we usually do on Thursdays. As you know, she never showed." Marjo frowned as she met his gaze. "They asked me if she'd been upset, if Stephanie was the type who might commit suicide. I told them, 'Hell, no, she wouldn't.'"

Stephen nodded. "I agree." He drew her to the back, to a more private corner. "Had Stephanie mentioned that she'd been having problems lately? I hate to ask you to reveal a confidence, but under the circumstances . . ."

Marjo glanced pointedly up the aisle to where Zane stood, surrounded by a small circle of people. "Her marriage wasn't happy, I'm certain of it, though Stephanie always preferred to keep her worries to herself. It's just that after ten years, I could read her pretty well. Something happened around two months ago, something that upset her and made her more closemouthed than ever. I tried to get her to open up, but she didn't reveal much." Marjo's eyes filled with anger as she looked over at Zane again. "I know that son-of-a-bitch changed Steffie. She hasn't been the same since she met him."

So her best friend had sensed dissension in his daughter's life, too. If only he'd pressed harder last Sunday when Stephanie had appeared unexpectedly at his house for brunch. She'd been restless and distracted, but when he'd asked if anything was troubling her, she'd put on a bright smile and brushed aside his concern. Then, as she was leaving, she'd hugged him impulsively for a long moment. He'd watched her leave, a thoughtful frown on his face, yet he hadn't called her back. Now, Stephen took a deep breath and wished desperately that he had. "Yes, I think Zane knows more than he's telling us."

Marjo fought a shiver. "I can't bear the thought of Stephanie somewhere in that dirty river. Why can't those inept cops find her body so we can give her a decent burial?"

"Maybe because there is no body."

Marjo's long fingers curled into his sleeve. "What do you mean? Do you think. . . ."

Placing a hand on Stephen's shoulder, an usher interrupted, requesting that they be seated as the services were about to begin. Stephen led Marjo to the last pew and sat down beside her.

Her eyes bright, she leaned close to him. "Stephen," she whispered, "do you know something?"

His mouth was grim. "Not yet."

Several friends and associates stopped on their way down the aisle, offering Stephen their sympathy and preventing further discussion. He shook hands with his attorney, Charles Hastings, and with his closest neighbors, the Whittakers. He supposed he should

16

have made himself more accessible as people had entered. But he hadn't felt like accepting condolences, however heartfelt. He didn't even feel like being here because he couldn't accept that Stephanie was dead.

Half listening to the eulogy begin, Stephen let his mind drift. Too much didn't make sense. Stephanie had been more introspective of late, but he'd stake his life that she'd never consider suicide. He'd ruled out an accident, too. He'd taught her to drive himself when she'd been fifteen, and she had always been a careful and conscientious driver. Though it had been raining that afternoon, the roads somewhat slippery, Stephanie had driven in this area all her adult life. She knew its hills and shortcuts and curves, knew every bush and tree and stop sign. And she'd maintained her car with almost religious fervor.

The most damning evidence was that there had been no skid marks. There would have been, had Stephanie tried to brake after losing control. But there was more here than the obvious. Perhaps she'd discovered something about Zane, about one of his shady operations, and he'd set her up. Stephen tightened with anger as he forced himself to consider that possibility. Of course, Zane wouldn't dirty his own hands, but he could have had one of his henchmen rid him of his wife's suddenly unwelcome presence, then send her car into the river to mislead them all.

Stephen's jaw clenched and he forced himself to relax as he wrestled with that thought. Perhaps she'd merely left Zane and he'd staged the accident to cover up his embarrassment. Or — and Stephen liked this scenario best — she'd planned the whole thing to get away from Zane and was now somewhere far off and safe. If only he knew . . .

The authorities had been of little help. The Grosse Pointe police were fairly small-town, and the Detroit police struggled daily to keep up with a staggering crime rate. They'd likely jump at the chance to accept the obvious and label it an accidental drowning.

17

Stephen wondered if Zane had cooperated with the investigation, such as it was. He'd become rich and powerful in a relatively short time, with rumors that tied him to the underworld abounding. And he had the appearance of a man who thought himself above the law. As Stephen stared at the back of Zane's head, he wished he could shake some answers out of the man.

Shifting in his seat, he found his thoughts scrambling around like so many mice in a maze. Perhaps he should go to the police anyway. He crossed his legs restlessly. They wouldn't believe him, nor could they spare the manpower to launch an investigation based on his wild speculations. Yet he couldn't do it alone. This sort of thing would require a man with police connections, lots of free time, and a taste for danger.

Suddenly, for the first time in days, Stephen felt a surge of hope. There was such a person. Luke Varner. The perfect man. And Luke owed him.

As Zane moved to the pulpit and began his remarks, Stephen leaned close to Marjo. He couldn't stand listening to more, and he couldn't stand waiting any longer. "I've got to leave. I'll be in touch." She nodded as he rose. Leaving the coolness of the church, he blinked into the late afternoon sunshine as he headed for his Lincoln.

Luke was probably still living on his houseboat up on Lake St. Clair on Michigan's eastern shore. It would take only one phone call to be certain. Getting behind the wheel, Stephen started the car. It was a nice day for a drive.

The fish weren't biting. Luke Varner removed his bare feet from the rail along his back deck and got up from his canvas chair. Anchoring his pole in its brace, he reeled in and secured the line. Twilight was usually a good time for fishing near the dock, but the fish were elsewhere tonight. Raising his tanned arms toward the cloudy sky, he stretched, easing the kinks from his shoulders. He'd been sitting still for two hours and that was about one too many for his restless nature.

Moving toward the galley, he heard the voice of his friend, Josh Kemper, echo in his head. *You've got to learn to relax.* Josh had sounded more like the doctor he was than an old friend. Luke had spent nearly twenty years honing his skills, he'd reminded Josh, teaching himself to be always alert, to sleep lightly and seldom, to move soundlessly, to hear noises others didn't, to be vigilant and ever ready. And now, for the past six months, he'd had to set all that training aside and learn to relax. Easier said than done. Maybe I'll never learn, Luke thought as he poured himself a glass of cold milk.

Walking back onto the open deck of his houseboat, he squinted into the setting sun. A radical change of lifestyle has to be one of the hardest things a man ever faces. Bad enough if it is by choice, but if it goes against the grain, it's uphill all the way, every day. He took a long pull on his milk, feeling the liquid cooling his insides as it drifted downward.

Another something he had to return to, watching everything he ate and drank or face the possibility of ulcer surgery. The same ulcer he'd had at least ten years, flaring up several months ago. Job related stress, Josh had said. And the booze he'd drenched it in for a while there hadn't helped. No question about it, life at times was a bitch, and getting older a pain in the butt.

Forty years old today. The middle of the span, and reputed to be the day life began. For some maybe. His own had taken a severe downhill spiral two years ago when they'd found his wife, Kathy, dead of a drug overdose. Everything had changed for him that day, Luke acknowledged. For a long time after that, he'd gone through the motions of living, but like an unfeeling automaton. Colors were no longer bright, food had no taste, and laughter was something he couldn't quite manage.

Propping one foot on the waist-high rail, Luke leaned forward, recalling the rage he'd felt immediately after the funeral of the poor, mixed-up woman he'd buried, remembering her as the lovely young innocent she'd been when they'd married. The fact that soon afterward Sonny Poston, who'd been responsible for her death, had wound up in a coffin of his own hadn't eased the pain, though at the time Luke had thought it would. If revenge hadn't been the answer, and relaxation didn't seem to be, then what?

Maybe it was too late for him. Maybe he'd become more animal than man, all the goodness, the humanity, in him buried with his dead dreams and disillusioned wife. Certainly there'd been plenty of his fellow officers at Police Headquarters who'd thought he'd lost it, some who probably still did. He'd thrown himself into his work, but he'd had difficulty controlling his thoughts. And his temper. Finally, six months ago, there'd been an incident where he'd whirled out of control. Captain Renwick, he'd come to realize, had been right to relieve him of all his duties and put him on enforced leave, though at the time it had been a bitter pill to swallow.

If he ever wanted to return to duty, he'd have to come to grips with his loss, to get his head straightened out, to deal with the delayed reaction to his anguish. That's what the captain and Josh and a few others had told him. A man he knew had led him to this houseboat, told him to fish and to heal. He'd found the former far easier to do. Some days, Luke wasn't certain he wanted to go back, to work undercover again, to brush shoulders with the scum of society day in and day out. Other days, he missed it like hell.

If not that, then what? Money wasn't a problem, but desire was. He simply couldn't think of a thing he wanted to do, except drift on the lake and wait for the fish to find him. Besides, police work was the only thing he knew how to do, the job he'd been trained for. And he'd been damn good at it, until Kathy's death and the loss of his control, his objectivity.

Forty years old. Too young to quit, too old to start over again. Or maybe too tired, too worn out, with too many memories that shared his pillow every night. Maybe when he mastered the fine art of relaxation, something would occur to him.

The sound of a car approaching along the dirt road that led to the dock caught his attention. He had few visitors and desired even fewer. Without much enthusiasm, Luke drained his glass and moved to the stairwell that led to the dock.

Stephen pulled his Lincoln next to a dark van with shuttered windows and turned off the engine. Climbing out, he removed his jacket and tie, throwing them on the front seat. He turned then and stared down the weathered dock toward the houseboat anchored at the far end. He hadn't had any trouble finding Luke Varner's place. Captain Renwick had given him good directions, and a warning. Luke had come a long way, but probably still wasn't himself, the captain had said, so don't expect too much.

Stephen had met Luke Varner five years ago, on an insurance investigation that had involved one of Stephen's companies. Luke had been in charge of it. He'd been able to provide important information, at some risk to himself, and had helped Luke crack open a case of widespread fraud. That little caper had gotten Luke promoted to detective.

He hadn't seen Luke in half a year, since shortly after Varner had been forced into taking a leave of absence from the department. Stephen had heard of his problems, the accusations against him, and had gone to visit him. He'd seen the empty eyes, the haunted look, the pain. He'd reached for the phone and called a man he knew who was selling a houseboat. By the weekend, Luke had moved aboard. Since then, Stephen had inquired about him from time to time through friends at the precinct and heard he was healing, but slowly. Not unusual for a man who'd been to hell and back.

They weren't exactly close friends, but they'd stayed in touch, each man respecting the other. Twice Stephen had helped Luke when he'd needed something or someone. He figured Luke owed him. Now Stephen was about to call in his markers. Walking down the pier, he knew Luke Varner was a man who honored his debts.

Stephen saw Luke waiting for him in that quiet, watchful way he had. He was tall, several inches over Stephen's six feet, his body slim and hard looking, the muscles of his bare chest firm and without spare flesh. He wore only white, rolled-up deck pants. His dark hair was cut short and more sprinkled with gray than Stephen remembered. His face was lined from the sun and years of living, more craggy than handsome, most would say; and he hadn't bothered to shave. His eyes were pewter gray and serious, with no hint of surprise at this unexpected arrival. His stance, though not hostile, wasn't warmly welcoming either. Undoubtedly his police training had taught him to keep his expression unreadable.

As Stephen reached the steps, Luke held out his hand. "Stephen, it's been some time."

Stephen shook the hard, callused hand. "Yes. How are you, Luke?"

Varner shrugged as he took a step backward. "I'm here. Come on board." Leading the way into the comfortable living area, Luke indicated a chair. "Would you like a drink? I have beer, milk, or . . ."

"A beer would taste good." Stephen lowered himself into the corner of the brown corduroy couch and watched Luke disappear into the galley. The place was neat and clean, if not terribly homey. The side windows were cranked open to the evening breezes, and the gentle rocking was not unpleasant. There wasn't another vessel around for some miles, though. Stephen wondered how Luke handled the isolation, the loneliness.

From the corner of his eye, Stephen saw movement. A large cat unfolded itself from a footstool and moseyed over, lazily sniffing him from a careful distance. It was beige with yellow streaks and barely curious, amber eyes. "I see you have a roommate," Stephen said, holding a hand out to the cat.

"Yeah," Luke answered, searching for the bottle opener. "He wandered aboard one day and never left. He's a little crotchety, like me, and not too crazy about people. We get along fine."

"What do you call him?"

"Benjamin. He's got some teeth missing. Probably been in as many fights as I have. I have to cut up his tuna. Damn nuisance." Luke returned carrying a brown bottle and a glass of milk. Handing Stephen the bottle, he sat down in a plaid recliner opposite his uninvited guest and waited.

Needing a moment to collect his thoughts, Stephen took a long swallow of beer as Benjamin wandered back to his perch. He indicated the milk. "On the wagon?"

"I'm afraid so. I have a doctor friend who's itching to practice with his brand new scalpel, so I'm trying to behave."

Luke had been hitting the bottle pretty heavily after his leave from the force. He looked far healthier now. "It's not easy, I know. I've got high blood pressure, and those damn doctors are always after me. No caffeine, whiskey, or cigars. I have trouble following orders. They don't leave you with much."

"There's always sex."

"I'm sure that's the next thing to go." He placed his left ankle on his right knee and met Luke's eyes. "Seriously, are you doing okay?"

"Some days."

23

"Thinking of going back to work yet?"

"Not really."

"Don't you miss it, the challenges, the satisfaction?"

Luke set down his glass, shoved out the leg rest, and rearranged his lanky frame. "Why don't we cut to the chase, Stephen. What's up?"

Stephen let out a long breath. "I'd have thought you might have heard about it on the news or read the story in the paper."

"I don't own a TV, and I stopped getting the paper. What story?"

"Last Thursday, my daughter, Stephanie, lost control of her BMW off Lakeshore near her home and wound up in the Detroit River. She's presumed drowned."

A loss, now that was something Luke could relate to easily. "Damn, Stephen, I'm sorry. I . . . *Presumed* drowned? Do you suspect foul play? Are they doing an autopsy on her?"

"They haven't found her body."

A horse of another color. Luke rubbed at the stubble on his chin. "Are you sure she was in the car?"

"The police report includes a witness, a man walking his dog nearby, who claims he's her neighbor and recognized Stephanie as the driver. So far, they've found only her purse and one shoe."

Considering possibilities, Luke frowned. "The current along there can be fairly strong. The body could be quite a distance away by now. Or caught in a pile of river debris along the way."

Uncrossing his legs, Stephen sat forward. "Ever have a hunch so strong it won't leave you alone?"

Hell, yes, he had, regularly and often. Intuition. He'd solved more cases relying on instinct than on facts. "You got a hunch?"

"Two ideas occur to me, and I don't know which to go with. Do you know Zane Westover, Stephanie's husband?"

Everyone at HQ had heard of Zane Westover since he'd hit town from Cleveland some years ago. Clever white collar criminal, operating several businesses, some legit, some not. Mostly, he imported antiques and artifacts from Europe and Africa through a Canadian affiliate. There'd been heavy suspicions that he also dealt in stolen goods he managed to smuggle in, but they'd never gotten enough proof. The word was that Zane had several judges and a couple of city council members in his pocket, which was why he'd never even had a parking ticket. "Yeah, I've heard of him. I didn't know your daughter had married him."

"Against my wishes. I believe their marriage was rocky, but Stephanie was always good at covering up her feelings. My first theory is that she found out something about Zane, something that could hurt him, and he arranged the so-called accident. The police report showed no skid marks to indicate she'd been trying to stop. They haven't released the report on the car yet."

"You're thinking that someone could have tampered with the brakes."

"Yes. She lives at the top of a steep incline. If she got in unaware . . ." Stephen was unable to complete the thought. "She was on her way to meet a friend at the little theater where she does volunteer work. Only she never got there."

He hated to ask, but he needed to know. "Was she depressed? What about suicide?"

"Absolutely not. Her friends agree. Not Stephanie."

"And you think Zane Westover is capable of murder? Let's hear from the cool, dispassionate businessman on this one, not the grieving father."

"Both of them say he is, without a doubt."

Luke studied the man sitting on the couch. Stephen Sanders had inherited money from his family, then proceeded to make even more. He was shrewd and intelligent, not one to go off half-cocked. He'd stood

25

firm and unafraid during the harrowing investigation Luke had conducted. And he'd shown compassion and understanding when Luke had needed help a few months ago. If Stephen had suspicions, they were undoubtedly well founded. "What's your other hunch?"

"That Stephanie wanted out of a bad marriage, faked her own death and took off."

Keeping his features even, Luke sipped his milk. "What exactly is wrong with her marriage that she'd go to such extremes? Why not divorce? Why not come to you? You're not exactly without influence."

Stephen propped his elbows on his knees and shook his head. "Damned if I have any answers, just guesses. It was no secret that Zane wanted children — and was upset that Stephanie hadn't gotten pregnant. She'd never mentioned divorce to me, but maybe she had to him and he'd refused. I believe Westover's a small-town hood who made a pile of dirty money and then wanted status to go with it. He came here looking to marry class, to climb the social ladder, to buy respectability. He found what he wanted in Stephanie, then found he couldn't control her. It wouldn't surprise me if he'd threatened her — if she'd mentioned divorce."

It wasn't unlikely that a man, especially a dangerous man, would arrange his wife's death rather than lose a lot of money in a divorce settlement. "What threat could he use on her?"

"I don't know. As to why she didn't come to me, that one really hurts. Her mother died when she was only seven, and we've been very close. I'd even thought maybe she hated to admit she'd made a mistake in marrying Zane after I'd warned her against him. But Stephanie wouldn't disappear just to salvage her pride. Maybe Zane threatened to harm me. There's no love lost between us."

Luke finished his milk thoughtfully. "Maybe Zane's threats weren't against her or you. Maybe she left so he wouldn't hurt someone else she loves. Have any idea who that someone might be?"

"We're a relatively small family. Other than me, there's only her grandmother, Juliana Richards, who's eighty-two, and my brother and his family, but they live in Los Angeles. Stephanie has a lot of friends. Marjo Collins is probably the closest. I can't imagine why anyone would threaten any of us."

"How about a man? Could Stephanie have been having an affair and been found out?" Releasing the chair's footrest, he got up and moved toward the galley.

Stephen's response was quick and tinged with just a shade of indignation. "Not Stephanie. She might walk away, but she wouldn't be unfaithful."

Luke came back, chewing on a granola bar. "Is that a fact? Every woman is some father's little girl, and some women do have affairs. If we're going to work together, you're going to have to set aside your father hat and explore all possibilities."

"Then you *will* help me?"

He had all but said that, hadn't he? Surprised at how much the case appealed to him, Luke offered a granola bar to Stephen, then sat back down when the older man shook his head. There were so many elements here that were puzzling, and puzzles had always fascinated him. "You got a copy of the police report and maybe a snapshot of Stephanie?"

Stephen stood and reached into his pocket for his wallet and a folded envelope. "Right here." He handed both to Luke and stood waiting.

Luke studied the picture. Long blond hair falling past her shoulders. Nice bones and a mouth that gave him pause, full lips just barely open. Her eyes were deep blue and held a touch of shyness. Her expression was pensive, with a hint of vulnerability. She was almost too slender. The word fragile came to mind. "Is this recent?"

"Yes. She wears glasses sometimes, the oversize

27

kind. She's about five foot seven, maybe a hundred fifteen pounds and . . . and she's all I have in this world." Stephen sat down heavily.

Luke set the picture and report aside and sighed deeply. He was being reeled in like a fish on a line, and he knew it. He also knew he owed Stephen Sanders for past favors. Finishing his granola bar, he stood and walked to the back of the houseboat. "Come out here a minute, Stephen. I want to show you something."

Slowly, Stephen walked out. He was prepared for the refusal, prepared to be told that all Luke wanted to do was sit out here and fish after what he'd been through. He wouldn't remind him of debts owed. The man had been wounded deeply and was entitled to heal in his own time. Coming alongside, Stephen looked down at the spot on the boat, where Luke was pointing. "What is it?"

"Maybe you can't read it since it's upside down. It's the name of my boat. *Lifeline*." Luke straightened and met the older man's troubled gaze. "Lifeline, that's what you handed me a while back, remember?" He saw Stephen nod, saw him fight the hope that sprang into his eyes. "Good, because I have a long memory, too. I'll do the best I can to find Stephanie. If she's alive."

Swallowing hard, Stephen touched his arm. "Thank you."

"Don't thank me till we find her." He moved back inside and turned on a table lamp. From a cluttered desk in the corner, he picked up a yellow note pad and sat down to make a few notes. "I'll study the police report and talk to a couple of guys I know downtown. I want to go over the car. I assume they've brought it up?"

"Yes." Stephen sat on the edge of the couch.

"I'll need you to do some checking at your end, some information you can get faster than I can. Inquire about her bank accounts, see if she's recently

28

withdrawn any substantial amounts of money. Disappearing doesn't come cheap. Find out if Zane has any big insurance policies on her. Since you're in the business, that shouldn't be hard for you." He scribbled on the pad as he spoke.

"Of course. I should have thought of that."

"I want to talk with the eye witness, the guy with the dog. Later, I'll visit this Marjo friend of Stephanie's and the Westover hired help. Meanwhile, I want you to make a list of all of Stephanie's likes and dislikes, her favorite things to do, foods she likes, recreational choices, medical history, taste in clothes, list of friends. Everything and anything you can tell me about her." Standing, he handed Stephen the sheet of paper.

"What about Zane?"

"For now, let's keep him out of this. If our preliminary findings indicate foul play, we'll move in that direction. But if they point to the fact that Stephanie *wanted* to disappear, then we don't want to tip our hand to her husband. If she's running, then most likely, it's him she's running from."

Stephen stood and placed the folded paper in his shirt pocket. "Tell me your gut feeling. Do you think we have a chance of finding her?"

Luke walked with him toward the stairs. "If she's planned this alone, planned to drop out of sight and start a new life for whatever reason, the chances are good. Let's face it, most ordinary citizens are amateurs at this sort of thing. And usually they're working out the details under emotional duress. Somewhere along the line, she's made a mistake, or will make one. When she does, it'll lead us to her."

"I certainly hope so."

"One thing I want to make clear, Stephen. If I find her — and there's no guarantee I will — and she doesn't want to return, that'll have to be her decision. I believe in live and let live. I'm not dragging her back to you, or anyone else, against her will."

"I understand. I don't want that either. I just want to know she's alive and safe." He clasped Luke's shoulder briefly. "I really appreciate your help."

"Let's not celebrate quite yet."

"We haven't talked about your fee."

"Let's just say you paid in advance for this one. You can cover my expenses, if it comes to that. I'll be by sometime tomorrow and we can compare notes."

Stephen stepped up onto the dock. The dark scent of water and fish hung in the heavy summer air. A cricket nearby serenaded with its monotonous tune. He took a deep breath. "I may even be able to get to sleep now. Good night."

Leaning on the railing, Luke watched him return to his car and drive away. The moon peeked out from behind a cloud, and a night bird flew past and settled in the welcoming arms of a weeping willow. From his pocket, he removed his pipe and clamped it between his teeth. He'd given up smoking some time ago, very reluctantly and not without considerable discomfort. But he still loved the smell of tobacco, so he occasionally puffed on a pipe. But tonight he didn't light it.

Hearing his stomach rumble, he thought of a steak, rare, and a big salad. Despite the milk and granola bar, he was actually hungry, something he so rarely was anymore.

He felt something else, too. A rush of adrenaline, the possibility of challenge. It felt good to be thinking about a case again. This was right up his alley. Maybe he wasn't ready to go back to his structured unit yet, but listening to Stephen, he'd felt the juices begin to flow, a flutter of the old excitement.

Walking inside, he picked up Stephanie Westover's picture. Was she still alive? Did that two-bit hood she'd married arrange her watery death? Or did she take off to begin over somewhere? And if that, then why? Her eyes stared back at him almost wistfully. *Where are you, lovely lady?*

Benjamin meowed, stretched and gazed at him with

accusing amber eyes. "All right, I'll get us some dinner."

In the galley, Luke opened the cupboard and stared up at his bottle of scotch. Just one would taste good, though it would probably rip at his insides.

He reached for the bottle and a glass. What the hell. Too squeaky clean was goddamn boring.

Chapter Two

Stephanie stood staring into the mirror, staring at the face of a stranger. The many disguises she'd used on the long trip — through strange cities and busy airports — had seemed temporary, almost a game. But this was more permanent and lent a frightening reality to an already scary situation.

Gone was the long blond hair that had hung past her shoulders, replaced by a shorter cut, dyed a warm brown and softly curling about her face. Gone also was the makeup padding she'd used to flesh out her hollow cheekbones in order to alter her facial construction. That was no longer necessary, nor could she have worn it every day.

The eyes that studied her were different, too. The deep blue had been changed to a dark brown. She'd set aside her glasses and stepped into one of those quickie optical places where they'd given her an eye exam and a pair of tinted contacts in about two hours. Amazing what a difference just hair and eyes could make. The worried look was still there, though, brown eyes or blue, as well as the wariness and the fatigue. Work on that, Stephanie, she thought.

No, not Stephanie, she reminded herself. Stephanie Westover was gone, drowned in a terrible accident. She'd gone to the library and looked up the newspaper account of her own death. It had given her an eerie feeling, despite her determination. She was Juli

Richards now—and had her new social security card to prove it. Surprising how easy it was to get one of those. She'd checked that information out by phone before she'd left Michigan. She'd told a few careful lies and had her new number and card in hours. Lying was getting altogether too easy.

Turning from the mirror, she moved to her closet. A sparse wardrobe, all brand new. And different from the clothes she'd chosen in the past, deliberately so. Before her wardrobe had been conservative, mostly with designer labels since she'd had plenty of money throughout her twenty-seven years. But the things hanging neatly in a row had come off the rack and were casual and youthful. Stephanie knew she could easily pass for five years younger with her new hairdo and clothes. Little things like that could make such a difference.

She reached for a pair of jeans and pulled them on, snapping them over her flat stomach. Her waist was still slim, but that would soon be changing. Her breasts had already enlarged, and there was a new tenderness to them. She could do very little to disguise her shape except camouflage her upper body with loose, floppy tops. Reaching for a pale yellow, baggy shirt, she slipped it on and examined herself in the mirror. It would have to do.

Keeping her makeup to an absolute minimum would foster the illusion of youth, and would be a departure from her former ways. Not that she'd ever made up heavily, but she knew how, what with her theater training. Now she'd let the freckles she'd cleverly hidden show through. And she was devoid of all jewelry, though that wasn't such a big change either as she'd never worn much. Glancing at her left hand, she rubbed the spot on her third finger where her wedding ring had rested for just under two years. She'd left it on her night stand at home, as often was her habit. She'd had no difficulty walking away from her ring or the man who'd given it to her. Cocking her head at her mirror image, she ruffled her new feathery haircut. The stranger resembled a college co-ed, not a Grosse Pointe housewife. So far so good.

Closing the closet door, Stephanie walked over to the fourposter maple bed and picked up her new canvas purse. Just this morning, she'd sewn into the lining something too valuable to carry around, something she must put into a safety deposit box as quickly as possible. But she knew she needed two pieces of identification in order to establish a bank account. She had the social security card. A driver's license was next. She had a plan, and she prayed it would work.

Earlier this morning, she'd phoned a driving school and enrolled herself in a crash course. She'd explained she'd grown up in New York City and had never needed to learn to drive, though she'd driven a tractor on an uncle's farm years ago. That would explain why she didn't have a license from another state to surrender, yet had a working knowledge of driving. Armed with her certificate from the school, she'd go to a nearby Florida Driver's License Examining Station and apply for her license. When she had her temporary, she'd hustle to a bank and get that box. Then she could at least stop worrying that her purse, which contained the package, would get lost or stolen.

With a sigh, Stephanie strolled over to the second-story window. A lovely sunny day with blue skies. A tall royal palm tree swayed gently in the slight breeze coming off the nearby lake. A typical summer day in central Florida. Angling her head, she saw the discreet sign on the front walkway: Barbizon Hotel for Women. A quaint old Southern tradition, and she'd been delighted when she'd found the charming inn. Tucked back among the trees on Orlando's Edgewater Drive, it offered a sanctuary she badly needed. A temporary home, but she felt fairly protected within the stuccoed walls surrounded by huge cypress trees heavy with dangling Spanish moss.

34

The days and nights of running, of constantly looking over her shoulder, of changing her looks and her destination in her frantic need to throw off anyone who might try to trace her were over. For the time being. She had no illusions that she might not have covered her tracks well enough, or that she'd forgotten some small revealing detail. During the weeks of organizing, she'd gone over and over her plan with the thoroughness only fear for her life could have brought about. Yet at the last minute, Zane had managed to outsmart her.

It was a miracle that she'd escaped the watery grave he'd planned for her. Actually he'd only accelerated her schedule, but he didn't know it. If he suspected that she hadn't drowned, that she was alive and had something he desperately wanted, he'd never stop searching for her. And he was far more used to games than she. If she could manage to outwit him from now on, it would be a first. But she was driven by a very strong incentive, the deepest need she'd ever had. She pressed a protective hand to her abdomen. For her baby's sake, she *would* get away from him. She simply had to.

After she had her driver's license and the bank arrangements were made, she'd hole up for a while in this quiet room. If and when she felt secure, perhaps she'd venture out and look for a job. A safe job where she could meld in with the crowd and go unnoticed. A job as different from something Stephanie Westover would do as night was from day. A job that the new Juli Richards would be drawn to. It, too, would be temporary, but it would give her something to do other than sit in this silent room and worry.

The rumble in her stomach reminded her she hadn't eaten in a long while. The hard knot of fear induced by days of anxiety had abated somewhat. She'd gotten sick in a couple of the airport restrooms and again on the plane, but she hoped that by now she could keep down a light meal. She couldn't afford to lose more weight. She'd experienced some bleeding, probably caused by that torturous swim, and it had frightened her. But that, too, had disappeared.

Just to be certain, she'd gone to a doctor yesterday, giving him a false name and address. After her tests, he'd assured her that both she and the baby were fine. He'd given her vitamins, a diet plan, and had told her to get plenty of rest. Twelve hours of sleep last night, behind a locked door had helped. If she hurried, she'd have time to stop for a bowl of soup before her first driving lesson.

With a trembling hand, Stephanie pocketed her key and grabbed her purse. One thing at a time, she told herself. She'd have to take it step by step and not let the panic take over. She'd go to the school and pretend she didn't know much about driving. Looking both ways in the hall and seeing no one, she closed the door firmly behind her, tested the lock, and, satisfied, headed for the bus stop.

Zane walked up the back stairs ahead of his attorney. "I think it's time, with the focus on the accident, that we move the package to a safer place." Reaching the landing, he turned to the left. "Not anywhere in the shop, but maybe that storage unit we used last time." He opened the first door. "What do you think, Bob?"

Bob Triner followed him into Stephanie's bedroom, shoving his thick glasses higher on his thin nose. "Sounds good to me. The building's in a remote location, and no one could possibly trace it to you."

Zane strode to the antique desk and stooped down. "That's what I thought." He slipped his hand behind the center drawer and felt around. With a frown, he stood. Carefully, he removed the drawer and turned it over. Nothing. "I know I taped it right here."

As Bob watched, Zane removed the other three drawers and came up empty-handed. Growing worried, he yanked the desk forward and searched the back and underside. Not a sign. Slowly, his fear mounting, he stood. "Son-of-a . . ." He jerked around and moved to the dresser, pulling open the top drawer.

"You sure you didn't already move it somewhere else?" Bob asked in his low, softspoken way.

"Of course, I'm sure," Zane snapped. "You think I could forget something this important?"

He rummaged through all the drawers, then shifted his attention to Stephanie's night stand. By the time he'd searched that and her dressing table, he was shaking with anger and disbelief. Tugging open the closet door, he shoved clothes aside, kicked shoe boxes open and dragged things off the top shelf. "I don't understand."

"We shouldn't have left the package in her room so long," Bob offered. "We should have—"

"Yeah. Maybe we should have done a lot of things."

Bob ran a hand through his thinning hair. "What if it was Stephanie?"

Zane swiveled about angrily. "What do you mean?"

"Just what I said. Suppose Stephanie took the diamonds. She's gone, isn't she? And so are the diamonds."

"Shut up!" Zane emerged from the closet, his eyes narrowing as he struggled with his fury. "She wouldn't dare."

"Wouldn't she? If she planned to leave—"

"She's never touched the others."

"Maybe because she didn't *find* the others."

"Damn!" Zane's eyes landed on Stephanie's white silk nightgown draped across the foot of the bed. Furiously, he ripped the fragile material down the center, wishing its owner were within. He tossed the ruined gown into the wastebasket and balled his hands into fists, trying to get his rage under control. There were people he had to answer to—one in particular—a man

37

with little patience. "If she did this, I'll get her. I'll find her and she'll regret the day she was born." He yanked open the door. "Come on."

With a worried frown, Bob followed him out.

Luke leaned against a cement pole and looked up at the red BMW high on the hoist in the police garage. "What do you think, Charley? Did someone mess with those brakes?"

Wiping his hands on a greasy rag, Charley ducked his head as he came out from under the car. "Sure did. A very small hole, Luke. In the brake line." The mechanic stuffed his rag into the back pocket of his overalls. "Otherwise, this car's been well maintained, tires like new and not a rust spot anywhere."

He'd come to Charley because he trusted his judgment more than the reports he'd been reading. "I'd thought as much. There were no skid marks, nothing to indicate the driver had been trying to stop the car. Because someone made sure the brakes wouldn't work, right?"

Charley nodded. "Yeah. And the one who did it took a chance. See, it's really small. It took a while for the brake fluid to leak out. If she'd have driven the car a couple of hours earlier, might have been a different story."

Luke thought to play devil's advocate. "Is it possible that when the car hit the water and sank, the brake line was penetrated by rocks or debris?"

Charley shook his head. "Hey, man, you know the way the brake line's positioned, that's not possible. If you want to crawl under with me, I'll show you. A perfect round hole, made by an ice pick or something shaped like one. I'd put money on it."

"I believe you, Charley." The mechanic's findings changed things considerably. Not suicide, not an accident, but murder. Or attempted murder. Luke followed Charley to the small cluttered office, thinking

38

aloud. "She rolled across two lanes of traffic, a median strip, up over a curb, down a grassy embankment — and just barely missed a tree. I'd guess she was conscious and steering. The tracks on the damp grass are straight, not zigzagging as if she'd been trying to gather enough traction to stop."

"More than likely she was so scared she froze and was gripping the wheel. She was damn lucky not to hit a passing car." Charley flopped into his swivel chair. "I see what you're getting at. All right, let's say someone set her up and she was awake and steering. The power windows were all up. The minute the car was submerged, the power went out, naturally. Is she a big, strong woman? It's damn hard to open a heavy car door under water against all that pressure."

Easing a hip onto the corner of the desk, Luke tossed him the picture of Stephanie. "Looks fairly average to me, with the ordinary strength of a young female, I'd guess. Could a door have popped open on impact?"

"Unlikely."

Exactly what he'd been thinking. "Were either of the doors open when the diver went down?"

"Yup, the driver's door." Charley leaned back, causing his aged chair to squeak, and ran stained fingers through his sparse hair. "You're asking could she have survived. She'd have to be one hell of a good swimmer. I'm familiar with where she went in. It's rocky and the current is strong."

"I know." Luke stood, returning the picture to his pocket. "But the instinct to survive might turn an average swimmer into a champion."

"That's true. Are you officially working on this case? I thought you were still sitting out a medical leave."

"Unofficially checking out a few things for a friend. I owe her father a favor or two."

Charley gave him a lopsided grin. "Either way, it's good to have you coming around again, Luke." He got up, letting his swivel chair bounce back up after him. "I've got to get back to work."

"You've been a big help. Thanks." Luke left Charley's office and made his way to his van. He needed to look into a couple of things before he went to see Stephen. Climbing behind the wheel, he headed for Lakeshore Drive.

"Stephanie was a pretty good swimmer," Stephen said as he sat back in his favorite easy chair and handed Luke another photo. "Here's a picture of her with Marjo, taken at a swim meet. They both competed in college, but it was Marjo who won all the ribbons."

Luke took the snapshot and sat down in the deep-cushioned leather chair in Stephen's den, facing the older man across a low coffee table. The concerned father seemed more relaxed today, Luke noted, though he toyed longingly with a cellophane-wrapped cigar. "I imagine Stephanie competed in swim meets in pools. Did she swim much in lakes or perhaps in rivers where she might have had to fight a current?"

"I have a place up in Canada, in Grand Bend. Stephanie swam in that lake a great deal, from childhood on. A river? I don't imagine so." He leaned forward, his dark eyes hopeful. "You found some clue. You think Stephanie was in the car, but that she swam away from the accident?"

"I don't know. I'm trying to determine if she was capable of doing just that. I drove by the scene of the accident a while ago. As I said yesterday, there's a pretty fast current there. Did Stephanie keep up her swimming since college? Did she and Zane belong to any clubs in the Pointes where she might have taught swimming?"

"She didn't teach it, but she loved to swim. They belong to the yacht club, but the members are mostly boaters. Zane has a sailboat and a cruiser with an

40

outboard. You're familiar with the yacht club, aren't you?"

Luke crossed his long legs. "As a matter of fact, I've just come from there. It's exactly three-point-two miles downstream from where Stephanie's car left the road."

"I hadn't thought of that. Stephanie could have pushed her way out of the car and made it to the yacht club. I'll bet that's what she did." His voice rose with his excitement.

"Stay calm, Stephen. We're just conjecturing here. I'm saying it's possible. It was a warm day, and though the water would have been chilly, it wouldn't have been unbearable. It's fairly rocky along the yacht club property where she'd likely have approached. The boats are all docked on the far side. But a strong, determined swimmer could have made it and emerged by the wooden stairs with only minor scrapes."

Stephen made an effort to curb his exhilaration. "Let's say she did that. It was daylight, between four and five in the afternoon. She risked being seen. Or perhaps she waited until dark. We should try asking around at the club. Maybe someone saw her."

"Someone did." Luke made a questioning hand gesture. "Or thinks she did. A teenage towel girl."

"Who?"

Luke took from his pocket a small notebook and flipped it open. "Tina Mayberry, one of the clubhouse attendants. She says she thought she saw a woman who looked like Stephanie—she calls her Mrs. Westover—hurry along the hallway, then disappear into the women's locker room. The woman was wearing something dark, and was dripping wet. But when Tina called out her name, she didn't stop, so Tina assumed it wasn't Stephanie. Later, when she read in the paper that Mrs. Westover had drowned, she assumed she'd been mistaken."

Stephen's voice was almost shrill. "That's it then. She's alive. I knew it!"

41

"Hold on now. A glimpse by a young girl who—"

"Isn't this girl reliable?"

Luke hated to raise false hope. Still . . . "Actually, I think Tina knows Stephanie fairly well. She worked with her at the little theater. They've been rehearsing *Oliver.* Mrs. Westover had been helping her learn lines. She thinks Stephanie's neat. Her word, not mine." Luke closed his notebook and tapped it thoughtfully against the back of his hand. "Tina wanted to ask her a question, so she hung around. But no one came out except a frumpy-looking woman in an old raincoat and tennis shoes, a scarf wrapped around her head."

Stephen had trouble containing himself. "A disguise. She probably hid a change of clothing in the locker room the day before. Have the police been around to question this girl?"

"No. They consider Stephanie to be a drowning victim, which she might still be. And yet . . ."

"And yet, things don't quite add up, do they?" Restlessly Stephen rose and moved to the built-in bar at the far wall. "Can I get you a drink?"

"No, thanks."

Stephen fixed himself a generous bourbon and branch, then resumed his seat. He took a grateful sip of the warming liquid, well aware that he wasn't supposed to drink hard liquor. But this business about his daughter had frazzled his nerves. Besides, he felt fine physically and was damn tired of those doctors always dictating to him.

"What did you find out at the banks?" Luke asked.

"Stephanie and Zane have two accounts jointly. No unusual sum has been withdrawn from either, going back six months. Zane has a separate account with his attorney for business purposes, and the transactions have been stable there, too. I also checked and there've been no recent insurance policies purchased on either of them. Although they're both insured, their coverage isn't extraordinary for people of their means."

Luke had expected as much. From what he'd heard of Zane, the man wouldn't be obviously careless.

"I have something else for you." Stephen downed a healthy swallow of bourbon before turning back to Luke. "Charles Hastings is my attorney and a valued friend. He called me today and told me something that Stephanie had asked him not to pass on to me. Charles felt, under the circumstances, that I should know. It seems that Stephanie went to him two months ago and discussed divorcing Zane."

The news didn't surprise Luke. "Did she sign the papers?"

"Yes."

"And we presume Zane was served?"

"The process server Charles uses has it on his records."

Luke ran a hand along his jaw, his mind considering possibilities.

"I'd suspected as much," Stephen went on. "My thinking was that Stephanie wanted a divorce and Zane refused her, so she decided on a way out. She planted her purse and shoes in her car and started it rolling downhill, causing it to land in the river. And then she took off somewhere. But now you've found someone who probably saw her at the yacht club, dripping wet. So she went in with the car, intentionally or accidentally. Then she climbed out at the club, picked up her disguise and disappeared. What do you think?"

Luke decided to share what he'd learned from Charley with Stephen. "Yes, I think she went in with the car." He glanced at a page in his notebook. "The neighbor who'd been walking his dog, Carl Osborne, talked with me, and he swears Stephanie was in the driver's seat when the car whizzed past him. She looked frightened, so I doubt if she intended to land in the river. But there's something else. The police mechanic found a hole in the brake line."

Stephen's eyes narrowed as he absorbed the news. "Zane. He tried to kill her." He jumped to his feet. "Damn, I'll—"

"Take it easy. Remember your blood pressure. If he did, we'll get him. But we have to prove it first."

Luke's calm, steady voice had Stephen sitting down heavily. With no small effort, he brought himself under control. "You're right." He rubbed a trembling hand over his eyes. "How do we do that?"

"Slowly, methodically, so our case is airtight. And by considering all angles. Stephanie could have punctured the brake line herself, trying to make the accident look like murder, but miscalculated somehow and things started to go wrong. We don't really know the woman that kid saw was your daughter. If Stephanie did go in on purpose, she took a hell of a chance. Tell me, is she a risk taker?"

Stephen shifted his gaze out the window to the clouds drifting along in a peaceful summer sky. Everything looked all right with the world, but it wasn't, not in *his* world. "Stephanie looks fragile, but she has a surprising core of strength. If the stakes were high enough in her mind, I'd say she'd take the risk. And I'd bet she'd make it, too."

Luke wished he had her father's confidence. "We still don't know why she would do it, if she's alive, or where she is. All right, she wanted a divorce, and let's say Zane wasn't willing. To stage her own death, possibly make it look like he tried to do her in, seems a bit extreme. Why wouldn't she just empty her bank account, jump on a plane and disappear?"

For the first time since last evening on the boat, Stephen looked troubled. "You don't know Zane. Stephanie was like a prize he'd won and didn't want to lose. I think you hit it on the head when you said he undoubtedly threatened her or someone she loves, and she felt trapped. Perhaps she thought if her plan worked, if Zane thought her dead, she'd be free. Pos-

44

sibly the police would suspect him of killing her, even lock him up. But if not, he wouldn't go looking for a dead woman. If she'd just disappeared, though, he'd move heaven and earth to find her."

Luke's frown was worried. "He's that obsessed?"

"That and more."

It might prove interesting to talk with Zane Westover, Luke decided, to watch his reactions and determine if he really believed Stephanie was dead. But the time wasn't right yet. "You mentioned Stephanie still kept a bedroom here in your home. Would you mind if I took a look in there?"

"Not if it'll help." Stephen stood. "It's very much as she left it two years ago." Walking to the curved stairway, he pointed up. "It's the second door on the right. Do you want me to go with you?"

"That won't be necessary, thanks."

Luke took his time climbing the stairs, noting the highly polished balustrade, the rich carpeting, the faint scent of flowers in the air. Must have been nice for a young girl to grow up in a house like this, he mused, thinking of Stephanie. Had she ever been mischievous enough to slide down that shiny bannister? Or sit at the top when her parents had entertained, before her mother's death, and eavesdrop a bit? Had she strolled down these very stairs on her way to her first high-school prom while a nervous young man waited at the bottom?

Where did the dream go wrong, Stephanie?

The room was airy and sunny, and not nearly as girlish as he'd expected. But then, Stephanie had been twenty-five when she'd left her father's house. The furniture was white pine with an heirloom spread draped over the big double bed. Luke walked to the cushioned seat that ran along a bank of windows overlooking a large side yard guarded by an old leafy maple. He could picture the slender blond woman curled up there, reading a favorite book.

A glance in her bookcase told him little of her

45

present taste, since it consisted mostly of classics and a few childhood treasures. On top of her desk was a picture of a much younger Stephen, his arm around a smiling woman with short, blond hair. Stephanie's mother, most likely, from the resemblance. Alongside the framed photo stood a Mickey Mouse bank from Disney World, still filled with coins, he noticed, as he hefted its weight.

He tugged at the top drawer and discovered a loose knob. A neat stack of papers and memorabilia were inside. A short note reminding Stephanie of a luncheon date, written in a somewhat shaky handwriting and signed Grandmother Juliana. A rose, dried and crumbling, pressed between the pages of a diary with not a word written on any of its pages. Who had given the flower to her? he wondered. There was a brass four-leaf clover with a tag attached reading Good luck, Steffie, from Marjo. And a pale peach-embossed invitation to her wedding to Zane Westover. He shut the drawer and kept wandering.

A bouquet of deep blue, dried flowers in a floral teacup was the only thing on her night stand. In its solitary drawer was a citation from the Grosse Pointe Little Theater for her contributions three years ago, along with a couple of snapshots of various stage productions. One showed her smiling at the camera as she stood next to a striking, dark-haired woman, both of them holding a clipboard. The brunette resembled the woman in the picture Stephen had shown him earlier, Marjo Collins. Luke stuck the photo in his pocket.

In the corner of the room was a stereo housing an impressive collection of records, from early Beatles albums to classical. Why hadn't she taken these with her? he wondered. Strolling to the mirror over her dresser, he removed a poem on yellowed paper. Evidently cut out of a magazine, it had been stuck into the frame. From Elizabeth Barrett Browning's *Sonnets from the Portuguese,* he read:

46

"How do I love thee? Let me count the ways. . . ."

Returning the clipping, he stood looking about. He hadn't learned very much. It would seem that Stephanie was neat and feminine and sentimental and romantic, a woman who liked music and reading and lunching with her grandmother. Luke walked to her closet and found it held very little, a few casual outfits, all with expensive labels. He'd have guessed as much. Stephanie had grown up with money and all it could buy. The comfortable life. And she'd married a wealthy man. Why had she wanted out of that good life?

Luke found Stephen in the library and showed him the picture.

"Yes, that's an old picture of the two of them. Marjo's beautiful, but a little wild."

"Two opposites, Stephanie and Marjo, would you say?"

Stephen nodded. "Stephanie likes fun, but she's quieter, more conventional. Marjo's outspoken, opinionated, and swears like a sailor. She lives north of here in a new condo complex that overlooks the water. That's where she moved last year after her divorce."

Another beautiful young woman whose dreams had gone astray. Who said that money and looks brought about happily ever after? Luke sat on a leather footstool and leaned forward. "I need to know more about Stephanie. Did you fill out my list?"

Stephen opened the sheet of paper Luke had given him. "Not all, but I can answer your questions. Favorite foods. I'd say any kind of fish, green salads, and coffee ice cream. She loves that stuff. She loves Italian food, dislikes Mexican. As to clothes, she dresses well, but conservatively. Nothing flamboyant. Medical history . . . as far as I know, she's healthy. Oh, she does have allergies, hay fever and the like, but who in Michigan doesn't? She had the usual childhood diseases, has all her own teeth and broke her left leg once in a fall from a horse. She rides beautifully."

There didn't seem to be anything Stephanie couldn't do well, at least in the eyes of her father. It was sounding a little too pat. Someone had put that hole in the brake line. If not Zane, then someone else. "Who doesn't she like, Stephen? Who doesn't like her? I know she's your daughter, but she must have run across a couple of people she didn't hit it off with."

Stephen bristled a bit. "A few. She didn't like Leona. She was a live-in maid Zane hired when they first married. Stephanie found her going through her things and fired her. Zane didn't much like that, but Leona didn't return. And she doesn't like Chester, Zane's chauffeur who seems more like a bodyguard. As to who doesn't like her, I can think of only one man. Andrew Collins, Marjo's ex-husband."

"Okay, tell me why."

"Stephanie told Andy off on several occasions, accused him of sleeping around. He denied it, but sure enough, Marjo caught him, threw him out without a cent, then divorced him. Marjo's parents died in a plane crash when she was still in college. They left her a lot of money, and everyone thought Andy married her for the good life she could provide. I think Andy blames Stephanie for his marriage breaking up. Wrongly, of course."

Of course. "And Marjo doesn't resent Stephanie for spotting Andy's weakness when she didn't?"

"No, they're very close."

"Confidants, would you say?"

"If Stephanie confides in anyone, it would be Marjo."

Luke put his notebook away and stood. "Is there anything else you can think of about your daughter that might help me know where to start looking?"

Frowning thoughtfully, Stephen rose. "Not offhand."

"Did she ever work before her marriage? I mean, for pay, a job."

Again, Stephen sounded slightly defensive. "No, but she volunteered more hours a week than most people work for pay. She worked at Cottage Hospital, at that little theater group and for the Detroit Symphony committee. Any of that helpful?"

Luke started toward the door. "You never know. I'm going to hang on to these pictures, if you don't mind." He turned, his hand on the doorknob. "Tell me, did Stephanie date much before Zane? Were there many men in her life?"

"She knew some men from around here, boys she'd grown up with mostly. People tend to stay with their own kind in the Pointes, to marry within the group mostly. She dated, but I wouldn't say a lot."

"How long did she know Zane before marrying him?"

A muscle in Stephen's jaw twitched. "Six months."

Long enough, in some cases. "Do you think she loved him?"

"I think she *thought* she loved him."

Typical fatherly answer, after the fact. "I'll be in touch." He went down the brick steps that led to the circular drive, got in his van and paused to reread his notes.

A picture was emerging, but slowly. He needed to talk to others who knew Stephanie, because her father's vision of her was obviously colored a rosy hue. Not unusual, just not informative enough. Stephen wanted to believe, he *did* believe, that his daughter was all things bright and beautiful. And maybe she was. But maybe she wasn't.

A sweet, well-mannered, well-to-do woman whose main function in life so far has been charity events doesn't disappear just because she gets tired of the scenery. She married an outsider who'd somehow wormed his way into the inner sanctum, yet people stayed friendly with her. She kept her own counsel, a trait Luke admired. Still, something wasn't adding up, and he didn't know what. But he would. The puzzle pieces would fall into place in time. And he had a lot of that.

Picking up his cellular phone, he called information, scribbled down the number and then dialed again. The phone was answered on the second ring. Deepening his voice, he asked for Zane Westover. In her lazy drawl, the housekeeper told him Mr. Westover was out until six. He thanked her and hung up. It was only three. Starting the van, he headed for the Westover home.

Eula Johnson had worked for the Westovers for nearly a year, he'd read in the report. Luke wanted to talk with her alone. Perhaps Stephanie's cleaning lady, the person the police indicated had probably been the last one to talk with her, could shed some light on her odd disappearance.

"I can't believe it, Detective Varner." The pudgy black woman dabbed at her eyes. "I can't believe I'm never going to see Miz Stephanie again. She wouldn't hurt a fly, that one. Why is it the good die young, do you s'pose?"

Why, indeed. Luke gazed about the spotless kitchen decorated in sunny yellow and white, and empathized with Eula. She'd unhesitatingly let him in moments ago when he'd flashed the credentials she'd only given a perfunctory glance. "You got along well with Mrs. Westover then?"

"Yes, sir." She poured him a cup of coffee, then eased her bulk into the chair opposite him in the breakfast nook. "She likes things clean. But she's not nasty about it, you know. She's real kind, to all peoples." Eula honked her nose loudly before stuffing the tissue in the pocket of her starched white uniform. "I don't know what more I can tell you. I already talked to them other officers."

Luke sent her an understanding smile. "This is just routine follow-up. Would you mind going

50

over the events of that afternoon again for me?"

While she launched into her story, which he'd read in the report, his eyes scanned the room. As he'd expected, the alarm system buttons were located near the back door, with a similar set by the front entry, he was certain, and perhaps a third in the master bedroom. Only the green light was blinking. A glance at the two open kitchen windows confirmed that the system had been deactivated. Eula evidently was airing the house and so had disengaged the alarm. It was his lucky day. He turned back and nodded as she finished her recitation.

"Did Mrs. Westover seem depressed lately, or sad or short tempered, or perhaps distracted?"

"No, sir, she's been her own sweet self just like always."

"You work here five days a week. Was she gone a lot more recently?"

"No, not so you'd notice. 'Bout the same."

"Did she bring any new friends home while you were here?"

"She never had many folks in. Just Miz Marjo." Eula smiled, and her cheeks blossomed. "That one, she's full of the devil, always laughing. She coaxes Miz Westover out nearly every week, and I tell her, go. Good for you to get out."

Funny how Stephen and now Eula still spoke as if Stephanie were still alive. "How about Mr. Westover? Did he take his wife out much?"

A subtle shift in her expression, a narrowing of her eyes, and Eula's thick fingers nervously pleated a corner of her uniform. "Mr. Westover's a busy man, gone a lot."

"Do you think he loved his wife?"

Eula shot him a worried look, as if she found these questions a whole lot different from the others she'd been asked. She glanced toward the archway, looking as though she half expected her employer to appear. "I don't get personal with people I work for."

51

Luke decided to try another route. "Are you married, Eula?"

Her shiny face broke into a smile. "Yes, sir. Twenty-two years come January. Joe drives a cab."

"Twenty-two years. These days, that's a record. I'll bet Joe's affectionate, hugging you when he comes home, a sweet-talking man. Am I right?"

She giggled girlishly. "Yeah, he sure is, even after all those years and six kids."

"Did you ever see Zane Westover act that way toward his wife?"

She sobered quickly. "No, sir. He's a cool one, that man. Don't smile much either."

"Did you ever hear them quarrel?"

Eula was back to fussing with the skirt of her uniform. Finally, she gave a quick nod. "Miz Stephanie's real soft spoken, but Mr. Westover gets awful mad, yelling, banging doors shut. This one time, he kept it up for half an hour. It was late afternoon, and I grabbed my pocket book and walked to the bus stop that day. I hate to be around fighting like that."

"How long ago did that quarrel take place, Eula?"

"Don't rightly know." She frowned, thinking. "Wait, I remember. Right after Easter, 'bout two months ago."

"And when you came back the next day, was Stephanie the same as always?"

"She stay in her room all day, never come out once. She open the door a crack and tell me to just do what I usually do and no special stuff."

"Had she been crying, could you tell?"

"Don't know. Her face was real white and she had her robe on all day. I took her some lunch on a tray, but she only drank the tea."

"Do Mr. and Mrs. Westover have separate bedrooms?"

"Yes, sir, but there's a door between."

Luke glanced at his notebook. "Do Chester Morton and Bob Triner come over often?"

She shook her head. "That Chester, he here all the time when Mr. Westover's home. Mr. Triner shows up once in a while, and when he comes, Mr. Westover take him in the study and lock the door. I don't like that Chester, him and his smelly cigars. Mark my words, that man's bad news."

Luke stood. "Do you suppose I could have a look in Stephanie's bedroom?"

Eula's eyes narrowed as she gave a quick shake to her head. "No, sir. Mr. Zane don't let no one in there. After she gone, I went in and started straightening up. He come in and shoo me out, tell me don't go in there again."

He'd expected as much. He'd move to Plan B, Luke decided as he glanced toward the refrigerator. "Could I have a glass of ice water before I leave? It's getting warm out there."

"Sure, you can." She reached for a glass and walked to the refrigerator.

Standing with his back to the door, Luke opened it slightly, shoved in the lock, then closed it quietly. Eula turned and brought him the water. He drank half and smiled his thanks. "That hit the spot." He checked his watch. "Are you almost finished for the day? I could drive you to the bus."

She shook her graying head. "I got to clean the silverware in the dining room yet. Then I can leave. But I thank you."

Luke walked outside and listened for the soft closing of the door, then her footsteps as she left the kitchen. The street was deserted as he climbed behind the wheel.

In minutes, he'd driven his van around the bend from the hilltop home and returned on foot to the side of the Westover house. The late afternoon sun filtered through the large maples that dappled him with undulating shadows as he peered into the first window. The library. He moved along, then stopped at the wide bay window. There Eula was, silverware spread out on a cloth on the large dining-room table, her efficient hands rubbing on a fork. Ducking down, he inched along to the back door.

Years ago, he'd learned to move quietly, quickly, carefully. He was fairly certain no one else was in the house, but Westover could return unexpectedly with his bodyguard in tow. He checked the .38 strapped to his ankle, reassured by its presence.

Creeping up the back stairs, Luke paused at the top. Double doors painted white were on the far left. He eased over and peeked in. Bingo. Softly feminine and decorated in peach and pale blue, it had to be Stephanie's. He closed the door behind him.

His training had taught him to go through a room without leaving a trace. His instincts had taught him to discover every secret hidden there. Luke stood still, his eyes circling. A large room, with three wide windows looking out toward the back yard. A huge closet along one wall, an archway leading into her bath. White furniture again, except for an antique desk. He checked that first and found all the drawers empty.

He moved to the night stand and found no lamp, but rather a fat white candle in a brass holder. A well-read book of poetry lay alongside. Next to it he saw a wide gold wedding band and a second ring with a diamond large enough to choke a mule. Stephanie had left her rings here. Zane had surely been in her room since her disappearance, yet he hadn't gathered them up either. Puzzling.

Standing at the foot of her bed, his eyes traveled up the pale blue spread. He could picture Stephanie lying there, her golden hair spread on the pillow, the candlelight flickering and reflecting in her hesitant blue eyes. Luke shook his head. What the hell was he thinking? Annoyed with himself, he glanced toward the window and spotted something white in the wastebasket.

He held up the thin gown with both hands and saw it had a tear down the center. More than that, it

54

looked as if it had been deliberately ripped. Had Zane torn Stephanie's gown from her during a quarrel? He dropped it back into the basket and moved to the dresser.

Feeling like an intruder, he opened the first drawer. Underwear, silky and fragrant, all in disarray. The second drawer held more of the same, slips and scarves, also tumbled. She'd been so neat in her father's house. Neat people rarely changed and became careless. Someone had searched these drawers before him. The next two, filled with sweaters and summer tops, were also in a jumble.

The closet door squeaked slightly, and he held his breath a long moment. Shoe boxes with lids askew were jammed to one side, while a variety of shoes were scattered every which way. The clothes were shoved to one side, some with pockets pulled inside out. The searcher had been here, too. What had he or she been looking for? Luke wondered.

Stephanie's curved dressing table had a wide mirror and a bench seat. He walked over to examine the jewelry box placed off to one side and was surprised to find it unlocked. Looking inside, he was even more surprised. Several old pieces, more diamonds in the form of bracelets and necklaces, a pearl and ruby ring, and a stunning emerald pendant. Enough here, if she'd have taken it, to finance several years of comfortable living. Curious, Luke decided as he closed the box.

Her makeup was expensive and professional. She'd undoubtedly learned about brands and methods of enhancing her appearance in the little theater where she'd volunteered her time. He'd have to look into that. He held her bottle of cologne to his nose and inhaled her preferred scent. Light, yet seductive in its subtlety. Experience had taught him women usually stayed with one brand of perfume most of their adult lives. Something to keep in mind.

A bentwood rocker sat by the window and held a

Raggedy Ann doll in its well-worn arms. The doll, with only one eye and ratty red hair, seemed out of place in the room's perfection. He stood, looking at the walls. A Toulouse-Lautrec print of two cancan dancers was the only picture. And no photos, not one. Not of Zane or Stephen—or even herself. Odd.

Luke stuck his hands into his pockets, frowning. Again, he'd learned some . . . but not enough. He had the impression of feminine colors, of gentleness, of flowers and soft scents. And yet he felt that something sinister had walked here. There was more to Stephanie Westover's disappearance than appeared on the surface, he was certain.

He tried the connecting door, certain it would be locked, and it was. Leaving the room as silently as he'd entered, he paused at the open railing. He could hear Eula humming to herself downstairs. Swiftly, he tried the door next to Stephanie's room and found it locked also. He could easily have picked the lock, but it was getting late and he didn't want to push his luck. There'd be other days.

Moving like the cat he'd often been compared to, Luke crept downstairs, waited a moment to make sure the cleaning lady was still occupied, then left as quietly as he'd entered.

Back in his van, he started the engine and drove down the winding street toward Lakeshore Drive. Rolling his shoulders to relieve the tension, he stopped at the intersection and pulled out Stephanie's picture. What had that quarrel two months ago been about? he wondered. Had that triggered her desire for a divorce? Or, more recently, had discussion of divorce prompted her need to run? Who had ripped her gown and when?

For a long moment, he studied her face. There was a vulnerability there that had drawn him from the start, and the realization didn't please him. He scowled, searching for the objectivity that rarely failed to be there for him.

Luke sucked in a deep breath of air, then swore softly under his breath. Instead of summer flowers and the nearby lake water, Stephanie's scent drifted to him. *To hell with this.*

With a squeal of tires, he whipped around the corner. It was time to visit Captain Renwick. If he was going to work on this case, officially or unofficially, he'd have to have some cooperation. He'd also have to be in top shape, which he wasn't exactly certain he was, mooning over a woman's picture.

Maybe it was time he found out. He headed for the Beaubien Street Police Station.

Chapter Three

The captain's bunions hurt. He'd been working behind a desk for twelve years now, but the source of his discomfort was an unwelcome leftover from all the years he'd worked in the field, the hours on his feet, walking a beat, standing on stakeouts on cold cement. Wiggling his toes, he shifted his cigar from the left side of his mouth to the right. He didn't need Luke Varner in his office today to add to his problems. The fact that he'd once walked a beat with Luke's father kept Renwick from revealing his annoyance.

"You know our motto down here as well as I do, Luke," Captain Renwick said as he leaned back. "If you can reasonably close a case, do it. We've got too damn heavy a workload to investigate every angle."

Luke steepled his fingers as he sat in the chair across from his superior's cluttered desk. "Yeah, I know. Not enough money, time, or good men. That's why I've come to you with a proposition." He watched closely as Renwick slowly puffed on one of his stinking cigars. Through the gray smoke that hung in the air of the small, glassed-in office, he met the older man's probing gaze and waited.

Six months and he hadn't heard a word from Luke, and now here he sat, looking fit once again, clear-eyed, relaxed. The captain thoughtfully tapped an ash off into his overflowing ashtray. But that was on the

58

outside. How was he on the inside? Part of his probation had included regular checkups with his doctor, Josh Something-or-other. He'd read the reports telling him that Luke was off the sauce, behaving, healing.

Luke had been good once, one of his best, though he'd often been a little loose on procedure. He'd always gotten away with it, until his wife's unexpected death had him throwing the rules out the window. His file was filled with a number of infractions. It also contained an even greater percentage of successful cases. For that alone, he owed it to the man to hear him out. "All right, let's have it."

"I want to work on the Westover case, the so-called accidental drowning. I don't think she's dead. Her father, Stephen Sanders, is a friend, and I owe him a favor."

So that was it, a favor. The Luke Varner he knew wouldn't walk across the street for ten grand if he didn't want to. He also wouldn't walk away from a debt. "What makes you think she didn't drown?"

Luke shrugged lazily. "A couple of things. I've been nosing around. Look, I know you're understaffed and this is going to die on the books. I also know you don't want to put me back to work officially, not until you're sure I can handle myself. I want to work on this unofficially, but with your sanction. I need to use the precinct's facilities—the lab, the garage, the police artist—and I want my badge back. I'll work alone, but I'll keep you informed. If I come up empty, so be it. But if I come up with some answers on this one, maybe we can talk again."

It wasn't an unreasonable request. Still, Renwick remembered the day Luke's partner had had to pull him off a man he'd almost killed with his bare hands. "I suppose you're working on the angle that Zane Westover did away with her and staged the accident as a coverup? We checked out his alibi and he's clean. He was in Cleveland from early morning until we informed him."

Luke shrugged. "Some men have a long reach. I have a few suspicions."

Renwick bit down hard on his cigar. "I don't suppose you're going to tell me what they are?"

"They're only hunches right now. As soon as I get something solid, I will. Have you got anything recent on Westover?"

He debated telling Luke, but only for a moment. Maybe it was time to play it out. If he solved the drowning accident, plus got Westover behind bars, they'd not only get two cases off the books, but he'd have a damn fine detective back full force. "A week ago, we made a bust at the Canadian border. Diamond smuggling, camouflaged in a shipment of artifacts. Uncut stones worth about a million. In the right hands, the value could easily triple. The young punk we caught named Westover on this end of things. That little shop he's got on Jefferson."

"I'd like to talk to that young punk."

"I would have, too. Unfortunately, he made a run for it and a border cop wasted him."

"Who was he?"

"A third level man. Unimportant."

"Did he say anything else?"

Renwick shook his head. "But we found something on him. A shipping order from an art dealer in Toronto. Alex Quentin."

Luke had heard of the tall, dapper man known as Mr. Q. Both Canadian and U.S. officials had been trying to get something on the slick dealer for a decade. Though his mind was racing, Luke kept his features even. It wouldn't do to look too anxious. "I imagine you'd like to put both Westover and Quentin behind bars."

"Damn right. Mr. Q's smart and very careful. Westover, on the other hand, has a hair-trigger temper. If he's involved in his wife's disappearance, that might be the mistake we've been waiting for. Are you thinking maybe the little woman discovered his sideline and he had someone push her car into the river?"

"Could be." He'd barely touched the corners of Stephanie Westover's life, yet the thought of a man she'd trusted coldly killing her filled Luke with an anger far too personal. "So maybe you get two for the price of one. What do you say, Captain?"

"Do you know the woman? Emotional involvement got you in hot water once before."

Luke remembered Sonny Poston, too, the man who'd provided his wife with enough cocaine to kill her. But this was different. "I've never met her."

"You know we're cooperating with the Grosse Pointe police on this one. I wouldn't want you stepping on any toes."

He had a few friends uptown. He'd manage. "I get along okay with the boys on the Hill."

For another long minute, Renwick studied Luke. He'd taken a lot of chances in his career. Some had paid off, some hadn't. He pulled open his top drawer, rummaged around, and found what he was looking for. It seemed like he was about to take another long shot. He slid the badge over to Luke. "You screw up on this and the next time I keep this permanently. You got that?"

Luke shoved the badge in his pocket. "If I screw up this time, I'll hand it over to you myself." He stood and offered his hand. "I appreciate this."

"You better. It's my ass on the line, too. And one more thing."

His hand on the knob, Luke paused.

"You can use the facilities, but I can't provide backup. I don't have men to spare. You're going to be alone on this one."

He'd worked alone before. At times, he preferred it. With a nod, Luke left the office. Outside the door, he drew in a deep breath and wiped his damp hands on his jeans. He hadn't realized just how much he'd wanted this chance until he'd walked in to see the captain.

He took a moment to look around. Homicide was on the first floor, at the back, as if guarding its secrets from casual visitors. A study in industrial beige, Luke thought. Pale beige walls, cream-colored desks with formica tops, dark tan tile on the floor. The lone female officer, Sergeant Mary Margaret O'Malley, had a bouquet of deep purple lilacs on her desk, the color a sharp contrast. It was an altogether drab room, smelling of sweat and disinfectant and smoke. But he'd missed it nonetheless.

As he stood in the archway of the nearly deserted squad room, Sergeant O'Malley glanced up. Her round face registered surprise, her clear blue eyes welcome.

"Luke," she said, leaning back in her desk chair. "You're looking good."

He'd always liked Megs, as everyone called her. He admired and respected her for being a tough cop and a loyal friend. She'd been his last partner, the one who'd pulled him off a man he'd nearly killed. She was smart, strong, and compassionate—a hard combination to beat.

Luke stepped closer and gave her one of his rare smiles. "How goes it, Megs? Still putting them away?"

Megs ran a hand through her short red hair. "Whenever I can. Are you back to stay?"

He shrugged. "We'll see. How's Dennis?" Megs's husband worked out of a west-side precinct and was a hell of a nice guy.

"He's fine, thanks."

Luke leaned against her desk and toyed with a paper weight in the shape of a red heart. "Who you teamed with these days?"

"Lombardi."

He knew him—a big, lumbering man who played it by the book. "Must be a big change for you."

She grinned, then glanced around the room. Seeing no one near, she leaned closer. "It sure is. Can you

62

come back?"

Straightening, Luke set down the paper weight. "Could be. You still want me—after all that?"

Her eyes softened with affection. "Any day."

Luke nodded. "Thanks, Megs. I'll be in touch." In the hallway, he headed for the stairs, then stopped at the sound of a familiar voice.

"Hey, Luke, nice seeing you," Dick Hayes, the desk sergeant, called out as he passed.

"You, too," Luke told him. Yeah, it was good being back. With a lighter step than when he'd entered, he climbed the stairs. On the second floor was a man he wanted to see.

Kevin Kiefer's office was little more than a large broom closet. Filled to overflowing with a drawing board and two filing cabinets, it looked even smaller. Perched atop his stool, the tall, lanky police artist looked up as Luke tapped on the open door and stuck his head in.

"Luke! Long time no see."

"You keeping busy or have you got time to do something for me?"

Kevin shoved aside the paper he'd been working on. "What do you need?"

Leaning over the drawing table, Luke handed him the picture of Stephanie. "This is a woman we're looking for. We think she might not want to be found. I wanted to kick it around with you, see how you think she'd go about changing her looks to mislead anyone searching for her. And then ask you to do a sketch based on those changes. What do you think?"

"Not too tough an assignment." Kevin studied the photo. "Nice facial bones. Long blond hair. She'd probably start by cutting that, either shoulder length or real short. We could do a sketch both ways. And she'd likely dye it darker, which would make quite a difference. Some women use wigs, though not usually the younger ones. She could get glasses. That would add another change." As he talked Kevin started sketching, using several colored pencils. A couple of rapid strokes and he had the shape of a head.

"She already has glasses, big ones that she wears sometimes."

"Ahhh. Okay. Then, we'll try a few sketches with glasses. She could also get contacts and have them tinted another color. Her eyes are blue, but she could go green, or brown or gray." His busy pencil kept moving. "If she's really into this, she could use makeup to add a scar, let's say, though most women would be too vain to do that. But freckles are easy to add and would also make her look younger probably." From a glass, he picked out a brown pencil. "I doubt if she'd go from this pale blond to black, but I'll do one like that, too, okay?"

"You're the boss." Luke watched, fascinated. He'd seen Kevin do his stuff countless times, but the artist's skill never failed to intrigue him. A totally different person was emerging on paper, yet with the same facial structure, the same nose and mouth as the woman in the photo. In another minute, Kevin seemed satisfied and handed him the first sketch.

Luke nodded, pleased. "This is great."

"Let me do a couple more, with another eye color and a different hair style. We don't know what she'd do, so this is purely guesswork." He set to work. "So, you back with us to stay?"

"Not officially. I'm working on a special case."

"How're they biting up your way?"

Luke gave him a quick fish story, just long enough for Kevin to finish several other sketches. Taking them, he nodded. "I owe you, buddy. Thanks for the quick service."

"Anytime. See you, Luke."

Carefully, he placed the sketches in the file folder he'd brought, along with Stephanie's picture. He'd have to get some copies made of the sketches. As soon as he had a definite lead, he'd need to have them ready. Hurrying down the stairs, he made his way out-side.

Diamonds, the captain had said. A handy business, owning an import shop if you're going to smuggle contraband into the country. If Stephanie had discovered Zane's illegal activities, Luke found it hard to believe she'd been brave enough, or stupid enough, to confront him. Or—and Luke was beginning to dislike this possibility—perhaps they were in on it together and she'd fled with a particularly large cache while he staged her death. That would explain why she'd casually left behind a small fortune in jewelry in her bedroom. Maybe filing for a divorce was a ruse, and Zane planned to collect on her insurance, gather up her jewels, and join her somewhere out of the country later. The woman in the picture he carried didn't look capable of that kind of deception, or of hurting her father. Neither had Ma Barker, he supposed.

Luke checked his watch. Six in the evening and he hadn't eaten since breakfast. Not good for his healing ulcer. Walking through the parking lot, he decided he'd stop for something before visiting Marjo Collins. He really should phone ahead.

He opened the van door. No. Surprise visits often yielded more information. From her picture, Marjo looked to be a knockout. Zany and opinionated, Stephen had labeled her. We shall see, Luke thought as he maneuvered out into afternoon traffic.

The woman in the white silk jumpsuit stood in her open doorway and studied his photo ID while Luke studied her. Pictures didn't do Marjo Collins justice. Rich black hair falling past her shoulders, flawless skin, and a figure that reminded him he'd been without the softness of a woman in a long while. Luke cleared his throat. "Satisfied?"

Deep violet eyes fringed with incredibly long lashes looked up at him. "Come in." She turned and walked into a sunken living room decorated in white and black with red accents. Bending, Marjo picked up a short, squat glass and drained the contents before whirling back to face Luke, who'd followed her in. "I'm getting damned tired of this. You're the third officer I've had show up on my doorstep. You guys think I drugged my best friend, propped her behind the wheel, and shoved her car into the river?"

"I seriously doubt anyone thinks that," Luke answered carefully. A spitfire, but then, he thought he understood. She was hurting over the loss of a friend.

Suddenly, Marjo ran out of steam. She waved him toward a chair while she went behind the bar. "Sorry. I'm a little edgy. Would you like a drink?"

"No, thanks."

Marjo dropped ice cubes into her glass. "On duty?"

"No, an ulcer that prefers milk."

"Milk." She made a face as she poured herself a hefty splash of scotch.

Luke chose a chair by the sliding glass wall that opened onto a spacious patio. A large free-form pool lay just beyond and, some distance past that, he could just make out the river. The room they were in could easily accommodate fifty for cocktails. Not your average little working girl's condo, he decided. "Nice place you have here."

Marjo curled up in the corner of the couch, pulling up her long legs, and lit a cigarette. "What is it you want to know, Detective Varner?"

"Everything you didn't tell the other police officers."

She narrowed her gaze as she sipped the dark amber liquid. "Why is it you don't seem like a detective?"

"What do I seem like?"

Marjo's eyes skimmed his lean frame, starting with the watchful gray eyes set in his angular face. He had on a black cotton shirt, jeans that fit his hard thighs like a glove, and worn boat shoes. "Like Steve McQueen on a bad day."

66

Luke laughed out loud and was surprised at the sound. "McQueen played a lot of cops."

She blew smoke into the air-conditioned room. "And a lot of con men. Which are you?"

"Whatever I have to be. At the moment, I'm a cop. A cop with a friend named Stephen Sanders who's hurting. What can you tell me about Stephanie that he wouldn't know about his daughter?" He watched a glimmer of respect move into her eyes.

"I like Stephen. His daughter and I had been close friends for ten years. I loved her like the sister I never had."

"Do you want to help me find out what happened to her?"

Marjo set down her glass. "Yes."

"All right. Who were her enemies?"

"Enemies? She didn't have any. If you'd known Stephanie, you'd understand. She was innately good. She didn't do nice things when people were watching. She did them when no one would ever find out. She was very private."

"You mean secretive?"

"Not really. We shared a lot of confidences, especially when we were younger. She had a silly side she seldom showed the world. And she was an incurable romantic. That may have been her downfall."

"She saw Zane Westover as her knight in shining armor?"

"God, yes. I tried to tell her, but she wouldn't listen to me, or anyone. I think she realized her mistake shortly after the wedding, but it was too late."

"You think Zane's responsible for the accident?"

"Damn right I do." Marjo ground out her cigarette in a large crystal ashtray. "And let's not call it an accident. It was murder. I want you to nail that bastard." Reaching for her glass, she took a long swallow.

"Stephen tells me that your ex-husband isn't too fond of Stephanie. Is that true?"

She gave a short laugh. "Andy's a weak man.

Stephanie spotted it, I finally learned it, and now everyone knows it. But if you're thinking Andy had anything to do with this, think again. Andy's not bright enough to steal a piggy bank much less kill someone."

He made a note to check out Andy Collins anyhow. Ex-wives weren't always the best judges of a man's character. Luke crossed his legs. "Everyone's capable of murder, Marjo, under the right circumstances."

"What would be Andy's motive?"

"You tell me."

She shook her head. "You're on the wrong track. Try sniffing around her husband, or some of those creeps who follow him around."

"I take it you don't get along with Zane?"

She gave him a hint of a smile. "I knew you were a bright fellow the moment I saw you."

"What do you know about Chester or Bob Triner? Did Stephanie talk about them?"

"Stephanie was closemouthed about her personal life after her marriage, and rarely complained about Zane or even those two clowns. She got along all right with Bob, but she once told me she thought Chester had been brain damaged in the ring, the way he did Zane's bidding without question. I don't know anything more except that he made her nervous."

"How was Stephanie's love life?"

Marjo's eyes widened. "You don't pull punches, do you? I'll let you in on a little secret, Mr. Cop. Women talk about their love lives some before they marry, seldom after."

"Bullshit, lady. Men talk. Women talk. That's the way it is." Calmly, Luke held her angry gaze. Though he admired loyalty, this wasn't the time for it. He hadn't intended to ask the question, but now that he had, he realized he wanted to know.

"Maybe."

He heaved a patient sigh. "I can't help find her killer if I don't know the truth about her marriage, especially since you seem certain her husband's responsible."

She braced herself with a long sip. "I'm reading between the lines with this, okay? I don't think Zane made her terribly happy in the bedroom. Stephanie wasn't very sexually experienced when she married. She didn't experiment much, even in college. She was in love with love, I used to tell her, waiting for Prince Charming to set the bells ringing with his magic kiss. I wish I could have convinced her that that never happens in real life."

Luke thought of Kathy, the early months of their marriage, and wished he hadn't let himself remember. "Are you so sure it doesn't?"

She looked at him then, deep and long. "Yeah, I'm sure and you ought to wise up, too." Rising, she moved to the bar.

A cynic. But then, so was he. "What did Stephanie do at the little theater?"

"Anything and everything. We all do."

"Including makeup?"

"Sure. She's really good with makeup." Marjo picked up her fresh drink. "That is, she *was* good with makeup. I have to keep reminding myself she's gone." A bit unsteadily, she wound her way back to the couch. "What else do you want to know, Mr. Cop? Ask away."

"Did Stephanie ever mention a favorite city, one she had visited or would one day like to visit?"

She frowned, trying to follow his thinking. "Why would you want to know that?"

"Humor me."

"My guess would be Boston. She spent a summer there, working in little theater, before she married. She thought Boston was full of history and romance." She lit another cigarette and inhaled deeply.

"Does Stephanie smoke?" He hadn't noticed an ashtray in either of her bedrooms, but that didn't prove a thing.

"Yes, like a chimney. Next question."

"Why are you sitting here all alone drinking yourself silly?"

She flashed a lopsided smile. "Why not, Mr. Cop?"

"Marjo, I lost someone I once loved, too, and I drank to ease the pain. It only hurt more." He walked over and held out his hand. "Why don't you give me that glass and let me take you out for dinner somewhere?"

She looked up at him, her eyes suddenly shiny. "Why, Detective Varner, you're not as hard-boiled as I'd thought." She shook her head and clung to her glass. "Thanks, but another time. We all handle things in our own way, you know. I'll get over Stephanie's death. But it's going to take a while. If you'd nail the son-of-a-bitch who hurt her, I'd recover faster. Will you do that for me, please?"

Luke tried a long shot. "What if she didn't drown? We don't have a body."

Something flickered in her eyes for a moment, something resembling hope. Then it was gone. "Nothing would please me more. You've been listening to her grieving father grasping at straws. But I stopped believing in Santa Claus some time ago."

"Thanks for talking with me." At the door, her voice pulled him back.

"One more thing I remember. Stephanie hated the cobra. It gave her the willies."

"Cobra? What cobra?"

"The one Zane has tattooed on his left bicep. I've never seen it, but she said it was quite large, the body coiled and waiting, the head all puffed up and ready to attack. Cobras are patient and deadly. You might want to give that some thought."

He might, at that. From his shirt pocket, he took out a card, wrote on the back, and handed it to her. "This is my home number. If you think of anything else, call me."

Closing the door behind him, Luke strolled slowly

toward his van. It had been an interesting interview. He couldn't help feeling sorry for Marjo Collins. He knew exactly how she felt, and then some.

A hell of a lot of mixed-up, lonely people in the world, Luke thought as he started the engine. He needed to get back to his houseboat, to the comfort of his solitude and his grumpy cat. Marjo had given him a lot to think about. In an hour, she'd provided some of the missing puzzle pieces that Stephen hadn't had. With a sigh, he drove through the brick arches and out of the luxurious condo community, then headed north.

The moment he turned onto the dirt road leading to his small marina, he knew something was wrong. The security guide lamps on the corners of his houseboat were always on, night and day. He'd fallen into that habit to insure that passing boats could spot him, even in foggy weather, out on the lake or at anchor. All four lamps were out tonight.

Luke turned off his headlights, then coasted to a stop in his usual parking place. No other vehicle in sight. He waited for his eyes to adjust to the dimness. Soundlessly, he slid out of the van and crouched alongside, his gaze skimming the area. The moon, not quite full, was nonetheless helpful as were the low yellow lights along the length of the dock. He wondered if his uninvited guest was gone or still around. Bending, he retrieved the .38 from his leg strap and released the safety. Holding his arm down and out of sight, he moved into the shadows of the pier.

Slowly, testing each step for the loose boards he knew were there, he eased toward his home, his eyes alert and searching. Suddenly, he heard Benjamin's loud feline squeal, followed by a man's voice swearing ripely. Luke froze, waiting. In another moment, two shadows separated themselves from the stairwell, one bulky and towering, the other much slighter. As they stepped forward into the moonlight of the pier, he recognized Zane Westover from pictures he'd seen and guessed the hulk with him was Chester.

"Find what you were looking for?" Luke asked, his voice level. He kept his finger on the trigger, the gun behind him. He was a damn good shot, and now that his intruders were out in the open, he wasn't worried.

"Ease up, Varner," Zane said calmly. "We just want to talk with you."

"Is that a fact? Do you always break in and search a man's home before talking with him?"

Chester took a step forward and blinked his small eyes. "When you didn't answer our knock, we thought you might be sleeping." His smile was mean and ugly.

"Uh-huh. What do you want?"

Zane touched the knot of his perfect tie as if to reassure himself it hadn't loosened. "More importantly, what do *you* want? I understand you've visited my home and that you questioned my housekeeper. I don't like people snooping around."

"That makes two of us."

"Why were you questioning Eula?"

"In case you haven't heard, I'm a police officer. Your wife's body hasn't been found. I'm investigating, which means questioning various people, including your maid, who might have been the last person to see her alive. That's my reason for visiting your home. What's yours for visiting mine?"

Zane ignored the question. "My sources downtown tell me Stephanie's death has been ruled accidental and the case is closed."

"You ought to get new sources. A case is rarely closed until a body has been found and examined."

"I thought you were on a leave of absence?"

"I'm back." In the dim light, Luke saw Zane's face take on a speculative look.

"You don't think she's dead, do you?" Zane asked.

"Do you?" He could almost see Zane's mind weighing that.

"Where could she be, if she isn't somewhere in that river?"

"You tell me."

Zane's temper flared. "You're goddamned cool, aren't you, Varner? You didn't just lose your wife, the one person who meant more to you than anyone else in the world." He stopped, seeing the quick tensing of the detective's body, suddenly realizing the parallel. He remembered the stories he'd heard of Varner's wife dying of a drug overdose and the way her death had affected the cop's control. Maybe he could make use of it. "Then again, you do know how that feels, don't you? And you also know how it feels to track down the man who ruined her, to make him pay. Maybe Captain Renwick needs a reminder of how you work, of your lack of control. . . ."

Luke felt his trigger finger twitch. "Don't push me, Westover. It'll be your last mistake." He didn't need a gun to handle him. His fists would do. How dare Westover bring Kathy's death into this? First he'd tried to play on his sympathy, then to threaten. Luke wasn't buying either tactic.

"Boss, let me handle him." Chester took a step forward.

Zane's arm held him back. "It's all right, Chester. I think the detective's a reasonable man. A man with a job to do. Find her for me, Varner, and bring her back."

"I didn't say she was alive."

Zane's eyes narrowed. "I pay pretty well."

"I don't work for hoods." He watched Chester's beefy hand move to his inside pocket. Swiftly, Luke raised his gun and aimed it at the bodyguard's heart. "I wouldn't if I were you. You're on my property and trespassers have been known to get accidentally shot."

Chester's lips curled. "Look, buddy . . ."

Luke kept his face expressionless.

Zane stopped Chester again, his patience gone. The gentlemanly look he'd cultivated so carefully disappeared, replaced by the deadly eyes of the thug he was. "Don't be cute with me, Varner. My wife, should

73

she be alive, seems to have taken something of mine. Something I'm *not* happy about losing. I want it back. If you find her, tell her that for me. And remind her that I'm not a patient man. Let's go, Chester." He started down the pier.

With a grunt, the bodyguard followed. Still holding his gun, Luke watched them. Almost to the embankment, Zane turned, his face in shadow.

"I get the feeling you're on your own with this, Varner. You'd better keep looking over your shoulder. Until I get back what belongs to me, one of my men will be breathing down your neck every second." Turning, he marched up the dirt road with quick, angry strides, his hulking bodyguard behind him.

Luke waited until they were out of sight, then drew in a long, cleansing breath of air. Even the fish smelled better than those two. He went on board, tossed his gun onto a table and looked around. It would seem he wasn't the only one who could search a room and leave it looking undisturbed. He had no doubt that Zane and Chester had explored every inch. He also knew he had nothing of interest to them on board, which was probably why they'd waited for him.

From his favorite stool, Benjamin meowed a complaint at the unusual disruption of his evening nap. Luke bent to scratch his scruffy chin. "Quite a night, eh, Benjie? I'm not sure I like the changes around here any better than you do."

Strolling to the back railing, Luke shoved his hands in his pockets and stared up at the night sky as if he might find some answers written among the stars. In his mind's eye, he pictured Stephanie Westover in the photo Stephen had given him and in the sketches Kevin had made. Her father saw her as sweet and true, capable of no wrongdoing. Her best friend, Marjo, saw her as inexperienced, foolishly romantic, yet innately good. But neither of them knew

74

something of Zane's was missing.

Diamonds. From what the captain had told him, it had to be diamonds that Zane was missing. Several million dollars worth of diamonds. Perhaps her husband hadn't loved her, but obviously he hadn't considered her a thief. It would seem that Stephanie had disappeared at the same time the diamonds had vanished. A coincidence? Maybe. Interesting.

Maybe Zane had pushed her too far and she'd decided to get even with him in a big way. She'd realized her marriage was a mistake, asked for a divorce, and he'd refused. She'd still wanted out so she'd come up with another plan. Hit him where it would hurt the most. Take the diamonds and run.

Luke rubbed his stubbly jaw. It didn't fit with her past actions or the picture that had been forming in his mind as he'd pieced together fragments of her life. Yet experience had taught him that most people were like the tip of an iceberg, often revealing only a tiny fraction of themselves to even their closest companions.

Maybe little Stephanie had fooled them all. The possibility of a diamond package put a different light on things. Odd how let down he felt at that thought. Only a couple of days and he felt as if he knew Stephanie Westover and she'd disappointed him. He'd poked through her possessions, her life, touched the silk of her ripped nightgown. And now he was feeling as if she were just another scheming thief.

Well, he'd needed this jolt, Luke told himself as he went into the galley and poured himself a glass of milk. From the beginning, he'd been gazing at her picture and thinking soft thoughts. No more. He had his perspective back. Tomorrow, he'd do more checking, and later take a shot in the dark and try Boston, her favorite city. Guilty or innocent, he meant to find Stephanie Westover because Stephen had asked him to. And he'd let the courts decide her fate, as a police officer was supposed to do.

Despite his fine speeches to himself, Luke drank his milk and tasted regret.

Someone was watching her, she was certain of it. Stephanie leaned back against the rough bark of a large palm tree and let her eyes skim the people strolling by on the winding walkways. Pulling up her knees, she leaned her arms on them and studied each person who passed, searching for something familiar in a glance or a walk.

She'd altered her looks as much as humanly possible with her limited abilities, yet she knew no disguise was infallible if the searcher was determined. And she knew Zane was determined. She had something he badly wanted, and there'd be no stopping him from stalking her if he thought she was alive. He would send Chester, perhaps even Bob, or hire new people. His dirty money had spoken loud and clear to so many already. After learning about the things he'd done, how could she think he'd stop at anything?

Somehow she'd slipped up and he'd discovered she'd been planning on running. He must have had Chester tamper with her brakes, before he casually kissed her goodbye, going out of town on business to secure his alibi. How like Zane.

Just that morning, she'd run an errand, parking in front of the house, believing her car to be in top form. How had Chester been able to do his dirty work and not be seen? It couldn't have been a coincidence that her brakes had given out on the very day she'd planned to escape. Her every instinct told her that Zane was behind it all.

Had he also unearthed the secret she'd tried so painstakingly to hide from him, the baby he so badly wanted? she wondered with a thumping heart. If only he believed that she'd washed downstream, a drowning victim never to be heard from again. Had he acted the aggrieved husband, quietly mourning the loss of

76

his beloved? Love. Zane didn't know the meaning of the word.

Stephanie plucked a blade of grass and stuck it into her mouth as she squinted up at the clouds leisurely floating by. She wished she could enjoy the peace and tranquillity of this place where she'd finally stopped running. If only that prickly feeling, the sense of being watched, would go away. Was it her fear or her overactive imagination that had her feeling this way? In either case, if it continued, she'd simply have to pull up stakes and go searching for another temporary haven. And she'd have to do it soon, before roaming about became too difficult for her as her pregnancy advanced. At all costs, she had to protect the child growing inside her.

At least she had her driver's license and her safety deposit box, and the package safely inside the bank. Stephanie sighed deeply, wondering if this nightmare would ever end.

She felt terrible about leaving her dad without a word. Most likely, he was the one grieving. And Marjo, of course. How she longed to talk to them both, but she didn't dare. Zane had paid eyes and ears everywhere. She was careful with the people she'd met at work, surface acquaintances to whom she gave guarded responses. Maybe later, when everything calmed down and she felt safe again, she'd call Marjo. If anyone could keep a secret, that woman could.

But Marjo would want to know why she'd run, and Stephanie would have to tell her about the baby. She could hear Marjo now, asking why she simply hadn't gotten an abortion. That might have been her friend's answer to the problem, but it was not Stephanie's. She desperately wanted this baby, someone of her own to love. She had so much love stored up to give. Maybe she could explain all that one day to Marjo, and hopefully Marjo would understand. She was a good friend, and Stephanie could sure use a friend.

And a cigarette. Her body still craved the habit that

77

had been such a part of her since her midteens. But then, she'd had to give up a lot lately. If all worked out, it would be worth it. If not, if Zane found her, he would carry out his threat and see her dead.

For the hundredth time, she went over the events of that day in her mind, searching for some small thing she might have done that could lead him to her. The unexpected accident had pushed her plans to escape several hours ahead of schedule, but at least she'd been on her way. Upon arrival, she'd retrieved the bag she'd planted earlier in the week in the airport locker. She'd used only disposable paper bags and cheap canvas totes that couldn't easily be traced.

The first case of nerves had hit her in the restroom as she'd changed herself from a dumpy baglady into a sophisticated redhead. She'd gotten sick, but she'd kept going. She'd fastened the plastic-wrapped package around her middle. The tickets she'd purchased, all with cash, had been one-way, the route somewhat circuitous. Detroit to Chicago to Atlanta to Orlando.

Twice more she'd changed identities, and twice she'd gotten sick again. Still she wondered if all her maneuverings had been enough. If only she knew how Zane had reacted when her body hadn't been found, whether his naturally suspicious mind had him immediately sending someone searching for her. Was that someone, even now, watching her from behind a tree or waiting for her back at the Barbizon?

Maybe she should have stayed in her room longer, not gotten this job. But after a week, the walls had been closing in on her and the nightmares had kept her edgy and tense. Being outdoors, walking anonymously among people, both cheered and worried her. Stephanie's stomach rolled queasily. Hugging herself, she leaned forward and closed her eyes. Will I ever be able to relax again? she wondered.

"Hey, Juli," a female voice called. "Time's up."

Rising, Stephanie waved to Brenda, the woman who'd hired her only yesterday. Her lunch break was over, and it was time to get back to work. Returning to the employee's lounge, she opened her locker and changed her clothes. The last thing she slipped on was the large black head mask with the rounded ears. Taking a final look in the mirror and seeing herself in the bulky costume, she nodded in satisfaction. Yes, now she felt relatively safe.

Stepping outside as Minnie Mouse, she wandered leisurely down the winding roads of Disney World, ready once again to meet and greet the children who'd come for a day of fun.

Chapter Four

It was nice weather for a swim, better than the day Stephanie Westover had chosen for a dip. Luke stood on the grassy embankment on Lakeshore Drive, looking down into the choppy waters that had swallowed up a red BMW last week. And maybe Stephanie herself, though he doubted it.

She'd left her house at four that rainy day, her cleaning lady had told the police. Turning, he squinted into the late afternoon sun as he gazed up toward the narrow, winding street that ended at Lakeshore. He could just barely make out the Westover house at the top of the hill. From that starting point, the car with its useless brakes would have picked up momentum, and it would have been going quite fast by the time it hit the grassy area before plunging into the water not far from where he stood.

Sinking fast, she'd have been fighting panic. Her survival instincts could have enabled her to shove open the door and squirm out. A good swimmer, she'd have hit the surface quite rapidly. At that point, most people would have made for shore and safety. But not Stephanie. If his intuition was on target, she'd emerged, looked around, and headed for the yacht club, three-point-two miles downstream. Shoving his hands into his jeans pockets, Luke began to walk.

He'd left his van parked on a side street, intent this

afternoon on retracing Stephanie's moves, flying by the seat of his pants on this one. He could be wasting his time or hit pay dirt and learn something. Walking at a pace that he felt would keep abreast of a swimmer rushing along with a strong current, he kept going, his eyes on the wooden stairs set into the pilings that bordered the old clubhouse grounds. Once there, he stood, hands on his hips, mentally tracking his ghostly swimmer.

She'd have been nervous about being seen, he was certain, so her moves would have been furtive. The rain that day would have kept activity around the club to a minimum. Emerging, she'd have hurried along the path, climbed the stairs that zigzagged up the side of the building to the second floor where the women's locker room was located, and dodged inside. That's where she'd have encountered the towel girl who thought she'd seen Mrs. Westover. Luke stood in the shade of a tree, conjecturing.

Evidently, Stephanie hadn't run into anyone except the towel girl who'd had only a glimpse of her. She'd probably stashed some clothes in her locker earlier — tennis shoes, a raincoat, and scarf the girl had said. The river water wasn't too clean so she'd probably taken a quick shower, dressed, and sneaked quietly out. No car and not wanting to be seen, what would she have done next? Too chancy to call a cab. Turning, Luke gazed around. Suddenly, he broke into a sprint. A city bus was lumbering down the boulevard street, heading toward town.

The bus stop was located almost directly across from the yacht club. A large posted sign warned everyone to have the right change. Luke dropped in his coins and took a seat behind the driver. The man looked pleasant enough, and since they were alone for the time being, Luke decided to do a little probing.

"Nice day."

"Yup."

"Are you a regular driver on this run?"

"Yup."

"Were you working last Thursday?"

"Yup."

They stopped at a red light and Luke leaned forward, holding out the picture of Stephanie as she would have looked that day. "Do you remember seeing anyone who resembled this woman?"

The driver removed his sunglasses and studied the picture a long moment. He shook his head. "Nope."

"She disappeared that Thursday, the day of the accident along here." Luke pointed toward the river. "Do you remember that?"

"Sure do. Some rich dame drove her sports car into the drink. Police cars all over the place. Tied up traffic for hours."

"I can imagine." Another thing bothered him. She had to have planned her escape, hiding money in her locker also. Or else, where would she have gotten the bus fare? "You ever let anyone on who maybe doesn't have the right change or enough money?"

"Hell, no. Why should I?"

A heart of gold, this guy. Luke tapped the picture against the arm of his seat. "And you don't recall seeing this woman, maybe wearing a raincoat with a scarf on her head?"

The driver shrugged. "It was raining last Thursday. Everyone was wearing raincoats. People come, they go — all day long. I don't pay much attention." Pulling to the curb, he wheezed the bus to a stop and pressed open the door.

Terrific. A man who saw everything and observed nothing. Luke watched two black women carrying shopping bags climb aboard. Cleaning ladies for the large Grosse Pointe houses along Lakeshore most likely. Chattering, they moved toward the back. Returning the picture to his pocket, Luke shifted his gaze out the window.

If she'd have called anyone to help her, Marjo would have been the logical choice, and he knew Stephanie hadn't contacted her. She wouldn't have hitchhiked, he felt certain. No, the bus was the only answer. He leaned forward again. "Where does this bus end up before turnaround?"

"Downtown Detroit at the Sheraton Hotel by Washington Boulevard." The driver glanced over his shoulder at Luke. "Hey, man, maybe your lady wanted to duck out on you, you know?" He gave a sympathetic grunt. "I say, let her go. We're better off without 'em."

A bus-driving philosopher. However, Luke couldn't have agreed more.

It took forty minutes for the bus to pull up alongside the Sheraton Hotel. Luke stood on the sidewalk, wondering what Stephanie would have done next. She'd had a bad shock and a rough swim. She probably never rode city buses under normal circumstances, but that day she needed to get away from the area where she might be recognized as quickly as possible and grabbed her first and best option. Most likely, she also needed to get out of town. Her type wouldn't consider a Greyhound or even Amtrak, he figured. A plane would be her choice.

"Hey, buddy, you catching this limo?" a voice behind him asked.

Swiveling, Luke looked at the man in uniform, then at the long black vehicle parked at the curb. The airport limo, of course. "You bet," he answered, reaching for his money.

Taking a seat, he settled back, comfortable that he was on the right track.

Two hours later, he wasn't nearly as confident. Thoughtfully, he leaned against a pillar in the Detroit Metropolitan Airport terminal and watched a variety of travelers rush past. He'd shown Stephanie's picture to two limo drivers, but neither had remembered seeing her. Flashing his ID, he'd approached the supervisors of a dozen airlines and asked permission to show her pictures to agents on duty. Over fifty people and not one had shown a glimmer of recognition. Damn frustrating, Luke thought as he gazed around.

His eyes stopped at a seating area designated for smokers. Stephanie, Marjo had told him, was a heavy smoker. Strolling over, he sat down on one of the chairs and continued studying the area. He felt sure she'd taken the bus and most likely a cab or limo to the airport. By then, she'd surely needed a cigarette. Maybe she'd sat in this very section, wondering where to go. Her purse, containing her wallet, was in the river, so where had she gotten the money? If she'd formulated a plan to disappear, it had evidently been changed that day by the hole punched in her brake line. She'd had to improvise.

Luke noticed a woman dressed in slacks and carrying a raincoat walk past. Had Stephanie managed to buy some passenger's clothes perhaps? Glancing up, he saw the women's restroom directly across the wide aisle. A thought occurred to him and he rose, moving toward the service area.

Half an hour later, he stood at the front of the utility room alongside the shift supervisor who'd assembled her cleaning women together after he'd explained his problem.

"Ladies, I need your help. A young woman's missing and we have reason to believe she was here a week ago Thursday evening about this time. She may have used one of the restrooms to change her clothes before boarding a plane. I'd appreciate it if you'd carefully examine these pictures and tell me if you've seen *anyone* who resembles her."

Spreading the pictures on the low table, he then stood back and watched the seven women in uniform huddle around and lean down. His hopes took a downward spiral as one by one he saw the heads shake, heard the negative mutters. A chunky gray-haired woman lingered longer. He stepped up to her. "Does she look familiar?"

"No, sir, she don't," Bessie Norton said. Straightening, she looked up at the tall police officer. "But I did see something odd last Thursday. Was this lady wearing a raincoat maybe?"

Luke kept his expression bland. "We think so. And perhaps a scarf and tennis shoes."

Bessie nodded as the other women filed out. "A little before seven that night, just before quitting time, this lady went into one of the stalls in the restroom at the far end of Concourse A. She was walking slow and tired like, and was pretty wet, bits of hair sticking out from under her scarf."

"Uh-huh," Luke said encouragingly.

"Sounded like she was sick in there, you know. She took her sweet time, so I got busy emptying the trash. Next thing, I turn around and she's disappeared. At the sink, there's this tall woman wearing a fancy green dress and high heels. She's got red hair and long fingernails to match." Bessie gave a laugh. "That lady never done a lick of work in her life, I'd bet on it."

Luke frowned. "Are you saying you think the woman went into the stall in a raincoat and tennis shoes, then came out dressed like that?"

"Wasn't nobody else in there, 'cept me. I thought maybe she'd slipped out and I didn't see, but then, after the redhead left, I found the bag."

"What bag?"

"From Saks, it was, so I got nosy and looked inside." She gave a satisfied grunt. "There they were, the raincoat wrapped around those wet shoes, a scarf, and ladies panties. The panties, they was silk. I could tell."

Luke recalled seeing Stephanie's silken underthings back in her Grosse Pointe bedroom. "What did you do with the items?"

85

"Put 'em back in the bag and threw it away with the rest of my trash. What'd you think?"

"Right. What'd this redhead look like? Was she heavyset or slender? Round face or long? Did you catch the color of her eyes?"

"Nah. I only saw her a minute. But she wasn't heavy, more on the skinny side. She smiled at me in the mirror, kinda shy like, you know?"

"Was she wearing makeup?"

Bessie narrowed her eyes, trying to recall. "Bright red lipstick, I remember, like her nail polish. She was classy, you know?"

"Was she carrying anything?"

"Yeah, one of those big shoulder bags. Canvas, I think."

Luke smiled down at her. "Thanks. You've been a big help." With a nod to the supervisor, he left the room.

Wandering, he found Concourse A and stopped in front of the restroom the attendant had mentioned. It was located about ten yards from a semicircle of gates, all belonging to American Airlines. If Stephanie had changed into a disguise in that ladies' room, she'd probably done so just before boarding her flight. Walking closer, he scanned the gates, reading the departure times after seven and the destinations.

New York/Boston, Chicago/Los Angeles, and Dallas/Miami. That about covered the country coast to coast. Like looking for a needle in a haystack. Jamming his hands in his pockets, Luke strolled back into the terminal.

Yet he felt a shiver of excitement. His instincts told him that Stephanie Westover had been here that Thursday. How she'd managed to come up with a wig and new clothes, along with red fingernails, he hadn't figured out yet. She'd gotten sick in the restroom while changing her appearance, from nerves or from having swallowed some river water. But, determined as ever, she'd gotten on a plane and gone somewhere.

Walking out into the muggy twilight, Luke hailed a cab to take him back to his van. He didn't know precisely where she'd flown yet, but he would. And the logical place to start was her favorite city.

Boston.

Nervously, Stephanie closed the door to the phone booth and sat down on the small seat. Leaning back, she set her change purse on the shelf beneath the phone and took a deep breath. Should she, or shouldn't she? Dare she do it?

Two weeks and she was going out of her mind, slowly but surely. Never had she felt so isolated, so alone. But phoning was so risky. Then again, she was at a random booth on a street corner, not in her room at the Barbizon. Marjo would never give her away. And even Zane didn't have the ability to bug phones. Calling her father was out of the question. If he knew she was alive, his nature would force him to act. But she could rely on Marjo. And she badly needed to hear a familiar voice.

Heart in her throat, Stephanie inserted the first coin. The operator came on and told her how much more to deposit, then she waited. Four rings. It was late Saturday afternoon. Maybe Marjo wasn't home. Maybe . . .

"Hello?"

"Marjo?"

A pause. "Yes. Who is this?"

"Now, don't faint on me, Marjo. This is Stephanie, and I'm very much alive."

A gasp. "Oh, my God!"

"It's really me. Are you all right?"

Marjo took a deep, steadying breath, then another. "I'm not sure. Where are you?"

"Are you alone?"

87

"Yes."

"I'm in Florida."

"Steffie, I can't believe this. I went to your memorial service. I . . . Stephen! Have you called your father?"

"No, and I don't want you to, either. Promise me, Marjo. No one must know I've called you. *Promise me.*"

Marjo sat down on her white carpeting, taking the phone with her. "I promise. I feel like a blithering idiot. I've got a thousand questions. What the hell happened?"

Stephanie let out a trembling sigh. "It's a long story. I had to get away from Zane."

"I knew it. That son-of-a-bitch. Did he hurt you? If he hit you, I'll —"

"No. I'm all right." The afternoon in the study, the rage on Zane's face, came back to her, and Stephanie shuddered. "He threatened to kill me if I divorced him. I couldn't see a way out, so I made plans to disappear. I was going to leave that night, after you and I had dinner, but Zane must have found out. The brakes were totally gone."

Marjo groaned. "So you did go into the river. Good God!" Rising, she dragged the phone by its long cord and walked to the bar. If ever she needed a drink, it was now. "How did you make it?"

"Sheer willpower, I think. Is my father all right?"

"Healthwise, yes. But he can't accept your death. He's hired a cop to look for you."

Oh, no. That was one she hadn't figured. "Who is he?"

"Name's Luke Varner." Marjo dropped ice in a glass and poured. "Low-key and kind of dangerous looking, with the scars to prove it. I talked to Stephen yesterday. Luke learned that someone punched a hole in your brake line."

Stephanie felt the blood drain from her face. Suspecting was one thing, but hearing the truth was another.

"Are you all right? I shouldn't have told you. . . ."

"I'm okay."

"Why would Zane want you dead, Steffie?"

"Because I filed for divorce. And because he must have discovered I have some information on him, proof of a crime he committed and tried to cover up."

"You've got evidence against him? Lord, Steffie, you've got to be *very* careful."

"I'm trying to be. I've heard my father mention Luke Varner. A cop with a hair-trigger temper. I went to so much trouble. Do you think he might find me?" That was all she needed, another violent man after her.

"I wouldn't rule it out. The man's persistent as hell." Marjo took a long swallow. "But you know, I think if push came to shove, I'd trust him."

"Neither one of us is very good at judging men, in case you haven't noticed."

Marjo allowed herself a smile. "You've got a point there. So what are your plans? Where in Florida are you?"

"Orlando, and my plans are vague. I shouldn't have called, but I'm so damn lonely." She felt her control slipping.

"I'll fly to meet you. Together we can—"

"No, I can't take the chance. Does Zane suspect I didn't drown, do you know?"

"I can't say. He certainly acted the grief-stricken husband at your service. He put his arm around me, and I shook it off. If looks could kill—"

"And you haven't seen him since?"

"No. The cops have been here questioning me, twice. And Luke Varner was here. I talk to Stephen every few days. What do you want me to tell him?"

"Absolutely nothing. His life depends on his not knowing."

"All right. But are you okay? Do you need money?"

"I've got it under control." Sure she did. "I've got an apartment, a new name, a nothing job. But I may be moving on soon."

Marjo felt the frustration mount. "Is there anything I can do to help?"

"You have already, just hearing your voice."

"I'm so glad you're alive, Stephanie. But I'm worried about you. What if—"

"Don't start the what if's. I do enough of that on my own."

"If I'd have known that Zane was making your life unbearable, I'd have hired a hit man."

Stephanie laughed for the first time in weeks. "You're a treasure, Marjo, and I miss you terribly. There is one thing. Could you distract Luke Varner? I don't want him finding me."

Marjo sipped her scotch. "Distract him . . . as in sex, you mean? Forget it. I've got a feeling no one distracts Mr. Varner unless he allows it."

Just her luck. Turning, Stephanie noticed a car drive slowly by the phone booth, its lone occupant eyeing her. She shuddered. "I've got to go. I'll be in touch."

"Please do. And you take care. I love you, Steffie."

"Me, too. 'Bye." Blinking back tears, Stephanie hung up.

In a green service van parked outside Marjo's condo, Chester Thomas waited for the second click, then hung up the phone as a big smile creased his ruddy cheeks.

The boss had been right, as usual. Zane Westover was one smart man, and Chester felt grateful to be working for him. They'd had this van for some time, but never had it come in so handy. After their chat with Luke Varner, the boss had sent him over with special instructions. He was to stay in the van until he saw Marjo Collins leave her place; then he was to pick her lock and bug the house. Thirty minutes and he'd been back in the van.

He'd rather have rigged the phone, but Zane thought that was too dangerous. The telephone company's equipment could detect listening devices too easily. But the tiny bugs he'd planted in every room would go unnoticed by most people. Naturally, you could only hear one side of the conversation, but, after days of parking in the neighborhood and listening, today he'd heard plenty. And he'd recorded every word Marjo had said to that lying bitch who'd run out on the boss. She'd pay big now and Chester hoped Zane would let him be the one to do her in.

Picking up the phone, he dialed the Westover house.

Nothing like the exciting life of a cop, Luke thought as he left the airport parking lot and headed for the expressway and home. The movies and TV depicted detective work as one thrill after another, with shoot-'em-ups an everyday occurrence. Nothing was further from the truth. There was some of that, about three percent. The rest was monumentally boring, wrapped in endless, detailed paperwork.

Hot and tired, Luke struggled with Friday night rush-hour traffic. He'd spent an entire week in Boston doing tedious legwork. Dull, draining, and fruitless.

He'd scoured the city, visiting little theater groups around the South End where he'd learned from Stephen that Stephanie had lived during her summer there. He'd shown her pictures to stage managers, acting companies, apartment managers, allergy doctors, coffee houses, and ice cream parlors. Not a trace.

Zipping his van around a slow-moving truck, he realized he'd come to two conclusions. It was unlikely that Stephanie Westover was now or had recently been in her favorite city of Boston, and he could squander away half his life going about the search city by city.

The country was too damn big, and they had too few clues as to where she'd gone. He'd go home, rest up, feed his cat, and maybe spend tomorrow fishing. But first he'd check in with Stephen and Captain Renwick to see if there'd been any developments in his absence. If there were new leads, he'd follow up on them. If not, he'd wait until there were.

Police work involved a great deal of waiting, a fact that gnawed away at Luke's impatient nature. But he was experienced enough to know some things couldn't be rushed.

Gazing up into a cloudy sky, he wondered if it would rain soon. The fish came to the surface in droves on a rainy day.

Humming to herself, Marjo held her face up to the shower spray. Stephanie was alive! She still could hardly believe it. She'd underestimated her friend's strength. That had been one hell of a swim to survival. What had she discovered about Zane that prompted such a daring escape? And why had she chosen Florida, of all places? So many questions there hadn't been time to ask. Pivoting, she let the water rinse the shampoo from her hair, then turned the faucet off.

Quickly, she wrapped a towel around her hair, then took another and began drying herself with it. If only she could tell Stephen and relieve the poor man's mind. But she'd honor her friend's request, knowing Stephanie was right. Stephen's life would be in danger if he knew her whereabouts. Clearly Zane would stop at nothing to get his way.

Marjo shivered at the thought despite the heat of the bathroom. She opened the door to dissipate the steam and shrugged into a long white terrycloth robe, belting it at the waist. Reaching for her comb, she paused in midmotion, listening. She'd heard something, a noise coming from the direction of the living room.

Holding the pointed end of the comb out as a makeshift weapon, she crept out into the hallway and peered into her large living room. All was quiet, and nothing looked disturbed. Feeling foolish, Marjo let out a rush of air and went back into the bathroom. She was letting her thoughts spook her. Small wonder after her suspicions about Zane Westover had been confirmed by Stephanie.

Removing the towel from her head, she ran the comb through her hair. There was a lot Steffie hadn't told her, but Marjo was good at reading between the lines. That slime ball had surely hurt her somehow; she was certain of it. Steffie had paused too long when she'd asked the question. Oh, how she'd like to see him pay. Shaking her hair back, she turned off the light and left the bathroom.

Running away was only a temporary answer, Marjo thought as she walked to the bar. Surely Steffie didn't intend to keep on the move, hopping from city to city, always looking over her shoulder and fearing that Zane might find her. She dropped ice into a glass. The next time her friend phoned, she'd be more prepared. She'd insist that Steffie allow her to help. Whatever evidence against Zane she'd found, they'd use it to get him behind bars where he belonged.

Pouring scotch, she began to plan. They'd hire a lawyer, the best. Threatening someone's life, even if that someone was your wife, was illegal. They'd stack up the proof, then move on him. Luke Varner, she guessed, would be only too glad to help. Marjo bent her head back and took a long swallow.

"Make me one, too, will you?"

Startled, Marjo nearly choked before she dropped

the glass onto the thick white rug. Scotch and ice splattered in a wide arc as she swung about, hoping she'd been mistaken about the familiar voice. She hadn't been.

Zane Westover's dark eyes met her shocked gaze as amusement touched his thin lips. "Where are your manners, Marjo, not offering your guest a drink?"

Gripping the lapels of her robe with trembling hands, Marjo swallowed a hard lump of fear, trying desperately to regain her composure. "How'd you get in here?"

"I have my ways." He stepped closer, raising his hand toward her. "You're even more beautiful without makeup."

She moved back quickly, out of his reach. He looked threatening, dressed in black shirt and pants as well as black sneakers. On his hands, he wore tight leather gloves. She pulled in a deep breath. "Don't touch me. Do you think now that you're wife's dead you can move in on me?"

Zane gave her a knowing smile. "Come now. We both know Stephanie's not dead."

"Not dead?" Marjo tightened the belt of her robe, her mind frantically searching for the right thing to say. How could he know? "Did the police find her? Where is she?"

She'd never seen eyes turn so cold, so menacing. "You tell me," Zane said, moving closer.

Marjo twisted abruptly toward the center of the room. She needed a weapon, desperately. "I don't know what you're talking about."

Undeterred, Zane followed. "I think you do."

She bent to grab the heavy crystal ashtray from the coffee table. Ashes and butts flew as she picked it up and raised her arm high. "Don't come any closer."

Zane stood very still. "Tell me what I want to know and I won't hurt you."

She didn't believe him. Gripping the ashtray, she

94

spread her feet for balance, waiting for the right moment. How she'd love to split his arrogant face wide open. "Threats, Zane? I think you'd better get the hell out of my home. I could nail you for breaking and entering."

In a swift movement, he snatched the silver candlestick from the table and smashed it down hard onto the glass top. Shards sailed in every direction, settling on the thick carpeting.

Marjo flinched and stepped back, sheer terror almost making her drop the heavy ashtray. The bastard wasn't buying her bluff, but she had no choice except to continue. "My neighbors next door probably heard that and are calling the police."

"Your neighbors are out for the evening, and the people on the other side are away for the weekend." He narrowed his gaze. "Do you think I've come this far by taking stupid chances?"

Fury made her reckless. "You can step out of the gutter, but the stench clings to you forever. You thought you could get clean, gain respectability by marrying Steffie. You're not fit to polish her shoes. You're a cheap crook, and you'll always be just that."

"Damn you . . ." Raging inside, Zane lunged to grab her across the shattered table.

Marjo took aim and hurled the ashtray with all her strength. But the heavy weight threw it off course and it merely grazed Zane's shoulder, infuriating him further. Realizing this, she turned to run, but he was too fast for her. With a sinking heart, she felt his hard fingers close around her upper arms.

"Do you want a second murder on your record?" Marjo blinked as he whirled her about to face him. "The police know there was a hole punched in the BMW's brake line. You won't get away with this."

That damn Luke Varner. One day, he'd make him pay, too. Zane drew her up close, watching terror jump into her eyes, enjoying the moment. She was almost as tall as his own 5'9" so they were nearly nose to nose. He watched the pulse in her throat pound and toyed with the idea of shoving her to the floor and taking her. He liked a little fight in his women, a little struggle. It was always more satisfying that way. A pity he couldn't spare the time.

He squeezed her upper arms. "I was in Cleveland that day, remember?"

If she kept him talking, perhaps she'd get another opportunity. Her foot was resting on a large chunk of broken glass, the edge cutting into her flesh. If only she could get to it. "You wouldn't mess up your manicure by doing your own dirty work. Slime like you hire others, but you were behind it. How Stephanie could stomach having you touch her is beyond me."

Zane banked his anger, knowing he'd make her pay in the end. "She loved it. Did you know she was a virgin when I married her? But I taught her, and she loved it."

"Bullshit! She told me what a lousy lover you were."

"You lying slut! She couldn't get enough of me."

Marjo forced a derisive laugh. "I always told Steffie she should have tried out for the stage."

His face twisted with hatred as his fingers pressed into her flesh. He'd had enough of this cat-and-mouse game. He gave her a backhanded slap that swung her head about. "And I always told her you were a lying bitch. But you're going to tell me the truth tonight, aren't you, Marjo? If you want to keep that beautiful face of yours from being carved up, that is. Or would you rather I got Chester from out in the van and had him come in and persuade you? Chester gets off on cutting up pretty women, and he's got a brand new switchblade."

Her cheek stinging, Marjo fought down the panic. She mustn't let him see how truly frightened she was, because she was certain Zane was capable of hurting

96

her very badly. She wouldn't even let herself think of Chester. "I don't know anything," she said as calmly as she could.

Swiftly he shoved her onto the couch, and before she could recover, he slapped her again across her lying mouth. Breathing hard, he smiled in satisfaction as he saw new red marks appear on her pale cheeks. She raised her hands in a protective gesture that failed to move him as he leaned down close to her.

"Your house is bugged, Marjo, every room. We recorded the telephone call from Stephanie. We know she's in Florida somewhere. And you're going to tell us where."

His smile was deadly. It made Marjo's blood run cold. Realizing he'd only heard her side of the conversation, she tried to think, to outwit him. She'd have to play along without giving too much away. "She didn't say where in Florida."

His hand cracked across her face again, even harder. He heard her cry out in pain as she slid to the floor, onto the broken glass. "I'm going to give you one more chance to tell the truth before I get really rough. *Where is she?*"

Her hand closed around a chunk of glass, praying he hadn't noticed the movement. Let him lean down, just a little more. "I don't know where."

Suddenly an idea struck Zane, the perfect way to make her talk. He yanked her up and hauled her to her feet. His shoes crunched on broken glass as he dragged her toward the patio. As he paused to unlatch the sliding glass door, he felt a stabbing pain in his shoulder and let out an oath.

Whirling, he saw she had a piece of glass in her hand, and was raising it again to strike him. Furious, he seized her wrist and squeezed until she dropped the weapon. Still holding her, he touched his wound gingerly and decided she hadn't done too much damage. The cut wasn't deep, though it was already bleeding.

He glared at her. "You're going to regret this."

Viciously, he shoved the glass doorwall open and dragged her out onto the patio. Marjo almost stumbled in her anxiety to pull away from him, but his fingers were like steel clamps on her arm. Her face was nearly numb from his bruising slaps, her feet were bleeding, and her robe was hanging open. She had to find a way to get free of him—and quickly. "Why are you doing this?" she asked. "I don't know anything more."

At the pool's edge, Zane stopped. "We'll just see about that." Untying the belt, he whipped the robe from her, still holding her one arm. Despite the heat of a summer evening, he saw her shiver and knew it was from fear. He suddenly felt powerful, invincible even. How did this pitiful creature think she could outwit him?

"So you'd have hired a hit man to get rid of me, eh?" He laughed, low and throaty. "It's going to take a whole lot more than you and your pathetic friend to stop Zane Westover. I've got big plans, baby."

She had to keep him talking, goad him on. Then his gigantic ego would take over. "You're not smart enough to pull off anything really big." She narrowed her eyes. "Or are you?"

"Not smart enough?" Zane's laugh rang out again. "Baby, I'm about as smart as you're apt to meet. You should have played your cards right and gone after me."

Marjo tried to ignore the pain of his grip on her flesh. "You're not rich enough for me, Zane. What can you possibly make in that little antique store?"

"Peanuts, sweetheart." He leaned close to her face. "But I've got more money than even you could spend. My dear wife stole a couple of million from me, but I'll get it back. And I've got more than twice that amount coming in in another month."

"I don't believe you."

There was no reason not to tell her, Zane decided. He was going to kill her anyhow. Let her die knowing what she might have had. "Believe it. Diamonds, baby, worth around ten million. Drifting across the border right into my hands, nice and easy. And those dumb cops can't tie me in to a thing."

Marjo's mind was racing. What had Steffie stolen from him? What could she ask that would divert him long enough to ease his hold on her? She needed only one chance, just one. "Impossible," she said with derision. "Those border cops are sharp."

"The hell they are. We've been shipping things through right under their noses for a couple of years. My partner up there's almost as smart as I am. Never been arrested, either of us."

"Maybe I *am* impressed."

Zane had grown weary of taunting her, despite her obvious beauty. He let his eyes roam lazily over her breasts and down her naked body. Even banged up and bruised, she was some looker. "Too bad I don't have time to show you what a real man is like."

He was insufferable. Fury overcoming her fear and even her good sense, Marjo shifted her head and spit in his face. Bracing herself for the blow, she didn't have long to wait as his hand struck her cheek once, then again. She felt a slight ringing in her ears and stifled a groan.

"Enough!" Zane snarled. "Where is she? Tell me now, or I swear these are your last few moments alive."

Marjo took in a shaky breath. "All right. She's in Miami." She let herself go slightly limp as if in defeat, hoping he'd buy it.

Cruelly he jerked her chin, forcing her to face him. He studied her eyes, trying to determine if she was telling him the truth. He'd always prided himself on being a good judge of people, their motives and weaknesses. Marjo looked frightened and cowed, subdued. He'd never seen her that way before. She was probably thinking he'd set her free once she told him. Zane narrowed his eyes. "You'd better not be lying to me."

"I'm not. Now, please, leave me alone." She hated to ask, but thought Zane was the type of man who felt ten feet tall if a woman begged. She prayed she was right. "You've got what you want. Let me go, please."

He raised an amused brow. "Let you go? My dear Marjo, you know a little too much for my peace of mind." Gripping both her arms, he shoved her into the pool at the three-foot end and heard her gasp in surprise.

"What . . . what are you doing?" Marjo stammered as she found her footing.

"Teaching you a lesson," Zane said as he knelt alongside. "Goodbye, Marjo." With that, he clipped her a hard blow on her chin, saw the shocked surprise in her eyes just before they drifted closed. She slumped and he caught her, then moved her into a floating position, face down. Leaning over, he held her by one arm as, with his other hand, he kept her head under water.

Evidently, he'd knocked her unconscious for there was no struggle left in her, he was relieved to see. He counted to himself slowly, then cautiously released her. Her body bobbed a bit on the surface of the water as he let go of her arm, then gently floated away. Slowly, she drifted from him along the edge of the pool, her long hair shimmering in the underwater lights like a dark curtain around her head.

Zane dipped his hand in and splashed water on his cut shoulder, not removing his shirt, then stood. He shook the excess water from his gloved hands and wiped the palms on his pants. He wasn't even breathing hard. With head cocked, he listened intently. The night breeze rustled the leaves of a nearby tree. Otherwise, there was only silence. He glanced over his shoulder and saw that Marjo had glided toward the deep end. Satisfied, he went back inside.

Planning ahead, he'd worn gloves, so there'd be no fingerprints. Reaching into his hip pocket, he drew out a screw driver and within moments had broken the lock to the patio. The police would surmise that there'd been a forcible entry, perhaps a rejected lover. The man and Marjo had quarreled, fought in the living room; then he'd drowned her. Perfect. Pocketing the tool, he walked to the front door and opened it cautiously.

The van, with Chester inside, was parked across the street and up two doors, the motor quietly idling. Odd how in this swanky neighborhood there were so few street lights, the nearest halfway down the curving street. High, well-tended shrubs bordered each unit. He smiled again as he thought how safe the rich bitches who lived here must feel. Soon they would think differently.

Stepping outside, Zane shut the door behind him and stood looking around for a minute. No one about that he could see. Walking purposefully, he made his way to the van.

Miami. He'd make a few calls and send Chester to Miami immediately. And he'd put a tail on Luke Varner, just to be sure. Soundlessly, he opened the van door and climbed in.

"Let's go," he said to Chester, then rolled his injured shoulder.

"You hurt, boss?" Chester asked, shifting into gear.

"It's nothing. Get going." Zane looked up at a nearly full moon and wondered if Stephanie, somewhere in Miami, was also gazing at a peaceful sky.

Sleep well, baby, he thought. Your days are numbered.

Luke poured himself a tall glass of milk, then tilted his head back and drained half of it. Taking the glass with him, he walked into his living room and sat down wearily in his plaid chair. Benjamin eyed him sleepily from his stool perch, then drifted back to dozing. The houseboat swayed lightly in the gently rolling water and the ever-present smell of fish teased Luke's nostrils. A midnight moon shone in through the open aft windows, and a summer breeze tangled with the flag dangling from the pole. Luke was glad to be home.

It had been a long twenty-four hours—a long two weeks, if the truth be known—and he was feeling the strain. The three-hour drive each way to Matt's cabin hadn't exactly refreshed him, but he'd been glad to see his old friend.

He'd known Matt Lewis forever, it seemed. They'd grown up on the same block, played football on the same high-school team, and dated some of the same girls. They'd even lost their virginity on the same night, at Matt's house when his parents had been out of town. Luke smiled and swallowed more milk as he thought of that nervous evening, and so many other days and nights he'd shared with his old friend.

They'd gone on to college together, Matt studying law while Luke had opted for law enforcement. They'd stood up at each other's weddings and been there for each other when they'd buried their wives. Ginny Lewis had died of cancer five short years after their wedding, and though Matt rarely spoke of her, Luke was sure his friend had never gotten over her death. I'm married to the law now, Matt was fond of saying, and she's a demanding old broad.

He'd needed a favor, so he'd called Matt and they'd met at his friend's cabin on the lake up near Tawas. They'd talked long into the night, Matt smoking his pipe and Luke chewing on the stem of his. Matt had stroked his graying beard and sipped from his ever-present jug of port wine as they'd shared their

102

thoughts. Luke had felt better afterward, he acknowledged. Matt was sensible, down-to-earth and very reliable, only a few of the reasons he was such a good attorney.

Finishing his milk, Luke leaned back in his chair and contemplated the next move in his efforts to locate Stephanie Westover.

The phone jangled, interrupting him. He considered not answering, then decided that wouldn't be such a hot idea. He reached for the instrument and barked a rather unfriendly hello.

"Is that you, Luke? It's Stephen."

Luke came instantly alert. The man's voice was almost shrill in his excitement. "Yeah, it's me. What's up?"

"I know where Stephanie is."

Chapter Five

"Okay, so where is she?" Luke asked.

"In Orlando, Florida." Stephen felt better, now that he'd finally reached Luke at home. His anxiety had had him pacing. "I've been trying to reach you all day."

"I had something to take care of. How do you know she's in Orlando?"

Stephen let out an exasperated sigh. "I forgot to mention something that afternoon we talked. When Stephanie married, I gave her some municipal bearer bonds. I just learned this morning that one has been cashed in Orlando."

Silently, Luke thought that over.

But Stephen was too excited to be contained. "I was going through some papers yesterday when I remembered the bonds. It's dangerous to keep bearer bonds around, as I'm sure you're aware, because there are no names on them. They belong to the bearer, whoever that might be. But they yield high interest and they're readily accessible in case you need cash in a hurry. When Stephanie insisted on marrying Zane, I had a feeling that one day she might need money fast. It turns out, I was right."

"How much did you give her?"

"A hundred thousand dollars worth."

With effort, Luke kept from whistling long and low. "You're a very generous father."

"I'm a rich man, Luke, and Stephanie's my only child."

He was beginning to realize how devoted a parent this man was. "How do you know one of the bonds has been cashed?"

"Yesterday, when I remembered the bonds, I called the municipality named on them and asked to be notified if one was cashed. You see, when one is presented for payment at a bank, it has to be forwarded to Michigan for authorization before the money is released. My contact there, Gerald Wise, called me at home this morning. I'd told him how anxious I was."

"I see. And what was the amount submitted for payment?"

"Five thousand. But I haven't told you the best part. The bearer's name is Juli Richards."

Luke rubbed his chin thoughtfully. "That could be anyone, Stephen. Maybe the bonds were stolen, or lost, or—"

"No, wait." Stephen's voice was impatient. "Juliana Richards is Stephanie's grandmother's name. My wife's mother died shortly after Stephanie married. Don't you see? Stephanie adored her grandmother, and has taken her name."

"Maybe. Does Zane know about these bonds?"

"I doubt it. She probably kept them in a safe place. Zane has a safety deposit box, she once told me, but her name isn't on it. I gathered he used it more for business purposes, though I'd love to take a peek inside. At any rate, I asked Stephanie not to tell him she had her own money, and I feel she didn't. I'd wager that's what she used to finance her disappearance. What do you think?"

A hundred grand plus a cache of diamonds. Small wonder little Stephanie hadn't bothered to pack the family jewels. Luke sighed, feeling suddenly drained. This case was becoming more complex by the day. And at the other end of the phone, a father desperate with new hope was waiting for his answer. He tried to sound positive. "I think it bears looking into."

Stephen paused, obviously disappointed that Luke wasn't more enthusiastic. "I'm sure it's her, Luke. I can feel it in my bones."

"Yeah, all right. I'll catch a plane in the morning for Orlando. What's the name of the bank she's using?"

"The First Financial Center it's called. The main branch downtown. She probably chose it because the bigger the bank, the more anonymous the customers are and the less chance there'd be of anyone noticing her and remembering."

"You've got a point." Luke pulled out the side table drawer and removed the telephone book. "I'll be in touch."

"Do that. Do you need any money?"

"Not now, thanks. Call you soon."

"Good luck, Luke."

Luke yawned. He wasn't thrilled about what might be just another wild-goose chase, this time to Florida. But he had to check this out. That meant he'd have to again leave Benjamin with Herman Eubanks, the old codger whose houseboat was anchored about five miles north of Luke's. Herman would be pleased, but Benjamin still hadn't forgiven Luke for his Boston trip.

Reluctantly, he looked up the number, called the airline, and made reservations for an early flight leaving the next morning. Taking a chance that he could locate him this late, he dialed the captain's number. Though he'd spoken with Renwick yesterday, he needed to update him. Leaning back, he counted the rings, then straightened when he heard the captain's gruff greeting.

Afterward, because he had a hunch, he called Mary Margaret O'Malley at home. There were things Megs could help him with and would—outside the department rules.

Stephanie gasped, then clamped her hand over her mouth to keep from crying out. No, it couldn't be true. It just couldn't.

She glanced up, reassuring herself she was alone in the Disney World employees' lounge. Someone had left the *Orlando Sentinel* morning paper on a chair, and she'd been idly reading it after eating her lunch. The headline on the article on page four had all but jumped out at her. GROSSE POINTE SOCIALITE FOUND DROWNED. Oh, God, no!

Stephanie's hands were shaking so badly she could scarcely hold the paper still long enough to finish the short news report. Marjo Collins had been found drowned in her back yard pool on Saturday, the article stated. Stephanie bit down hard on her knuckles, fighting back a scream that threatened to escape.

Marjo was a powerful swimmer, her endurance amazing. Drowned? Impossible. She scanned the article again. The police had found evidence of a break-in, a struggle. There were bruises on Marjo's arms and face, indicating she'd fought with her assailant. *Dear God!* Yet it appeared that nothing was missing from her home, so they were ruling out robbery.

Shuddering, Stephanie faced the truth. Zane had gotten to Marjo, she was sure of it. Not him most likely. Probably Chester had done it, for Marjo was tall and quite strong. Had Zane somehow learned that she'd phoned her? Guilt washed over Stephanie as she realized she'd signed Marjo's death warrant with that selfish call.

But how had he found out? Surely even Zane wouldn't have the capability to bug someone's phone. Had he threatened Marjo, forced her to talk?

Trembling, Stephanie set the paper aside and struggled with a wave of nausea. Hugging her arms, she closed her eyes, mourning Marjo's evidently painful death. The high cost of befriending Stephanie Westover. Was her father next? Had all her careful plans, her brave escape, been for nothing? Was Zane's long reach going to kill everyone she loved?

Feeling a flutter inside, she pressed a hand to her stomach, trying to allay her unease. She was almost three months along in her pregnancy, too soon to feel life. Yet she felt her child's presence as surely as if he'd moved. For her unborn baby, she would have to be strong. She couldn't let Zane win.

Stephanie took a tissue from her pocket and wiped her eyes. Oh, how she regretted the loneliness that had caused her to phone Marjo. Or had Zane coincidentally sent Chester to pay her friend a visit on the same night she'd happened to call? She would never know. But she couldn't take another risk. She'd have to quit this job, move from the Barbizon, relocate.

Thinking back, trying to recall her conversation with Marjo, she decided she hadn't disclosed very much. But she had mentioned the city she was in. Still, Orlando was large and teeming with tourists. Perhaps if she moved to one of the suburbs, stayed inside for a while and lost herself in a sleepy little Southern town . . . She didn't need the money from a job. Yes, that's what she'd do, for now.

Oddly, she'd felt almost safe, hiding behind the mask of Minnie Mouse, for a brief time. Rising on shaky legs, Stephanie went in search of Brenda, the woman who'd hired her, to reluctantly turn in her notice.

In his rented Buick, Luke drove along Orange Avenue toward the center of town where the bank was located. In Orlando only an hour and already he was sticky and damp from the early afternoon heat and humidity. The Monday flight had been noisy and crowded with parents and children excitedly anticipating a Disney World vacation. The few businessmen aboard had looked annoyed at having to be squeezed in among the chattering throngs. When the child

108

seated next to him had spilled her breakfast milk all over herself as well as his pantleg and shoe, Luke hadn't been overjoyed either. But he'd helped the poor frazzled young mother mop up.

The woman behind the car-rental counter had given him a map, circling the location of the bank at Orange Avenue and Michigan Street. He checked it now to make sure he was on the right track. Finding he was, he squinted into the sun and spotted the sign up ahead. He turned into the lot, stuck his sunglasses on, then left the car.

"Miss Carpenter's office is over there," the harassed teller at the first window told him, indicating with her outstretched arm the general direction of the manager's office. "Sorry you had to wait, but it's the first of the month and we always get a rush when the Social Security checks come in." She flashed him an automatic smile, then turned to her next customer.

Luke knocked once on Miss Carpenter's glass door and waited until she beckoned him in. "Nice of you to spare me some time," he began as he stretched out a hand to shake her carefully manicured one. While calculated charm wasn't natural to Luke, he needed this woman's help and wasn't above using whatever means necessary to get her cooperation.

While she examined his police ID, Luke looked her over. This branch of the First Financial Center was housed in an older building that had seen better days. Miss Carpenter, he couldn't help thinking, had also had her prime some time ago. Her blond hair was a little too brassy, her makeup applied with too heavy a hand. She was a little overweight which wouldn't have been so obvious if she'd chosen clothes a size larger and a bit less youthful.

She raised her thick false eyelashes and gave him a toothy smile. "What can I do for you, Detective Varner?"

"I understand you recently received approval from a Michigan municipality to cash a bearer bond in the amount of five thousand dollars for a Juli Richards. Is that correct?"

"I don't know, but I'll check for you." She stood and walked to the door, her tight skirt clinging to every bulge.

"While you're at it, I'd also like to know what accounts she has here, and if she's rented a safety deposit box."

"Certainly." Miss Carpenter left, returning in five minutes, in her hand a three-by-five card. Resuming her seat, she flashed him a victory smile. "Juli Richards did cash a bearer bond ten days ago, approved by the city of Livonia, Michigan, through the First Federal Savings and Loan Corporation. She has a checking account with us, opened that same day, and a safety deposit box."

"Can you tell me the amount in her checking account?"

Miss Carpenter hesitated, folding her ringless fingers together. "Do you have a court order or a warrant, Detective Varner?"

He'd been prepared for the possibility of reluctance. Bank personnel liked to play by the book. Warrants and court orders took time and required explanations he was unwilling to give right now. Crossing his legs, Luke sent her a sincere look. "I realize my request is somewhat unorthodox. I'm working on a missing-person case." He handed her his card. "You could call that number and ask for Captain Renwick for verification."

Miss Carpenter studied him a moment, then shook her head, obviously deciding to trust him. "That won't be necessary. You have an honest face."

Luke watched her bat her eyes almost coyly as she picked up the card again. On her desk was a picture of a teenage boy. Luke guessed she was divorced and getting desperate. He was getting her message, but he wasn't in the market.

"Juli Richards has forty-five hundred in her account, and the notation reads that she took the other five hundred in cash." She looked up at him. "Has she committed a crime?"

"Not that I know of. Has anyone else been inquiring about her?"

"I don't believe so."

He gave her his best winning smile. "Would it be possible for me to examine her safety deposit box?" He was fully aware he was really pushing on this one, but saw no harm in trying.

She looked disappointed, undoubtedly realizing she'd gone as far as she could without breaking the law. "I'm sorry, but that's against bank regulations. It also is a violation of our customer's privacy. If you could bring me a court order, I'd be happy to accommodate you."

"Perhaps later. I'd like her address, please."

She looked doubtful, then studied his card again. Finally, she wrote the address down and handed him the paper.

Luke stood. "Do you personally recall meeting Juli Richards?"

Again, that apologetic smile. "I wish I could help you, but this is a very large bank and I don't have time to meet many of our customers."

He pulled out the pictures of Stephanie and showed them to her. "Do any of these look familiar?"

Miss Carpenter scanned the photos quickly. "No, I'm sorry."

Tearing a sheet from his notebook, he scribbled down the address of a motel he'd spotted and decided to use. "This is where I'll be staying. Now that you know we're looking for Juli Richards and what she looks like, I'd appreciate it if you'd call me should she come in."

Miss Carpenter rose and took the sheet from him. "I'll red-flag her account and call you *personally*." Running her tongue over her red lips, she smiled invitingly at him.

111

Luke nodded his thanks and got the hell out of there. The Miss Carpenters of the world made him uncomfortably sad. And she'd reminded him of Marjo Collins minus the class.

In his car, he read the address she'd given him. The Barbizon Hotel for Women on Edgewater Drive. If Stephanie was there, this was all coming together too easily.

He'd never trusted easy answers.

"Yeah, boss, this is the first chance I had to call you." His eyes on the door to the motel office, Chester stood in the phone booth across the street. "I was all set to catch the flight to Miami when I saw Luke Varner in the airport. He picked up a ticket to Orlando, so I hurried and had mine changed and followed him."

Zane leaned back in his leather desk chair. So the bitch had lied to him after all. "Good work, Chester. Did he see you?"

"No. The flight was full of kids and tourists. I kept my eye on him, though. He rented a car and drove to a bank." He checked his notes. "The First Financial Center it's called. Downtown. He was in there quite a while, but I kept watch on the door. I thought if I went inside, he'd make me for sure."

"Good thinking." For once, Chester was using his head. "Where are you now?"

"Across from this motel. Varner's in the office. I can't tell whether he's checking in or asking about Stephanie."

"You stick with him, you hear? Don't let that cop out of your sight, and don't let him see you."

"Got it."

"And call me later when you get a chance. If I'm not here, try the car phone. This has top priority, Chester."

"Okay, boss. Talk to you later."

"You're doing great. I won't forget this."

Chester hung up the phone, Zane's praise ringing in his ears. Angling the door, he kept his eyes on the tall man talking to the guy behind the counter. The sun was glinting on the motel window, but he could still make out the two men.

Pleased, he leaned on the booth's doorframe. The boss was happy with him. Everyone thought he was a little slow, just because he'd gotten hurt in the ring a couple times. Running his hand through his blond crewcut, Chester smiled. He'd outsmart that cocky Varner and bring Stephanie back to Zane. He'd show them all that Chester Thomas was a man to be reckoned with.

Chewing on an unlit cigar, he peered across the street.

"Juli, you were wonderful with Clara Masters," Sandy Burke said as she handed Stephanie a cup of coffee and sat down on the couch alongside her. "How did you know the right things to say to make her want to stay?"

Stephanie took a sip of the coffee, grateful for its warmth. Despite the Florida heat, she'd been feeling chilled all day, and more than a little queasy. She turned toward Sandra. "She's so frightened, Sandy. Frightened of leaving the familiar, of returning to her abusive husband. Yet she's scared to death he'll find her here and be even worse to her. I know how she feels because I've been there. I just acted on instinct."

Sandy brushed a lock of limp blond hair from her face. "Your instincts are sure on target." She glanced through the archway and into the next room where Clara lay curled up on a cot at the far end. "I think she may be able to sleep now."

"I hope so. She's exhausted, poor thing." Stephanie shook her head sympathetically. "And she's only twenty."

113

Sandy's world-weary gaze shifted to the woman beside her. Juli Richards had come in to Safe Harbor, the shelter for battered women that Sandy and her mother operated out of an old renovated storefront on the outskirts of Winter Park just north of Orlando, on Sunday afternoon. She'd come to volunteer, she'd said, willing to do anything that needed doing, and they'd been thrilled to have her.

But Juli was hardly the average volunteer. Despite her collegiate looks, that fresh face, the youthful haircut, and the attractive clothes, there was something in her eyes that made you look twice. There was compassion mingled with determination and an occasional hint of buried pain. Sandy had seen a lot of troubled women come and go over the past five years, and Juli Richards wasn't the typical battered woman.

"You can't be much older than Clara," Sandy went on. "Most of our volunteers have similar backgrounds. Was it your father who abused you? Or a boyfriend, a husband?"

Stephanie gripped the coffee mug in both hands. She would share just enough with Sandy to satisfy her, but she mustn't say too much. Shelters like Safe Harbor were run by a whole army of closemouthed women, but one loose tongue could be dangerous. "My husband," she answered softly.

Sandy nodded, shifting her bulky frame more comfortably on the shabby couch. "With me, it was my father. Started coming to my bedroom when I was eleven. When I put up a fight, he hit me until I stopped fighting him. When my mother tried to stop him, he hit her."

She'd heard it before, at the shelter where she'd volunteered her time in Michigan and on the evening news countless times. Still, the stories of violence and its after-effects never failed to move Stephanie. She reached out a hand to touch Sandy's arm. "But you're here and it's over."

Setting down her empty cup, Sandy nodded.

"Yeah, it's over—and the bastard's dead. But then, so's my sister."

"Your sister?"

"Monica wasn't so lucky. She broke her ankle that summer, had a cast on it. Mom and I weren't home, and my father wouldn't let her be. She couldn't run, but she fought him anyway. He beat her senseless. Mom walked in on it and stabbed him with a butcher knife, but it was too late. Monica died. But so did he, thank God." She swung bleak eyes to Stephanie. "I couldn't cry, you know. Not for him. They didn't charge my mother." She nodded toward the room where Clara lay. "Now every young girl who comes in looking like that is another Monica to us."

Stephanie squeezed her hand. "Yes, I know."

"Damn men. Not a decent one left, if there ever was one."

"There are a few. My father's one."

"He's rare then. I went to a shrink for two years. They're free through the county services." She glanced down at her misshapen form, her baggy dress. "He told me I let myself get fat so no man would want me." She gave a short laugh. "Well, it works. But I don't give a shit. I'm better off with women for friends. A man comes near me and I start to choke up, you know. I can hardly breathe. What do you make of that?"

Stephanie shrugged. "Anxiety, I suppose. Every man reminds you of the one man you should have been able to trust, and couldn't."

"You sound like you've taken some psychology courses. Did you go to one of those Ivy League schools?"

"No, but I did go to college and I did take some psych courses, for all the good it did me."

"And some guy hoodwinked you anyhow."

"Education and money alone can't prevent a woman from being vulnerable. And there are always men who will take advantage of that vulnerability."

She heard the bitterness in her voice, but was helpless to change it.

Sandy's kind eyes met hers. "I'll bet there's a story in you. You want to tell me? I'm a good listener."

Stephanie smiled. "Thanks. You've probably heard worse, but I'd rather not." She stood, hoping to end this cozy chat. She liked Sandy, but things were getting entirely too confidential. "Do you have that list of possible employers I can call for Clara? And we'll need a doctor's appointment. She's pregnant."

Sandy got to her feet. "She didn't tell me."

"She told me. Only two months, and she's awfully afraid this last beating might have harmed the fetus." Stephanie walked to the scarred wooden desk by the window and sat down.

"That's when most women come in," Sandy commented, "when the safety of their children or unborn babies is threatened."

Yes, that's when we finally wake up, Stephanie thought as she located the sheet she needed. "Here's the list of clinics. I'll try to get Clara an appointment for tomorrow."

"Great. I've got to check on Mom in the kitchen. You want some more coffee?"

"No, thanks." The last cup hadn't set too well as it was. Rummaging in her handbag, Stephanie found an antacid and popped it in her mouth. Maybe she should consider giving up caffeine for the duration of her pregnancy. She was jumpy enough without it. Chewing the tablet, she picked up the phone and dialed the nearest medical clinic.

Safe Harbor. If only it were, she thought as she heard the busy signal and hung up. She'd moved her few belongings from the Barbizon yesterday after finding a small house for rent in the quiet suburb of Winter Park. After settling in, she'd gone for a walk and found this building with its welcoming warmth offering shelter to abused souls. She'd wandered in.

Sandy's mother, Hannah, was an overweight

woman in her mid-fifties who wore a bib apron and moccasins. She also wore a friendly smile much of the time and her eyes were deep blue and wonderfully warm. Stephanie had felt the pull of that warmth immediately and had decided on the spot to volunteer. Rarely given to impulses, this was one she didn't regret. In two days, she felt at home at Safe Harbor.

The reception room was small, furnished with donated furniture that had seen better days. Through the arch were two large rooms, each offering six cots, and a small but serviceable bathroom. The kitchen, presided over by Hannah, was huge and spotless, smelling of wonderful things put together with skill on a low budget and from donations. All the beds were currently occupied by a variety of women, three with toddlers. Yet no one really in need was ever turned away, Sandy had said proudly. If only I can hide here until I need to move on, Stephanie thought.

Again, she picked up the phone and dialed, then waited for the clinic to answer.

Luke had the eerie feeling of being followed. His hunches seldom misled him. After paying the man at the motel desk, he chanced a seemingly casual glance out the front window. A busy boulevard with plenty of late afternoon traffic. A diner next door and a heavy-set man in a phone booth across the street, too far away to see clearly. On the one hand, it could be Chester. On the other, it seemed unlikely. But if so, how the hell had that thug found him?

Still, only foolish men took unnecessary chances. Luke pocketed his room key and caught the eye of the counterman. "Is there another way out of here besides the front door?"

Looking as if the question wasn't at all unusual, the young man pointed to a hall. "Down that way leads to the service area. There's a door that goes to the parking lot on the other side."

"Thanks." Luke hurried along the passage and

peered out the door. Looking both ways, he saw that no one was in the lot except a thin black woman pushing a maid's cart along the walkway. He hurried to his Buick.

Maybe it was nerves, he thought as he started the engine. Maybe not. Checking his map first, he shifted into gear and headed for the Barbizon Hotel for Women.

The winding road along Edgewater Drive bordered a lake and some lovely homes. Luke was too busy checking his rearview mirror to appreciate the scenery. When he was convinced no one was following him, he slowed his speed. It wasn't long before he spotted the discreet sign and turned into a long drive flanked by huge cypress trees literally dripping with heavy moss. The pink stucco three-story building with pillared portico had an antebellum aura, exactly the type of place he felt might appeal to a woman like Stephanie Westover.

He stopped the car in a designated space and sat still for a moment. Just what kind of a woman was Stephanie Westover? he asked himself, not for the first time. A model daughter. A good and caring friend. A runaway wife. A liar and a thief. It kept coming back to that. Much as he hated the premise, he'd have to keep the missing diamonds and the hundred thousand in bonds in mind. He got out of the car, noticing there were only three others parked in the small lot.

The lobby offered an abundance of greenery, a Spanish tiled floor and rattan furniture. The young woman behind the polished mahogany desk, clad in shorts and a halter top, her pony tail bobbing, seemed out of place in the hushed atmosphere. Chewing her gum with gusto, she looked up as Luke walked in and gave him a big smile.

"Hi. I'm Myra. Can I help you?"

"I'm looking for someone. Do you have a Juli Richards living here?"

118

Myra flipped through a registration book bound in red leather. "Yeah, we do. Oh, wait. Sorry, she checked out yesterday." She looked up in apology.

So much for too easy. He frowned at the teenager, wondering why they had someone so young working in a sedate place like this. "Did she leave a forwarding address?"

Again, the young lady glanced through several pages. "Nope."

Of course, she wouldn't. Luke reached for his ID and showed it to her. "Police officer. Would you show me through the room she vacated, please?"

Myra's eyes widened. "A cop. Gee whiz, sure." She opened a drawer, grabbed a ring of keys and stood. "This way." She led him to the stairs. "I watch 'Jake and the Fat Man.' I know how you cops operate." She cracked her gum as she walked.

Luke watched her small bottom rotate as she climbed. "Is that so? How long have you worked here?"

The girl giggled. "I don't. I'm filling in for my sister. She's at the beauty shop. It's real slow most afternoons." At the second-floor landing, she turned left. "Juli Richards was in Room two-ten." At the door, she paused. "What'd she do, anyway?"

Luke gave her a conspiratorial look. "I can't say. You know how it is, official police business."

"Right, right." She unlocked the door and stepped aside.

Obviously feminine, with chintz curtains and a lacy bedspread, the room was clean and neat as a pin. Expertly, he looked through closets and drawers, but found not even a piece of paper in the bright pink wastebasket. "Was the place cleaned after Miss Richards checked out?"

"Don't know, but probably," Myra answered. "This is a real clean place. You through? I got to get back to the desk."

"In a minute." Luke walked into the small bath-

119

room. From experience, he knew it was the best place to find traces of the former occupant. Sink and tub spotless. He picked up the plastic wastebasket and leaned close to look inside. Carefully, he ran his finger along the sides, then paused to examine his findings. Several brown, somewhat curly, medium-length hairs. If these belonged to Juli Richards, she'd likely cut her hair and dyed it brown. At least he'd know which picture to show around. Luke set the basket down and left the room.

"Find anything?" Myra asked as they reached the lobby.

"You've been a big help. Did you ever substitute for your sister when Juli Richards lived here?"

She shook her head as she sat back down at the desk. "I'm only visiting for a few days. I live in Tallahassee."

"Well, thanks again."

"Sure, anytime. I like cops."

Suppressing a smile, Luke strolled out. His practiced gaze scanned the parking lot. No new cars since his arrival and no one around. Glancing at his watch, he decided he'd have enough time to drive back to his motel and phone that overly eager bank manager before they closed for the day. He needed to alert her to call him when Juli Richards notified them of her change of address.

Climbing behind the wheel, he heard his stomach growl. And I'd better get something to eat, he thought. My ulcer sounds unhappy.

Dusk was settling in around the small motel as Luke left the diner and strolled to his room. The traffic had thinned noticeably and few people were out walking. A family of five splashed around in the motel pool. He'd deliberately chosen a location off the beaten track. Cautiously, he'd parked his car at the far side of the lot, where it was hidden from street view by a clump of overgrown oleander bushes.

Walking slowly but with senses alert, he circled the area, scrutinizing every building, car, and person he saw. He still hadn't been able to shake the feeling of being observed, and it was stronger here. But after twenty minutes of being unable to spot anything suspicious, he entered his room.

The double bed looked mighty inviting to Luke as he stretched wearily. Up since five, he was feeling the strain of a long day. It was taking his body longer to readapt to the endless hours required for investigative work. Yet when he lay down, he had trouble turning off his restless mind. Perhaps he'd better check in with Stephen, knowing how anxious he was.

Stephen answered on the second ring. "It's Luke. Just wanted to let you know I'm here and settled in."

"I've been hoping you'd call. I've got some bad news."

The man sounded terrible. "What is it?"

"They found Marjo drowned in her back yard pool."

Luke took a moment to respond. "Drowned? I thought she was a competitive swimmer?"

"She was. The newspaper article said there were several bruises on her, and there'd been a forced entry. They have no suspects, but I sure as hell know who did it or ordered it done."

"Don't mention any names on the phone, and don't reveal the name of the city I'm in. We need to take extra precautions. Did the police contact you?"

"No. Why would they?"

"Just wondering. What else did the article say?"

"That there'd been an open bottle of liquor and some was spilled on the rug. They're hinting that she was drinking and got careless. I don't buy it, do you?"

"She was drinking pretty heavily the night I was there, but a forced entry doesn't sound like she was entertaining a friend. Frankly, I got the impression she could hold her liquor."

121

"She could. Damn it, Luke, first Stephanie, now Marjo. When will that son-of-a—"

"Hold it, hold it. I know you're upset, but get a grip on yourself. We can't accomplish anything if we get all emotional."

"You're right, I know. I feel so damn helpless." Stephen splashed bourbon into a chunky glass and decided to skip the water. Luke Varner has ice flowing in his veins, he thought with a surge of anger. But that was exactly why Luke was the right man to find his daughter—a cool, dispassionate cop. He took a quick gulp, grimacing as the liquor slid down. "Have you found out anything?"

"Not much. The bank has her on file as a customer, but she's not at the address they gave me."

Stephen absorbed the disappointment along with the alcohol. "So what are you going to do next?"

"Tomorrow morning I start looking. Same kind of leg work I did in Boston. Sooner or later, she'll be in touch with the bank, and I've got them alerted to call me."

Stephen sat down wearily and ran a shaky hand across his jaw. "But for now you have very little to go on, right?"

Luke frowned, hoping the strain wasn't getting to be too much for Stephen. "I never said it would be easy. Or quick."

"I know. I don't mean to sound so impatient. It's just that—"

"You cared about Marjo. I don't blame you. She impressed me, too."

Stephen remembered then, remembered the compassionate side of Luke Varner, and felt ashamed of his quick anger. "She was like another daughter to me," he added, realizing Varner would understand.

Luke cleared his throat. This was getting them nowhere. "Did you happen to remember any more details of Stephanie's life—something you might have forgotten to mention? Some information that might point me in the right direction?"

With effort, Stephen shifted his train of thought. "I know she must be having trouble with her allergies in . . . in that state, so there're the doctors to check. And any little theater companies, of course. She likes the symphony, too."

Luke struggled to hold back an exasperated sigh. A woman on the run from a threatening husband would hardly be sitting around enjoying a symphony, but he restrained himself from mentioning that to her father. "Anything else?"

"For a while there, she volunteered her services at a home for abused women. I told her I wasn't crazy about her spending time in that tough neighborhood, but she did it anyhow. Stephanie's not very good at taking suggestions from others."

Yet she'd fallen under Zane Westover's slick spell. For the life of him, Luke couldn't picture the Zane he'd met with the woman he was hunting. Or at least the woman he thought Stephanie was. Maybe his perception of her was all wrong. He brought his mind back to Stephen. "All right, I'll check out that angle. Anything else?"

"She likes animals, especially cats. When she was little, she used to drag home the mangiest-looking kittens you ever saw and insist we keep them. But Zane wouldn't let her have animals in the house."

Animals. Terrific. All he had to do was check the dog pounds of a dozen communities, along with countless veterinarians' offices. He sat down on the bed and began unbuttoning his shirt. "Okay, thanks. I'll be in touch."

"When?"

"When I have something to report. Goodbye, Stephen." Luke lay back, a frown on his face.

What didn't make sense was why, with a hundred thousand dollars in bonds and several million in uncut diamonds, Stephanie was hanging around Orlando. Florida was the gateway to a whole assortment of Caribbean islands. Anyone with money could get lost down there—and stay lost. Was she perhaps waiting for an accomplice to join her before she took off? Didn't she know that cashing the bonds would reveal her whereabouts to an alert father who remembered giving them to her?

Reaching into his travel bag, he pulled out the sketches of Stephanie Westover. He studied the pictures for quite a while, memorizing the details of her face. Then he looked at the photo from which the sketches had been made. The difference was in the eyes. The camera had captured what the artist hadn't quite been able to do.

Her eyes were guileless.

Could a woman fake that? Luke wondered as he lay back on his bed.

Chapter Six

Whenever Chester Thomas got nervous, he would sweat. Not just a little. Large beads of perspiration popped out on his florid face, stained his armpits, and made his thick hands slippery. This morning he was wringing wet, his shirt sticking to his broad back, his cotton pants damp on his heavy thighs. And he had good reason to be nervous, he realized as he drummed his stubby fingers on the dash of the rented car, his cigar stub clamped between his teeth.

He'd lost sight of Luke Varner, and Zane was going to blow his stack.

He'd watched the motel office from the phone booth across the street for some time yesterday. After a while, when Luke still hadn't come out, he'd decided he'd better move in closer. Peering through the glass door, he'd seen that the desk clerk was all alone. Hurriedly, he'd gone in and questioned the guy, who'd said no Luke Varner was registered.

That hadn't surprised Chester, since he'd figured Luke wouldn't be dumb enough to use his own name. But when he'd described the cop, the desk clerk didn't seem to recall seeing anyone like that come in. Chester could have sworn that had been Luke he'd seen walk into the office, yet why would that young guy lie to him? For a moment, he'd had half a notion to grab the clerk by his shirtfront and scare him just a little, see if fear would improve his memory. But the boss had said no rough stuff, so he'd left quietly.

He'd searched the parking lot from corner to corner, but found no trace of the Buick he'd seen Luke driving earlier. Had that shrewd cop somehow spotted him and ducked out, even switching cars? He wouldn't put it past him. Zane had said he'd checked him out and Luke was as crafty as they came.

Zane. How the hell was he going to explain blowing this important operation to him? Yanking his handkerchief from his pocket, Chester ran it across his face and wiped his hands. He'd driven around after that, gone back to the bank, even checked the car rental company Luke had used. No sign of the man. Finally, exhausted and nervous, he'd checked into a Motel Six and spent the night worrying. This morning, he'd come back to the motel where he'd lost Luke and now sat with his motor idling, staring at the office, though he wasn't sure why he was here.

Just like he wasn't sure where to start looking for Varner. Jesus, Zane would kill him!

With damp fingers, he shifted gears. He'd put off calling Zane for now, just drive around some more and pray he'd get lucky. For his health's sake, he'd better.

Zane Westover wasn't a man who looked on mistakes kindly. Chester stepped on the gas pedal and coasted down Orange Avenue.

By Wednesday evening, Luke had decided that Stephanie's allergies weren't bothering her enough to seek out a doctor and that she definitely wasn't spending her time working on a little theater production. Parking the Buick in his usual spot at the rear of the motel lot, he rolled his shoulders to relieve the kinks. He was used to leg work, but he'd never get used to the frustrations it involved.

He'd spent hours on the phone and more hours visiting medical clinics and theater groups. No one recognized her picture nor did the name Juli Richards ring a bell to anyone. He'd even called a few animal shelters—to no avail. For an amateur, the woman was damn good at hiding out.

Walking past the motel dinette, he glanced inside, automatically scanning the few late evening customers. Tired of the menu there, he'd treated himself to a steak in town before returning. He missed his own cooking, the solitude of his houseboat, and his cantankerous cat. Rubbing the back of his neck, he wondered when he'd get back to them.

"Hey, buddy. Got a minute?"

Luke paused at the door of the office, then nodded to the young desk clerk who held the door ajar. "Sure." Moving inside, he saw the room was empty of other guests.

"Thought you'd like to know, there was a guy asking about you that first afternoon you checked in," the clerk said as he stepped behind the counter.

"That so? Did he give his name?"

"No. He was short and stocky with a blond crewcut. He was smoking a cigar, a real muscular guy. He didn't use the name you registered under, but he described you to a tee."

Luke stuck his hands in his pants pockets nonchalantly. "Uh-huh. What'd you tell him?"

"Told him we didn't have anyone by that name registered and that I hadn't seen any guy fitting that description." His smile was cautious. Obviously, he was wondering if he'd done the right thing.

Silently applauding his instincts, Luke gritted his teeth. How had Chester gotten a bead on him? "He been around since?"

"I thought I saw him yesterday cruising by in a gray Toyota, but I can't be sure it was him. He never stopped in again."

Luke removed his money clip, found a fifty, folded it, and passed it to the clerk. "Thanks."

The young fellow let out a relieved breath. "Anytime. I believe in people leaving people be."

Luke nodded. "A good philosophy. Tell me if he comes around again and you'll earn another one of those."

"Yes, sir. Oh, and you had a message this afternoon." He reached behind him and removed a pink slip from a wooden slot. "A Miss Carpenter called from the First Financial Center. Said she had a new address for you." He handed Luke the paper. "I wrote it down."

"Great. Thanks again."

Walking to his room, Luke read Juli Richard's new address. P.O. Box 337, Orlando. Damn!

Driving around town, his eyes constantly darting from the rearview mirror to the traffic ahead, trying to spot a gray Toyota, was taking its toll on Luke's nerves, he acknowledged as he stopped to pump gas into his Buick. He was jumpy and irritable, and his ulcer was tired of the strain. He wasn't afraid of running into Chester, but it was easier to avoid him. If the bodyguard popped up, Luke might just have to use his fists to discourage the burly guy from remaining in Florida. In his present mood, he rather relished the thought.

Paying for the gas, he squinted into the noonday sun, noticing everything and everyone. He was ready to leave this town, find Stephanie and haul her pampered ass back to her daddy. With all his money, maybe Stephen could protect her from Zane and his apelike bodyguard. It was also likely the police might want to talk with the missing Mrs. Westover. She'd lifted those diamonds from her husband, but Zane had stolen them before that.

Not that she was likely to go peaceably with him. He'd told Stephen that he wouldn't force his daughter to return. But that had been before he'd known about the diamonds. Classy socialite or not, a thief was a thief. Feeling grumpy, Luke pocketed his change and got in his car.

He'd checked with the bank, then the main post office, and had learned the branch where Juli Richards had a box. Rolling down the street, he saw the familiar flag flying over the beige building set back from the street. He parked, noticing that Uncle Sam was doing a thriving business today. Luke sauntered inside.

Box 337 was located amid a cluster of mail boxes on a side wall of the large office. Through the archway, four busy clerks took care of the customers, each taking a number as they entered. He'd been told on the phone that the afternoon mail delivery would be completed by one. It was ten to. Luke draped himself on a bench set against the wall and picked up a discarded newspaper, prepared to wait a while.

By three o'clock, he'd read the paper, several leaflets, and the wanted bulletins, and he'd counted the bricks on the wall facing him. It was likely Stephanie wouldn't pick up her mail daily. After all, how many people knew of her box here? The bank, and that was probably it. Another dead end. He could check with Miss Carpenter to see when they sent out the monthly statements, but that could be weeks away. With a heavy sigh, he walked over to the enclosed phone booth.

In the phone book, he found listings for four shelters for abused women, two in Orlando and two in the suburb of Winter Park. Might as well try, he decided, dialing the first number.

Minutes later, he hung up scowling. A tight-lipped broad if ever he'd spoken with one. Of necessity, she'd be reluctant to give out information on anyone staying or working there, he supposed, trying to be fair. Ripping out the page, he returned to his car, hoping he'd be able to make more headway in person.

Someone in this damn town had to have seen or

heard from Juli Richards. And by God, he would find that person.

With a sophomoric squeal of tires, Luke drove off.

Someone was tailing him. Though he couldn't spot a gray Toyota in the rearview mirror, Luke felt certain someone was dogging his moves, and had been much of the day. His hands easy on the wheel, the tension locked inside, he drove just under the speed limit, his eyes ever watchful.

He'd visited the first shelter in midtown Orlando and had come away feeling the women there had never seen Stephanie. The second, located in a somewhat seedier section, catered mostly to Hispanics. The one English-speaking woman had convinced him she didn't recognize Stephanie from the pictures he'd shown her, so he'd started out for the shelter in Winter Park, the feeling of being watched growing stronger.

Making a quick, unexpected turn onto a side street, Luke drove half a block, then jerked the wheel and roared down an alley. Coming out at the far end, he heard a car following, though still not very close behind. He'd been right.

Zigzagging through sparse late afternoon traffic as much as he could without attracting the attention of a policeman, Luke maneuvered back to Orange Avenue. The wide, main thoroughfare seemed a better place to lose someone than the narrower side streets. Stopping for a light, he caught sight of a red-faced man with a fair crewcut in a tan Toyota two car-lengths behind him. He hadn't gotten a clear look at Chester that night on the dock in the moonlight, but the man surely resembled him. The desk clerk could have mistaken a tan car for gray.

Rushing away from the intersection, he concentrated on losing the bulky bodyguard. Luke had never been one to underestimate an opponent. A former prizefighter, Chester would undoubtedly know many ways to hurt a man. Stephen had indicated that it was

Chester who'd bruised, then drowned Marjo—a woman of some height and strength. It would be far more sensible to shake him than face him. Luke stepped up his speed.

It took him a good half an hour, driving a complicated route, but he finally felt as though he'd lost Chester and found Safe Harbor, the third shelter on his list. Even so, he sat in his parked car across the street for ten minutes before walking across and entering the building.

A bell over the door tinkled in welcome. The room smelled of cabbage and sweat. A large blond woman, who'd probably once been quite pretty but now seemed a bit shopworn, looked up from some papers on her desk and viewed him through suspicious blue eyes.

"Yes?" she said with not a trace of welcome in her voice.

Luke flipped over his ID and showed it to her. "Detective Varner from Michigan. I'm looking for someone who might be working as a volunteer here. Do you know a Juli Richards?"

Something flickered in the woman's eyes for an instant, then she dropped her gaze and shook her head. "Never heard of her."

Instinct told him she was lying. Calmly he removed the picture of Stephanie that the police artist had sketched, the one that showed her with short brown hair and brown eyes. "Does this woman look familiar?"

"No, she doesn't." The woman returned to her paperwork.

A small handmade sign on the desk had her name on it: Sandy Burke. Luke put on his charming smile. "Sandy, I need your help. Juli Richards is in danger. I have to find her." He heard a baby crying in the next room, and hushed voices came through an arched doorway while he waited for Sandy to look up.

"I already told you I don't know her."

131

"I think you do."

Sandy shrugged. "Think what you want." She was acting indifferent, but her insides were tensing. She had to protect Juli, as she'd protect any of the women at Safe Harbor, residents or volunteers. Juli had said her husband had abused her. How did she know this guy was really a cop? Badges probably weren't that hard to come by. Men stuck together, helped each other out. For all she knew, this tall fellow *was* Juli's husband. His stance, his steel gray eyes, looked dangerous. Sandy felt her chest grow heavy with alarm.

Struggling for patience, Luke anchored his hands on the edge of the desk and leaned nearer. He watched her eyes widen. Good. He would use fear if he had to. "You don't seem to understand. I'm a police officer, and you're keeping me from doing my job. Now, I don't have jurisdiction in Florida, but I sure as hell can call the local cops and have them here, questioning you, in the next five minutes. You want me to do that?"

She'd call his bluff before she'd reveal Juli's whereabouts. "Go ahead, call 'em."

"Damn it, lady, I've had it with you!" His voice rang out, echoing through the suddenly quiet building. Then he heard shuffling footsteps, and a dumpy older woman appeared in the archway, holding a meat cleaver.

"What's going on here?" Hannah Burke asked.

Luke spoke, controlled anger evident in his every word. "I'm looking for Juli Richards, and I'm not leaving 'til I find out where she is."

"Sandy, call the police," her mother instructed, still clutching the weapon. Several women were huddled behind her, their faces nervous and fearful.

"I *am* the police." Again, he brought out his ID and held it out to the older woman. While she studied it, he took a deep breath. "Juli's husband has tried to kill her once. She escaped to Orlando, but he's sent someone after her. The next time, this man won't bungle

132

the job." From his jacket pocket, he removed the newspaper article on Marjo's death and tossed it on the desk. He'd found a back issue after talking with Stephen. "We also feel he's responsible for the recent drowning of Juli's best friend."

He watched Sandy's face turn pale as she read the report. The older woman lowered the cleaver and walked over to peer over her daughter's shoulder. He'd have to be straight with these two. They'd obviously been protecting battered women for a long while. It was more than a job to them. It was an obsession.

"I have reason to believe Juli's nearby," Luke went on. "I need to get to her before her husband's accomplice does." He placed a card on the desk. "Her real name is Stephanie Westover. That's her father's phone number in Michigan. Call him and verify what I'm telling you."

Having finished reading the clipping, Sandy looked up at her mother. "What do you think?"

The older woman studied him for a long moment through intelligent eyes. Finally, she set down the butchering tool. "My daughter will call Juli, tell her you're here looking for her. If she wants to see you, we'll give you her address. If not . . ." She shrugged vaguely.

If she thought he was giving up that easily after coming so far, she was sadly mistaken. One step at a time. "Fine."

Sandy drew a tin box out of a drawer, riffled through several index cards, pulled one out, then dialed a phone number.

Luke put away his ID and the article while he waited.

Sandy shook her head. "There's no answer." She glanced up at her mother again. "She was supposed to be in sometime this afternoon. I called earlier, too, but she didn't answer."

"We may be too late." Luke whipped the card from

Sandy's hand almost before the woman realized it. "Thanks." He made for the door.

"Hey, wait!" Sandy yelled after him.

"You can't take that," Hannah cried out.

The two women got to the door in time to see the car that had been parked across the street zoom away.

"I'm going over to Juli's," Sandy said angrily. "How do we know he's who he says he is?"

Hannah stopped her with a firm grip on her arm. "Whoever he is, he's damn determined. I don't want you getting in his way. Call the police, then keep calling Juli." With a sigh, Hannah crossed herself. "Holy Mother, I hope he's on the level."

It was already dark by the time Luke arrived at the address on Safe Harbor's card. He'd stopped to check the map for the street location and had found it was only six blocks from the shelter. But, still wary that Chester might somehow be following him, he'd driven about aimlessly, then retraced his path by a rather circuitous route before parking two houses down from the small frame home where he hoped he'd find Stephanie.

The street lights popped on and still he waited, letting his eyes adjust. This area was a far cry from the Grosse Pointe neighborhood she'd left only a couple of weeks ago. The houses were modest, but well tended and not in disrepair, reminding him of the genteel poverty of his early years. Brave little flowers sat in window boxes and bordered grassy lawns. Several porches invited summer evening relaxation, some with hanging swings and a couple with comfortable lawn chairs. A pink flamingo standing on one leg decorated a side yard.

Stephanie had probably thought she'd be less apt to be found in these middle-class surroundings. The Barbizon had definitely been more what he'd expected. Getting out of the car, he wondered how the spoiled daughter of a rich man was faring in what had to be a major step down for her. Of course, she was likely only biding her time here for reasons unknown, until she could move on and cash in her millions. Disliking that scenario, but nonetheless having had to come to grips with it, Luke strolled up the walk leading to the porch.

The house was dark. He could hear the television in the living room next door blaring forth through the open front windows. A cat curled up on the porch railing of the house on the other side eyed him curiously. He rang the bell and heard it echo through the interior.

After several seconds, he pushed the bell again. No answering movement inside. There was no side drive and no sign of a car. Did she even have one? She could easily have walked to the shelter from here, but would she? And where was she this late in the evening when she'd been expected at the shelter earlier?

Uneasily, he stepped down and circled the small house. No fence surrounded the small yard. No garage either. The windows were too high to see inside. He returned to the porch. Removing his billfold, he extracted a small tool. Quickly, he looked about and, seeing no one, bent to his task. The lock clicked open. Pocketing both the tool and wallet, he stepped quietly inside.

The house had that rental smell about it. Recycled furniture and worn carpeting. In the dim light filtering through the window from the streetlamp, he could see the place was neat and clean, with an overstuffed couch and dark wood tables. He moved through the arch into the dining room.

Pausing, he listened as he inspected. No personal things around, not on the shiny buffet or the dropleaf table. He could see the kitchen beyond, also quite empty. Then he heard it, a sound coming from the hallway leading off to the right of the dining room. A moan. He hurried toward it.

He could barely make out a form on the floor. His hand searched for the hall light switch, found it finally and flipped it on. She was lying on a rug alongside the bed, her position awkward. Had she fallen or been pushed? He knelt quickly and felt for her pulse. Weak but steady.

Her hair was brown and short, but her features were the ones he'd memorized from the pictures he'd studied so often. He took a deep breath and recognized her scent. At last, he'd found Stephanie Westover.

Her face was very pale, her lashes dark against her cheeks. Sliding his hand under her shoulders, he raised her upper body slightly. "Stephanie, can you hear me?"

She groaned again, her eyes still closed. She moved her hand, and it settled fitfully on her stomach. She was wearing a loose top and a full skirt, her feet bare. He decided to take a chance and put her on the bed so she'd be more comfortable, hoping she had no internal injuries he could be making worse. But when his other hand slid under her, he encountered a pool of something wet and sticky. Drawing back, he saw that it was blood.

Chester couldn't have gotten here ahead of him. And he wouldn't have shot her, then locked the door on the way out. If not that, how had she gotten hurt? Getting a better grip on her, Luke lifted her onto the bed. Immediately, she curled into a ball and moaned again. He'd have to find the wound and see how serious it was, see if he could take care of it himself.

Stephanie flung her head back as she let out a small whimper. "My baby," she said. "Please, my baby."

Baby? Pregnant? That was one possibility he hadn't considered. Luke left her briefly, found the bathroom, and turned on the light. Grabbing a washcloth, he soaked it with cold water, wrung it out, and hurried back to her. Gently he wiped her warm face.

"Stephanie," he tried again, "can you hear me?

136

What happened?"

Her head thrashed as she doubled over, her hands pressing into her lower abdomen. "Have to get help," she muttered.

"I'm here now. I'll help you."

Her voice was weak, her eyes tightly shut. "My baby. Can't lose my baby. Not now. Not after all . . . all we've been through. Please, God, no."

Shifting her skirt, he could see she was losing a lot of blood and there was more on the floor. How long had she lain here? He couldn't take the time to clean her up. He didn't know where the hell the closest hospital was, but he had a map and he'd find it. Asking someone—anyone—was too risky. Gathering her into his arms, he held her close to his chest and walked through the dark, silent house toward the front door.

The ringing of the phone in the dining room startled him, but he held on. Probably Sandy from the shelter, Luke guessed. Limp in his arms, she whimpered again. "You're going to be all right, Stephanie," he assured her.

On the porch, he checked the neighborhood before hurrying down the stairs and to his car. She wasn't very heavy, but she was dead weight. From her nearly incoherent mumblings, he realized she was semiconscious. It was with some difficulty that he got her into the passenger seat. Getting behind the wheel, he shifted her so that she was lying down with her head in his lap. Perhaps she'd lose less blood that way, he reasoned as he checked the map for hospitals. Winter Park Memorial wasn't far.

Luke didn't switch the car lights on until he'd gone several blocks and turned a corner. Driving as fast as he dared, he swung onto the main thoroughfare. As he did so, a police car cruised past them going in the direction of the house they'd just left. Sandy had called them, most likely. Luke pressed on. As a rookie policeman, he'd assisted in the delivery of several babies, but he'd never happened on a pregnant woman who'd suddenly started bleeding.

He let go of the wheel and ran his right hand hesitantly along her side and over her belly. Not very far along, if he was any judge. With the loss of so much blood, she'd likely miscarried. And she seemed to know it from the few words he'd heard her say.

How had she survived the car crashing into the river and that treacherous swim, and not lost her baby then? he wondered as he picked up speed, one eye on the rearview mirror. Zane had badly wanted a child, Stephen had told him, and had been angry when she hadn't gotten pregnant. Did he know of this baby?

Luke felt the dampness of tears on his thigh where her cheek rested. Without thinking, his hand stroked the softness of her hair. "Don't worry. We're going to get you help."

"The name's Smith. Stephanie and Luke Smith," he repeated for the nurse standing beside him, clutching her clipboard.

"Smith." She filled in a blank. "And how will you be paying for your wife's charges, Mr. Smith?"

"Cash." Digging in his wallet, he extracted five one-hundred-dollar bills. "Will this do for starters?"

She took the money. "We need you to fill out the rest of this form."

From behind the curtained-off cubicle of the Emergency Room, he heard Stephanie moan. "Later." With a disapproving look, the nurse departed. Luke ducked behind the curtain, where the doctor on duty was checking Stephanie's vital signs.

"Smith, eh?" the doctor inquired, checking her pupils. He flashed Luke a knowing look through smudged horn-rimmed glasses. "We get a lot of your relatives through here."

He was young, but he wasn't stupid. Luke read his name tag and almost laughed. Dr. Derek Jones. "And the other half are yours."

"Yeah, more or less." Dr. Jones straightened and stuck his small flashlight back into the pocket of his lab coat. "Your wife's stable, but she's lost a lot of blood. We have to take her up to the OR and clean her out, of course."

"And the baby?"

"She lost the baby." Dr. Jones touched Luke's arm sympathetically. "I'm sorry."

Luke shifted his gaze to Stephanie's pale face. Young. She looked so damn young. Even sedated and in repose, she looked sad. He remembered the sound of her voice as she'd cried out her pain over the loss of her baby. "Yeah, I'm sorry, too," he said, and found he meant it. Whatever else Stephanie Westover had done, he strongly felt that she'd badly wanted this baby.

"You can wait in the room by the front door," the doctor told him as an orderly came in and pulled back the curtain in preparation for moving Stephanie.

"I want to stay with her."

Dr. Jones paused. "You can't come into the OR."

"Then I'll wait outside the OR."

Shrugging, the doctor shoved his glasses up onto the bridge of his nose. He met all kinds working Emergency. "Suit yourself," he said and left the cubicle.

Luke hated hospitals, hated the gruesome sights, the hushed atmosphere punctuated with painful screams, and the smell of blood mingled with disinfectant. As a policeman, he'd hung around far too many. As a husband, he'd identified his wife's overdosed body in one. As a friend, he'd sat with Matt Lewis for days while Ginny had struggled to die. For him, hospitals reeked of death, not life.

And here he was again because a tiny, unformed life had died before it had begun. Its mother, lying in medicated oblivion on an operating table through the

139

double doors he sat facing, would soon awaken and have to live with that. Two nurses had tried to chase him away from this privileged area, but he'd dug his heels in and stayed. Luke wasn't sure why.

Maybe because she looked so small, so alone, and only he knew where she was, *who* she was. She'd aroused his protective instincts, the ones he'd thought long buried. Luke slouched back on the plastic couch, resting his head on the seat back.

Since Stephen had told him her story and brought her picture to him, his thoughts had centered around Stephanie Westover. If she was alive, where she'd gone, why she'd left. Who she was and what kind of woman she was. Whether she was prey or perpetrator. He'd learned a lot, yet not nearly enough.

For an embittered man who'd some time ago all but given up the gentler sex, he'd felt oddly drawn to Stephanie from the beginning. He'd touched her things, inhaled her scent, memorized her features. She'd touched his life, dominated his thoughts, suckered him in. And then he'd learned about the diamonds. And the bonds.

Luke somewhat wearily ran a hand over his day's growth of beard. He, of all people, should know how misleading a man's perception of a woman could be. Kathy had been a sweet innocent when he'd met her, a lying tramp when he'd lost her. There were good women out there, he knew. Women like his mother and Ginny Lewis had been . . . honest and loyal and trustworthy. It was just that it took so much energy to separate the wheat from the chaff.

Glancing down, Luke checked the front of his shirt where he'd tried to remove the bloodstains in the restroom. He hadn't done a very good job. He leaned forward, balancing his elbows on his knees, and folded his hands thoughtfully. He wasn't quite sure why he kept wanting to believe in the goodness of Stephanie Westover when all the evidence pointed otherwise. Maybe because he was fond of her father, or because it would be a pleasure to remove Zane from the society he thumbed his nose at.

Or maybe it was hormonal. Turning forty had panicked his libido. Yet mostly he found the pursuit hardly worth the price. He was far more a cynic than a romantic. But there was something about Stephanie. She was lovely on the outside, and he didn't want her to turn out to be ugly inside. He wanted her to live up to her father's and to Marjo's vision of her. Perhaps just once more in his lifetime, he wanted to run across a woman who was more than she seemed, rather than less.

But he was honest enough with himself to admit it probably wouldn't happen.

The double doors swung open, and a short man in scrub greens came through, his face mask dangling from around his neck. He spotted Luke and walked over. "Mr. Smith? I'm Dr. Crandall."

Luke stood. "Yes, Doctor. How is she?"

"Your wife's going to be all right. An early miscarriage like this, for a healthy young woman, is more emotionally difficult than physically. She lost a lot of blood, however, so she'll be in recovery an hour or so. Then you can visit her in her room."

"I want to stay with her in the recovery room."

"We don't recommend that. The nurse in charge won't like it."

"I'll stay out of the way, but I want to be with her."

The doctor didn't care. It was nearly ten and he hadn't had dinner yet. He gave Mr. Smith a nod. "They'll be wheeling her out shortly."

"Thank you." Luke watched him walk away, then turned back to the double doors.

Jamming his hands in his pants pockets, he paced the short hallway. Why the hell am I being so stubbornly insistent? he asked himself. Stephanie Westover is another man's wife, no one to me except a party to a police investigation I am working on.

But she'd be frightened when she woke up. He

glanced down at his pants and saw the spot where her tears had soaked the material on the drive to the hospital. And she'd be devastated by her loss.

Personal feelings aside, she'd need someone to be there for her. And he was the only game in town.

She was whirling toward a tunnel, a large black tunnel. The mists were closing around her and there was nothing solid to cling to. Her hands reached out . . . closed over moist air that evaporated quickly, making the mouth of the tunnel more visible. She fought hard to keep from being sucked in, but the pull was strong and fierce, the winds pushing her forward.

Suddenly a face appeared above the tunnel opening. Dark and angry and scowling. Zane's brows were drawn together, and his eyes were accusing, his mouth a thin line of hatred.

"You took what was mine," he bellowed at her. "You had no right. I'll get you for this."

"No," Stephanie said, trying desperately to back away. "My baby. Please don't hurt my baby."

The wind picked up, blowing harder, the force pulling her forward as Zane's arms reached out. Unable to fight any longer, Stephanie felt the strength drain from her.

His words echoed in her head. "You had no right, no right, no right. . . ."

She screamed.

Eyes popping open, Stephanie struggled to sit up, on her face a look of sheer terror.

Seated next to her, Luke touched her arm, careful not to disturb the IV taped to the inside of her elbow. "It's all right, Stephanie," he said reassuringly. "You're okay."

She fought to keep her heavy eyes open as her chest heaved with labored breathing. A dream. It had been a dream. Zane wasn't here. But who was this man, and where was she?

142

The recovery nurse stepped closer, touching her other hand. "There, there. You must have been dreaming." Fingers finding Stephanie's pulse, the woman shifted her eyes to her watch. "You're coming along just fine."

Stephanie tried to swallow, but her throat was parched. "Where am I?"

"In the hospital," the nurse replied. A pause, then, evidently satisfied, she placed Stephanie's hand back on the bed and moved to check the monitor alongside the headboard. "You passed out, lost a lot of blood. But you're going to be okay."

"May I have some water, please?"

"Not just yet," the nurse said. "It'll only nauseate you. Soon though. Be patient, dear." Skirts rustling, she pulled the divider curtain, leaving the end open. "It's fortunate that your husband got you here when he did." She smiled at Luke. "He's been so worried." Swiveling on rubber-soled shoes, she left to check on her other patients.

Stephanie's eyes shifted to the man seated at her side, his hand on her arm. Her heart had thudded into her throat at the word *husband,* but she again saw that this man wasn't Zane. She let out a sigh of relief. "You're not my husband."

He gave her what he hoped was an encouraging smile. "Don't tell that to anyone here. They think I am."

She frowned, trying to clear the fog from her brain. "Who are you?"

"Luke Varner. I'm a cop. Your father asked me to try to find you."

"My father. Is he all right?"

"He's fine, but worried about you. He never believed you drowned in that accident."

Despite the medication, she felt a rush of alarm. "Zane. Does Zane know . . . know that—"

"That you're alive? No. Where you are? Not that either." He hoped not, at least. No one seemed to

143

have followed them.

Oh, thank God. Luke Varner. She tried to think, to remember. "My father told me about you. You have a bad temper. You don't look like a man who would kill someone with his bare hands."

"If that's a compliment, I'll take it." He slid a hand down her arm and wrapped his fingers around hers. "You should rest."

But something was bothering her, something she needed to know. If only she could think more clearly. "How did you find me?"

"It wasn't easy. The important thing is, I did." And before Chester was able to locate her. He watched her eyes drift shut, then saw her will them open again, battling the drugs they'd given her so she'd rest. Her mind hadn't closed in on the big one yet, the reason she was in here. Luke braced himself for it as she shifted restlessly, trying to focus.

"Have you called my father yet? Does he know where I am?" The fear returned, stronger than before. "You mustn't. Zane might have his phone tapped. I talked with Marjo and . . ." An unexpected surge of grief overcame her and a sob escaped from her dry throat. "Marjo, I'm so sorry."

Luke squeezed her fingers.

"I shouldn't have called her. Zane is capable of anything. *Anything.* If he knew about . . . about the . . ." The memory she'd been trying to bring forth came roaring back. She moved her free hand to her stomach and, as if in response, felt the responding cramp deep inside. Involuntarily, her fingers clutched Luke's as she groaned out loud. "My baby. Oh, God. My baby's gone."

That was why she'd been bleeding, why she was in a hospital. Squeezing her eyes tightly closed, Stephanie was unable to prevent tears from coursing down her cheeks. "It's true, isn't it?" she asked in a barely audible whisper.

Luke tightened his hold on her hand, feeling help-

144

less. "Yes, it's true."

She lay perfectly still while he watched the tears flow from beneath her closed eyelids. She didn't sob, didn't make a sound, which seemed all the more heartbreaking. She was brave and dignified in her sorrow, earning his respect. He could do nothing but let her cry it out.

He sat like that for long minutes, letting her cling to his hand with a fierce grip, the only other sign of emotion she displayed. Finally, he reached for a tissue and put it into her other hand. She seemed not to notice, still lost in her pain.

She was silent for a long time after the tears stopped, the colorless fluid dripping slowly into her arm. Luke could tell by her breathing and the restless movement of her hands that she was still awake.

Gone. Everything gone. Emptiness slowly replaced the pain inside Stephanie. Zane had stripped her of everything. He'd humiliated her, set her up, killed her best friend, and caused her to lose her baby. There was nothing left.

"He's won again," she said in a raspy whisper.

"No, he hasn't," Luke insisted. "You're alive."

Stephanie shook her head almost imperceptibly. "I wish I were dead."

Chapter Seven

Luke came awake with a start. The chair was too damn small for his long frame. Gingerly he shifted upright and stood, stretching to relieve the stiffness. In the glow of the dim night light across the small room, he glanced at the bed. Stephanie was sleeping, her breathing deep and even. The medication had finally knocked her out. He wished he had a dose himself.

Not really, he decided, reconsidering. He needed to be alert. Checking his watch, he found it was only three A.M. Another couple of hours and there'd probably be a shift change on the nursing staff. The last nurse had been nice, friendly, and empathetic. She'd even managed to bring him milk for his ulcer and cookies to appease his growling stomach. She'd also allowed him to remain with his "wife"—after he'd gone down to the front desk and coughed up another five hundred dollars for the private room. At this rate, he'd have to wire his Michigan bank for additional funds. Or Stephen.

Luke strolled to the window and stood looking down three floors onto the lighted parking lot below. He should call Stephen in the morning and let him know he'd found Stephanie. Then again, perhaps sending a wire would be safer. For a civilian, setting up phone surveillance was damn difficult, yet Zane had friends in high places. Friends as crooked as he, perhaps.

He walked back to the bedside and stood looking down at Stephanie. She was so slender there seemed hardly anything under the sheet that covered her. She looked fragile and vulnerable and sad.

You don't look like someone who could kill with his bare hands, she'd said to him in her foggy state. Well, lady, you don't look like someone who'd trick a man and run off with several million dollars worth of diamonds, either. Had she been planning to use the diamonds as leverage, so she could keep her baby from Zane?

I wish I were dead, she'd told him with such utter and quiet despair that he believed she meant it. She had to know that someone had tampered with the brakes of her car. She seemed to know it had been Zane, to know he'd gotten to Marjo as well. What had she done to cause her own husband to want to see her dead?

She looks innocent enough, Luke thought. But he'd seen innocent-looking women who'd been anything but. Had she duped a smart man like Stephen, and fooled a clever woman like Marjo, into believing she was innately good? He wanted to wake her this very minute and ask her if she had the diamonds stashed in her safety deposit box. He wanted to know how she got them away from Zane and what she planned to do with them. However, this was hardly the time to question her. Yawning, he sat back down in the uncomfortable chair.

Tomorrow, Luke thought as he propped his stockinged feet on the foot of her bed and leaned back, closing his eyes. He'd get the truth out of Stephanie Westover tomorrow.

"Christ Almighty! Can't you do anything right?" Chester flinched as he listened to Zane's tirade over the phone. He had it coming, he knew, but that didn't make it any easier to take.

"Twice. You had him in your sights twice, and you lost him both times." Zane swore ripely. "I shouldn't have sent a boy to do a man's job."

That hurt. At thirty-six, Chester was exactly Zane's age. To be called a boy was too much. "Boss, I'll find him. I *swear* I'll find him again."

"You damn well better." Outwardly calm, Zane sat at his crescent-shaped mahogany desk and toyed with a pencil, his elbow resting on the hand-tooled leather desktop. Anyone glancing in through the glass door of his office at the rear of The Antique Connection would never guess that inside he was seething. "Need I remind you that you're washed up as a boxer, too fat and too old? If I let you go—and that decision rests solely on how well you carry out this assignment—you have few options left. Do I make myself clear?"

Chester mopped his damp face with an already soggy handkerchief. "Yeah, boss. Real clear."

"Find Luke Varner and find him quick. Go back to the car rental company; maybe they know something. Shake down that motel clerk. Use force if you have to. Grease a few palms. Knock a few heads together. Go inside the bank where he spent some time. Do anything, but find him. Then stick to him like glue until he leads you to that bitch. Report in to me every day. I want results. Now!"

In his nervousness, Chester let the cigar fall from the corner of his mouth. "Right away, boss." He heard the phone at the other end slam down and ducked his head, as if Zane had thrown the instrument at him.

Hanging up, he dried his sweaty fingers. Jesus, he'd rather go ten rounds with Mike Tyson than face his boss when Zane was mad. Shoving open the door to the phone booth, he stepped out into the humid morning air.

Where the hell was Luke Varner?

148

In Detroit, Zane narrowed his eyes thoughtfully. He'd give the stupid lug a couple of days. If Chester didn't get results, he'd have to take matters into his own hands. He might have to think of something else. When push came to shove, he could rely on no one but himself. And there was always Stephen, his ace in the hole.

His eyes turning bright with anticipation, Zane snapped the pencil in half.

Stephanie woke as she so often did these days, all at once, her eyes opening and darting about, checking out her surroundings. The last few weeks on the run, often awakening in unfamiliar places, had done that to her.

The hospital room. Memories flooded her mind — of not feeling well and lying down to see if her discomfort would disappear, of trying to make it to the bathroom and falling alongside the bed, of blood gushing forth just before the darkness claimed her.

Automatically, her hand moved to her abdomen, and a swirl of remembered pain caught her in its grip, causing her eyes to close. She stifled the sound that threatened to escape, knowing it would do no good to cry again. Her baby was gone and no amount of tears could bring it back.

Foggily, she remembered being carried, being driven, being questioned. Her eyes opened again and moved to the man slumped awkwardly in the chair, his feet crossed and resting on the foot of her bed. Luke Varner. Ex-cop, violent avenger, troubled man — or so her father had told her some time ago. Yet Stephen had trusted Luke enough to ask him to find her.

Persistent, Marjo had said of Luke. Clever, too, evidently, for he'd found her when Zane hadn't. If her father suspected she hadn't drowned, then Zane probably did also. Did that mean he had someone search-

149

ing for her? Oh, God, not Chester! Stephanie shuddered at the thought.

The sky outside the window was barely lightening, so it had to be quite early. Through the closed door, she caught the faint drift of hushed voices, an occasional distant bell ringing. She wasn't in pain, so whatever they'd given her was still working. But at least the mists had cleared from her mind.

Turning her head to the side, she studied Luke Varner. Dare she trust him? She didn't know for a fact that her father had sent him, only that he'd said so. She couldn't risk calling to ask, not after what had happened to Marjo.

If he'd been hired by Zane, she'd be dead by now, she realized for he'd had ample opportunity to do her in. Instead, he'd brought her to a hospital, held her hand while she'd wept; and here he was, still with her. Why? she wondered. Now that he'd found her, what did he plan to do about it?

Even asleep, he looked rough and raw around the edges. He didn't have a kind face, yet he'd been kind to her last night. His hair was dark, with a generous sprinkling of gray, and cut short in what looked like an attempt to tame an unwelcome tendency to curl. His nose had been broken at least once, she guessed, giving him a hawkish look, and his unshaven chin was square, with a stubborn slant. Well, he would find she was equally stubborn, should he decide to test her.

He had lashes too long, too thick, for a man, but that didn't make him look in the least feminine. His eyes were gray, she remembered, not leaning toward warmth even when he'd watched her weep. Maybe warmth was foreign to his nature. Maybe police work in a big city squeezed all the warmth out of a man. But then, she hadn't known many warm men, even those who weren't in law enforcement. Except for her father, she couldn't think of a single one. Sad.

Too damn much sadness in this world. Why hadn't Luke Varner left her there on the floor to die? She'd

150

probably be better off. With a weary sigh, Stephanie closed her eyes.

"You awake?" Luke swung his feet off the bed and sat up.

Stephanie looked at him and saw a decided wariness in his cool gray eyes. Oddly it relaxed her more than confident self-assurance would have. All men, she supposed, hated being around weepy women and sick women, and last night she'd been both. "Yes. You needn't have stayed. You must be stiff as a board."

"I've slept in worse places." He rubbed a hand across his face.

She was sure he had. There were dark blotches on one sleeve of his shirt and along the side. Her blood, from when he'd carried her, she guessed. Not easy to harden your heart against a man who has hauled you to safety and bears the marks to prove it.

Luke checked his watch. "It's only five. You can get in a few more winks before someone comes in. You wouldn't want to deprive the nurse of her morning fun, shaking the patients awake."

Was that a hint of humor she heard in his voice? She wouldn't have guessed he'd be capable of much amusement. "I'm not sleepy. I feel a little floaty, but I'm awake."

He angled the chair closer to her head. He needed a shower and shave, some strong, black coffee and a lot of answers, not necessarily in that order. He'd go slowly, though, not wanting to start her tears again. "Are you hurting?"

"No." She found the button and eased the head of her bed up a bit so she could see him better. "I need to thank you for getting me here last night. That *was* you, wasn't it?"

"It was me." Luke propped an ankle on his bent knee. "Your father didn't know you were pregnant?"

"No one knew."

Her voice was emotionless this morning, a safeguard against pain, he guessed. "Not even Zane?"

Her eyes were huge and suspiciously bright as she studied him. She didn't seem inclined to answer.

"You don't trust me?"

"Should I?"

"Yes, but we can call Stephen and you can check with him if it'll make you feel better."

Her hand moved restlessly on the sheet. "I can't. The phone might be . . . Zane might get to him somehow."

"So you *are* afraid of Zane?"

Stephanie felt a flash of anger and welcomed it. It was so much easier to handle than pain. "Do you think I disappeared because I got tired of the Michigan weather?"

"I don't know. Why did you disappear?"

"Look, I don't owe you any explanation, and I don't feel comfortable talking with a stranger about my problems or my life. I don't know how you found me, but I'm grateful you were able to get me to a hospital. Now could you just go back and forget you did?"

Luke shook his head, never taking his eyes from hers. "I can't do that, Stephanie."

She let out an exasperated sigh. "Why not?"

"Because of Stephen. He's very worried."

That much, at least, she believed. "How did my father figure out I hadn't drowned? I went to the library here and read the newspaper account of my accident in the *Detroit News.* I was presumed drowned, only my purse and shoe found downstream."

"Stephen's a hard sell. I think at first he simply couldn't accept that you were gone. You'd always been a careful driver and all that. And his dislike of Zane played a part in that disbelief. He began to suspect foul play when no body was found. So he came to me."

"And you dropped everything and started looking for me?"

Luke shrugged. "There wasn't much to drop. I've been on medical leave from the Department for about six months. The fish weren't biting so I said I'd try."

"Just like that." Stephanie had never thought of herself as a skeptic. But trusting too quickly had gotten her into the mess she was in now. She'd learned her lesson the hard way. "I hadn't realized you and my father were such good friends."

Luke didn't miss the sarcasm, but chose to ignore it. "He was there for me once when I needed him. I don't forget something like that. I owe him."

"All right, you've found me. The debt is paid; the slate is wiped clean. You drag me back to my father and you walk away. Is that it?"

"No, that's not it. I have no intention of dragging you anywhere you don't want to go. I told Stephen I'd try to find you, but that I wouldn't take you back if you didn't want to return." However, the diamonds were another story. *If* she had them.

"Go back? I hated having to leave, but I can't go back. Zane would . . . he'd . . ."

"Try to kill you again?"

Her hand clutched the sheet reflexively. "How do you know he tried?"

"Someone punctured your brake line, and it wasn't accidental. Do you have many enemies?" He saw her face turn excessively pale and regretted his harsh words. But there was no prettying up some statements.

"No." Just her husband, the man who'd sworn to love, honor, and cherish her. But that had been a different Zane, the one brought out only for special occasions. The real man was totally different, she'd soon discovered.

"Of course," Luke went on, "we have no proof that Zane did it. Or ordered it done. Why would your husband want to kill you, Stephanie?"

Stephanie let out a ragged sigh. "Because I asked him for a divorce and he didn't want that."

153

Too simplistic an answer. "Most men don't turn to murder when their wives want a divorce. There has to be more."

There was. Quite a bit more. But would this hard man understand any of it? "Zane's not like most men. He became obsessed with me. Sometimes he had me followed. He had to know where I was every minute, who I was with."

"Why'd you marry him, Stephanie?" A very personal question, but the one that had been bothering him. She appeared to be intelligent enough. Why hadn't she seen through a man like Zane Westover?

Stephanie absently brushed at a lock of her hair. "A good question, one I've asked myself many times. He dazzled me, I guess." She shook her head. "Stupid. Like a teenager, I wanted romance. I wanted a family like the one I had before my mother died. My father loved her so much. Still does, I think. I thought Zane would be like that, loving and supportive, like my father. Zane can be very charming when he wants to be. You may find that hard to believe."

Marjo had been right. She was a romantic. "Yeah, I do."

"But I learned that he can turn that charm on and off, like water from a faucet. Do you know Zane?"

"I've met him." This would be a good time to tell her about the message Zane had given him for her, that he wanted her to return whatever she'd taken from him and that he wasn't a patient man. But her eyes looked so haunted he couldn't make himself say the words. He had her talking, probably helped along by the medication, and he didn't want her to stop. "I take it he changed after the wedding."

"Drastically." She stared off into middle distance, remembering. "In the beginning, he actually courted me, which sounds old-fashioned, but he did. Flowers, small gifts, taking me dancing. He was soft-spoken, with an offbeat sense of humor; he made me laugh. Suddenly, after we were married a few months, he started having outbursts over the slightest thing. He'd become so angry—so quickly—if he didn't get his way, yelling, smashing things. Once he rammed his fist into a closed door and cracked the wood all the way down."

"What'd you argue over?"

She turned to stare at him, as if coming to a sudden realization. He was questioning her, not exactly like a suspect at the police station under hot lights, but the results were the same. "Why am I telling you all this? I don't even know you." Her eyes felt grainy as she rubbed them with a less than steady hand. "Must be the medication."

Luke rose and angled his hip onto her bed so he sat facing her. "Because you need to tell someone, and maybe I can help."

Stephanie shook her head. "No one can help." The tears were building, and she fought to hold them back. She felt vulnerable. "I hate having anyone see me like this."

"It's all right."

"No, it isn't." Her voice was filled with self-derision. "But I can't seem to stop crying and I don't know how long this will last. I've never . . . never lost a baby before so I . . ." She ended on a sob she couldn't suppress.

Without conscious thought, Luke took her hand.

Her eyes, not quite overflowing, looked up to meet his. "Please don't be too nice to me. I'm liable to really fall apart if you are."

He smiled. "All right. Twice a day, I'll slap you around a little just so you . . ." He saw the fear jump into her eyes, darkening them. His fury rising, he squeezed her fingers. "Did Zane hit you?"

"No." She thought of that night in the study, the wiry strength of him, the arm raised high but not quite connecting, the humiliation that followed. But he'd never actually struck her. "No, he didn't hit me." She felt exhausted, as if she could sleep for a week.

She heard the door open, but was too tired to care who it was.

Carefully, Luke banked his anger at Zane. There was more to it, he was certain, but this was no time to go into that.

"Good morning." A white-haired nurse with an enormous breast-pocket handkerchief hurried in. "I see you're awake. Good. My name's Helen." She glanced at Luke and winked. "Husbands, Mr. Smith, are not allowed on the beds."

Properly admonished, Luke let go of Stephanie, but not before he again noticed the question in her eyes at the word husband. "Shhh," he whispered conspiratorially, then stood and moved out of the way.

Helen shook down a thermometer and stuck it into Stephanie's mouth. "You might want to step into the hall while I freshen up your wife before they bring in her breakfast tray."

"Actually, I think I'll go get cleaned up." He peered around the nurse who was removing a bowl and cloth from the night stand. "Can I bring you back anything, *sweetheart?*"

Stephanie raised a brow and shook her head.

"Okay. I've got a few calls to make; then I'll be back."

Stephanie pulled out the thermometer. "You're not going to call my father, are you?"

"No."

"Time enough later to tell the family, right, dear?" the nurse asked, radiating sympathy. "I'm so sorry about your baby."

With a quick wave, Luke turned toward the door.

"I lost two myself," Helen went on, "then had three healthy boys. You're still young. You and the mister can try again in no time." She whipped out a clean gown.

Glad to be going, Luke left the room. He had a lot to do, including a call to Captain Renwick. Stephanie was too frail, too run down, to make the trip back

156

even if she consented to go. And it was too dangerous leaving her here. He would have to find a safe place where she could rest and heal.

But first he needed some breakfast with lots of strong coffee.

For the first time in days, Chester smiled. Sitting at a booth in the restaurant adjacent to the motel, he watched Luke Varner walk hurriedly to his room, glance around, then slip inside. Patience paid off, he thought as he slid off the vinyl seat. Patience and a little friendly persuasion.

He'd waited until the skinny kid who worked behind the motel desk had ended his shift last night and caught him as he reached his car. Behind the cover of a big bush, Chester had rearranged the desk clerk's face until he was told that someone resembling Luke was a guest of the motel. Spitting out a mouthful of blood, the clerk had even remembered Luke's room number.

Chester had let the kid go then, warning him that a loose tongue would bring about a rematch. The fear in the youth's eyes had assured Chester that he'd stay home and lick his wounds for a while. Throwing a five on the diner table for the half-dozen cups of coffee he'd had while waiting for Luke, Chester left the restaurant and walked to his car.

Parked where he was, the nose of the Toyota just clearing a semi at the rear of the lot, he could keep an eye on Luke's room. He'd already sneaked into it last night and found only a small leather bag, a minimum of clothing, and no information. But he knew Luke was a careful cop who wouldn't leave clues around.

Climbing behind the wheel, Chester was pleased that he could also see Luke's Buick parked near an oleander bush. He ran a beefy hand over his chin and yawned expansively. Since talking with the desk clerk, he hadn't left the vicinity, knowing Luke would return sooner or later. He was nearly dead on his feet, but it had paid off. He hadn't the foggiest notion where Luke had been all night, and he didn't care. He had him in sight now, and he wouldn't have to be patient much longer.

When Luke Varner came out this time, Chester would stick to him like his shadow until Varner led him to Stephanie. His gut feeling was that the smoothie cop would find her, if he hadn't already. Then Chester would move in, let his fists sink into Luke's tough hide. Or his switchblade, if necessary. After that, he'd make Stephanie tell him where the diamonds were.

Chester stuck an unlit cigar in his mouth and smiled again. Yeah, he looked forward to making that skinny broad talk. And talk she would. 'Cause if he didn't come through for Zane this time, his ass would be in a sling for sure.

His eye on the door of Room 108, Chester waited.

Luke set his leather bag on the motel-office floor and pulled out his wallet. "I'm checking out," he said to the woman behind the counter. "Room one hundred eight."

"Yes, sir." She busied herself at the computer, entered the date and time, and waited until his bill printed out. Tearing it from the machine, she laid it on the counter.

Quickly, Luke scanned the figures, then handed her a hundred dollar bill. As he waited for his change, he glanced out the window. He'd already scrutinized the parking lot once and found nothing unusual.

He felt infinitely better, having stopped for a big breakfast after leaving the hospital, then gotten cleaned up and changed. He'd formulated his plans carefully, made a few calls, and hastily packed his bag. He had a few more things to do, but he wanted to go back and talk to Stephanie first. Oddly, he felt

158

uncomfortable about leaving her alone too long.

"Thanks," he said, accepting his change. "Say, where's the young fellow who usually works the desk? His day off?"

"No, he called in sick this morning. I'm filling in for him. Do you need anything else?"

"No, I just wanted to thank him again for something he did." Luke picked up his bag and gave her a parting smile.

"Have a good trip, sir."

"Thanks." With long strides, Luke headed for his car.

As he pulled out into traffic, a tan Toyota left the parking lot several car-lengths behind and followed at a careful distance.

Stephanie had color in her face this afternoon, her hair was combed and curling softly around her face, and they'd removed the needle from her arm. She lay lightly dozing as Luke closed the door and walked over to her bed. Then her eyes flew open.

"You're looking better," he said.

She gave him a wan smile. "So are you." As she touched the button and raised herself into a semisitting position, he sat down on the bed, near her waist.

"Helen's going to toss you out of here."

"No, she thinks I'm a devoted husband."

"Why are you masquerading as my husband?"

"To avoid unnecessary questions."

"The Smiths. Very original."

"I didn't have much time to make up a better story. When I carried you in, you were bleeding pretty heavily." He saw her absorb and accept that. "Stephanie, we need to talk about a couple of things."

Her eyes took on a wariness. "Like what?"

"Like the fact that you're in danger. The longer you stay here, the worse it could get."

Her heart began to thud wildly. "But you said Zane doesn't know where I am."

159

"He doesn't, not exactly. But he knows you're in Florida."

"He must have learned that from Marjo before she . . ." Stephanie choked on the rest, regret over her call to her friend causing a sharp pain in her chest. With difficulty, she swallowed a lump in her throat. "How do you know Zane found out I'm here?"

Luke debated about telling her that he'd seen Chester, then decided there would be time enough later to go over everything after he had her safely stashed away. "Let's just say, I have my ways."

Was this man really on the up and up? "How did you find out I was in Orlando?"

"The bonds. Your father told me he'd given you the bonds. He made arrangements to be notified when you cashed one, and he was. They told him the bank that handled the transaction, how much you received, and the name you used. Juli Richards. Your grandmother's name, I believe."

Only she and her father had known about those bonds or about Grandmother Richards. Luke Varner had to have conferred with Stephen. Stephanie let herself relax fractionally. "I guess I wasn't so clever, after all."

"You're not bad for an amateur." He still had a lot of unanswered questions. "Tell me, after you became aware of Zane's temper, why didn't you leave him and move back with your father?"

"My father has high blood pressure. He had a stroke a couple of years ago, not a bad one, but serious enough. And Zane knows I love him, so, of course, he used that knowledge. He told me if I left, my father would pay with his life. I never doubted that for a moment, and I'm worried that my leaving put my father in jeopardy. But my baby *had* to come first."

"So you devised a plan to disappear?"

"Yes, when I found out I was pregnant. Zane wants a child as obsessively as he wanted me to remain his

160

wife. I knew if I had a baby, he'd use the child to control me for the rest of my life."

"So you decided to run away and hope he wouldn't find you?"

She hated to trust him, but he already knew so much. And she was beginning to realize she might need his help. "I came up with a plan to get away. I thought I'd worked out all the details. Zane left for Cleveland that morning, and I was going to go through my normal day. Errands, then little theater, and finally dinner with Marjo. On the way home after dark, I'd planned to drive the car to the riverbank, get out, release the brake, and let it go into the water. I'd duck under cover and make my way to the back of the shopping center where I'd hidden a change of clothing and a wig next to a dumpster. Then I'd catch a cab to the airport, where I'd rented a locker and left another change of clothing, the bonds, and some money. I had it all carefully arranged—disguises, one-way tickets for a roundabout route, all paid for in cash." She sighed heavily. "But my plan ran into a snag."

To put it mildly. "You're quite a swimmer." There was admiration in his voice, and it wasn't just for her skill in the water. *If* she was telling the truth. A big if.

"I would have swum twice that distance to save my baby. Only . . . only it didn't work out, after all."

Before the tears reappeared, he switched tactics. "What about the package?"

Stephanie rubbed her forehead absently. "What package?"

Luke angled his bent knee and sat more comfortably. If the nurse happened in, she'd see only a husband and wife having a chat. "After Stephen asked me to investigate, Zane got wind of it and paid me a visit. He was beginning to doubt you'd drowned. He mentioned missing something you might have taken from him. He was pretty upset."

With a puzzled frown, she shook her head. "I don't know what he's talking about. I left everything—my clothes, my jewelry, even some of my mother's. I took nothing with me from that house except the bonds my father had given me and my baby. Zane didn't know about either."

Luke stared into her eyes a long moment. Could he afford to believe her? She was hardly in a condition to be questioned further, already tiring. "I have to get you out of here."

"Why? Do you think Zane would—"

"I don't want to take chances. I made some calls earlier. I've rented a houseboat on a nearby lake. We're going to drive there and stay aboard until you're feeling better."

"A houseboat? I don't know anything about boats. And I hardly know you." She began to shake her head, but he stopped her with a touch.

"It's too dangerous to hang around here. I live on a houseboat in Michigan. It'll be much safer out on the lake."

Persistent didn't cover it. Tenacious, maybe. Insistent even better. "Look, you're not responsible for me, despite what you may feel you owe my father. Go home. Tell him I'm fine. And I will be. Very soon."

He had no choice but to pull out the big guns. "Chester's in town." It gave him absolutely no satisfaction to see her turn paler than the sheets. "If I found you, he could. Do you doubt that he intends to hurt you again?"

She felt like weeping, like crying out, like running away. Would she never be free of Zane? She need no longer worry about her baby, but what if he harmed her father? She didn't want to be indebted to this man, yet she'd run out of good alternatives. "All right, I agree I must leave here. Still, I can't let you risk your life for me. We're strangers. Knowing me has already cost Marjo her life." Lowering her gaze, she shook her head. "I couldn't live with myself if anyone else is hurt because of me."

Luke was stunned. He couldn't remember the last

162

time someone had tried to protect him. He didn't welcome her concern, and he sure as hell didn't want to be deeply concerned about her. That kind of anxiety over another made you careless, then vulnerable. For her sake, as well as his own, he couldn't afford to be either.

Uneasy with this new assessment, he masked his expression with nonchalance. "Don't sweat it, lady. This is a job, not a lifetime commitment."

That brought her up short. His eyes were cool, unemotional. Then it hit her. He was on leave from the Department, at loose ends, unemployed. "A business proposition? Is my father paying you?"

"Yes," he lied. Anything to get her to agree to his plans. At the motel, he'd gotten that nervous feeling again, about someone following him. Although he'd seen no one that he recognized, Zane could have called Chester home and sent another of his goons, one Luke wouldn't recognize.

Stephanie told herself she should have guessed. Marjo had always told her she saw too much good in people, never noticed the rotten part of the apple until she'd bitten off a chunk. Long ago, she should have listened to Marjo. Her friend would be alive today, and she wouldn't be here in this hospital bargaining with a hired bodyguard.

Stephanie sank back into her pillows and closed her eyes. She was tired, so very tired. "All right."

"All right, what?" He'd been watching a variety of emotions play across her features, from surprise to disappointment and finally weary acceptance.

"All right, I'll go with you. Isn't that the answer you wanted?"

It was. Yet seeing her utterly drained and giving in disturbed him somehow. Luke reminded himself she'd been through a lot, physically and emotionally. She needed time to rest and regain her strength. He stood, trying to think of something to say that would remove

163

that resigned look from her face. "I'm a pretty good cook," he offered lamely.

She didn't open her eyes. "Good. I can't boil water."

"I've got a few details to settle. You rest, and I'll be back in a couple of hours." He saw her nod, her fair face lined with strain. He had an irrational urge to smooth back her hair, to tell her everything was going to be all right.

The diamonds, Luke reminded himself. She'd said she had no knowledge of a package, but he had to keep in mind that she'd been in the theater. She could be acting. He'd hardly expected her to confess, to tell him where they were at first mention. The diamonds were still missing, and Stephanie was the logical one to have carted them off. He'd get her well—and get her talking.

And he'd keep his hands off her. Luke turned and left the room.

Shift change was a busy time in most hospitals, with a good many people coming and going. The evening shift at eight was no exception. Chester stood in the supply room peering through the door that was slightly ajar. 612. That was Stephanie's room number and he kept his eye on it.

He'd followed Luke here, carefully staying well out of sight and in the shadows. He'd gotten as far as the sixth floor, but hadn't been sure which room Luke had gone into or who he was seeing. Around the corner, in one of the waiting rooms, he'd stood behind a large plant, lingering and watching. Finally, Luke had come out of 612 and hurried to the elevators.

After he'd gone, Chester had sneaked out and peeked in. Her hair was darker, but the woman in the bed was Stephanie, all right. Too many people were around to chance making her talk just then, so he'd stepped into the supply room, biding his time.

He had no idea why Stephanie was in the hospital,

nor did he care. Minutes ago, he'd heard two nurses chatting, one of them revealing that she was going to give Mrs. Smith in 612 something to help her sleep as she seemed unduly agitated. He'd have to hurry before the medication made Stephanie too groggy to answer his questions.

Fighting impatience, Chester watched. Two doctors were being paged, an orderly was wheeling someone on a gurney down the hall, and several nurses were huddled around the service desk four doors away. A number of visitors were leaving, chattering in the hallway as they vacated the rooms. Amidst the confusion, Chester slipped unnoticed into Room 612.

He closed the door behind him and saw in the dim light that Stephanie was asleep. With a smile curling his thick lips, he moved toward the bed.

Chapter Eight

Helen wasn't crazy about working the night shift. She'd finished up that morning at eight, but the hospital was shorthanded so they'd called her in early in the evening. Visiting hours had just ended, and here she was again. She stifled a yawn and checked out her charts.

There was usually less to do in a hospital nights, and often the hours dragged by. But there was one advantage. She got to visit with her favorite patients more. And this week, her favorite by far was the sweet-faced woman in 612, Stephanie Smith.

Checking the chart, she saw that Stephanie had been given something for her discomfort half an hour ago, after the outgoing nurse had noticed she'd been restless and unable to sleep. It surely couldn't have been that handsome husband of hers who'd upset her. Most likely, she was dwelling on the baby she'd lost.

Helen decided to look in on Stephanie to see if she was resting comfortably by now. If not, perhaps she could reassure her that there would be more babies in her life to come, as there had been for Helen and Raymond. Starched skirt rustling, she moved to the door.

"Helen," Marie called out, "have you medicated six-ten?" The stocky nurse came alongside Helen, chart in hand. "Mrs. Trent says she's had her injection, but there's no notation here."

Hand on the knob of the open door of 612, Helen

glanced at the chart Marie held out. "No, I haven't been near Mrs. Trent yet tonight."

Frowning, Marie moved away. "All right, thanks."

Helen went inside Stephanie's room. She noticed an odd smell in the air as she moved quietly to the bed. Like stale cigars, yet Mr. Smith hadn't smelled of smoke earlier that day. The light on the side table was on, casting a dim glow over her patient's fine features. Such a pretty woman, Helen thought as she straightened the rumpled bedding. She leaned over and picked up a pillow that her restless patient must have flung onto the floor.

Stephanie didn't stir, poor little thing. She was obviously exhausted and in need of the rest the sedative was allowing her. Gently, Helen smoothed her brow and found it to be cool and dry to the touch. Good, she wasn't overly warm. She'd be on the mend soon.

Turning, she noticed the door to the private bath ajar and moved to close it. There, the odd smell was even stronger. Glancing in, she could see nothing amiss. Helen pulled the door firmly shut and walked to the hallway door. If time permitted, she'd return later and check on Stephanie. She'd have enjoyed a chat, but she had to admit that the best thing for her patient right now was to sleep until morning if possible.

Visitors had departed and the hallway was all but deserted, except for several nurses at the station. Since it was quiet once more, Helen decided to leave Stephanie's door open to air out the stuffy room. As she was about to walk away, a tall orderly pushing an empty gurney approached her.

"Nurse, I may need your help," the man said as he stopped in front of Room 612.

Helen hadn't seen this one around before, though there was something oddly familiar about him. But then, there were so many new people these days. His hair was reddish brown and full, and he had a mus-

167

tache to match, as well as horn-rimmed glasses. The name badge on his lab coat told her his name was Robert.

"Yes, Robert, what do you need?"

He waved paperwork at her. "Room change ordered by Dr. Crandall. The patient in six-twelve, a Mrs. Smith. I'm to wheel her down to the fourth floor."

"Kind of late, isn't it?"

Robert look harassed. "We've been swamped. I haven't had a chance to come up and get her sooner. Doctor said she's out of danger and to move her from OB-GYN to general."

Pursing her lips disapprovingly, Helen shook her head. "These doctors, shuffling patients around like they were sacks of potatoes, and at all hours of the day and night." Briskly, she walked back into Stephanie's room. "She's asleep, Robert. I'll help you move her over. She's been medicated, so she may not be too responsive."

Stephanie felt strong arms lift her, then shift her onto something hard. Valiantly she tried to open her eyes but they refused to obey. "What . . . what's happening?" she whispered hoarsely.

"It's all right, dear," Helen assured her as she folded the sheeting around her. "Robert here is taking you to a new room, that's all. We'll notify your husband when he comes back."

Stephanie felt dazed, as if she were dreaming. A moment ago, it had seemed as though rough hands had yanked her about and a gruff voice had demanded something of her. But she couldn't remember what.

"Thanks, Nurse," Robert said, starting out the door.

"Sure. I'll miss her. She's a sweet one." Helen touched Stephanie's pale cheek. "Good luck, dear."

Helen stood at the door and watched the tall orderly wheel Stephanie down the hall and into a waiting elevator. Turning back to glance into 612, she frowned. The door to Stephanie's bathroom was ajar, though she was certain she'd closed it herself just before Robert had appeared. Odd. Maybe she should check it and . . .

A nurse jogged down the hallway, grabbing her attention. "Helen. Code blue. Room six-thirty. STAT."

"Right you are," Helen answered. She hurried along behind the nurse, ready to assist with the emergency. For now, she'd have to relegate Stephanie Smith to the back of her mind.

On the fourth floor, Luke pushed the gurney off the elevator and down the hall, turned right, and signaled for the service elevator. Two men in OR greens walked past him, deeply engrossed in conversation. His upper lip itched with the phony mustache, but he ignored it. At last, the doors slid open and he shoved a sleeping Stephanie inside.

It was fortunate they'd sedated her. He didn't have to waste time explaining his plan and possibly running into more opposition from her. She'd been subdued — a little too much so — when he'd left her earlier, but that could have changed. At any rate, he'd get her out more easily in her groggy state.

On the first level, he set the hold button, left the elevator and glanced about. Not much activity at this time of night, which was one reason he'd waited until now. Walking unhurriedly, he pushed the gurney toward the service door. Luck was with him, and the area outside the double doors was deserted. Quickly, Luke maneuvered his passenger over to the white pickup truck parked just past the entrance.

He opened the door and bent to lift her. "Here we go," he said, depositing her on the passenger seat. She moaned softly, then leaned her head against the seatback, sighed heavily, and returned to her dreams.

Luke shoved the gurney in the back and climbed behind the wheel of the truck.

Casting his eyes about until he was certain no one was around, he started the truck and steered past the delivery area and out of the hospital parking lot. He drove carefully, well within the speed limit, not wanting to catch the attention of a patrol car sitting in wait on a side street.

At the first light, he came to a halt and saw no cars behind him and only one stopped opposite him. He leaned over to Stephanie and saw she was curled into her seat, her breathing deep and even. Somewhat awkwardly in the cramped space, he shrugged out of the white lab coat and shoved it into the compartment behind the driver's seat.

The light changed to green, and Luke stepped on the gas pedal, heading toward the highway to the lake. With one hand, he removed the tight brown wig, then peeled off mustache and glasses. At last, he settled back for the drive, hoping the serviceable little truck would give him no surprises. He'd bought it earlier, after turning in his rental car, paying cash and no questions asked by the owner of a lot on the shady side of town. It was a little beat up, which was just what he'd been looking for. Less noticeable that way. The motor was somewhat tired, but hummed along quite nicely.

Luke had Stephanie's window up, his own rolled down to let in a trace of night breeze. Already nine, but the temperature still hovered close to eighty.

In an hour or so, they'd be at the lake and boarding the houseboat. He'd driven down earlier to make the arrangements and check out the accommodations with the owner, a wizened old fisherman named Howie. The sharp-eyed little man rented boats and fishing gear, and ran the only store for some miles around. He'd promised to wait for Luke, who'd told him he wanted the houseboat for a couple of weeks so

170

his wife would have a peaceful place to recover from surgery.

Luke's eyes constantly shifted to the rearview mirror, scanned the cars behind him. Traffic was light, and no particular car remained in his line of vision for long. He stepped up his speed and let himself relax a fraction.

Chester was hot, frustrated, and so tired he ached. He wasn't sure how long he'd been hiding behind the shower curtain in Stephanie's bathroom, but he knew it had been too damn long.

He'd almost had her, but that damn nurse had come in to check on her. Just before that, he'd had a grip on her, and though she'd been like a rag doll, her eyes never opening, he would have made her talk — if only he'd had a little more time. Then the nurse had come in and left the hall door open. He'd been stealing out to close it when that goddamn orderly had popped up.

Chester rubbed at his tired eyes. He hadn't had a good night's sleep since that bitch had run off. He'd never liked her. With so many women around with hot pants, why Zane had picked Stephanie, Chester would never figure out. She'd always looked at him like he was someone she wouldn't want to touch. He'd been glad when she'd left, if only she hadn't taken the diamonds. That little caper had changed his life.

Now the boss was pissed, and Chester's days were a living hell.

Nervously, he moved to the door and peeked out. The hallway was brightly lit, two nurses standing by the big desk, one behind it. The smell of medicine was giving him a headache. How anyone slept in this hospital with those damn bells ringing all the time was beyond him. And the tight-ass nurses with their rubber-soled shoes, sneaking around, were giving him the creeps.

He checked his watch. It was getting late. He needed to slip away unseen and get down to the fourth floor. Somehow he'd have to find the room they'd transferred Stephanie to. Damnable luck. He didn't want to consider the possibility that he couldn't locate her. That couldn't happen, not when he had to call Zane soon. Wiping his sweaty hands, Chester peered through the crack in the open door, waiting for his chance.

Stephanie became aware of being uncomfortable, of a cramp in her neck, the discomfort dragging her out of her foggy state. She shifted, fighting to awaken. She'd had dreams again, of a menacing voice snarling at her, of hard hands shaking her. Zane? Her eyes flew open.

Disoriented, she blinked and slowly pulled herself upright. She'd been lying on the front seat of a car, her head in a man's lap. Easing away, she recognized Luke and let out a gush of air. For a moment there, the fear had returned full force.

Luke stretched a hand out to steady her. "You okay?"

"I think so." Her voice sounded thick to her own ears. "Did you drug me?"

"Not me. The hospital staff gave you something to help you sleep. Evidently, it worked."

Shakily, Stephanie ran a hand through her hair. Lord, she must look a mess. Lowering her gaze, she saw she was wearing a hospital gown and had a light cover wrapped around her. "Where are my clothes?"

"Your clothes and the rest of your belongings are in the back of the truck. I went to your house and packed everything up."

A truck, not a car. And a vintage one at that. She braced a hand on the window ledge. "I see we're traveling first class."

172

Her sense of humor along with her feistiness was returning, a good sign. "Nothing but the best."

"Where are we going?"

"To the houseboat I told you about. We're nearly there."

"God, I hate this drugged feeling. Did you check me out of the hospital?"

"Not exactly. I kidnapped you."

"Oh, terrific. Are they going to have an APB out on us?"

He smiled. "You watch too much TV. Where would they begin to look for a Mr. and Mrs. Smith? They won't find us at the false address I gave them."

She turned to look at him. He looked pleased with himself. "We left without paying the bill?"

"I paid a thousand bucks on account. When this is all over with, we can call them and ask how much is still owed."

"You paid? You mean my father paid."

He wasn't about to correct her and open that kettle of worms, though he found her assumption unreasonably annoying. "Right."

"It seems he gave you a generous expense account. This magnificent truck, now a houseboat."

"Stephen's a very generous man." Luke angled off the main road. A couple more turns and he swung onto a dirt path and rolled to a stop. The vegetation surrounding the lake was thick and overgrown, the trees tall and moss covered. Few tourists knew of this out-of-the-way lake used mostly by local fishermen. A good place to lie low.

Quickly, he pulled on the wig and settled the mustache on his upper lip. It wasn't a perfect disguise, but it was better than none. He started up again, finding the uneven road a real test of the truck's shock absorbers.

Stephanie bounced up, then landed hard. As pain sliced through her, she groaned and doubled forward.

173

"Shit! I should have thought to get some pain pills for you." He glanced over at her as he slowed the vehicle. "Is it bad?"

"I'll live. I'd rather hurt a little than be so doped up I don't know what's going on." She felt a gush and the dampness then, and wondered how she was going to make her other more pressing needs known to this man she hardly knew. "What about supplies, food and such, for the houseboat?"

"The man who's renting it to us runs a store nearby. We'll stop there first." As he came around the bend, he saw the weathered building with a spotlight shining on a hand-painted sign that read Howie's. "There it is now."

"Charming. I hope they have what I need."

Luke pulled up near the door and turned off the truck. "Just give me a list. You're too weak to walk just yet."

"No. I'd rather go in and look around myself."

Damn stubborn woman. He got out and walked around, opening her door. But as he helped her out, she went limp in his arms, a wave of dizziness overtaking her. "Damn it, you're in no shape to go shopping. Tell me what you want, and I'll get it." His voice was harsh, but his hands were gentle as he placed her firmly on the truck's seat. She sat there catching her breath, not saying a word. "Well?" he demanded.

"I've just had a miscarriage," she said sharply. "I need feminine products, pads and things." In her anger and embarrassment, her face flamed.

He should have thought of that. He'd been so intent on planning their getaway that he hadn't given any thought to her physical needs. Irritated with himself, he looked away. "I'll take care of it. Anything else?" Eyes downcast, she shook her head. "Any food preferences?"

"No." Stephanie patted her damp face. "It's sticky hot in here. Will you just go?"

174

"I'll leave the door open. Maybe you can catch a breeze. Be back in a couple minutes." Luke left her there and went inside.

It took him no more than fifteen minutes to hurry through the deserted store, pick out groceries and necessities, and settle up with Howie.

The old man counted the cash and stuffed it into a banged-up metal box. "You're paid up for two weeks," Howie said, rubbing his whiskery jaw. "You reckon you might need longer?"

"It's possible. All depends on how well my wife does. We'll probably come back for more supplies in a week or so." Luke gathered up two bags stuffed full and shoved open the screen door. He placed the sacks in the truck bed and glanced inside the cab.

Stephanie was sitting up and holding a small calico kitten, rubbing its fur and looking wistful. She turned to look at him. "He just hopped up on my lap. Do you suppose he belongs to anyone?"

Howie appeared, carrying two more bags of supplies. "He's a stray, ma'am. Comes around looking for handouts. You'd be doing me a favor if you took him off my hands. I never cared much for cats myself." He handed the bags to Luke.

"Can we take him with us?" She waited until he met her eyes.

What the hell. If it would make her day. "Sure."

She smiled at him then, perhaps the first genuine smile of pleasure he'd seen from her. It changed her face, making her look happy and carefree when he knew she was neither. Luke turned away, fighting the softening, and took the bags from Howie.

"Did you get . . . everything?" she asked hesitantly.

"Yes, everything," he assured her as he closed her door.

Howie was looking at Stephanie's hospital gown. "Guess you folks checked out in a hurry."

Luke stepped between them. "You got the keys?"

175

Howie reached into the pocket of his baggy pants and withdrew a chain with three keys on it. "Like I said before, the motor needs a little coaxing. Be careful not to flood her. There's plenty of gas, and I loaded in some ice like you asked. You can park your truck alongside the shed next to the dock."

With a curt nod, Luke took the keys and climbed behind the wheel. He backed up and swung around, then headed for the dock about a hundred yards away.

"Did you happen to buy any strong soap?" Stephanie asked, stroking the kitten's soft head.

"Why do you ask?"

"I think our unexpected guest just might have a few fleas."

Just what I need, Luke thought.

It was nearly midnight before Luke found a secluded cove that satisfied him enough to drop anchor. He stood at the wheel on the bridge, examining the picturesque area of the huge lake carefully. In the wide beam of his lights, he could see thick vegetation and no sign of civilization. Large weeping willows bordered the shoreline. A sliver of a moon dangled in an inky sky. When he shut off the motor, only the distant sound of night birds could be heard, along with the gentle sloshing of water against the boat. He flipped off the lights, leaving only a small lamp burning. Yes, it would do nicely.

Rubbing the back of his neck, he rolled his shoulders and turned. Stephanie was lying on her side on the padded bench along the wall, sound asleep with the kitten curled up by her stomach, her hand curved around him. After showering and changing, he'd wanted her to get into bed, but she'd insisted on coming up with him, explaining that she'd rather not stay below alone. She'd tried valiantly to stay awake, but had quickly lost the battle.

176

Crouching down beside her, he ran a finger along the kitten's fur. Fleas. He'd have to do something about them soon or they'd be all over the boat. Just what he felt like doing at the end of a twenty-hour day. He reached for the cat and provoked a meow of protest.

Stephanie woke, her hand stopping his. "What are you doing?"

"I'd better give your friend a bath before we all have fleas."

She sat up. "I'll help you."

He headed for the stairs leading down to the living area. "Why don't you go to bed? I can handle this."

She followed him. "I had a miscarriage, not a heart bypass. I'm fine." But she felt light-headed enough to grab the railing to steady herself.

He saw and sent her a look. "Yeah, you're real tough, all right."

In the kitchen, Stephanie leaned on the red linoleum counter top and watched Luke run warm water into the sink. It was sweet of him to let her bring the kitten along, especially since she didn't think he was a particularly sweet man. Nuzzling up to her, the kitten sensed he was in store for trouble and tried to climb up onto her shoulder. "Easy there," she soothed.

The moment he hit the water, the kitten screeched loudly, his claws coming out and finding a home in Luke's flesh. Luke tried to keep the animal still with one hand while his other searched for the soap, but the cat was fighting for his life, squirming and splashing. "Damn it, hold still."

Stephanie moved closer. "Here, you hold him and I'll soap him down." Coming alongside, she rubbed soap into the wet fur. "There they are. Look at all those little black critters." They were moving toward the kitten's eyes and safety. She leaned forward and began to carefully soap the kitten's neck and head, murmuring softly.

177

Luke was getting scratched on his hands and arms, but there wasn't anything he could do to hurry up the process. He watched as she patiently searched out the insects, squeezed each one and dropped it into the water, then went back for more. The cat, reacting to her low sounds and gentle touch, was settling somewhat, realizing in the intuitive way of animals that she was trying to help him. He still struggled to be free, but not as desperately.

"You look like you've done this a time or two," Luke commented.

"I have. I helped out at an animal shelter in Detroit one summer when I was going to college." She gave a small laugh. "I wanted to adopt most of them. I did drag home several cats and a couple of puppies. My poor father just smiled and bought another food dish each time."

"You really care about him, don't you?"

"My father? Yes. He's the only man I've ever known who's everything he seems." Finished with the kitten's body, she concentrated on his small head.

"Stephen told me that Zane wouldn't allow animals in the house. That must have disappointed you."

A lot of things about Zane had disappointed her, but the list was too long to go into. "I knew that was how he felt, but I thought I could win him over. One day, while he was out, I went to a pet store and bought a cute little gray schnauzer. Three months old, all his shots, paper trained. When Zane came home, he went into a rage. Told me animals belonged outside and that if I wanted a dog I could go live outdoors with one." She sighed sadly. "The next morning, before I could take him back, the dog was gone."

"You don't know what happened to him?"

"I shudder to think." She sent him a level look. "Do you think a man who would punch a hole in his wife's brake line and drown her best friend would hesitate to kill a puppy?" She released the dirty water and turned

178

on the tap, shoving those disturbing thoughts from her mind. "Time to rinse."

By the time all the suds and fleas had been washed down the drain, the cat was exhausted. Drying him in a towel that Luke handed her, Stephanie murmured reassuringly to the cat, then looked up at Luke. "Thanks for bathing him. It was kind of you."

He'd been labeled a lot of things in his life—and as a cop. Kind hadn't been one of them. Uncomfortable with the thought, he shrugged. "Not kind. Practical. I didn't want to wake up with fleas."

Stephanie sent him a knowing look before turning back to the kitten. "How about calling him Casey? It's Gaelic for brave, and he certainly has been."

"Were you a language major?"

"No, literature, but I studied languages for the fun of it. I find words fascinating." She set the kitten down on the upholstered bench seat. "I think if Casey had a little milk now, he'd be ready for a long nap."

Luke poured milk into a saucer and placed it in front of the kitten. Casey stopped licking his foot, sniffed the milk, and then began lapping it up. "He's hungry—and I am, too. How about you?"

"I could scramble us some eggs," Stephanie suggested, putting away the towels.

"I thought you couldn't boil water?"

"I lied." She was watching his face as the words came out. Slowly, she folded her arms across her chest. "You're wondering what else I've lied to you about, right?"

"No, I—"

"Don't deny it. I could see it in your eyes. What exactly is it you think I've done to lie about, Detective Varner?" She shook her head. "It's funny, isn't it? You want me to trust you, but for some reason you don't trust me."

Luke reached into the cupboard for a frying pan.

179

"We're both tired. Let's not go into all this tonight. Let's eat."

"Never mind. I've lost my appetite." Turning on her heel, Stephanie moved toward the short hallway that led to the bedroom. He caught her at the door.

"Wait." He turned her, his hands on her arms. "I'm not used to trusting people. In my work, it's easier to stay alive if I don't. In my personal life, I married a woman I trusted. It turned out to be a mistake. Once you've been betrayed, it's hard to get it out of your mind."

"I understand betrayal. I've lived with it for two years."

"Tell me it hasn't changed you."

She softened reluctantly. "Yes, it has, and not for the better. Let's try to keep in mind that I'm not your wife and you're not Zane. Let's not make each other pay for someone else's sins."

"That's a deal." He slid his hands from her, but not before she noticed how the kitten had ripped his flesh.

"Oh, look at this." She pulled him back toward the kitchen. "I don't suppose you bought any salve or ointment? Maybe there's some in one of the cupboards. We have to put something on those cuts."

He took his hands from hers, unused to being fussed over. "I'll be fine." Moving around her, he placed the pan on the stove. "How do you like your eggs?"

She should have realized he wouldn't want her help. "Scrambled's fine." There was a toaster on the counter, and she slipped in two slices of bread, then stifled a yawn. That bed was going to feel awfully good.

But there was only one. Stephanie busied herself setting the small table. She was sure he was going to insist she take the bed, and she was equally sure she didn't want to share it, even though it was huge. The couch in the living area was long, but somewhat narrow. And he was a big man. She sighed. That was going to have to be Luke's problem. She simply couldn't cope with any more issues tonight.

He'd added freshly grated cheese to the eggs and had cooked sausages to go with them, plus the toast she'd buttered and milk. Prime rib couldn't have tasted better to her at that moment and she told him so.

"When you live alone, you learn to cook or you starve."

Stephanie leaned back, sipping her milk. "Do you like living on a houseboat back in Michigan?"

He shrugged. "It's peaceful, private, and inexpensive. What more could I ask?"

She looked out the open window, at the moon glistening on the water's surface. "This was a good idea. It appears to be a safe place. I know you're just doing the job you were hired to do, but I want to thank you."

Her evaluation of their situation was beginning to grate on his nerves. What he'd done for her had been above and beyond the call of duty, but he saw no way to tell her that. He'd been acting on instinct ever since finding her. And though it was relatively safe here, he didn't kid himself that they were totally out of danger. Zane was clever enough to find them — if he came in person and set his mind to it. And he just might. The man surely wasn't going to easily dismiss several million dollars.

And Luke still didn't know where the diamonds were.

Stephanie drew her legs up onto the seat as the cramps began again. "I wish we could let my father know I'm all right without endangering him."

Luke drew a folded yellow paper from his pocket and handed it to her.

She opened the sheet and read:

SUBJECT LOCATED STOP SAFE WITH ME
STOP MORE LATER STOP DESTROY THIS
STOP LUKE

"You sent him a telegram?"

"Safer than a phone call, wouldn't you say?"

"Probably. I hope he doesn't do anything foolish,
now that he knows."

"He's too smart to jeopardize your safety."

She folded the telegram. "Thanks for letting him
know. It would seem you've thought of everything."
Suddenly, she grimaced as another cramp took hold.

"Are you hurting?"

She wrapped her arms around herself. "Physically,
a little. Emotionally, I wonder if a woman ever gets
over losing a baby, even one she's never had the
chance to hold."

"Or a man. Don't you think a would-be father
grieves?"

Stephanie rested her cheek on her bent knees.
"You're asking the wrong person about how men
would feel. I don't know how their minds work, or
much about their emotions. You're a man. You tell
me."

"I don't think men feel things so differently from
women. They just disguise their feelings more." He
rose and cleared the dishes, then reached into his bag
and pulled out the flask of scotch he'd tucked in at the
last minute.

"Really? How would you feel right now if your wife
had miscarried?"

"Devastated." Luke found two small glasses and
poured scotch into each. "Drink this. We don't have
pain pills, but this'll do the trick."

She ignored his command and raised her eyes to
his. "Would you really be devastated?"

He propped his elbows on the table, taking a moment to seriously consider the question. "I wanted to

182

have a child with Kathy, but she was ten years younger than I am, and she wanted to wait. Now, I'm glad we didn't have any. But back then, if she'd lost our baby, I'd have been upset. How do you think Zane would feel—if he knew?"

Stephanie straightened and wrapped her fingers around her glass thoughtfully. "Angry because he's lost a chance at immortality, not because he actually wants a child to love. Zane doesn't know how to love." Bracing herself, she took a sip of the liquor and swallowed the heat. Knowing it would probably dull the pain in her body and mind, she downed the rest, then met his eyes as they carefully watched her. "What about you, Luke? Do you know how to love?"

"I'm not sure."

She stared at him a long moment, then nodded as if appreciating his honest assessment. Disentangling her limbs, she rose. "I think it's time I said good night." She picked up the kitten who didn't even open his eyes. A bit shakily, she left the galley and went to the bedroom.

Luke watched her walk away, then tossed down the drink and poured another. It would seem this trip was going to be damn hard on his ulcer.

She'd been sleeping almost nonstop for three days and nights. After that spurt of energy she'd shown the evening they'd arrived, he'd thought she'd be up and about the next day. But she rarely put in an appearance except for a minimum of two meals a day, which he had to coax her to eat. He checked on her periodically and found she truly was asleep, curled up with the kitten beside her. It was beginning to worry him.

He'd motored around the lake, scouting out other secluded spots to anchor. He'd fished and cleaned and cooked his catch. He'd read the couple of books he'd stuffed in his bag when he'd left home from cover to

183

cover. He'd listened to the small portable radio, though he could only pick up a country station. And he admitted he was lonely.

It wasn't an easy admission to make, even to himself. Back on his own houseboat, he rarely experienced loneliness. Now it was probably because he knew she was in there, a warm body who could talk with him and eat with him and share her thoughts with him. Stupid. Yet there it was.

On the evening of the third day, he decided to tempt her with a special meal—his homemade spaghetti sauce which he carefully assembled and had simmering for several hours. Stephen had mentioned her fondness for Italian food. The aroma alone should draw her out, he thought as he propped the bedroom door open. He'd just turned the guide lights on at dusk when he heard her come out on deck.

She had on white slacks and an oversize top. Her bare feet were silent on the polished wood deck as she walked over and sat down in the canvas chair next to him. He looked her over and saw that the dark shadows under her eyes had lightened considerably. With her face free of makeup, she looked barely twenty. Oddly, she seemed to have no vanity about her looks, never fussing with her hair or clothes. It wasn't the image he'd formed, based on his knowledge of her upbringing and previous lifestyle, but it was a pleasant surprise.

Luke propped his bare feet on the aft ledge and smiled at her. "Well, hello, sleepyhead."

Stephanie smiled, then turned her face up into the evening breeze. "I feel as if I've just come off a colossal hangover. Is that spaghetti sauce I smell?"

"Mmm-hmm. Are you hungry?"

"Not really. But the smell woke me. Maybe my subconscious is hungrier than I am."

"You should eat more. You're too thin."

She sent him a purely female look of censure.

"Thanks. You look terrific, too."

"I didn't mean that the way it sounded."

"Really? How did you mean it?"

"Only that you're a lovely woman. With a few more pounds, you'd be beautiful."

Stephanie was unused to flattery. Her father had always said she looked "very nice." Zane, even when they'd been dating, hadn't bothered to comment on her looks except to tell her she looked "fine." Marjo had often said she could look stunning if she'd work at it. Stephanie had never bothered. She'd always considered herself neat and fairly attractive, but beautiful? No. Disconcerted, she ran a hand through her hair. "I must look wonderful with these blond roots starting to grow out."

"Somehow I don't think Howie carries hair dye in his little backwoods store."

"Probably not." After they left the houseboat, she'd have to find a drugstore. But she didn't want to think about leaving this peaceful place just yet. A sound caught her attention and she looked up in time to see a silver fish leap high in the water, then skim back under. She noticed a pole hanging, supported by two hooks, just under the ledge. "Will you teach me to fish, maybe tomorrow?"

Her question surprised him. "Sure. You've never fished?"

She stretched her legs out and slumped back on her spine. "No. I learned to do all the acceptable things for young women from *good families*. But hardly any of the really fun, ordinary things."

"What acceptable things did you learn?"

"Ice-skating, skiing, horseback-riding, piano. When I was young, it seemed all I did was go from school to lessons to sleep, then start the same routine the next day. My father wanted me to be well rounded." She turned her head to look at him. He wore only denim cutoff shorts. His skin was bronze and tan, making her feel pale and anemic by comparison. "I suppose you learned to do all those other things without formal lessons."

"All except the piano." Luke angled his chair so he could more easily look at her. He didn't question why he liked to look at her, only accepted that he did. "I suspect we grew up in different worlds."

"Maybe not so different."

"Oh, I think so. I was a cop's son, and we lived in the city because that was a requirement for policemen then. My dad was an ordinary cop, one who walked a beat back when that was commonplace. But he was a good and honest cop. He didn't get killed in the line of duty; just didn't wake up one fine spring morning. Your mother, when she was alive, undoubtedly *had* a cleaning lady. My mother *was* a cleaning lady. But she had pride and dignity, and was a wonderful woman. So you see, we grew up probably ten miles apart, but it might just as well have been a thousand. Different worlds."

"Do you feel that two people have to have the same background in order to relate to each other as adults?"

"It probably helps. I notice you didn't marry some bricklayer or a guy who sells insurance door-to-door."

"My father began by selling insurance. My grandfather made him work his way up. My family didn't always have money."

"But by the time you came along, there was plenty."

"Yes, and I walked away from all of it."

"Not quite. You have a hundred grand in bonds. Most people never acquire that much spare cash in a lifetime." Not to mention the possibility of another three million in diamonds.

Stephanie sighed heavily, wondering why she'd started this stupid conversation, why she'd even left the unchallenging peace of her bed. "You're right. If I tear up the bonds and throw them overboard, will you accept me more easily, distrust me less?"

"Why do you care whether I accept you or not?"

A good question, one she should give some serious thought. "Damned if I know." Stephanie got to her feet. "Let's eat, not talk. Perhaps we can at least agree on food choices."

He rose and moved toward the kitchen. "It's only spaghetti. Not very fancy."

"Peasant dish though it is, I'll manage." She felt the heat of anger and wondered why she was allowing herself to get so worked up over nothing. She reached for the plates and all but slammed them onto the table. "Of course, I'm more used to caviar, truffles, and escargots. Served with champagne." She whirled about and glared at his back as he stood at the stove. "You've got me pegged as a rich little brat who grew up into a spoiled, wealthy, society princess, don't you?"

Slowly, Luke turned to see the red of anger darkening her cheeks. *So the sweet little daughter and the wonderful friend has a spunky side. Good.* A little healthy sparring would certainly relieve the boredom. And maybe he'd learn something besides. People often say things in anger they wouldn't otherwise reveal. "This little temper tantrum seems to prove my point. Mature, unspoiled women don't have them."

Jamming her hands on her hips, Stephanie moved a step closer. "You wouldn't know a mature, unspoiled woman if you tripped over her."

"I know when I see one who isn't. Can you tell me, with a straight face, that your father didn't spoil you? Damn right he did. Then along came Zane with hearts and flowers, and you married him, thinking that would continue." He was baiting her, and he knew it. Maybe it was cruel, but he was certain there were things Stephanie wasn't telling him, things he needed to know. "When his romancing didn't continue, you plotted your own disappearance and left

187

him. You ran because he'd threatened your father — and because you didn't want him raising your baby, you said. Was that really all there was to it, Stephanie? Or was there another reason?"

She sagged, her hands finding the edge of the table and using it as a brace to keep herself upright. Damn him for making her recall all that. "Yes, there was," she admitted shakily.

Here it comes, Luke thought. At last, she was going to tell him about the diamonds. "What was your real reason?"

Anger drained from her, replaced by remembered humiliation. "Because he raped me."

Chapter Nine

Rape. The missing piece to the puzzle, the one he hadn't thought of. Muttering an oath, Luke turned the burner under the spaghetti water off and drew her to the padded bench. Her hands were cool despite the lingering evening heat, and he wrapped his fingers around them. Her face was ashen, but her eyes were dry.

"Did you call the police?" he asked, because he thought she needed to talk about it and he needed to know.

Stephanie shook her head. "Do you know how hard it is to prove rape between husband and wife? I did go to an attorney, and he very kindly pointed that out to me. Zane didn't hit or bruise me. He merely held me down and had sex with me without my permission or desire. The attorney told me if they locked up every man who was guilty of that, they'd have to build a prison on every street corner." She drew in a deep breath. "Great commentary on today's world, isn't it?"

Luke watched her struggle to keep herself under control. The tears were there, waiting to fall, but she held them back, her lips trembling with the effort. As a detective, he'd run across a fair number of rape victims and knew what hell they lived with, many for the rest of their lives. Had that son-of-a-bitch thought that a marriage license gave him the right to force himself on his wife? He remembered the quarrel the maid—Eula—had said she'd overheard and felt like hitting something. But instead he slid his arms around Stephanie and drew her closer.

"What . . . what are you doing?"

"Come here, damn it."

"I'm all right."

"Yeah, you're tough. You don't need anyone. Well, maybe *I* need this." His touch just short of rough, he pulled her to his chest and tucked her head under his chin. "Maybe I need to hold you, to apologize for all those guys who hurt women. Go on, let it out."

She held herself stiff for several seconds, seated somewhat awkwardly and leaning into him, her cheek on his bare chest. Then she gave in, let her arms move up his back, and closed her eyes. The sob that escaped sounded as if it had come from her very soul, and maybe it had. Stephanie let go, let the agony rip, let the pain flow as freely as her tears.

She cried for her dead baby, her irreclaimable hope, her lost innocence. She felt Luke's hands stroking her hair and absorbed the comfort he offered without too much thought to the giver. He was right. She needed this—she needed someone to cling to so she could let it all out.

Luke held her gently, without pressure, feeling the grief slowly work its way out of her. Through her cotton top, he felt the bones of her spine clearly, and was moved by her frailty. She was the wrong kind of woman for him to go all soft over.

She was perfumed silk, and he was faded denim. She was vacations abroad, the Riviera, while he was fishing and camping. She was a Matisse painting in a victorian frame, a modern woman with old-fashioned desires for home and hearth. He was a cop, a man who'd walked on the edge for years, one who'd killed. There was a line here, an invisible boundary, that he'd better keep in mind and not cross. If he didn't, he might never be able to crawl back over.

Finally, Stephanie's trembling passed, along with her tears. He heard her hiccup her way to silence as he reached to the table and grabbed a handful of tissues to give her. He watched her blot her face and wipe her red eyes. She reminded him of a sad waif, yet she looked less pinched, less uptight.

"I'm sorry," Stephanie whispered, feeling embarrassed now that it was over. Luke was almost a stranger, but she'd soaked him with blood the night he'd found her and now she'd drenched him with tears. She wouldn't blame him if he pulled anchor and hauled her back to shore, then walked away. She blew her nose.

Looking up at him, at the angular lines of his face, the gray eyes that still seemed a bit distant, she wouldn't have thought this man capable of tenderness. She'd have been wrong. "You probably won't believe this, but I rarely cry."

"Really? I cry all the time."

She smiled at that. "So, are you going to feed me, or what?" She wasn't hungry, wasn't sure how much she could get down. But he'd gone to the bother of cooking, and he'd been kind. She'd eat if it gagged her.

"Wait until you taste my sauce." Luke went to the stove and turned on the burner. Inhaling deeply, he sampled a bit of his concoction from the end of a wooden spoon. Turning, he kissed the finger tips of one hand and made a smacking sound. *"Mamma mia!* That's scrumptious."

She found she could smile. Finishing up half an hour later, Stephanie had to agree that he knew his way around a kitchen. For someone who hadn't thought herself hungry, she'd cleaned her plate.

191

"You can cook for me anytime, Detective Varner," she told him, leaning back in her chair and feeling comfortably stuffed.

"I have been, in case you haven't noticed."

"I noticed. I really can't cook much. At the risk of having you label me spoiled again, I'll confess that I never had to, so I never learned. When I was young, my mother cooked. When she became ill, my father hired a live-in housekeeper who also knew her way around the kitchen."

"What about Zane? Did you cook for him?"

"Rarely. I made an effort and bought all these cookbooks, figuring if I could read, I could cook. But I couldn't please him. So he hired a succession of cooks, none of whom were able to please him either. Zane likes best to eat out."

"I'd rather eat at home."

"So would I." Another something they had in common. The list was short, but growing. Stephanie found herself curious about Luke, about his youth, his work, his marriage. He knew almost everything about her, yet she knew very little about him. If they had to be together on this boat, she at least ought to know his background. He was closemouthed, but perhaps she could draw him out. "Did your wife like to cook?"

"She took a stab at it when we were first married. She'd come from a fairly well-off family and had never needed to learn, like you. Some of her efforts weren't bad. In all fairness to Kathy, I worked long hours in those days, seldom getting home before the dinner had died waiting for me to show up."

She liked his honest assessment of that. How honest would he be about the rest? she wondered. "You said you trusted your wife and she betrayed you. How did that come about?"

She'd stripped the facade from her own past. He

supposed he should do no less, though he didn't know where to begin. He looked away and shrugged. "Who knows when a marriage starts to go sour? I sure didn't." He thought back to the beginning, when they'd each had fragile young dreams. "It isn't easy to rise in the police department of a major city. The competition's fierce, the work long and grueling, the hours unbelievable. I didn't want to be just a cop like my dad. I wanted to get into undercover investigation where I could call some of the shots. So I ate, drank, and slept police work. I thought I was working toward a better future. I didn't realize I was neglecting Kathy."

Stephanie had guessed as much. "She began to step out on you?"

"Worse. She got hooked on drugs. She was in a car accident before I met her, injuring her back. The doctors had put her on pain pills, and they gave her a buzz. She liked the feeling."

"God, I can't imagine why. They make me feel so listless I don't care about anything."

Luke toyed with a spoon, his eyes on the table. "Maybe that's what Kathy wanted. She was bored with the job she'd taken as a receptionist, so she quit. She latched on to this neighbor woman who liked to hang around malls. And bars. You can get anything, legal or illegal, in the kinds of bars they frequented. By the time I found out, Kathy was addicted. Cocaine."

"What did you do?"

"I put her in the hospital, a rehab center. The best program I could find. Six weeks later, she came home and swore she'd never touch the stuff again. Like a fool, I believed her. I found out later, she didn't even make it through the first week. Only now, she was more careful. She began to lie to me about where she'd been, who she'd been with. I

193

didn't leave her much money, trying to cut her off that way. They called me one day. She'd been picked up for shoplifting."

Stephanie leaned forward, feeling his disappointment and hurt, even though his recital was unemotional, his voice low and even.

"I got the charges dropped, first offense and all. Again, she made all these promises. I was skeptical by then, but I wanted so damn much to believe her."

Now she heard the pain. Silently, she waited for him to continue.

Luke swallowed, wishing he'd never started this but needing to finish, to get it over with. "Next came the men. They paid her, and she used the money to buy drugs. A vicious cycle, and an unending one. Finally, one day when I'd gone home and found her with a man, both of them higher than kites, I'd had it. I walked out on her."

"And divorced her?"

"I planned to. But a week later, she was found dead from an overdose."

"Oh, Luke." Stephanie touched his hand. "I'm so sorry."

Uncomfortable, he squeezed her fingers, then got up and walked to the sink. He needed a moment and hoped she'd give it to him. He simply wasn't used to spilling his guts, not to anyone. To have something to do, he put on a pot of coffee. Finally, he returned to the table and found her quietly watching him.

"I suppose, after that, you blamed yourself because you neglected your wife and she died of a drug overdose."

"Hard for me not to shoulder some of the blame. I was older, far more experienced. I should have noticed earlier that she was headed for serious trouble."

"Luke, a lot of men work long hours and their

194

wives don't turn to drugs out of boredom."

"No, they turn to alcohol, or other men. Show me a happy marriage and I'll change my tune."

"I can't, offhand. My parents had one, I believe."

"Maybe. Maybe if your mother had lived, things would have turned out differently."

"I don't want to believe that. You're a worse cynic than I am."

"Better a cynic than an unrealistic romantic."

"Point well taken." She badly wanted to know something, but hesitated to ask. What could he do but refuse to tell her? "My father told me that you went after someone once, with your bare hands. Who was it?"

"Sonny Poston, the drug dealer who kept supplying Kathy with that poison. I warned him, a number of times, but Sonny felt he was invincible."

"Did you do it? Did you kill him?"

Luke believed in justice unequivocally. But he wasn't naive enough to believe that the law was always just. He'd known that Sonny Poston was too smart for them to tie him to Kathy's overdose as surely as he'd known the slick drug dealer had been the one to make sure she got the stuff. So he'd decided not to wait until the law, which moved too slowly, might trip Sonny up on another charge and put him away for a short time. That wouldn't be nearly enough punishment. An eye for an eye. That was justice.

Now he would find out if Stephanie could handle raw truth. "In the line of duty, but yes, I did." He watched her eyes as she stared into his, unblinking, inscrutable. "How do you feel about that?"

"I think, in your shoes, I'd have done the same thing."

It wasn't the answer he'd been expecting. His evaluation of Stephanie Westover shifted with her simple statement. There was more substance to her than he'd thought, and suddenly he looked forward to stripping away the rest of her carefully arranged facade and discovering the real woman behind the mask. The few glimpses he'd had so far intrigued him.

Rising, he looked down at her. "Would you like to go out on deck with me and have a cup of coffee, just sit?"

"Yes."

Walking outside, she felt as if she'd somehow just passed an important test. And she felt good about it.

Luke lay on his back on the living-room couch, his hands crossed beneath his head, enjoying the familiar rocking of the houseboat. It was close to one in the morning, yet he still wasn't able to sleep. Too much caffeine, he supposed.

Or perhaps his conversation with Stephanie had stimulated him more than usual.

Over a cup of coffee, with the night breezes caressing them, they'd talked about city living versus country, about books they'd read, places they'd visited. He found her interesting, sensitive and bright, with a quiet sense of humor that appealed to the introvert in him. And there was something else.

He wanted her.

Luke rolled to his side, disgusted with himself. The last thing he needed was involvement with a wounded waif of a woman still very much married. A woman whose father had asked him to find her because he trusted him. He was absolutely certain Stephen hadn't intended that, when he found her, he should offer her the comfort of his bed. Yet that was exactly what he wanted to do.

196

Perfectly natural reaction, Luke told himself. Take a man who's been celibate for months, put him on the deck of a boat in the moonlight with a lovely woman who smells good and has a nice laugh and soft skin and *voilà!* You have a man who's as hard as the wood beneath his feet. Ah, nothing a grown man can't overcome. After all, he wasn't a teenager eyeing his first girl.

Then why the hell couldn't he put her out of his mind and get to sleep?

Restlessly, Luke shifted again, then went still. Cocking his head, he listened. There it was again, a noise from the direction of the bedroom that sounded like someone crying out. He was on his feet and moving down the hall in seconds.

Stephanie was thrashing about on the bed, evidently caught again in the throes of a nightmare. Luke knew all about nightmares, having gone through a horde of his own, especially back in his drinking days. She was frightening the kitten, who jumped off the bed and scooted out of the room. He moved to the bed, eased a knee on top of the tangled sheets and leaned down to her.

"No," she muttered, "stay back." An arm shot out, stiff and unyielding, as if holding someone away. "Don't touch me."

"Stephanie," Luke said, touching her shoulder. "Wake up."

"I don't want you near me." Louder now, more agitated. "No. Let me go, please, just let me go." She tossed her head back and forth, and her legs shifted restively. "Please don't hurt me."

He took hold of her shoulders gently. "No one's going to hurt you, Stephanie. It's me, Luke. Wake up."

Her eyes opened and she bolted upright. She gazed past him, staring with wide-eyed fright at

197

something only she could see. "Not the cobra. Oh, God, not the cobra." She trembled violently as her hands came up to cover her face.

Luke knelt beside her and gently pried her fingers loose. "Look at me. It's Luke. You're safe."

For a moment, she stared at him as if he were a stranger. Then recognition dawned in her eyes, and she sagged forward. "Luke," she whispered. "Thank God, it's you."

He shifted into a sitting position and eased her into the circle of his arms. She clutched him closer, her small hands squeezing his upper arms in her anxiety. "Shhh, it's all right," he told her. "You're okay now."

Stephanie took deep breaths, letting her heart slow down, letting the fear subside. She allowed Luke to comfort her, waiting for the horror of the nightmare to recede. Long moments later, she eased back from him a trifle. "I seem always to be thanking you."

"It was a bad one?"

She nodded against his chest. She shivered, remembering. "Zane was holding a cobra, and it was upright, coiled to attack. I begged him to move away from me, but he just laughed. Oh, God, I wish these dreams would end. I feel so helpless, so foolish."

He held her tighter. "Don't. You can't control your dreams. But they are just that, *dreams*." He leaned his back against the headboard and settled in more comfortably. "Marjo told me about Zane's tattoo."

"It's horrible. If I'd have known he had that thing on his arm, maybe I wouldn't have married him."

"You didn't go to bed with him before you were married?"

Perhaps it was the aftermath of the dream, or maybe the sense of isolation since they were alone in

198

the middle of a big lake, but she felt no embarrassment about their intimate conversation. "If I had, I *know* I wouldn't have married him."

"Marjo said she didn't think Zane made you happy in the bedroom."

Frowning, Stephanie angled her head back so she could look into his eyes. "You talked with Marjo about . . . about my marriage, my sex life?"

"I only asked because she seemed to think Zane was responsible for your accident. She didn't say much, adding that you rarely confided anything personal. Marjo was reading between the lines, I'd say. Told me that back in college, you were in love with love."

"She sure had me pegged."

"In these nightmares, is he raping you again?"

"Sometimes." Stephanie settled her cheek more comfortably in the soft hair of his chest. "Other times, I'm running from some kind of unknown danger and, suddenly, he's there, his arms reaching out. Just before he grabs me, I wake up." She shuddered involuntarily. "I want so badly to feel safe again."

Luke pressed her closer. "Try to get some sleep."

Drowsy and beginning to drift, Stephanie let herself relax against him. She remembered being held like this years ago by her father when she'd needed comforting. But not since. Not until now, with Luke. "Don't leave me, please."

Bending his head, he rested his cheek on her hair. "I won't," he promised, then wondered how in hell he could keep his word.

"I can't touch a worm." Stephanie's expression was one of distaste. "I can do all the rest, but not that."

Luke hid a smile as he dipped into the bait bucket

he'd bought from Howie. He extracted a fat, juicy worm and held its wiggling body up, revolting her further. He laughed out loud as she closed her eyes and averted her head. "Women! You're all sissies."

She retreated a step or two, watching him bait the hook from a safe distance. "Men! You're all gross."

Finished, he held the pole toward her. "Do you think you can manage from here on, or do you want me to throw your line out for you, too?"

"Smart ass." She grabbed the pole, held it in position and aimed her toss over the end of the boat. The weight of the worm arced the line out, then dipped it into the blue water. She turned to him with satisfaction and stuck out her tongue.

Luke grinned as he loaded his own pole and followed suit. Pulling over the canvas chair, he sat down and propped his feet on the rail. "You don't have to stand there. The sinker will let you know when you have something."

Stephanie moved the other chair up and sat down next to him. "So this is all there is to fishing, eh? Bait the hook, toss out the line, and wait."

"That's about it. A child of six can do it. And, if it's a male, he can even deal with the worm."

"And if it's a female, she can find some little boy to do it for her." She glanced over and saw the kitten watching her from the deck, head cocked as he sniffed the air. "Hold on, Casey. You'll have fresh fish for dinner soon." Tossing her hair back, she glanced up at a blue sky. "What a beautiful day."

He wasn't crazy about spending weeks floating around on a Florida lake, but he needed her fully recovered. She could use some color, he thought, watching her raise her face to the noonday sun. They'd been gone long enough for her hair to start growing out. "I think I'd like you as a blonde."

Self-consciously, she touched her brown bangs.

"I'm afraid to return to blond just yet. When we go back, I'll put the brown contacts back in." The thought of returning sobered both of them, she noticed. "Do you think Chester went back to Michigan when he couldn't find me?"

"I hope so. What do you think Zane will do to him if he returns empty-handed?"

Stephanie sighed. "Your guess is as good as mine. Zane's not very predictable. He might be very understanding about Chester's failed mission, or he might cause him to quietly disappear."

She was relaxed now, loosening up. Time for a little quiet probing. "While you were living with Zane, did you suspect he was involved in criminal activities?"

"Not until last spring. He was always very secretive, but then, I didn't really ask too many questions. Then one afternoon—last March, I think—we'd been talking in his study. Arguing really. He wanted me to go see a specialist, and I didn't want to."

"What kind of a specialist?"

"A fertility doctor. We'd been married a year and a half and I still wasn't pregnant. He seemed to take it as a personal affront to his manhood. It was all he talked about."

"Did he ever consider it might have been his fault, a low sperm count?"

She sent him a mock scowl. "The great Zane Westover less than perfect? You must be kidding. No, he was sure it was my fault. I was equally sure I wasn't in any great hurry to have a child with him. I'd begun to suspect he was up to something shady. He had these mysterious meetings, always late in the evening. Men would show up, and he'd take them into his study, lock the door. They'd be in there for hours."

201

"Did you meet any of them?"

"A few. A quick introduction and then Zane would hustle them away."

The cop in him was suddenly alert. "Do you remember any names?"

She frowned. "They were odd, nicknames I'd guess. One short, chubby man was called Fat Freddy. Another—tall and very well dressed—was Mr. Q. And there was this other one with a jagged scar on his face . . . Willy something or other."

Luke shifted his pole to the other hand. "What did you do while they were in his study?"

"I'd go to bed. I know that was awfully passive of me, but I was a little afraid of Zane by then—and of the company he kept. Marjo had just gotten her divorce, and she'd asked me to go to the Bahamas with her for a short vacation. Zane had a business trip planned for that week so I asked him if he'd mind. He hit the ceiling, screaming at me like a mad man. Accused me of wanting to sleep around as he was certain Marjo did."

"So you didn't go."

"No. Anyhow, that evening our argument was interrupted by a phone call. He was very cryptic on the phone, answering in monosyllables. He hung up and told me he had to go out. He left in such a hurry, he forgot to lock his desk. So I went through it."

"What did you find?"

"Plenty. It seems that about six months before Zane and I were married, he'd been involved in a hit-and-run accident. In a metal box at the back of a drawer, I found a copy of the police report listing him as the driver of the vehicle. And there was a copy of a letter he'd written to someone named Ralph Mallory. In it, he outlined how he'd put a certain amount of money each month into a bank account set up in Ralph's name for a period of five years in return for a great favor."

"What favor?"

Stephanie turned to face Luke. She'd debated the wisdom of telling him this story, then had decided to trust him. Her father trusted him, and, in this matter, she would also. If anyone could get Zane convicted, it was the man who sat waiting for her answer. "He's paying Ralph to go to prison for him for the hit-and-run accident."

Luke whistled long and low. "I'll be damned." He sat up taller. "What did you do with those papers?"

"I took a big chance that Zane wouldn't return for a while and drove to the library and made copies of everything, including the bankbook listing the monthly deposits. I was lucky. He wasn't back when I returned. So I put everything back the way he had it. And I took the copies and hid them. By the time he came home, I was reading in bed."

"Do you think he suspected you may have snooped in his desk?"

She shook her head. "I would have heard about it if he did. I don't think he believes I've got the guts to go against his orders. From the beginning, he'd warned me never to touch his desk or anything in his study."

Luke felt like hugging her. "Where did you hide the copies?"

"Under the carpeting in my closet. I pried it up carefully, slid the manila envelope containing the copies under and tacked the carpeting back down."

"I was in your closet. I wish I'd known."

"What were you doing in my closet?"

He shrugged. "Looking for clues to your personality so I could find you. Your father thinks you can do no wrong. Marjo said you were 'innately good'; even Eula thinks you're wonderful. I had to go looking elsewhere."

"And what did you learn from rummaging through my room?"

"I didn't rummage. I looked. I learned you were neat, a reader of good books, and still a romantic who likes the soft light of candles and dreamy music."

Stephanie sighed. "Ah, yes. I *was* like that. However, knowing that someone tried to kill me has changed me into a realist."

"I also learned that someone had been in your room before me. Someone who'd gone through each drawer and the entire closet, shoving things every which way, obviously looking for something."

"For what?"

"I thought you might know."

"Zane doesn't know about the envelope, I'm sure. I don't know what else it could be."

"I did mention that Zane seems to feel you took something he wants back very badly."

"I *told* you, I have nothing of his."

"What's in your safety deposit box at the bank in Orlando?"

She narrowed her eyes at him. "You're very thorough. The bearer bonds and the envelope of evidence against Zane."

He would let it go for now, before she got so upset she clammed up.

Stephanie stared out at the calm lake water, wishing she were more calm. Zane had gone through her things. What could he have thought she'd taken? It was too much to think about; she was getting a headache. Suddenly, the beauty had fled from the day. She held the pole out toward Luke. "I think I'll go lie down. I feel a bit drained."

I've given her something to think about, Luke thought, taking her pole. Maybe, when alone, she'd decide to tell him the rest. *If* she knew any more.

At the doorway, she paused and turned back. "Do you think we can use the evidence in that envelope against Zane when we return?"

Luke swiveled around to face her. "Have you decided to return, Stephanie?"

Even hearing the thought spoken aloud made her wince. "Oh, God, I don't know." She turned and left the deck.

Luke propped the two poles in the metal braces and leaned back in the chair. Stephanie Westover was either brutally honest or one hell of an actress.

If only he knew which one she was.

She was doing it again, sleeping most of the time to avoid thinking. Or was it to avoid him? It was afternoon. Yesterday morning he'd showed her how to fish, and she hadn't been out of the bedroom for more than half an hour at a stretch since. Sitting on the back deck, Luke felt his annoyance mount.

He'd brought her here to rest and heal, it was true. How long does it take a woman to recover from a miscarriage? he wondered. The doctor had told him a couple of weeks and she'd be good as new. It'd been over a week, and, to him, she looked much more rested and even seemed to have gained a little weight. She had to be hiding in there. Perhaps she hated to face what she knew she must: returning and testifying against the man who'd tried to kill her.

Luke knew why Stephanie was worried. Zane had friends in high places; even Captain Renwick had reluctantly admitted that. If Zane slipped through the cracks, avoided conviction, he'd be after her again. And this time, he'd make sure he succeeded. But with the evidence she had in the safety deposit box, they could get him on that charge and worry about proving the attempted murder of his wife afterward. Provided it was real and would hold up in court.

He heard a noise behind him and turned. She was standing at the rail, behind and to the side, staring out at the water, wrapped in a white terrycloth robe. "I didn't hear you come out. Feel okay?"

"Yes, fine." The wind whipped her hair about her face, and it felt good. "How deep is the water here?"

They were anchored about half a mile out from the nearest shoreline, and would move into the shelter of a cove only at night. "Thirty feet, maybe more. Why?"

"I thought I might swim a little. I feel sluggish."

"Can you? I mean, after the miscarriage and all."

"The . . . uh . . . physical effects seemed to have abated." She was relieved to find she could tell him something like that and not blush like a teenager. Perhaps she was getting used to him. She walked over where he sat and peered down at the water. Not much of a dive. "But I don't have a suit."

Luke crossed his feet on the railing and kept from smiling. "I won't look."

Slowly her head turned to him. His relaxed attitude hid a readiness only the most astute observer could spot. Watchfulness was such a part of him that it was almost second nature. His pale gray eyes looked bored—unless you really studied them and saw they were alert. He frightened her a little, and attracted her more than she liked. And his eyes were as aware as her own. "The hell, you say."

He gave her an exaggerated frown. "Such language from a proper Grosse Pointe socialite." Luke stood. "You're a big girl now. Forget the suit. I'll go in with you, in case you get overtired or cramp up."

He was wearing only the faded denim cutoffs, his legs lean and muscular, his chest brown and broad.

She'd had another dream before coming out, only this one couldn't be classified a nightmare. She'd been in bed, and Luke had been holding her. But his touch had been far less comforting than vividly sensual. If he went in with her, she wondered if she could keep her mind on swimming. "If I could swim several miles against the current in that filthy Detroit River, I should be able to manage in this quiet lake."

If that was a request that he stay aboard, Luke chose to ignore it. He uncoiled the rope ladder and slung it over the rail. "You want to use this and push off, or dive from the rail?"

There was no arguing with his determination. Stephanie untied her robe, thinking she'd best not hinder her recovery by overdoing. "I'll push off." She looked up at him. "Want to go in first?"

He waved his arm. "After you."

She'd decided against wearing just her bra and panties. Her breasts were still quite large from the pregnancy. So she'd put on black shorts and a black tank top that she usually wore under a shirt. Trying to swim in a shirt would be silly. Quickly, not looking at him, she removed the robe and tossed it onto the deck chair. Turning, she hoisted herself up onto the rail, swung around, and began descending.

Luke felt his body tighten in response to the clear outline of her figure in the form-fitting shirt. He swallowed and stepped closer to the rail, watched her push off and begin swimming away from the boat. Looking forward to hitting the cool water, he followed.

She was a powerful swimmer, as he'd known she must be. But he was no slouch himself and was soon abreast of her. Noticing him, she slowed to a stop and began to tread water.

"So, Detective Varner, do you feel up to racing me?" she challenged.

"You name it, Mrs. Westover."

Her smile slid from her face. "Don't call me that, please. If I'd have stayed in Michigan, I'd probably be divorced by now." She kept her feet moving as she brushed wet hair from her face. "I filed months ago. My attorney told me that with no-fault, it shouldn't take long."

He declined to point out that if she'd stayed in Michigan, she'd likely be dead. "You filed right after Zane forced himself on you?"

"No, after I found out about his hit-and-run. When he was served notice of the divorce, he came home angrier than I'd ever seen him. He told me he'd see me and my father dead before he'd allow me to divorce him. Then he came at me."

Stephanie lay back on the surface of the water, floating. "My life is such a mess. We're not really certain Zane knows for a fact that I'm alive. Sometimes I think I should just get the bonds and take off for parts unknown and never return. Other times, I think I should go back and try to nail him."

"What do you *want* to do?"

She closed her eyes against the sun and against harsh realities she hated to face. "I want to be free of Zane. For months, that's been my only thought. But wherever I go, he'll send someone after me. If I go back, he'll find a way to carry out his threats. Or he'll hurt my father."

Luke moved closer, catching her hand in one of his. "I'll help you put him away. But I'm not going to kid you that it'll be easy."

"There's a limit to what two people can do. Zane's got influential friends."

"We don't have to decide right now, but think about it. I believe we can get him. But you have to believe it, too. And you have to trust me."

She straightened, her legs arrowing downward, her

208

face very near his. "Do you think I'd have told you all this if I didn't trust you?"

Her eyes were a startling blue in the sunlight, coupled with the reflection of the water. "I mean trust me completely, in every way," he said as his arm touched her shoulder, bringing her closer.

She swayed, inches from him. His long lashes were spiky from the water, his mouth open and moving toward hers. He was going to kiss her, and she wanted him to. But something told her she'd be moving from one dangerous man to another. She was in over her head here, and it had nothing to do with the depth of the lake.

Pulling away, Stephanie jackknifed under and began swimming back to the boat.

The first clap of thunder broke the silence just after midnight. Stephanie woke with a start to find a frightened kitten all but sitting on her face. She pushed back from Casey and glanced out the window in time to see a flash of lightning streak across the sky. Moments later, it was followed by another burst of thunder from somewhere above.

Hugging the meowing cat, she got up and went closer to the window. Rain was falling in sheets almost too thick to see through. At least the storm will cool things off for a while, she thought as she opened the bedroom door.

Padding on bare feet, she made her way quietly to the back of the boat and stood under the overhang, just out of reach of the rain bouncing onto the wooden deck in huge droplets. Nature lit up the sky again with double flashes, then followed with the answering bursts of thunder. Mesmerized, she stood watching.

"Exciting, isn't it?" Luke asked from behind her.

Stephanie didn't move. She should have guessed that the storm would waken him, too. "Yes, it is. I had a window seat in my bedroom in my parents' house. I used to curl up there when it stormed and watch for hours. It's both frightening and fascinating."

He stepped nearer, standing behind her. "Most elemental things are."

Like a trip-hammer, her heart picked up its rhythm. Was it the primitive appeal of the storm, or the man close to her? She couldn't have said which. The rain splashed her toes, and Casey jumped from her arms, retreating to drier quarters. Stephanie turned.

The soft glow of the table lamp lit him from behind, haloing his head, yet hiding the expression in his gray eyes. It was odd how, during their days together, having him with her made the silence pleasant rather than oppressive. Now the room where she stood seemed warm whereas before he'd joined her, it had been cool.

Lightning streaked somewhere over the water behind her, and she studied his features in its brief flash. At times he seemed like a safe harbor, at other moments like a storm raging out of control. It was mostly his eyes that moved from a warm gray to an icy silver, depending on his mood. His mood right now was one of quiet determination.

"I was in that bedroom of your childhood, Stephanie," Luke told her. "I saw your window seat."

She was no longer surprised. "It seems you know a great deal about me."

"Not nearly enough." He took her hands in his and examined them in the faint light. He would not rush this fragile woman who'd been mauled and threatened. He would treat her gently so she would know there were men who wouldn't hurt her. Even shopworn cops like him.

Dipping his head, Luke kissed the palm of one hand, then the other, his lips caressing the soft flesh. When he raised his head to look at her, her eyes were huge and wary.

"Why did you do that?" she asked, her breathing uneven.

"Because I wanted to. Didn't you enjoy it?"

She was reluctant to admit the truth. "I don't want this."

He ran his eyes down her and saw her nipples harden through the thin cotton of her nightshirt. "Don't you?" He closed the gap between them by slipping his arms around her. His bare chest rubbed against her breasts, and he felt them grow fuller. She could deny him with words, but her body betrayed her. "I think you do." He lowered his head and touched his mouth to hers.

No, Stephanie thought, even as she swayed closer to him. I can't do this. But there was no pressure from his mouth, no insistence she could detect. He nibbled, he sampled, he teased. His tongue outlined the framework of her lips, then withdrew as he kissed her again. Lightly, playfully, coaxingly.

If he'd rushed or grabbed or devoured, she would have pulled back. But it was as if he felt that the mouth was for tasting and he did just that—lingering, savoring. She found herself rising on tiptoe, to give him better access, as her arms went around him. An unexpected pinpoint of desire began to take root and grow.

Slowly, the tip of her tongue inched out to meet with his, and he enticed it to follow back inside his mouth. There she was free to loiter, to explore, to learn him. When she withdrew, he didn't rush to follow, but instead shifted his mouth to the column of her throat and kissed her there.

211

Her eyes closed, Stephanie felt floaty. She wanted, yet was afraid to want. If he could make her forget, even for a little while, she would welcome the diversion. He made her breasts ache, made the restless void inside her long for fulfillment. But it would be risky for him and stupid on her part.

"Luke," she said, her voice husky, "I don't think you want to do this."

He angled to look at her. "Think again." He took her hand and placed it on his full erection, let her feel the heat. Her eyes darkened, widened. "Does that show you just how much I want you?"

"I'm not good at games."

"It's not a game. I'm very attracted to you. I thought that was obvious, even before I kissed you."

She felt him throb under her hand and felt herself grow damp. "I'm very attracted to you, too. I've been married, lived with a man for nearly two years. Still, I'm not quite sure how to handle this."

"Why not just go with it, see where it takes us?"

She searched for the right words. "I've never been a casual person." A bolt of lightning lit up the whole deck, and she saw his eyes turn pewter gray. When the thunder hit, she was jolted.

"Do you think what I'm suggesting will be casual, for either of us?"

"You could get hurt, knowing me, getting involved with me. Zane's a jealous man, vindictive and dangerous."

"It's too late, lady." He took her arm from between them and placed it around his neck, then ran a hand down the small of her back. Cupping her buttocks, he ground his erection into her softness and smiled when she involuntarily arched to meet him. "Way too late. And I'm not afraid of Zane."

This kiss was deep, passionate, breathtaking. His lips seduced, his tongue dove deep inside her mouth, his body molded to hers. His hands crept up under the long T-shirt she wore to caress her back, then shifted around to her front. When they closed around her swollen breasts, Stephanie could no longer hold back a moan of pleasure.

Her hands threaded into his hair, and she kissed him back. She was lost in need, struggling with passion, fighting a desire that threatened to buckle her knees. She wanted this man and the oblivion she was certain he could give her. But involvements were costly, and dangerous men played by their own rules.

That thought, creeping into her subconscious, sobered her and had her pulling back. Hadn't she bought into this dream once before, only to pay a very high price for her naiveté? Breathing hard, she placed a hand on his chest and held him off.

Aroused and unwilling to stop, Luke loosened his hold and searched her face. "What's wrong?"

Stephanie took a step back, straightening her clothes. "I can't do this. It won't work."

"You mean because of the miscarriage? The doctor said . . ."

She shook her head. "No. Because of me. I just can't."

Luke took a deep breath and let her go.

Stephanie stared up at him a long moment as the rain splashed onto the deck. "I wish I'd met you first," she said, then turned and left him.

Luke listened to the closing of the bedroom door. Lightning split the sky—high, wide, and handsome. "Sonofabitch!" he said out loud. The thunder clap that followed underscored his frustration.

Chapter Ten

Bob Triner was tired. Running his fingers through his sandy hair, he settled back on the leather couch in Zane's study. He'd just returned from his second trip to Orlando in as many weeks, and his eyes felt grainy from lack of sleep. Perhaps if he'd come back with good news, he'd have felt better. But he'd accomplished very little, which only served to fuel Zane's already volatile temper.

His employer was drinking too much, Bob noticed as Zane went to the built-in bar and poured himself a generous splash of bourbon, then added one ice cube. Zane, too, apparently hadn't slept much, leaving him jumpy and irritable.

"Maybe we ought to cut our losses and forget her," Bob suggested, his voice soft and reasonable.

Zane swiveled around so quickly he nearly spilled his drink. "And let approximately three million dollars worth of diamonds go, just like that?" He snapped his fingers angrily. Shaking his head, he walked restlessly back to the fireplace and stood facing his attorney. "Never. Besides, I have a score to settle with that bitch."

Bob pushed his thick glasses up higher on his nose and wished he were somewhere else, *anywhere* else. Under the best of circumstances, Zane was difficult. Lately, he'd become impossible. This obsession with Stephanie was getting on Bob's nerves. Not for the first time, he thought that he should seriously consider severing the relationship with Westover.

But, first, he'd have to try to solve Zane's current problem. "All right," he began. "Let's see what we have here. We know Stephanie got out of the car somehow, swam to safety, and made it to Orlando. Evidently, she'd discovered the diamonds and had been planning to run with them when the car accident brought about a change in her plans. We also know Stephen felt she hadn't drowned, hired Luke Varner to find her, and somehow they found out she was in Florida."

Zane took a long swallow of bourbon. "I wish to hell I knew how they learned that."

"Maybe Marjo called Stephen after Stephanie phoned her."

"Chester was listening on the bug, and we have the recording. She didn't call anyone before she died."

"Nevertheless, Varner knew and flew to Orlando. With Chester on his tail, he visited the First Financial Center, drove all over town—to animal shelters and allergy doctors—trying to trace Stephanie. Chester lost him, then found him again and followed him to the hospital where Stephanie was a patient. He almost got her, but again that slick cop took her out of there right under Chester's nose. Are you sure you want Chester on this? The man's not running on all cylinders."

Zane felt a fresh spurt of anger erupt and welcomed it. He'd questioned Chester's capabilities regularly and often, but he didn't want to hear complaints about him from Bob. "Don't go picking on Chester. You think it's easy to find a muscle man who'll do what you tell him, no questions asked?"

"And screw up regularly."

"How about you? You've been there twice now. Have you found her?"

Bob let out a sigh of exhaustion. "Maybe not, but I do know where the diamonds are, which is more than Chester learned."

Zane moved to his lounge chair and sat down. "You *think* you know where they are."

"What else would Stephanie have in that safety deposit box?" It'd been almost too easy to charm the bosomy blond bank manager into identifying the picture he'd shown her. Chester had said Stephanie's hair was shorter now and dyed brown. Bob had visited a client who was an artist and had a sketch made. Then he'd flown to Orlando and gone to the bank where Chester had said Luke Varner had spent some time. Most women opened up to Bob's nonthreatening, boyish approach, and Miss Carpenter had been no exception.

He'd given her a story about a missing sister who might have amnesia. She'd softened, telling him she'd never met the woman in the picture, but a customer named Juli Richards did have a checking account and a safety deposit box there. Juli hadn't been in in some time, according to bank records. The manager had stopped short of giving out the customer's address when Bob had pressed, saying only that it was a post-office box. "Stephanie's got those diamonds in that bank, and she sure as hell isn't going to skip town without them. She's gone to too much trouble to leave them behind."

Zane sipped thoughtfully. "How can an amateur like her find a fence for that much ice?"

"Stephanie's no dummy. Who'd have thought

216

she'd make it out of the Detroit River? Besides, money talks, Zane. You ought to know that. She's not far from Miami, a gateway to the Caribbean. My guess is, she's holed up somewhere, maybe waiting for the right buy on the diamonds. When that happens, she'll come back for them. And we'll have her. If Chester doesn't screw up again, that is."

"Not this time. I've got him scared shitless. He's practically living at that bank." Zane set down his glass, a worried frown creasing his brow. "I just wish we had another lead on her."

"I've searched that damn city from every angle. It's like she disappeared into thin air. But I believe she'll be back."

"You think she's with Varner?"

"It's a possibility. You said you've checked his houseboat and your sources at the Police Department, and no one's seen him. If she is with him, why would they just be sitting it out? And why was Stephanie in the hospital in the first place? I couldn't get those hospital officials to reveal a damn thing. Without a court order, they wouldn't let me see any records."

Zane drummed his fingertips on the arm of the chair. "Stephen's been around town, acting cocky and confident again. That man knows something. If we don't get a break soon, I may have to apply a little pressure there."

Bob leaned forward, intent on making his point. "You pay me for advice, so I'm going to give you some. Since that incident at the border, the cops have been watching your operation. My informants told me that that punk talked, naming names, and one of them was yours. You rough up Stephen, he winds up like Marjo, and the cops are going to tie

217

it to you, sure as hell."

Zane made an impatient gesture. "I'm not going to rough up Stephen. But I might have to persuade him to share his information with us, that's all."

"Damn, Zane, I'm telling you, that would be a mistake."

His temper climbing, Zane got up. "Hey! You don't tell *me* what to do. I tell *you* what to do. Let's remember who's working for who around here."

Bob didn't like the way Zane's eyes looked, wild and crazed. He sat back, giving in. "All right. If Varner finds her and brings her back, he'll put her in protective custody. You think she's going to tell the cops she found the diamonds on the lawn? If Chester doesn't find Stephanie and snuff her, you've got serious problems."

"They can't trace those diamonds to me. Besides, one more shipment and I'm through." He'd let Mr. Q handle the cops after that. His smooth Canadian partner prided himself on outwitting the police.

"Suppose she found out about the hit-and-run and that's the evidence she had against you that she mentioned on the tape from Marjo's phone?"

Zane drained his glass. "No way. There's only the bankbook locked away in back of a drawer. Stephanie's never touched my desk. You think I wouldn't have noticed if she'd have tried? Go look for yourself. Not a scratch on any drawer."

"I just wish to hell Chester didn't have a cloudy brain. Maybe I should fly to Florida one more time. I tell you, he's unreliable."

Zane walked back to the bar. "And I tell you, Chester's camping at that bank, and when she shows he'll grab her. Once he's got the diamonds, he'll take care of my dear wife." He poured another drink and tossed it back quickly. "I just wish I could be there to watch."

Bob saw the cold gleam in Zane's eyes and shivered despite the warmth in the room. When this business with Stephanie was finished, he would move on. Continuing to work for Zane Westover could be hazardous to his health and well-being.

Luke slouched in a canvas chair off the stern, his feet propped on the rail, a fishing pole in one hand and a pale blue cotton hat pulled low over his forehead. He was semidozing in the late afternoon sun, trying to keep his mind blank.

It wasn't working.

The reason was all too clear to him. Up on the bridge deck at the bow, Stephanie lay on a blanket, trying to get a tan and wearing next to nothing. She'd specifically requested he not come up. Crisply, he'd replied that he wouldn't dream of it. But dreaming of her was exactly what he was doing.

He closed his eyes, and saw her. His mind filled with how she'd felt in his arms, how she'd smelled and tasted. Damn, this wasn't like him, getting all in knots over a woman.

Of course, she wasn't just *any* woman, and it wasn't her fault. If anything, she'd taken great pains to avoid him since she'd left him standing on the deck in the rain last night. He didn't have room in his life for a woman, and even if he did, she wouldn't fit in. Yet he'd lain awake on the lumpy couch for hours, remembering the taste and feel of her, wondering what to do about the way he felt.

Luke shifted in the chair, settling the pole between his knees more comfortably. Zane had really done a number on her. She'd been deeply affected by the rape, by her husband's coldness and the loss of her baby. He could understand why she didn't want another involvement. Neither did he.

It's purely physical, he told himself, and that's all. He almost believed it.

So lost in thought was he that at first he didn't hear the sound. By the time he did, the motor boat wasn't very far away and was heading toward the houseboat. Squinting, he saw that it was the same cruiser he'd noticed yesterday at about the same time. Maybe thirty feet long and flying a red and yellow flag from the bridge. Quickly, he moved to the stairway and climbed.

"Stephanie," he called without preamble. "I want you down here quickly. There's a boat headed our way, and I don't want you seen."

She'd been lying on her stomach on a folded blanket, wearing only bra and panties, half asleep in the sun. But she didn't have to be told twice. She jumped to her feet and gathered her things, both modesty and her coolness toward him forgotten. "You can't see who's on board?"

"No, they're too far away yet. But moving up fast." He stepped aside as she hurried down the stairs. "I don't like the looks of it at this time of day. Fishing boats head out in the early morning hours." They'd seen a few off in the distance several times, but none had ventured near. Now here was this one, twice in two days. "Just stay in your room until I check it out."

She scooted down the hallway and closed the bedroom door behind her.

Luke stopped in the living room beside his leather bag and removed his gun, then stuffed it in the waistband of his shorts. Pulling his white T-shirt down to cover it, he walked out on deck. He resumed his seat at the railing, picked up his pole, and slumped back down. Adjusting the hat he'd found in the closet so it tipped down and shaded his face, he tried to give the impression of a lone, lazy fisherman.

The motoring sound got louder, and soon he could see the cruiser off the port side parallel to them, its speed slowing. Squinting, he saw that a bearded man was behind the wheel. At the bow of the boat stood another, a tall man wearing a cap with a bill, his face in shadow. As Luke watched, the tall one raised binoculars to his eyes and swung them toward the houseboat. Luke angled his hat lower and averted his gaze.

He'd give a lot right now if he'd thought to pick up binoculars, too. From this distance, neither man resembled his memory of Chester. His stomach muscles tightened. Soon enough, he'd find out whether the man looking so intently at him had been sent to find them. Luke's hand moved to rest on the shirt that covered his gun.

Suddenly, the boat's motor revved out of idle and roared to life. Luke risked a glance and saw the cruiser rise higher in the water and head on out toward the center of the lake. The man with the binoculars had set them aside and was staring ahead. Luke let out a relieved breath. Evidently, whatever they'd been seeking, they hadn't found.

He waited until the boat was well away, glancing all around to check out the area. After that first time, he and Stephanie had been swimming nearly every day, sometimes going to shore and walking awhile. Stephanie had claimed she needed the exercise, and he'd tagged along to keep an eye on her.

Yet they'd never seen this cruiser or any other come close.

Luke braced the fishing pole and went to the bedroom, knocked once and walked in. She was wrapped in her robe, huddled against the headboard, her face as white as the terrycloth. Her eyes met his, and he shook his head. "It wasn't Chester," he said.

She looked as though she might cry, but she didn't. Still, she was coiled with fear. He went to her, loosened the arms she'd wrapped around her bent knees, and pulled her to him. She clung, letting him chase away the panic.

Wordlessly, he held her, smoothing her hair, his touch one of comfort. I am becoming entirely too used to his being here to help me through the hard times, Stephanie thought. When they parted, she would miss his concern, his reassurances. And she would miss his touch.

After a while, she shifted away from him. "Luke, about last night . . ." She met his eyes, saw he was waiting and not inclined to help her say what needed to be said. "I hope you understand."

Yeah, he was a real understanding guy. "I know you've had some bad experiences and that you don't want to risk getting hurt again. I'm not crazy about taking chances either. But the plain truth is, I can't get you off my mind." He drew back from her, annoyed with his own admission. "It's probably because we're all alone out here, thrown together for days."

"Is that all it is?"

He sighed, not surprised that he hadn't fooled her. "I wish it were."

"It doesn't bother you that I'm still married?"

Hell yes, it did. "I don't usually go after married

222

women, but our being together here has hardly been usual. You've told me you don't love your husband, you've filed for divorce, and for all practical purposes, you can be considered legally separated. That's good enough for me."

She wanted to. God, how she wanted to try to forget with this steel-hard man whose touch was more tender than any she'd felt before. But memories kept getting in the way. She raised her eyes to Luke's face. "I don't want to make another mistake."

"I know."

But she didn't want uneasiness between them either. He'd become too important to her. Hesitantly, she placed her hand on his chest. "I need to work through this. Give me some time, please?"

"Sure." Seated here with her on the big bed, knowing she wore so little underneath that robe, had him shifting uncomfortably.

As he moved, Stephanie noticed the weapon he'd tucked into his waistband. "Why are you carrying a gun?"

"Because I didn't know who was coming toward us on that motorboat. I would've been a sitting duck if it'd been Chester."

That thought sobered her quickly. She scooted back alongside him. Casey jumped up, and Stephanie hugged the kitten to her, her thoughts causing her to frown.

Luke removed the gun and hoisted it in his hand. "I want to show you how to shoot this. It's a .38, light-weight, easy to handle."

Stephanie looked at the gun with distaste. "Is that absolutely necessary?"

"I wouldn't do it if I didn't think it was. I promised your father I'd keep you safe."

223

When it came to safety, he was the expert. She'd give in on this. "All right."

"We're only an hour or so away from Howie's store. I think I'll head back and use his phone. I want to check in with my precinct, see if there's anything new happening."

On the one hand, she was anxious to hear about home. On the other, she dreaded the possibility of more bad news. Burying her face in Casey's soft fur, Stephanie closed her eyes.

The captain's voice was grim. "Yeah, there's news. And you aren't going to like it one damn bit."

What now? Luke stood in the rear of the store at the phone, his back toward the front, hoping Howie who was stocking shelves couldn't overhear. Stephanie was wandering through the aisles, pretending great interest in gathering groceries. "Okay, tell me."

"Stephen Sanders had a stroke yesterday afternoon. He's in the hospital."

"Damn! You know any details?"

"His housekeeper—an older woman named Nettie who's worked for the family for years—called us. It seems Stephen's son-in-law paid him a visit couple of hours before it happened."

Zane again. He'd thought of him immediately but hoped he was wrong. "Will she swear to that?"

"Oh, sure, for all the good it'll do. Zane's got half a dozen witnesses that put him fifty miles from there at an all-day meeting. Says he hasn't seen Stephen except from a distance in public places since the memorial service for his wife."

"He's lying."

"Hell, I know that. Proving it is another thing. Besides, even if we could, a visit from a former son-in-law could hardly be construed as threatening enough to bring about a stroke."

"What's Stephen's condition?"

"Alive, aware, but he can't talk."

"Can he write?"

"Not yet, he can't. Maybe, in time, doctors say. But Stephen's been sloppy. Told more than one of his cronies that he hates the sight of Zane. With his past history of a previous stroke, a judge would probably say he was using his medical condition to get at Zane."

Luke hated to admit it, but Renwick was right. "Have you seen Chester around lately?"

"Nowhere in sight. Zane's attorney, Bob Triner, was in. He very nicely told us that if we don't stop questioning his client every time something happens he's going to file a harassment complaint. He's got us—and he knows it."

"Anything else?"

"We've been watching Zane's activities like a hawk, but he's keeping things clean. We've searched every shipment headed to his place. Nothing. We've got a mole over there in the warehouse, but he hasn't overheard a thing of value. How you coming at that end?"

"I found her, but I still don't know if she's got the goods."

"After all this time? What are you doing, playing footsie with her, thinking it'll loosen her tongue?"

It was too close to the truth to anger Luke. "She had a miscarriage. I've got her in a safe place until she's recovered."

The captain paused, digesting that. "Zane doesn't know about this?"

"I don't think so."

"How long before she's recovered?"

"Soon."

Captain Renwick knew Luke wasn't a man who could be pushed. He liked doing things his way, in his own time. Since Luke was on the case unofficially, he'd have to wait him out. "What do you figure on doing next?"

"Telling her about Stephen. Seeing if I can locate the package." Though he was becoming increasingly convinced that Stephanie didn't have the diamonds. If she didn't, where were they and who had taken them? Zane evidently thought she'd run with his cache. How much, if anything, had Stephen revealed to Zane before his stroke? Luke wondered. Surely he'd destroyed the telegram Luke had sent him.

"Think you'll be heading this way soon?"

"It's possible. I'll call to update you again as soon as I know."

The captain scratched his head. Luke sounded distracted, anxious to hang up. From her pictures, he'd thought Stephanie Westover a beautiful woman, with style and class. She didn't look like Luke's type, yet the man sounded as if he were developing a personal interest in this case. That had been his downfall in the past. Warnings were all but wasted on Luke. Still, he had to try. "You watch yourself, Luke. Westover's bad news, and you've got his woman. If he finds you, you may not live long enough to bring her back."

Luke knew better. He answered anyway. "She's no longer his woman. Call you later."

Luke took another five minutes to put in a call to Megs, just to check things out unofficially. Hanging up, he walked to the front and found

Stephanie looking longingly at a cigarette display. "No you don't. Those things are bad for you."

"Everything I like is bad for me." She studied his unreadable expression. "Learn anything?"

"Later." Taking her arm, he led her over to the counter where Howie was waiting for them. Luke dug out his wallet to pay for the few things Stephanie had gathered, but he was more interested in information. "Noticed a big cruiser earlier today," he drawled conversationally as he patted his fake mustache. "Flying a red and yellow flag. You know who owns it?"

Howie looked up from totaling their purchases. "Yup. Belongs to a big, bearded fellow by the name of Daryl. Rents it out to fishermen by the day. Why? Did he give you some trouble?"

"No. What made you ask?"

"Daryl's kind of tough, you know. Came up from Haiti a while back. Used to be a gunrunner. Brags about it all the time. Good man to stay away from."

Exactly what Luke intended doing. Daryl sounded like a man familiar with the underworld. He also seemed like someone Zane might hire. Luke picked up the bag of groceries.

Howie wiped his face with a dingy handkerchief. "You going to keep the houseboat another week?"

"Might as well. We're paid up through next week." With a hand at Stephanie's back, he guided her through the door. "Let's get going," he said quietly, hustling her along.

"What's wrong?"

"Nothing I can put my finger on. I'll feel better when we're on the boat and out on the water."

A midafternoon sun beat down on Stephanie's head as she sat curled up on the bench seat of the bridge watching Luke guide the houseboat toward the center of the lake. He'd been distracted since their visit to Howie's store, and she wondered at the cause. He would tell her in his own sweet time, she'd come to realize, for that's just how he was.

Luke. She'd become dependent on him very quickly. She was smart enough to realize this wasn't wise, yet feeling a shade too vulnerable to do anything about changing it. And it involved more than a need to be kept safe and comfortable when the postpartum depression crept up on her.

Luke offered possibilities. Like the ad on television for Master Card. Suddenly, possibilities beckon. A man who could make her feel protected and cherished was a rare find. And he'd made her feel desirable when she'd been ready to bury her hopes for love. Yes, endless possibilities.

She had to be brutally honest with herself, though. Was sex all he wanted? It was not even close to what she wanted. She wanted to give in to the terrible need most women have to be close to someone, a particular someone who understands that need. And perhaps shares it.

Did men really have such a need, albeit buried deeply? Or was their need much more basic, really just physical but cloaked in soft words so women would buy the whole package? Stephanie wished fervently that she'd dated more often in college and shortly after, experimented more, made a study of men as Marjo had. She'd been wrapped in her romantic fantasies instead. Now here she was, uncertain which of her instincts to follow.

What kind of man was Luke Varner? Did he still love his wife, the way Kathy had been when first

228

he'd known her? Did he want to care again, or would an occasional sexual encounter be enough for him? He seemed to care, yet there was something so guarded about him, as if there were parts of himself he was unwilling to share with another.

Did he want her for herself, or did he see her as some kind of challenge? Would she make a fool of herself if she gave in to him, or would he be the one who could truly make a difference in her life? She'd stopped believing there was such a person. But lately, with Luke, she'd resurrected that frail dream. Maybe . . .

Stephanie heard the sound of the motor being cut off, then watched as Luke dropped anchor. She leaned back, waiting for him to join her.

He had been standing at the wheel, his eyes searching for signs of another boat while his thoughts were centered on how best to tell Stephanie about her father's stroke. He felt she was recovered enough to handle the news. He was equally sure he didn't want her falling apart on him if he was wrong.

In the end, he opted for the straightforward approach. Safely anchored near a secluded cove, he sat opposite her on the back deck and told her about his conversation with the captain. To her credit, though she turned pale with shock, she didn't cry.

"Oh, God," Stephanie whispered, fighting a rush of nausea. "That bastard."

"His housekeeper, Nettie, she's pretty reliable, isn't she?"

"Very. She's been with Dad since before my mother died." She closed her eyes, leaning her head back. "I worried when I left Zane might go after my father if he suspected I was alive."

229

"Don't beat yourself up over it."

She took a deep, calming breath. "You say he can't talk. With the first stroke, his speech was hard to understand for a while, but he never lost it altogether. Is he paralyzed?"

"The captain only knew what I told you."

Stephanie stared out at the water a long moment, then looked at him. "I've got to go back."

"I thought you'd feel that way."

"I left to keep the baby from Zane, so eventually my father would be free of him and so I could build a new life. Now, the baby's gone, he's after Dad, and I'm still running." She touched his hand. "Luke, we've got to put Zane away so he can't hurt people."

"I'm ready when you are."

"How do we do it? There's the hole in my brake line and Marjo's death, and now his visit to my father."

Luke shook his head. "We can't tie him positively to any of those. But we have the hit-and-run evidence in your safety deposit box."

"That would do it, wouldn't it?"

"I'd have to have it checked out. I'd feel better if we had that bankbook. Papers can be faked, but bankbooks can't. What did you plan to do with that evidence?"

"I was going to keep in touch with Marjo, and if I ever heard that Zane was bothering my father, I'd planned to inform the police. When we get back, I can go to the house and get the bankbook if you feel we need it. Oh, I forgot. My keys were in my purse in the car."

"Zane's probably had the locks changed by now. Why didn't you give Stephen the envelope to begin with and just ask him to keep it for you?"

"Because he wouldn't have. When it appeared I'd drowned, he'd have opened it and would have felt compelled to proceed against Zane. And I wasn't convinced that information alone would put Zane behind bars. If Zane even suspected Dad had something on him, he'd arrange to have him killed. I couldn't risk that."

"We'll make sure we have enough evidence to nail Zane before we go to court."

"Did you ask about Chester?"

"He hasn't been seen around, so he's probably still in Florida."

"That boat you asked Howie about — are you thinking Chester might have traced us somehow?"

Luke shrugged. "It's possible. I don't want to take any chances. We're relatively safe here for tonight. Tomorrow, I want to wait until dark, then take the houseboat back late enough so we won't run into Howie. We'll drive the truck back to Orlando. Zane's men might be watching the airports, so it might be smarter to take the train. When we get to Michigan, I have a friend who has an apartment we can use, one Zane couldn't know of. I'll show Renwick the evidence you have, and if he thinks it's necessary, *I'll* go get the bankbook. We don't want to tip our hand to Zane or he'll close out the account and destroy the book."

"I should be the one to get it."

"It's too risky for you to go back into that house."

"Are you a cat burglar, too?"

"When necessary. I'm a little more experienced at this than you, don't you think?"

She knew he was right. "My father must be paying you a bundle of money for you to be taking all these chances."

Luke had had enough of that line of thinking. "Stephanie, he's not paying me anything."

She frowned, confused. "You're just doing this rescue operation out of the goodness of your heart?"

"Let's just say, I owe Stephen."

Stephanie sat back. "How is that?"

He was tired of her thinking he was merely doing a job for money when it had become a whole lot more. "About six months ago, I was in bad shape. Working too many hours, not giving a damn about much, drinking heavily whenever I wasn't working. There was a drug bust, and I ran into this guy named Sharkee, one of Sonny Poston's men. We were taking him in, but he had a smart mouth, kept talking about Kathy and how Sonny used to brag about . . . well, about being with her."

She guessed what was coming and waited.

"I lost it. If my partner hadn't pulled me off Sharkee, I'd have killed him. There were several witnesses. I got suspended, put on medical leave. I decided to hell with it. With no job to interfere, I was free to drink night and day. Stephen found out and came to see me."

Luke smiled then, a surprising slash on his sober face. "Your father's quite a guy. Took one look at me and gave me hell. Cleaned me up, arranged for a friend to sell me his houseboat, and plunked me on it—with a fishing pole, a bucket of bait, and nothing stronger than milk. He tossed me a lifeline, and I grabbed it. He did what several of my lifelong friends hadn't been able to do—made me care enough to quit." He remembered the flask of scotch in his bag. "Well, almost quit."

"Odd that Dad never told me that story."

232

"He's not the kind of man who would. So, when he came to see me, to ask me to look into your disappearance, I told him this one he'd paid for in advance."

"But it's costing you—this houseboat, the trip here."

"Stephen will reimburse my expenses when it's over."

She was still unclear about one point. "You told me once that taking me back wasn't part of the deal, only finding me and making sure I was all right. Once you found me and took me to the hospital, your job was over. You could have gone back."

"No, I couldn't have. By then, I knew Chester had followed me. I couldn't leave you to him."

"I see." She'd thought he was going to say that he'd learned to care about her. Had hoped he would. Ever the romantic, Stephanie thought, disgusted with herself. Glancing up at the sky, she stood. "I think I'm getting too much sun. I'm going to my room to read for a while."

He frowned, confused by her abrupt mood change. "Want something to eat?"

"No, you go ahead." Stephanie skipped down the stairs.

Watching her go, Luke wondered if he'd ever understand women.

Chapter Eleven

"I'm not sure this is a good idea," Luke said as he lowered the rope ladder over the rail. "I'd feel better if we stayed on board and out of sight today." He'd been uneasy since that cruiser sighting, though the boat had sped away and not been seen since.

Stephanie sent him an exasperated glance as she slipped off her sweat pants. "It's our last semicarefree day for what may be a long while." She looked up at the bright noonday sun. "It's beautiful, and we haven't seen a boat all morning. Besides, I've packed our lunch. I'm looking forward to a picnic. Please, Luke."

Luke frowned, but he stepped out of his deck shoes. "All right."

She hated that worried look. "You don't have to come with me if you'd rather not," she said with a sigh. "I'll just swim over and walk around awhile and—"

"You're not going anywhere without me." He tossed his shirt onto the chair. "We've come too far for me to let something happen to you before I get you safely home." At the rail, he tested the roping. "Besides, what if you ran into a crocodile?"

Stephanie eyed him suspiciously. "There are crocodiles in this lake?"

Luke kept his features even as he put the strap of the insulated bag over his head and shoulder.

"Sure. And stingrays, possibly water snakes."

"Stingrays are only in salt water, aren't they?"

"Are they?"

She batted at his arm. "Stop this. I'm going." Before she could change her mind, she eased herself over the rail and pushed off.

Close behind her, Luke followed, swimming leisurely alongside. It was less than a mile to shore, and though they hadn't seen any boats since leaving Howie's yesterday, he still wasn't relaxed. The bearded owner of the cruiser sounded exactly like the kind of man who'd do most anything for money. With every other stroke, Luke let his eyes skim the area.

Heavy, prickly grass grew down into the water's edge. Stephanie climbed out, stepping gingerly. Water snakes weren't poisonous, she remembered, but she didn't want to encounter one anyhow. Wringing out the end of her long T-shirt, she moved between the trees as Luke came up behind her.

Pausing to catch her breath, she leaned against a tree trunk. The sandy soil was a dirty gray underfoot rather than tan, the weeds thick and overgrown. Not a great place to go hiking barefoot, she admitted. But, since she'd insisted on coming, she'd manage. Hearing a noise, she looked up. A large, black crow sat on a limb, cawing at them. "Looks like we're not alone, after all."

Luke ran a hand over his short hair, skimming off the excess water. "I think I read somewhere that they have wild parrots around here, too."

"You're just trying to scare me." She turned toward him and wished she hadn't. Wearing only cutoff shorts, his broad chest inches from her, he made her breath catch in her throat. Then she noticed the piece of leather hanging from his belt. "You brought a knife?"

"Honey, I seldom go anywhere without some sort of weapon." He didn't mention that his gun was at the bottom of their lunch bag. He glanced back toward the houseboat bobbing gently in the lake. A peaceful scene. Then why did he have this uncomfortable feeling? He took Stephanie's arm. "Well, are we going to walk or stand here?"

She started through the trees. But she'd only gone a dozen feet when she cried out. "Oh, damn!" Hopping on one leg, she stopped in a clump of thick grass and sat down. "I think I stepped on something."

Luke moved to her side and took hold of her foot. A spiny green frond was embedded in the sole just above her arch. "I'm not sure what this is," he said, touching it gingerly. "But it's sharper than hell." Pulling the bag around, he dug inside for his Swiss Army knife. "I can't pull it out with my fingers."

"I hope it's not poisonous," Stephanie said with a frown.

"I doubt it." Using the flat edge of the small knife, he braced with his thumb and tugged. It took several seconds of maneuvering before the sliver came free. Luke then took a paper towel from the bag and held it to the spot which had begun to bleed. "I think you'll live."

Stephanie leaned back against a tree limb, her foot in his lap. "Thanks, Doc." The sun could barely be seen through the thick leaves overhead, making the temperature at least twenty degrees cooler here in the shade. As Luke zipped the bag closed, she glanced to the side and smiled. At the base of the tree was a cluster of wild honeysuckle, over aways a huge oleander bush. She forgot her discomfort as she leaned forward to caress a fragile blossom.

236

"Aren't these lovely out here in this wilderness?"

Luke watched her pick a flower and stick it in her hair.

"Imagine, finding beauty among these gnarled and twisted old trees." Stephanie sighed, suddenly pensive. "One of these days, I'm going to have a place with a garden and fill it with flowers." Suddenly shy, she sent him a nervous glance. "I guess you think I'm silly."

He scooted closer, turning her to face him, and touched her cheek. More beautiful than any flower, he thought, but was too embarrassed to say it. "No, not silly. A little romantic, maybe."

"That again." She let out a deep breath.

Yes, that again, even after all she'd been through. "Don't change." He lowered his mouth to hers.

The kiss was gentle, easy, undemanding. Yet it sent shock waves through her nonetheless. Shifting for better access, Stephanie wound her arms around him and let him take her under.

She could feel the tension in him, yet he didn't press. That more than anything won her over. Daring to take the lead, she inched her tongue into his mouth and heard him moan low in his throat. At last, Stephanie eased back because she was beginning to enjoy too much.

The eyes that stared into his in the dappling shadows were huge and a little frightened. Giving himself a minute, Luke brushed a strand of hair from her cheek. The attraction between them was getting more difficult to ignore. "It seems we have a little problem here."

"Yes." She leaned back, her hands touching the bark of a tree behind her. "But we don't have time for this problem right now. We have to go back and put my husband in prison."

237

His jaw twitched at the word husband, but he allowed himself no other reaction.

"Isn't that right?" she asked.

Luke brought himself under control. "Yeah. We empty your safety deposit box when the bank opens and return to Michigan."

It was hard to concentrate when all she wanted to do was lie down with him, to feel that clever mouth on hers again. "The bonds and envelope, you mean?"

"Is there anything else?"

There was that question again. "I've already told you there isn't. Why do you keep asking?"

It was time to say it out loud, he decided. "Zane's been under police suspicion for some time for smuggling diamonds in from Africa. We think they're routed through Canada and across the U.S. border, hidden in antiques shipped to his shop. That *something missing* that he mentioned to me—I think it's the diamonds from the last shipment. I'm told there was over half a million in uncut stones, worth around three in the right hands. Zane thinks you have them."

Stephanie's eyes widened. "But how could he think that? I rarely visited his shop."

"A snitch told the cops Zane sometimes has an antique piece sent to his house."

Stephanie swatted at a buzzing fly. "He does. Last Christmas this lovely old armoire arrived and, more recently, a Queen Anne desk that he gave me for our anniversary. It's in my bedroom."

"A package of diamonds could have been hidden in either of those pieces. In a secret compartment or taped to the back of a drawer. Did you ever see anything like that?"

She was getting angry. Really angry. He didn't believe her. Why else would he keep on with these

238

questions? He thought she'd taken several million dollars worth of diamonds and had them in her safety deposit box.

Giving in to her rising temper, Stephanie clenched her fists, but kept her voice even. "I want you to come to the bank with me. I'll open that box in front of you. Obviously, I'm supposed to believe every word you tell me, but you think I'm a common, devious thief." She leaned closer now, furious. "You didn't come to find Stephen's daughter. You came to catch a thief. Only the laugh's on you, Varner. I don't know where the hell the diamonds are."

Furious, Stephanie got to her feet, ignoring the slight pain in her foot. How could he kiss her one minute and accuse her of a major crime the next? Needing to get away from him, she started back to shore.

Luke felt like hitting something hard. Instead, he started after her, giving her a moment to work off her temper.

He'd handled that badly. There was some truth in what Stephanie had accused him of. He *had* believed she had taken the diamonds. At first. For quite a while, actually. Until recently. But he no longer did.

He was right behind her, still within the protection of the trees, when he heard the distinct sound of a motor. Grabbing Stephanie's arm, he pulled her back. "Wait!"

"What?" Stephanie asked, responding to the tension in his voice. With a quick movement, he had her on the ground, his arm keeping her low. Peeking through the tall grass, she saw the smaller craft pull alongside their houseboat. "Where'd they come from?"

"It's the cruiser. Damn! I should have followed

239

my instincts." Squinting, he saw a figure leave the cruiser and hop on to their deck. He was too far away to make out much, but it was clear that the man disappeared inside the living quarters.

"Won't he be surprised when he finds we're not there?"

"No, I think he knows we're not. Somehow, he's been watching us. He's figured out that we regularly leave the houseboat around noon most days. We got careless and established a routine. He's using it to his advantage."

"But who is he? Chester, do you think?" The very thought had her shivering despite the heat.

"Maybe, but I doubt it." He had only himself to blame, Luke thought, growing more angry by the minute. If Stephanie hadn't gotten upset with him, they'd be deep in the woods by now and wouldn't have heard the cruiser approach.

"You think Zane hired that gunrunner to come after us?"

"Something like that." Suddenly the man appeared on deck and stood looking toward the strip of land where they lay in the tall grass. Luke watched him raise a hand to shade his eyes and then study the area for several minutes. Finally, he left, jumping back onto the cruiser. In seconds, it was off, the motor on low to keep the noise level down.

"What could he be looking for? I don't have anything with me linking me to Stephanie Westover."

Luke sat up, choking back his fury. "It doesn't matter. He hopes to get two birds with one stone. Most likely, he's planted a bomb set to go off in a couple of hours when he's pretty sure we'll be back on board."

"A bomb! Oh, God." Shivering, she sat up, the

damp shirt feeling suddenly cold on her shoulders. The sun was hidden behind a growing cloud cover. "I'm never going to be free of Zane. *Never.*" She turned to him as realization hit. "He could have killed you this time as well."

"But he didn't."

"We can't be sure he planted a . . . anything. What if you're wrong and he was just searching for the diamonds you say Zane thinks I stole?"

Luke shook his head as he leaned back against a tree. "He knows you're pretty clever by now and that you wouldn't have the diamonds with you. He's probably also figured out I'm with you. You're right, though, we don't know for certain there's a bomb on board."

"So what do we do, take a chance and go back?"

"Not yet. We wait, at least until dark. If it hasn't blown by then, I'll swim back and—"

"I'm going with you. This is *my* fight, remember?"

Luke shifted to study her. Her eyes were wide, full of frightening possibilities, yet she wanted to go with him. He touched her cheek because she needed comforting. And maybe he did, too. "We can argue about that later." He gazed up at the gray sky, darkening with rain clouds. "We may have a long wait. We could have some lunch to pass the time."

"I couldn't swallow. You go ahead."

He felt the same. Gently, he pulled her over so she lay against his chest. He wasn't good at apologizing, but there was something that needed saying. "Stephanie, for the record, I do believe you don't have the diamonds. I admit I wondered in the beginning. But not since getting to know you. You can choose to believe that or not."

241

"Thank you for saying that." She settled against him, needing his strength right now. But a sudden thought had her sitting upright. "Casey! Luke, the kitten's still on board."

"Yeah, I know." He pressed her head back onto his chest as he checked his watch. Only one o'clock. Lord, but he hated stakeouts.

Stephanie was dozing when she blew. The shock of the blast had her awakening with a start and crying out. Then Luke's hand pressed her to the ground.

It was one time Luke wished he hadn't been right. The explosion sent pieces of wood and metal flying high into the air before they dropped back into the lake. Waves swirled about as fire roared through the vessel. Next to him, Stephanie squirmed closer, both of them watching in horrified fascination.

Even from this distance, they could smell gas fumes tainting the muggy air. Nervous birds flew from the shelter of the trees, screeching in protest. Stephanie buried her face in Luke's shoulder, and his arm tightened around her.

It was over in minutes, the charred remains sinking rapidly. The sputtering flames died out, and all Luke could see was a lone life raft bobbing on the undulating water. Once more, it was quiet. Still he held her close, waiting while she worked her way through her terror.

Finally, Stephanie lifted her head, feeling drained. "The kitten, Luke. He—"

"I know." The kitten was the least of their worries.

It had been years since she'd felt so unable to make a decision. "What do we do now?" she

242

asked, her voice husky.

"We go deeper into the woods and lie low."

"But why? It's still light. We can find a trail. There's got to be a road on the other side of these trees somewhere." She was anxious to be out of there, out of Florida.

"There is, but it's too dangerous right now. Hired killers don't take things for granted. He'll probably come back in the cruiser and circle the area, scanning the shoreline with those binoculars. Then he'll get in a car and ride around the surrounding roads, just to make sure. After all, there's a slim possibility we could have found the bomb and jumped clear in time."

She was too weary to argue. When he stood and pulled her to her feet, she rose willingly. As he turned and began walking, she followed close behind him.

He knew she was tired, frightened, and uncomfortably damp. But he couldn't take the time to comfort her further. Luke didn't stop until they'd walked half an hour. It was much cooler in the shade of the thick foliage overhead. They were deep in the woods now, and he doubted if they could be seen either from the lake or the road.

Earlier, he'd studied a map of the area, and he knew the only road was easily five miles east of them. He'd worry about the way out tomorrow.

Stephanie seemed to be dazed and looked ready to drop. He positioned her under a tree, and without a word, she sank to the ground. "Sit here until I put together some kind of shelter."

He felt the first drop of rain as he reached for his knife. So far, he hadn't seen lightning, nor had he heard thunder, so it was probably just a light summer shower. But wet nonetheless, which they didn't need right now. There was a huge rubber

243

plant where they'd stopped, plus lots of fallen palm fronds. Working quickly in the waning light, he cut off several broad leaves and twisted them together with moss roping, fashioning a makeshift lean-to alongside the largest tree. When he was satisfied that it would offer some protection, he grabbed more moss and spread it on the ground for cushioning.

"Best I can do," he told Stephanie.

Feeling numb, she let him guide her under the overhang where she sat down on the mossy flooring. It was dim and dry under the shelter, and she fell back on the moss gratefully.

Joining her, Luke rummaged in his bag and pulled out a T-shirt only barely damp. "Here, use this to dry off with or put it on."

Fighting the shivers, Stephanie turned her back, whipped off her wet shirt, and put his on.

Luke saw that she was trembling again and he wasn't certain whether it was from the evening coolness, the dampness, or the aftermath of fear. She needed some rest; they both did. But first some heat. Again he reached into his bag and brought out his flask. He poured scotch into the silver cap that would have to serve as a cup and held it toward her. "Drink this. It'll warm you."

Obeying like a small child, Stephanie drank, coughed, then swallowed the rest. She felt the liquid heat slide down, but she couldn't seem to stop shaking. Hugging herself, she watched Luke drink, then grimace before putting aside the flask and bag. When he turned to her, she struggled to prevent a sob. "Hold me, please." Blindly, she reached out for him.

He held her, running his hands along her back, along her shoulders and up into her damp hair, warming her, soothing her. "It's all right, honey.

244

You're safe now."

"He . . . he tried to kill me again, Luke. When? When will he stop?" She heaved with dry sobs, her voice quavery.

"We'll get him, Stephanie. I promise you." Luke felt the anger he'd banked earlier, shoved it away again. She needed him now. He'd take care of Zane Westover when the time came. And it would—soon.

Stephanie tilted her head back, trying to read his eyes in the dim lighting. "You saved my life twice now. I don't know how to thank you."

"I'm not expecting thanks."

"You mean it's your job, right? Just your job."

Did she still think that? "No, honey, that's not what I mean. It stopped being just my job a long while back."

It wasn't everything, but it was enough. "Make love with me, Luke. For days now, I've wanted you to."

It was what he'd been waiting to hear. He framed her face with his hands, his thumbs caressing her soft mouth, then touched his lips to hers. Slowly, slowly. He drew the kiss out. She hadn't been romanced much, he was certain. And he wanted that for her, at least this first time between them.

Luke couldn't see very well, so he went mostly by feel, his hands moving under her shirt where they unfastened her bra and shifted to close over her breasts. He heard her draw in a shaky breath as he bent to taste her. She was cool and firm and unbearably sweet.

Hesitantly, Stephanie ran unsteady fingers over his lean, hard chest; then she touched her lips to his shoulder and let them linger there. She needed, wanted, but didn't know how to ask. "I'm not very

245

good at this."

He lifted his mouth from her throat. "Who said? You're doing fine."

Eyes closed, she traced the planes of his face and found the small scar. "How did you get this?"

"It doesn't matter, not anymore." He lay down on his back, silently swearing at the confines of the small area, then eased her over and on top of him.

It did matter, the violent life he led, but she wasn't going into it. She waited while he shoved off the rest of their clothing, then felt his hands cup her breasts. His touch was so gentle, so different, that she wanted to weep. Instead she lowered her mouth to his.

He knew she had a lot to forget. He also knew that she expected him to erase all that had gone before, a tall order. The knowledge slowed his hands, gentled his touch. Until he felt her grow heated and lose patience. She pulled him closer, her mouth suddenly hungry and seeking.

Quickly he shifted until she was beneath him and reaching for him. When he entered her, she was more than ready. With a sigh, she arched against him, wrapping her arms and legs around him, losing herself in him. He began to move then, and heard her sounds of pleasure.

He was all wrong for her and he knew it, but it didn't seem to matter. He no longer heard the rain falling against their flimsy shelter, no longer was aware of discomfort. Desire was a tidal wave, rising fast, taking him with its powerful pull.

Stephanie forgot her fears, forgot there were people out there who were after her, even forgot where she was. She gave herself up to the security of arms that held her tight, to the pleasure of the mouth that kissed her. She set aside the real world and clung to the man who'd shown her a new one.

246

Stephanie awoke feeling cramped and chilly. The space next to her, where Luke had lain, was empty. Sitting up, she noticed that it had stopped raining and a weak sun was trying to rise in the pale morning sky barely visible through the leafy trees. She crept out of the shelter and looked around. He was nowhere in sight.

He wouldn't leave her; she knew that. Knew it, yet couldn't fight a rising panic. She spotted his bag on the ground and felt a little better. Perhaps he'd just needed a little time and space.

She had much to thank him for: for listening to her father, for coming after her, for saving her life twice. And last night, for making her feel very female and cared for, if only for a short time. When she heard a noise through the trees and saw Luke approaching, she brushed back her hair and warned herself not to make too much of their love-making. A case of mutual need satisfied was the only sane, sensible way to look at it.

Her eyes were watchful, her stance hesitant, Luke thought as he walked up to her. She was wearing only his wrinkled T-shirt which skimmed her at midthigh. She couldn't know how long he'd lain looking at her when he'd awakened and found her still asleep. And wouldn't know from him, for he was all wrong for her. Had always been, would always be. Yet this wasn't the time to tell her that. This was the morning after, and she badly needed reassurance.

He stepped close and touched her cheek. "How is it you look so good after spending the night in a rain shower huddled under a couple of leaves?"

He was a rotten liar, but she smiled at the compliment anyway. "Good bones, I guess."

His arms slid around her, bringing her in close contact. After a moment, he felt her relax, her hands creeping up his back. He rested his cheek on her hair, savoring this moment before they would have to start back. Before he would have to return her to her sick and waiting father as he'd promised, then round up the bad guys, if he could.

"I've checked around. Can't see any signs of anyone."

She spoke into his throat. "Do you think whoever set the bomb believes we . . . we drowned?"

"Probably." He eased back to look at her. "But we're still not going to take any chances."

She'd already taken a big one last night, by asking him to make love. But now his thoughts were elsewhere. "What do you think we should do?"

"Make our way to the road. Hitch a ride back to the truck. Drive into Orlando and proceed with the rest of our plan."

"Fine." Her hands dropped from him. "I'm ready."

No, she was not. Her eyes were vulnerable and frightened, but she was trying not to let him see. "Are you sorry about last night?"

She shook her head.

"Stephanie, will you believe me if I tell you I thought it was wonderful?"

She let out a sigh. "Probably not. I've been lied to for so long I don't know what to believe."

"Then believe this." He kissed her, kissed her softly, then more deeply. Needing to convince her, wanting to believe himself. It had been so long since he'd let himself care about a woman that it scared the hell out of him to find himself in that velvet trap again. Yet he couldn't easily dismiss Stephanie's hold on him. He would deal with all that awaited them later. Right now, she was here, in his arms, and it felt so damn right.

Breathless, she drew back, her hands on his chest, her eyes searching his.

He pulled her into intimate contact. "Tell me you want me as much as I want you."

It was so much easier to talk about physical needs than emotional wanting. She allowed herself a small smile. "I want you. Badly."

In moments, he had her back under the shelter, on the ground and out of her clothes. "I thought we were in a hurry to get going," she protested halfheartedly as his busy hands warmed her skin.

"Banks don't open until ten. It's barely five." Luke reached for her. "Come here."

Luke stopped the truck on the street behind the First Financial Center, shifted into park, and turned to Stephanie seated alongside him. "Now, you know what to do?"

"Yes, but I don't agree. I think you should go in with me. I would like you to be there when I open that safety deposit box."

He shook his head impatiently. "Look, we've been over this. I believe you have nothing in there except the bonds. It's entirely possible that Chester—or one of Zane's other goons—is lurking around here somewhere. Even though the houseboat exploded, they're not going to give up easily. If Zane's learned you have a box here—and there's a good chance he has—then this would be the logical place to have someone watching. If he shows, I'll make sure he spots me, and I'll lead him away."

Stephanie was nervous just thinking about Chester. "You don't know that man. He's vicious."

"Stephanie, I've dealt with his kind before. I want you to go in the back way and empty the box, then leave by the front door. If I'm parked across the street, it'll mean I haven't spotted him. If I'm not there, you scoot on over to that beauty shop two doors up and call a cab like we discussed." He reached in his pocket and handed her some bills, enough to cover the forty-mile cab ride.

"I can cash another bond," Stephanie said, not wanting to take his money. Most especially not after last night. And that morning.

They'd tramped through the woods for what seemed like forever, finally finding the road. A farmer in overalls who was driving a load of chickens, had picked them up and dropped them near Howie's. Luke had sneaked back and gotten their truck without alerting the nosy little storekeeper. They'd driven back to Orlando then, stopped in a store for some clothes and checked into a motel to get cleaned up and changed. Now, after a quick lunch, they had to get the bonds and envelope out of the safety deposit box and make it to the railroad station in time for the late afternoon train.

But just the thought of leaving Luke, of being without his protection when Chester might be lurking out there, had her heart hammering.

"You can pay me back later, if that's worrying you. I'll meet you at the station by the ticket counters as soon as I make sure no one's following me."

"What if you can't shake him?"

"Hey, let's have a little confidence here. I *will* get rid of him." He touched her chin, tilting her face up. "I thought we were going to trust one another?"

"I trust you. It doesn't stop me from worrying." She leaned into him, her face in his neck. "I felt a lot safer on the boat." Until yesterday.

So had he, but he didn't think he should tell her.

250

"We'll get this behind us and be on the train in a couple of hours. Just follow the plan."

Stephanie nodded, then shifted to kiss him because she badly needed to. She wished it didn't feel like the last time. Reluctantly, she tied the scarf Luke had insisted she wear around her head. Slipping on her sunglasses, she scanned the parking lot. It was midday and several people were coming and going, the walkway to the bank's door never empty for long. She took a deep breath, opened the door, and stepped down.

Luke watched her walk away, his palms sweaty. There was no question about it, personal involvement made his job a whole lot harder. For the next little while, he'd have to be the levelheaded detective not the smitten lover.

Shifting into gear, he cruised around to the front of the bank and coasted to a stop across the street. Lazily, he climbed down from the truck's cab and shoved his hands into his jeans pockets. The traffic was light for the middle of a hot summer day. He walked a few steps along the parking lane, checking out both people and vehicles. He didn't miss a beat when he saw the tan Toyota four car-lengths away with someone obviously sitting behind the wheel, his face shaded.

Pay dirt, Luke thought as he turned and casually strolled back to his truck. He heard the engine of the Toyota start up. Since he wanted Chester to follow, he paused as he opened the driver's door and glanced back, scowling in his direction, making sure the man saw him clearly. The moment he swung away from the curb, the Toyota shot out into traffic, the second car behind him. Luke smiled.

He'd been involved in a number of car chases, but usually he'd been in the car following. Shaking a driver intent on catching him wouldn't be easy, Luke was well aware of that. And he also knew that Zane must be out of patience by now and all over Chester to deliver Stephanie—or else. As he drove, he hoped Stephanie would follow his instructions.

It took more than thirty minutes before he felt fairly certain that he'd lost Chester. His eyes still darting from the traffic to the rearview mirror, Luke picked up speed and headed west on Highway 436.

The old building wasn't in the best of neighborhoods, but then, very few train depots were. He maneuvered the truck into the parking lot, grabbed the ticket, and parked in a nearly full lane. Stepping out, he settled his bag onto his shoulder and just stood there a moment, checking every which way. Seeing no one he recognized, Luke headed for the door.

Stephanie wasn't anywhere in sight, either. Damn, he hoped she hadn't taken it upon herself to do something dangerous. What if Chester had lost him, then doubled back just as she'd come out of the bank? No, he wouldn't think along those lines. Keeping a watchful eye out, he went to the ticket counter.

Tickets in his pocket, Luke strolled toward the gates. Amtrak did a larger volume out of this area since the opening of Disney World. There were lots of people who didn't like to fly, it would seem. The platforms were crowded with passengers pulling luggage or carrying bags, porters pushing carts, people meeting trains. Luke found the gate for the Detroit train with a change in Chicago, and headed down the stairs toward the coaches already beginning to load. Maybe Stephanie had decided to wait for him down there.

But a short walk later, he still hadn't caught sight of her. Trying not to worry, he reversed his steps. Halfway along the platform, he stopped. A short, stocky man with a blond crewcut was hurrying along beside a slender, brown-haired woman wearing jeans. Stephanie! His heart leaped into his throat as he skirted an older couple and rushed after them.

When he saw the burly man glance over his shoulder and recognized Chester's face, Luke broke into a run. How the hell had Chester followed him to the depot when he had been so certain he'd lost him? Am I losing my touch? Luke wondered.

Some distance ahead of him, the woman climbed into a passenger car, followed by Chester who seemed to be shoving her up the stairs. The train they'd entered was the one heading for Detroit. Luke arrived at the steps, lunged aboard, and stopped to look around. Chester was not in sight.

To the left was a baggage car, to the right a compartment car with most of the doors open and a few people in the aisle. He shoved past a porter assisting an elderly woman and glanced in each open compartment as he rushed through. A movement at the front of the coach caught his attention, and he stared ahead. When his gaze locked with Chester's, he saw the man's eyes narrow malevolently.

Luke walked toward him, experiencing an adrenaline rush at the scent of danger. He clenched his teeth tightly together, feeling the comfort of the weapon wedged in his waistband. The man has piggy eyes, mean and humorless, he thought as he stopped in front of Chester. "Where's Stephanie?" he asked.

Though Luke stood a good six inches taller, Chester didn't flinch, his fists hanging at his sides

253

like hard knots. "You tell me, copper."

Luke's eyes flew to the nearest compartment. With a quick push, he opened the door. It was empty. Moving faster than most people would think he could, Luke grabbed Chester's shirt front, shoved him inside, and kicked the door closed. Chester recovered from the surprise move and swung, but Luke managed to sidestep the punch.

He'd never liked to play defense, even in football. Offense was the position he felt comfortable in. Luke widened his stance, feigned once to the left, then threw a right that slipped off Chester's wide chin, followed by a left that caught him in his fat belly. The air whooshed out of Zane's goon, but Luke didn't allow time for recovery, his fists pummeling Chester's face and thick neck with bruising blows.

Chester wasn't down for the count though and kicked wildly, catching Luke with a hard blow to the left knee. The pain shot through Luke, and he took a couple of steps backward. The pause gave Chester enough time to catch his breath and come back swinging.

The first punch landed on the corner of Luke's left eye, very near his old scar, but the next one just glanced off his shoulder. Luke got his second wind and advanced on Chester, backing him up to the hard edge of the upper berth. Grabbing his ears, he banged the tough's head several times on that metal edge, then let fly smack into the solar plexus. Chester's eyes glazed over and he doubled forward, then slumped to the floor.

Knuckles bleeding, his breathing coming in short puffs, Luke leaned over him and slapped him several times until he rallied. "Where is she, damn you? If you've hurt her . . ."

"I don't know, honest." Chester's hands came up,

trying to shield his face. Blood oozed out of the corner of his mouth, and there was a generous cut along one cheekbone.

Luke grabbed Chester's collar, jerking him up. "Who was that woman you came on board with?"

Chester gagged, his arms flailing. "What woman?" he croaked.

"If you're lying to me—"

"No, I swear."

Luke let him drop to the floor. Chester touched his mouth gingerly and grimaced when he saw blood on his hand. Moaning, he looked up at Luke. "What do you want with that slut, anyway? She's not worth—"

Luke's fist exploded in Chester's face. Half a dozen more quick punches followed. It would be the last sentence Chester would utter for a while. A red haze was all Luke saw as his hands kept hitting long after Chester had crumbled into unconsciousness. Finally, sweating profusely and nearly out of breath, Luke straightened. From a distance, he heard the warning whistle signaling the train's imminent departure.

He had to find Stephanie.

Quickly, he ducked into the small bathroom, rinsed his face and hands, and dabbed them dry with a towel. He looked at the heap on the floor. Chester hadn't moved. Easing out of the compartment, he closed the door and walked over to the porter chatting with a passenger near the exit.

"My friend in Compartment eight doesn't wish to be disturbed. He's recovering from an accident and needs lots of rest."

"Yes, sir," the porter said, touching his fingers to his hat.

Luke stepped down, his eyes scanning the platform. Only a few stragglers to be seen. He hurried

255

into the station.

His knee was throbbing like hell, and the damn scar had opened up again. Holding his handkerchief to the cut, he rushed through the terminal, searching, growing frantic. In desperation, he hobbled back down the platform.

Standing at the arch leading to the gates, he paused, wondering how he was ever going to find her. If she wasn't here, he'd have to go all the way back to the bank and see if he could track her. Slowly, he made his way toward the train for Detroit, checking to see if she'd gone that way and making sure Chester hadn't recovered enough to get off. He was limping past a large concrete pillar when he heard his name whispered. Tensing, Luke swiveled.

Stephanie rushed into his arms. He groaned as he hugged her, as much from relief at seeing her as from the pain Chester had inflicted on him. For a moment, he just clung to her.

"Oh, God," Stephanie whispered, "I thought he'd gotten you. I thought I'd lost you."

Luke swallowed and leaned back from her, his aches forgotten. "Would losing me bother you?"

But Stephanie was looking at him, seeing the blood coming from the cut by his eye, the disheveled look of him. "What happened to you?"

"I'll tell you later. First, answer my question. Would losing me bother you, Stephanie?"

Her hands tightened around his waist. "Yes."

Chapter Twelve

"New York?" Stephanie hurried along the platform, trying to keep up with Luke. "Why did you buy tickets to New York?"

"Several reasons." He held her hand tightly in his, shifting the leather bag to his other shoulder. Since finding her, he didn't want to let go of her. "Number one: someone hunting for us is less apt to look on a New York-bound train. Number two: the train for Detroit left while we were standing there talking. And number three: Chester's on that train." As he talked, he searched the cars, looking for the one containing Sleeper Compartment 22.

So that was what had happened to his face. Though he was rushing, she could see he was favoring his left leg. The cut at his eye had opened up, and his knuckles were scraped and bloody. She wondered how Chester had fared. "Luke, you're hurt. We should have a doctor look at you."

"Can't spare the time, and we can't get anyone involved right now. There'd be too many questions." He stopped at the next set of steps. "Here we are. Up you go."

The porter smiled a welcome. "Good afternoon." He checked the tickets Luke held out. "Yes, sir. Compartment twenty-two, right down there, middle of the car. Dining room in the opposite direction, three cars forward." He brought forth his clipboard. "And the name, sir?"

"Mr. and Mrs. Luke Smith," Luke answered. He leaned closer to the portly man. "Honeymoon trip. I expect we'll stay mostly to ourselves." From his pocket, he withdrew a folded bill and slipped it to him. "Do you think you could scare up a bottle of chilled champagne for us?"

The porter's sunburned face split into a big smile. "Yes, sir. And congratulations."

Luke thanked him and followed after Stephanie who was already standing by their compartment. Inside, he dropped the bag and let out a deep breath as he heard her lock the door. The whistle sounded, signaling imminent departure. It couldn't be soon enough for Luke. He wanted to get out of this town in the worst way.

Stephanie turned toward Luke as he pulled the shade down on their wide window. "So we're the Smiths again, I hear. What was your secret little chat with the porter about?"

He took her in his arms, pulling her close. "I told him I had a beautiful woman in here and didn't want to be disturbed. He understood perfectly."

"You didn't!" She touched his cheek carefully. "I wish we had something to put on this cut."

He had a few questions he wanted answered, but he'd let her play nurse first. "In my bag, there's a shaving kit. The styptic pencil will stop the bleeding."

"This is going to sting." He didn't even flinch. "Think you're tough, do you?"

"Not so very." Not tough enough to resist her, though he knew better. She'd said that the thought of losing him bothered her. Had she meant it, or was it the fear of being alone that had made her say it?

"Once we're home, you may have to have this restitched. Or plastic surgery if the scar heals crooked."

He grinned at her. "Honey, this face, scars and all,

258

is going to stay the way it is. No doctor's going to cut away at me. In my work, a pretty face can be a problem. I've got enough problems."

"Your face is pretty, scars and all."

His arm slid around her. "Not as pretty as yours."

"Why, thank you, Mr. Smith. Now, let me see those hands." Her eyes widened as he held out his hands. "Good God, Luke. Is Chester alive after the way you used these on him?"

He shrugged. "I don't know. I think he only passed out."

She felt a little queasy. "You don't know? You mean you might really have killed him?"

"Stephanie, I thought he had you. I spotted him, and there was this woman walking with him. She had short brown hair like yours, and she was wearing jeans. I followed him onto a car, but when I caught up with him, she wasn't there. I needed him to tell me things."

"And did he?"

"He said he didn't know where you were. I didn't know if he was telling the truth."

"So you beat him up."

"Not until he said some things about you I didn't like."

"Oh, Luke." She moved closer to embrace him. "You got all these cuts and bruises because of me. I wonder how many more you'll get before this is over."

"It's nothing for you to worry about. I've lived through worse." As she moved back from him, her hand touched his knee and he winced.

"I thought I saw you limping. Stand up and take off your pants."

He smiled. "Best offer I've had today."

"Don't be so cocky." She watched him slide his jeans down, her eyes widening at taking in his discolored and swollen knee. "We need an ice bag for that. Is there a buzzer in here somewhere so we can call the porter?"

"He'll be here soon. I asked him to bring us some champagne."

Stephanie raised a brow as she smiled. "Well, well. What's the occasion?"

"It tastes better than aspirin. Besides, I thought you might want to sip a glass while you elaborate on that little conversation we had out on the platform earlier."

"Oh, that." Stephanie rose and went to the bathroom, dampened the end of a towel and returned to him.

"Did you mean what you said?"

"Every word." Gently, she dabbed at his cuts.

Luke swallowed. His mother had cared for him, of that he'd been certain. And Kathy, in the beginning, had declared her love often and sincerely. But since then, no one. He'd decided he could live without someone special in his life. Relationships took so much time and energy, and commitments came with a price tag. The thing was, until meeting Stephanie, he hadn't honestly known how much he wanted to hear again that someone cared deeply.

"Sometimes," he began, talking to her bent head, "when people are upset or worried, they say things they wouldn't under normal circumstances."

Stephanie finished, set aside the towel, and raised her eyes to his. "I meant what I said, but I want you to know that my feelings don't obligate you in any way."

"It's just that I'm not the sort of man you should have."

She crossed her legs and raised a questioning eyebrow. "Really? And what kind of man is that, oh wise one?"

He shrugged, keeping his expression bland. "An Ivy League man who wears silk shirts and likes the

260

opera. Someone from your side of the tracks. You misjudged Zane. Stephen wouldn't like your making another mistake. And I would definitely be a mistake."

"Why would you be a mistake?"

"Because I can't be what you need. I live on a houseboat—with a grouchy cat who matches my mood most of the time. I'm forty years old, I've got an ulcer and insomnia. I've seen things, rotten things you can't even imagine, things that keep me awake nights. I've killed, Stephanie, and that haunts me. You should run from me."

In that moment, for Stephanie, everything fell into place. In Luke's eyes, she saw his terrible need and the tenderness she'd been seeking. Love. The feeling had exploded inside her last night as he'd held her close to his heart. She felt it again and knew she wasn't mistaken this time.

"I ran away from a man recently. Now I'm reaching out for another."

He would give her one more chance. Just one. "I'm not an easy man, Stephanie. Not the kind of man you should want."

She put her finger to his lips. "If you tell me again about the kind of man I should want, I'm going to put a cut next to your other eye. I admit I made a bad choice with Zane. You didn't do much better with Kathy. People make mistakes. That doesn't mean they can't ever get it right. However, I can understand why you wouldn't want to get involved with me. I'm still married to a man who will stop at nothing including murder to get his way. That alone would stop most men, those with good sense, anyway."

Luke searched her face as he took hold of her hands. "I've been accused of not having much good sense, regularly and often. I'm not afraid of Zane. I am afraid I can't give you the kind of life you de-

261

serve."

"Deserve? That's ridiculous. How about the kind of life I want? I want a home, and I don't even care where it is. I always hated the house Zane chose. I've never been happier than these last couple of weeks on that houseboat."

It was sounding too close to what he wanted to be believable. She still hadn't thought it through. "But what about my work? I like it. I'm good at it. I don't want to quit being a cop."

"Why would you?"

"Could you live with the fact that I deal with criminals, large and small, every day? That when I leave I might not return because one of them got lucky?"

Her fingers flexed within his, but her gaze didn't waver. "People get run over by buses, too."

She was being so damn reasonable. "All right, what about lifestyles? I like sitting around and fishing, country music—and I don't even own a tie. And you, you like *ballet!*"

She smiled at that. "I do. And Anita Baker and k. d. lang and the Boston Pops. I don't mind fishing, and who asked you to wear a tie anyway?" Stephanie shook her head. "Look, I'm not trying to talk you into anything. I'm merely trying to point out that your mountains are molehills. None of this stuff matters. Not if the feelings are there and they're real."

Luke kissed her then, a long, lingering kiss filled with expectations. He'd been right when he'd told the captain that Stephanie was no longer Zane's. She was his.

His mouth moved over hers, his aches forgotten as he gathered her close. She tasted so good, so sweet and—

The knock on the door was sharp. "Mr. Smith, sir," said a deep voice. "Your champagne."

262

Stephanie pulled back and smiled. "Mr. Smith, perhaps you ought to pull up your pants and answer the door."

Later, much later, Luke lay with his back to the wall of the lower bunk in Compartment 22 feeling comfortably sated in every way, something a man in his vocation seldom felt. The train hurtling through the night offered a measure of safety. His bruises were numbed courtesy of a considerable amount of champagne, and his appetite was appeased by a halfway decent dinner in the dining car, where they'd finally wound up after showering and changing. His other, more pressing appetite had just been satisfied by the woman who now lay within the circle of his arms, looking as contented as he felt. Life, as it so seldom was, was good, at least for now.

"This apartment we're going to in Detroit," Stephanie said, her voice languid, "does it belong to a male friend or a woman?"

"Are you jealous?" He kissed her ear lingeringly.

"Depends."

He laughed. "All right. A man. His name's Pete Myers, and he's been on the force almost as long as I've been there. Pete's never married and has women strung out all over town."

"Are you so certain he'll relinquish his bachelor pad just because you ask him?"

"Pete knows I wouldn't ask unless I had a real need. He'll bunk in with one of his ladies. Hopefully, we won't be there long. It won't be the Ritz, but it'll be safe."

Stephanie shifted to face him. "I've never stayed at the Ritz."

"You've probably never stayed in a place like this either. The building's old, with no elevator, and Pete's on the third floor."

"Race you up the stairs, old man."

Luke smiled and tucked her head under his chin.

But Stephanie's mind was restless. "What do you plan to do when we arrive?"

He'd been doing a lot of thinking the last few days, and finally he'd formulated a plan. Admittedly, there was some danger to it, but that couldn't be helped. "I plan to go to Zane's house and get the bankbook."

She frowned. "Zane comes and goes at odd hours. He could return unexpectedly. Or he could have gotten guard dogs or a new bodyguard or two."

He hugged her to him with what he hoped was reassurance. "You have to trust me. I'm very careful. It's the only way to stay alive in this business. Besides, Zane doesn't know you have copies of the hit-and-run information. He would have no reason to be suspicious or to beef up his home security with dogs or extra men."

"But by then, Chester will undoubtedly be back. They'll have guns. Luke—"

"Relax, honey. I've been doing this for years and I haven't been killed yet. Just think about how good you're going to feel when they lock Zane away."

Stephanie released a nervous sigh. She would have to start getting used to having misgivings where Luke's work was concerned if she planned to be with him. If she didn't know what Zane was capable of, maybe she'd feel better. Maybe.

She reached up to touch his face. "I just don't want to lose you before I've really got you."

"Lady, you've got me. You've really got me." He trailed his fingers down her throat and around the soft underside of her breast and saw her eyes darken. "Does that feel good?"

"Mmm." She moved closer, burying her face in his neck. "Oh, Luke, it feels so good that it makes me afraid."

"Afraid of what?"

"That I'll wake up."

"This isn't a dream, Stephanie. This is very real." He kissed her, his tongue moving inside her mouth possessively. His hand slid down her, parting her legs, opening her. He threw back the sheet and raised himself above her as her eyes opened. "Very real."

Stephanie arched as his fingers found her. Stunned by her own abandon, she moved against him.

She was wet and ready. Luke entered her with one long thrust, heard her moan a welcome. Slowly at first, then faster, picking up the rhythm.

The loud knock on the door startled both of them.

"Got some evening tea for you and the missus, sir," the porter in the hallway said in his Southern drawl. "Nice and hot, just like you asked for."

Luke froze for a moment, then decided the man speaking really was the porter he'd been dealing with.

Stephanie felt Luke's pause. She gripped his back harder. "Don't stop. Let him go away. Please, don't stop."

He smiled. "Don't worry, honey. I don't plan to."

Luke knew that, as Mrs. Westover, Stephanie could give him permission to go into Zane's home, since she was technically still married to the man. With permission, he wouldn't have to break in and get the bankbook. But he didn't want to tip his hand to her wily husband and give him time to destroy any evidence still on the premises.

That was why the day after they arrived he stopped at the station to pick up one of the unmarked vans. With a new wig and full beard in place, he drove to Grosse Pointe, hoping Stephanie would listen to him and stay put.

They'd flown in from New York late last evening and had taken a cab to Pete's apartment. In Manhattan, he'd stopped long enough to buy Stephanie a red wig. Together with oversize sunglasses, she'd looked totally different. Both in disguises, they'd still been uneasy at the Detroit terminal and while he'd made arrangements to rent a car, right up until they'd locked the apartment door.

Luke had called the hospital first, pretending to be Stephen's brother, and had been told that Mr. Sanders was resting comfortably but was still unable to speak. That had upset Stephanie, although she knew she couldn't risk going to see her father yet. Next, he'd checked in with the captain, brought him up to date, and they'd gone over his plan. He'd been more than a little surprised when Renwick had agreed with his strategy.

The respect he'd been used to getting before his breakdown was back in the captain's voice, and Luke welcomed its return. It had been a long haul, but he was beginning to feel on safe ground again, with his career, with his emotions. Part of the reason was Stephanie and his unexpected feelings for her.

She'd been worried about his leaving today, he could tell, but she'd hidden it well. It had taken Luke a while to convince himself that they could make it together after all this was over, but he was beginning to think along those lines. And the rest of the world be damned.

But first things first. He had Zane Westover to take care of before Stephanie could be free.

He'd called the Westover house earlier and, with a few well-worded questions, had learned that the maid was alone there. It would be a real test, seeing whether Eula Johnson recognized him or was suspicious. Luke pulled the van up in the circular drive, grabbed his tool box, and got out. Standing on the

266

wide porch, he rang the bell.

Eula swung open the door. "Yes?"

"I'm from Central Security Systems, ma'am." Luke flashed his fake ID card. "Here to service the alarm system."

"But it's not broke," she said, frowning.

"No, ma'am. But it's an intricate system and we do regular checkups every three months. It's in the new maintenance contract Mr. Westover purchased." Patting his mustache, he gave her his best earnest smile.

"Just like checkups at the doctor's, eh?" Eula chuckled and pushed open the screen. "Come on in, then."

So far, so good. "Thank you, ma'am."

She led the way through to the back of the house. "You been here before, I s'pose, so you know where that box is in the basement."

"I sure do." He waited while she opened the basement door for him and snapped on the light. "I won't be long."

"I'll be right here in the kitchen if you need anything," she said as he descended the stairs.

Luke found the control center quickly. He didn't want to waste time, for Zane or one of his cronies might return unexpectedly. While he could handle himself, he wanted to avoid tipping his hand. Opening his toolbox, he found a screwdriver and went to work.

He had his friend, Tony, to thank for his electrical knowledge. A master electrician, Tony had taught Luke enough basics to get by and several specialty moves, such as the deactivation of security systems, which was something he'd had to do more than once. The trick was to reprogram the system in such a way that the power was off while the monitors upstairs indicated that the alarm was active. Peering into the box, he saw that this system was a bit different than any he'd worked on before. He hoped he wouldn't screw up.

When he returned to the kitchen, he found Eula cleaning the stove. "All finished, ma'am," he told her, closing the basement door.

"Everything okay down there?" she asked, wiping her hands on a towel as she walked to the front door with him.

"Yes, ma'am. You're all set." He walked off the porch and then climbed into the van. He had one more stop to make before returning to Stephanie, but first he'd have to change his appearance again. Whistling, he left the Westover house.

Cottage Hospital in Grosse Pointe was surrounded by stately, affluent homes in a quiet neighborhood. Parking his rented station wagon in the back lot, Luke checked his appearance in the visor mirror. A different wig again, this time a sedate gray with matching mustache. Not bad. Maybe he'd grow a mustache himself one day, he decided as he climbed out. Wearing dress slacks, a white shirt, and the striped tie he'd borrowed from Pete's closet, he walked purposefully to the main entrance. He'd always hated ties and shirts with starched collars, but he had a role to play and the costume was appropriate.

Working undercover for years, Luke had learned early that few people questioned someone who seemed to belong, a person who looked as if he knew where he was going. It was hesitant, nervous people that earned suspicious looks. He'd checked on visiting hours and had found them to be generous. Nodding to a passing nurse in the hallway, he made his way to the bank of elevators.

Stepping aboard the first available car, he joined a weary-looking man holding a large floral piece.

When he'd phoned last night, he'd been told that Stephen was in Room 209. Arriving on the second floor, he found it and quietly let himself in.

It was a private room, and Luke was grateful for that. Stephen lay on his back, his eyes closed. He looked pale and a little thinner, but otherwise unchanged. Luke moved to the bed and touched his arm.

Stephen's eyes opened, flew wildly about the room, then settled on Luke. There was no recognition in them.

Luke stripped off his mustache. "It's Luke Varner, Stephen." He saw the surprise in the older man's eyes, followed by acknowledgment. Stephen moved his chin slightly and made a clumsy attempt to nod. Luke pressed the fake mustache back into place.

"I wanted you to know Stephanie's all right. We're back, and I've got her in a safe place."

Stephen blinked rapidly, seemingly agitated.

Luke sat down on the edge of the bed and leaned closer. "I don't want you to worry. I know where there's evidence against Zane, enough to put him behind bars for a long while. I'm going to get it very soon and give it to the police. Once Zane's in custody, Stephanie can come out of hiding."

Stephen tried desperately to form an answer, but couldn't quite make it. He made a low, growling noise in his throat, a sound of frustration.

"Don't try to talk. When this is all over and Stephanie can come to see you, I know you'll recover faster." He saw a tear Stephen couldn't control roll out of the corner of his left eye. Luke glanced away so as not to embarrass him. "She's in good health, but worried about you. I'm going to her after I leave here. I'll tell her you're going to be fine and out of here in no time. Right?"

Again, the older man tried to nod. One of his arms lay very still, but he brought the other up and

269

gripped his visitor's fingers more tightly than Luke would have guessed possible from the frail look of him.

"There's a lot to tell you, but I'll wait until you're home. The important thing is your daughter is fine and safe. I promise you, I won't let anything happen to her." But he needed to know something. "The day of your stroke, did Zane visit you? Blink once for yes, twice for no."

He waited, then saw Stephen deliberately blink once. Luke nodded, then squeezed the older man's hand. "I understand. I'd better be going." He stood and smiled down at him. "You concentrate on getting well, and I'll be back soon."

Luke could have sworn he saw a ghost of a smile on Stephen's face. But maybe it was only wishful thinking.

Walking softly, he opened the door and glanced out. Not too many people about. He saw the red light indicating the stairwell and decided not to risk being recognized. It seemed unlikely that Zane or any of his men would be around, but years of caution had taught him anything was possible. Quickly he made his way downstairs and walked briskly through the double doors leading to the back parking lot.

Behind the wheel, Luke was anxious to get back to Stephanie. He whipped the station wagon out of the lot and headed south on Kercheval, toward Pete's apartment building.

Within moments, a late-model, white Chevrolet pulled into the lane two car-lengths behind the station wagon. The man behind the wheel was cunning, patient, and very dangerous.

270

Chapter Thirteen

Stephanie peeked between the slats of the ancient Venetian blinds, scanning the parking lot adjacent to the apartment building, and still couldn't see a trace of Luke returning. He'd been gone an awfully long time.

The late afternoon sun bounced off the rusty fire-escape steps and the two teenage boys playing catch in the alleyway three floors down. It was a section of town long past its prime, but she scarcely noticed. Her eyes kept watching for a blue station wagon and the man she loved.

She dropped the slat back into place and moved to the couch, curling up on it. Twenty-seven was a little late in life to fall in love for the very first time. Stephanie supposed most women had been this route several times by that ripe old age. But she was experiencing the ups and downs, the highs and lows, like a lovelorn teenager. And the lows were very scary.

The worst part was that should things work out between Luke and her after all this, she'd have to pretend she wouldn't be anxious about him every minute he was out of her sight. Or maybe she'd get used to this . . . this waiting and wondering and worrying. Obviously lots of women were related to police officers or men involved in other dangerous work. Somehow they managed to get through the hours without screaming. She would, too. Hopefully.

Maybe if she weren't personally involved in this case and hadn't experienced Zane's cruelty firsthand, or if she had someone to talk to, someone she could call, like Marjo or her father, or if she hadn't finally found a man who seemed like the other half of her that she hadn't even known was missing — maybe then she wouldn't be so frightened.

Three short knocks sounded at the door. Smiling with relief, Stephanie rushed over and unbolted the lock. Before sliding back the chain, she paused, remembering Luke's instructions. "What's the password?"

"Casey," Luke answered from the other side, pleased she'd remembered to ask. Together they'd chosen the safest password, realizing that only the two of them knew the name Stephanie had given the ill-fated kitten. The chain slid back and Stephanie all but leaped into his arms. "Hey, that's quite a welcome," he said, walking her backward into the room.

"I've been worried." She dropped her arms and noticed he was holding a fragrant white sack in each hand. "Mmm, I love Chinese food."

Luke kissed her forehead and went to the kitchen. "Good, because I've got a ton of it here."

"What took you so long?" she asked, following him in.

While he opened cartons to reveal steaming hot meat and vegetables, Luke told her briefly what he'd done at Zane's house. "So tonight, after dark, I'll go back, slip in and get the bankbook."

Setting out plates, Stephanie looked skeptical. "What if what you did doesn't work and the alarm goes off?"

"Then I'll get the hell out of there."

"It's a silent alarm. You won't know."

Luke sat down and cut into an egg roll. "I disconnected the alarm."

"I know it's hooked up so it'll ring at the Grosse Pointe Police Station as well."

272

"Yes, but I redirected the circuit."

"Something could still go wrong. Why don't you just get a warrant and search the house?"

He sampled a bite of sweet and sour pork and shook his head. "You can't just get a warrant because you want to search someone's house. You have to prove to a judge that there's just cause."

"Damn, why didn't I take that bankbook with me when I left?"

"Because Zane would have discovered it was missing by now, and he'd have covered his tracks. But you're worrying too much. I'll get the bankbook and take it to Captain Renwick right afterward, to make sure there's no hitch. I've already alerted him."

Stephanie chewed on her pepper steak disinterestedly. She'd been hungry until she'd started thinking about Luke returning to that house. "Why don't I put on my red wig and sunglasses, drive the station wagon and act as lookout? I could signal you if someone approaches the house while you're in there?"

Luke sent her a long-suffering look. "I appreciate the offer, but I work alone." He needed to switch the focus of their conversation before she worked herself up further. "I stopped in to see your father."

Stephanie flashed him a look of alarm. "What if someone recognized you at the hospital?"

"Stephanie, I wore a wig and mustache. Are you going to stop all this and believe that I do this sort of thing regularly and often — and have for over fifteen years?" Of course, luck played a large part in the scheme of things, as Luke was well aware, but he saw no need to tell her that.

He was getting annoyed. She sensed it and realized she was displaying very little confidence in him. "I'm sorry," she whispered. "I know you're careful. It's just that . . ."

Luke leaned over and kissed her. "I know. Now, you want to hear about Stephen?"

"Of course I do. How is he? Did he know who you

273

were?"

"After I took off the mustache, he recognized me. He looks okay, a little thinner. He tried to talk, but couldn't quite manage." He didn't go into Stephen's paralysis on one side, thinking it could very well be temporary and would only alarm her. "I told him you were safe and with me, and he gave a nod and tried to smile."

Stephanie blinked back tears. "I wish I could at least speak to his doctor and ask what the prognosis is."

He touched her hand. "Soon as this is over, I promise. I told your dad I was getting evidence on Zane together and that we're going to nail him this time." Luke reached for the fried rice, spooned some onto his plate and offered the carton to her. When she didn't take it, he looked up.

She'd put down her fork and had her hands to her mouth, again fighting tears. "What's wrong, honey?" he asked, turning to her.

Stephanie swallowed a lump of emotion. "I want to get him so badly, Luke. For what he's done to my father — Dad may never fully recover — and for Marjo. I still can't believe she's gone."

Luke slipped an arm around her. "We *will* get him. And let's not forget what he tried to do to you. If you hadn't had your wits about you when your car hit the river, you'd be gone, too." The thought spoken aloud, he pulled her closer.

"I've never hated before, Luke. I'm not comfortable with the feeling, but I do hate Zane."

"Go ahead and hate him. Just don't get careless until he's behind bars."

She met his eyes, needing reassurance. "There's no way he can get out of this, is there?"

There were always ways, Luke was well aware. Money talked, and smart attorneys could be had. But this one time he'd skirt the truth because Stephanie needed to hear something hopeful. "Not this time.

274

We're going to make Zane pay." He glanced at his watch, keeping track of the time.

Stephanie became aware of the minutes ticking away. "When do you plan to leave?"

"I made a couple calls. Zane's got Rotary Club tonight, a dinner meeting. He never misses."

Stephanie nodded. "I remember. He was so anxious to become a Rotarian. I think he feels it's prestigious."

"While he's there glad-handing, I'll visit his house." Luke dug into the fried rice.

"Did you find out if Chester's back?"

"Renwick says he is. Told me Chester looks like someone beat him up. Asked me if I knew anything about it."

"And what did you say?"

Luke gave her an innocent look. "I told him an ex-boxer like Chester probably has trouble staying out of fights."

"He guessed, I imagine."

Luke shrugged. "The man's alive. I did what I had to do."

The hard cop talking. She didn't like to hear it, but that was also part and parcel of what Luke Varner was, and she'd have to live with it. But not tonight. "Zane's meetings start at seven, as I recall. We have two hours before you have to go. I don't want to eat. I want you to hold me, to make love to me. I don't want to think, just feel."

Luke shoved his plate aside, got to his feet and held out a hand.

It isn't dark enough, Luke thought with a frown as he flattened himself against the back wall of the Westover house. Summertime daylight lingered, and he wished it didn't as his eyes scanned the neighborhood through the trees. Around the bend of the curving hilltop street, several kids were playing hide-and-seek.

An older couple with a dog on a leash had passed by a few minutes ago. Otherwise, he'd seen no one.

He'd parked some distance away and strolled casually toward the house, hoping he'd be mistaken for a new neighbor out for an evening walk if he were noticed at all. Then he'd ducked onto the shaded grounds of the silent house and made his way to the back.

A lamp had been left on in the front room, and there was a light on in the kitchen at the rear. The upstairs was dark. Stephanie had told him Zane had a gray Mercedes that Chester usually drove. It was nowhere in sight. Confident that he was alone and unnoticed, Luke removed his small tool kit from his pocket and bent to the back door.

When the lock opened he let out a relieved breath before slipping inside. Hurriedly he moved through the house to where Stephanie had told him Zane's study was located. Pausing there, he let his eyes adjust to the dimness again after the glare of the kitchen light. It was utterly quiet as he stood before Zane's den.

The door was unlocked. From inside his jacket, Luke pulled out a flashlight with a dimmer shield, went in, and looked around. The wall facing him consisted of built-in bookshelves filled with volumes and a few knickknacks. There was a cozy corner fireplace and, in the opposite corner, a large television with a leather couch and two chairs facing it. On the opposite side of the room was a huge desk. Luke moved to it.

Checking carefully, he noticed that Zane was either very neat or very cautious. Nothing on the top except a desk lamp, an ashtray, and a pen in a holder. Sitting down on the leather swivel chair, Luke examined the drawers.

All were locked. There seemed to be a master lock on the center top drawer and a separate lock on the second drawer on the right. Luke retrieved his tool from his pocket and went to work.

It took him less than a minute to open the central lock. Beaming the flashlight into each drawer, he examined the contents, careful not to disturb the order. He found nothing of interest. Closing the last of these drawers, he studied the second lock. A more intricate one, obviously added after the desk had been purchased. Concentrating, Luke picked up his tool.

This one took longer, but finally gave. Shining the light, he looked inside. Empty. Absolutely empty. Damn!

Discouraged, Luke stood. He'd laid the story out for Captain Renwick and they'd both agreed that there was a possibility of conviction based on the evidence Stephanie had already given them. But the bankbook would have strengthened their case. Zane must have gotten worried when he'd learned Stephanie was still alive, and he'd destroyed everything, probably even closing out that bank account. Luke would check that out.

Pocketing the flashlight, he decided he'd visit Zane's bedroom on the off chance he could find something incriminating there. He left the study, quietly closing the door, and crept along the hallway to the back stairs. Halfway up, he heard a door open and slam shut, followed by the sound of voices.

Decision time. He could hurry up and hide in one of the bedrooms, or he could take a chance and perhaps overhear something important. He flattened his back to the shadowy wall opposite the hand railing and strained to hear. Male voices, coming closer.

Something heavy dropped onto the glass top of the kitchen table, followed by a scraping noise as if a chair were being pulled out.

"I don't like it," Zane said, his voice high-pitched.

"Boss," Chester said, "you got to let me go after him. After what he done to me, Luke Varner's mine."

Luke's hand closed over the .38 tucked into the waistband of his jeans.

* * *

For the second time in one evening, Stephanie found herself pacing in the small confines of the apartment. After tonight, it will all be over, she told herself. As he'd held her in his arms just an hour ago, Luke had assured her that the end was in sight. He'd get the evidence, give it to the captain, and be back with her as quickly as humanly possible. Warrants would be issued. Then Zane and the questionable people he surrounded himself with would be picked up, locked up. Nothing would go wrong, Luke had assured her.

Why, then, did she have this uneasy feeling?

Think of our future while I'm gone, Luke had suggested. Stephanie leaned her head back in the overstuffed chair and tried to concentrate. He would take her to his houseboat tonight, if she wanted, he'd said. Yes, she wanted. Wanted to get out of this dingy, unfamiliar place that made her nervous, to go somewhere with fresh air and open waterways.

He'd told her about Benjamin, his grumpy cat, and how the two of them often took the houseboat out into Lake St. Clair, anchored at a peaceful spot and lazily fished the hours away. Sometimes whole days. Right now, that thought held a lot of appeal.

But she was anxious to see her father, assure him that she was unharmed, and spur him on to recovery. Once Stephen was home, his health improving daily, maybe she could relax. Until the trial.

Luke had warned her that she'd have to testify against Zane. The very thought of sitting in a courtroom, up on the witness stand, answering questions about the dangerous and cruel man she'd married, gave her the chills. Though she was wearing jeans and a long-sleeved cotton shirt, Stephanie shivered. She could picture Zane's dark eyes on her, as he tried to intimidate her as he so often had in the past.

But no more. Luke would be in the courtroom, his

solid presence lending support. Then they'd put Zane, and probably Chester, away for a long while. She and Luke would be free. Free to live their lives without always looking over their shoulders. Free to build a life together, if that was to be. She had to hang on to that thought.

Restlessly she got up and walked into the kitchen. She didn't really want anything, but just to have something to do, she put water on to boil for tea. The little she'd eaten sat like a queasy lump in her stomach. She leaned against the door frame, picturing Luke in Zane's house, in his study, getting the bankbook, sneaking back out. By now he should be on his way to Police Headquarters, or perhaps already there. Why hadn't she asked him to phone her the minute he'd left Zane's house, so she'd know he was in the clear?

The kettle whistled, and she poured hot water into a teacup. Carrying the cup, she wandered back into the living room. Maybe she'd look for a magazine to read and —

Three sharp raps sounded at the door.

With a relieved smile, Stephanie leaped up and slid back the bolt. Remembering, she paused, her hand on the chain. "What's the password?"

There was only silence. Another knock and she jumped back, startled, the worry returning. Why wasn't Luke answering? "What's the password?" she asked again.

"Stephanie, let me in," came the reply.

The voice didn't belong to Luke.

"Shut up and let me think," Zane said, scowling at Chester. Seated at the kitchen table, he stared down at his folded hands. He'd have to handle this very carefully, or everything could blow up in his face. He'd worked too hard and too long to let that bitch spoil things now.

279

One more shipment and he'd be set for life. He'd just finalized the arrangements with Mr. Q earlier tonight. Day after tomorrow, just after midnight at shift-change time at the tunnel. Nothing would go wrong. Not this time.

Zane raised his gaze to Chester's face. Most of the swelling from the beating the bodyguard had received had gone down, except around his split lip. He had a purplish bruise on one cheek and had had to have stitches at the back of his head. Nearly all of his hair had been shaved off, leaving him looking more menacing and more thuglike than ever. Chester has outgrown his usefulness, Zane decided. But tonight, he still needed him.

"Tell me again what Bob said," Zane commanded.

"It's like I told you, boss." Chester sat down heavily. "Bob had this hunch that either Stephanie or Luke would try to see her old man at the hospital as soon as they got back in town. So he sat it out, and sure enough, that's where he picked up Luke's trail, at Cottage Hospital. Followed him to this old apartment building off Jefferson—you know the one, red brick and—"

"I don't give a shit if it's red brick or green. Get on with this."

On the stairway, Luke frowned. Leaving the hospital, he'd kept his eye on the mirror, but he'd been watching for the wrong man. Bob. Had to be Bob Triner, Zane's attorney. Why had Bob been so anxious to locate Stephanie? To score points with Zane, or was there another reason? Luke felt the first twinges of panic, like a fluttering fist in his gut. Cautiously he moved down two steps, straining to hear.

"Yeah, sure." Chester wiped his hands on his handkerchief. "So Bob phoned me from the lobby of the building across the street. Said he was going in soon, that he'd take care of Varner and bring Stephanie back here to you."

Zane narrowed his eyes. "I don't get it. Bob take

care of Luke Varner? That's a laugh. I'm not sure he's got the muscle or the guts to bring Stephanie in, much less take care of that crafty cop. Something doesn't add up here. Did Bob say anything else?"

"No, boss. Just told me to sit tight. But I got worried; that's why I called you at your Rotary meeting and asked you to come home. I say we go help Bob out. We can take care of Stephanie like we talked about, snuff her and dump her body downriver. When they find her, they'll think she floated down from the car accident. And then I'll take care of Varner." He rubbed his big hands together, like a child looking forward to a treat. "Nothing easy and quick for him. I'm gonna enjoy seeing that bastard squirm."

Zane gave a short, harsh bark of a laugh. "You've had several opportunities, and you haven't taken care of Varner yet."

"I almost had him on that train," Chester said defensively.

"But he was too fast and too smart for you." Chester was stupid, underestimating Varner, Zane realized. And he decided maybe he had gotten careless and underestimated someone, too. Bob Triner's new tough stand was definitely out of character for the mild-mannered tax attorney. He'd never even seen Bob swat a fly.

And there was still the matter of the missing diamonds. Mr. Q was getting impatient—and was holding their disappearance against Zane. He needed to save face.

"This is one I think I have to handle myself." Abruptly Zane stood. "Come on. We're going to that apartment. And I don't want you to do anything unless I give the order. You got that?"

"Yeah, boss, I got it."

On the stairway, Luke heard the sound of retreating feet, then the door closing, the lock clicking. He held his breath a moment, then crept down the stairs. The kitchen light was still on; he couldn't risk leaving that way. In the fading light of dusk, he made his way to the dining-room window.

As he carefully unlocked and opened the window, he saw the gray Mercedes pull out of the drive and turn left, heading down the curving street. Heart pounding, he squeezed through the window, closed it, and hurried toward his rental car.

He *had* to beat Zane and Chester to the apartment house. And he had to figure out what Bob Triner's involvement in all this was. With squealing wheels, he raced forward. He'd promised Stephen he'd take care of Stephanie, keep her safe. He meant to keep that promise.

He knew his way around the narrow old streets and downtown alleys, knew every shortcut the city had to offer. He'd spent far too much time wandering around it. Tonight, those years paid off as the rented car surged forward.

He broke out in a cold sweat as he drove, trying not to conjure up scenarios. Stephanie would stay put, she would *not* open the door, she would be safe. But even so, he knew she was impatient and braver than she should be.

Praying, Luke pressed down on the gas pedal.

"Bob, is that you?" Stephanie's hand on the chain was damp and shaking.

"Yes. Let me in, Stephanie."

Of the few men Zane trusted, Bob Triner was the only one she'd liked. The man was gentle and seemed trustworthy, and she'd often wondered why he worked for Zane. But she couldn't imagine how he'd found her. "What are you doing here, Bob?"

"I need your help." His voice was low, persuasive, and confidential as he leaned closer to the door. "I have proof about Zane's activities. I've only recently learned about how vicious he really is. Let me in and together we can expose him."

She felt a rush of gratitude, someone else was catching on to Zane. Bob could wait with her until Luke returned. Then, with their combined evidence, they could really nail him. Cautiously, Stephanie opened the door.

It really was Bob, standing there wearing a somewhat rumpled brown suit, his tie hanging loose. "Are you alone?"

Triner put on a smile and held out his hands. "All alone."

Slipping the chain back, she let him in. It was nice to have someone to worry with. "I'm glad you're here," she said.

Pushing his glasses up on his face, Bob glanced around the room, then swung his myopic gaze to Stephanie. "I saw Luke Varner leaving earlier. Where was he headed?"

"He's gone to the house to get something. He should be back soon. How'd you find us?"

"I was at Cottage Hospital when Luke came in." Bob eased his lanky frame onto the ottoman and leaned forward, his elbows on his knees. "Whatever he's after must be real important. Is Luke breaking in?"

Stephanie perched uneasily on the edge of the couch. She'd always been relaxed around Bob. She forced herself to take a steady breath. As Zane's attorney, Bob would probably have lots of evidence in his files on Zane's less-than-honest activities. They would need his cooperation. She decided to trust him. "I have proof of something illegal that Zane was involved in some time ago, but one important piece is missing. Luke is getting it for the police."

"About the hit-and-run?" he asked quietly.

Of course, he would know about that. "Yes. Bob, why is it you've worked all these years for Zane when you knew he'd done some terrible things?"

Bob shrugged. "He pays well."

His eyes were distorted by the thick lenses, she

283

noticed. "Money isn't everything." There was disappointment in her voice.

"That's easy for you to say. You've always had plenty, a great house, big cars." He thrust himself to his feet, plunging his hands into his pants pockets. "Do you know what it's like to spend years working your way through college, then law school? Never having enough to eat or nice clothes." He waved an arm through the air, indicating the room. "You see this place? It's a palace compared to where I had to live back then."

Uneasily, Stephanie glanced toward the door, wishing Luke would hurry. "But you got out of that. A tax attorney can make a lot of money. You didn't have to work for a murderer and a crook to get somewhere."

Bob grinned then. "You know that Zane had someone rig your car and that he killed Marjo?"

She scooted back into the corner of the couch, uncomfortable with the direction of their conversation. "I guessed as much. Is that the kind of proof you have about Zane?"

He began to pace, running bony fingers through his thin hair. "I know lots of things about Zane, things that would get him locked up and they'd throw away the key."

"Good. When Luke comes, we'll go to the police."

Turning, he stepped closer. "I don't want to wait. Let's go now."

"I promised Luke I wouldn't leave until he returns."

"They won't need the stuff about the hit-and-run after I get through talking." He held out his hand. "Come on."

She was beginning to get nervous. Bob's voice was suddenly more assertive than she'd ever heard it, his tone more demanding. At any minute, Luke would be here. She would focus on that and keep Bob pacified and talking. "We've waited this long. Surely another few minutes won't matter. Tell me what you have on Zane."

284

"Zane." Bob made a disgusted sound. "He thinks he's so smart. But he's going to find out real soon that he's not the clever one. Do you know why he wants to find you real bad?"

"Because I filed for divorce."

Bob shook his head as if dealing with a backward child. "Not anymore. It started out like that. I'd warned him that it was dangerous, rigging your car and all. But he figured sooner or later you'd leave him, and his ego couldn't handle that. The reason he wants you now is the diamonds."

Stephanie frowned as she looked up at him. "What diamonds? I don't have any diamonds."

Bob's smile was crooked. "*You* know that and *I* know that, but your darling husband is sure you have them. And why shouldn't he be? Hurting his ego by leaving him would have been one thing. Hurting his bank account is far worse. You were the logical one he'd suspect. They were hidden in the antique desk in your room. Who else would have access? The perfect crime."

Her head was beginning to hurt. "I don't understand any of this."

Bob stepped closer, his lips curling in resentment. "Why couldn't you stay away? Even after that stupid Chester went to Florida, you could have taken off. You could have dodged that cop, too. But no, you had to come back and spoil things." A trace of spittle escaped from his mouth, and Bob swiped at it.

It was becoming all too clear. Her heart lurched. Luke had been wearing a disguise at the hospital, yet Bob had recognized him. He must have been watching for him. Stephanie struggled to appear calm. She had to buy time. "Who did I spoil things for, Bob?"

He grinned then, a smile tinged with insanity. "Don't play games with me, little rich girl. You know damn well Chester doesn't have the brains to pull this off, nor do any of those other muscle men who hang around Zane at the shop." He leaned to her, his eyes wild. "I took the diamonds."

She had to keep him talking. "But where had they come from?"

He shook his head at her naivete. "Smuggled in from Canada. Zane has connections, I'll give him that. They were hidden in the panels of cars, wrapped in plastic bags buried in truck loads, stuck at the bottom of the shopping bag of a little old lady on a touring bus — all setups. Sometimes, we used the bridge, other times the tunnel."

"These shipments went to the antique shop?"

"At first they did. But I always thought that was dangerous and stupid, so later they were concealed in certain antiques that were delivered to Zane's house. The grandfather clock in the vestibule, an armoire, your desk." He smiled again. "Clever, eh?"

"Did you think this up?"

"Yeah, I did. But did Zane ever give me credit for masterminding his lucrative plan? Never. Still, I showed him. I got the last package, and I've been hanging around waiting for the next one. The biggest haul yet, ten million. Couple days and it'll be here. And I'll get that one, too. I just had to revise my plan a little since you didn't blow up with that houseboat."

Stephanie gasped. "You. You were the one who set the bomb?"

"Yeah. Did you think it was Chester? He's too dumb, didn't you know? But not me."

No, not him. He was close enough in the small room for Stephanie to smell his stale breath and nervous sweat, but she held her ground. Anything to keep him talking while she prayed Luke would hurry back. "What are you planning to do, leave the country?"

Bob straightened, rubbing his face. "I didn't set out to steal from Zane, you know. But when your car went in, I figured *why not?* Zane already hated you. I figured he'd blame you and I'd bide my time. Then one day I'd quietly disappear — with millions in gems.

With that much money, you can live like a king on a lot of little Caribbean Islands. The poor boy who grew up working two jobs just to get by would hire others to work for him. And I wouldn't have to take any shit from anybody ever again."

"Don't you think Zane will eventually figure things out and go looking for you?"

"I'm sure he doesn't suspect me. If you hadn't returned, he'd have kept on believing you ran with them. You messed up my plans, Stephanie." Suddenly he grabbed her arm and yanked her to her feet. "You're going to have to pay, you and Varner. If I get rid of the two of you, Zane will still think you have the diamonds stashed somewhere." His fingers curled into her flesh, bringing her closer. "I have to kill you. I can't risk having Zane or Mr. Q discover I tried to double-cross them. You see that, don't you?"

Fear had her weak and desperate, but she fought to keep her eyes on his face. "Luke's probably already at Police Headquarters with all the evidence. They'll arrest Zane tonight. If you just leave now, no one will know who has the diamonds."

Bob's face was inches from hers. "No one except you."

She'd never seen a man, not even Zane, look at her with the madness of death in his eyes. But she recognized it immediately. A scream rose in her throat just before she felt a damp hand close over her mouth.

"Don't make a sound. We're going to walk out of here, nice and easy, friendlylike. If anyone spots us, we're slightly tipsy lovers with our arms around each other. You understand?"

Stephanie didn't answer, just struggled against the iron grip of his hands. She felt his fingers tighten on her flesh and moaned.

He'd never carried a gun, never needed one before. Now Bob found himself wishing he had a weapon. "Do you understand?"

Left with little choice, she nodded.

"That's better. Now, I'm going to open the door, and we're going to walk down to my car. I'm taking my hand away, but if you scream, it'll be your last one." Still holding her by one arm, Bob took his hand from her mouth and unbolted the door.

Stephanie decided to risk a question. "Where are you taking me?"

"To a nice, quiet, deserted warehouse not far from here. By the time they find your body, I'll be on a cruise ship." He giggled in anticipation as he slid back the second lock.

Now or never, Stephanie thought, and gave a mighty twist to her body, wrenching away from his grasp. She watched him swivel toward her, his face furious. She was certain she'd have only this one opportunity, so she'd have to make it pay. Bracing a hand on the TV, she eased back her right leg, then swung it forward in a powerful kick.

The hard rubber tip of her tennis shoe connected with soft flesh as she scored right between his legs. She heard him cry out and bend over, grabbing himself, falling back against the door. Turning, she raced to the only other way out. Yanking up the blinds, she shoved open the window.

She didn't take the time to look back and check Bob's condition. Hurrying out onto the rusty landing of the fire escape, she slammed the window shut. Hand on the railing, she started down.

The muffled sound of cursing drifted to her. Hang on, she told herself as she hit the second-floor landing. It was then she saw that the rest of the fire escape leading to the ground had disappeared, probably broken off some time ago. It was too far to jump without risking a broken neck.

Stephanie looked upward and saw no one. Fearful that this detour had cost her precious minutes, she reversed and started back up. When she hit the third floor, she glanced at the window and saw that it was still closed. She climbed on, picking up her pace, praying the rickety metal stairs would hold her weight.

The apartment building was five stories high. As she neared the top, she heard footsteps below her. They were coming closer. Squinting to see better, Stephanie climbed over the low parapet onto the roof. Looking back down for a second, she recognized the top of Bob's dark head moving upward. Frantically, she turned.

She'd never been on the roof of a building in her life. Filthy blacktop, papers swirling in the night breezes, pigeons cooing in the far corner, and several bent TV antennas dotting the area. Shouldn't there be stairs leading down? Leaving the edge, she moved quickly to the other side, hands outstretched so she wouldn't stumble.

Only when she'd landed in the river had she been more frightened than she was now. She willed herself not to panic, to keep her mind on the task of finding the door leading to the steps. She heard a shuffling noise and a curse, then saw that Bob had reached the top.

Stifling a scream, she searched frantically for the stairs.

Where on earth was Luke?

Chapter Fourteen

Emerging from an alley, Luke drove the last couple of miles with the needle hovering around eighty. Where in hell were the patrol cars when you needed them? The streets were oddly deserted as he finally screeched to a stop in front of his friend's apartment building and jumped out of the car.

He raced through the small lobby and took the stairs two at a time. On the third floor, he ran down the hallway and stopped at Pete Myers's door. As he reached into his pocket for the key, he saw that the door was ajar. *Jesus!*

Luke took out his gun slowly and cautiously shoved open the door. Moving inside, he saw that the place was empty. Then he noticed that the window in the living room was wide open, the old Venetian slats pulled up high. His heart hammering, he stepped out onto the fire escape.

Street lights had come on, and he could see that the rickety stairs ended a short distance below. He scanned the parking lot and saw no movement. Turning he looked up. Whoever had opened that window had to have gone up. And whether that was Zane, Chester, or Bob, he had Stephanie with him.

Climbing rapidly, Luke made his way to the roof, gun drawn.

* * *

Bob crouched low, his eyes narrowing. Then he smiled. There she was, the little bitch. Huddled in the corner, clutching in her hand something that she'd evidently found on the floor of the roof. Didn't she know there was no way she could stop him this time? He'd come too far, taken too many chances not to pull it off.

Slowly he inched toward her, calm now. All his life, people had commented on how calm and unruffled Bob Triner was, and he'd taken it as a huge compliment. He'd almost lost it in there when Stephanie had kicked him. But he was back in control now.

The wind had picked up, Bob noticed as he moved closer. Good. She could scream all she wanted up here and no one would hear her. His hand went to his pantleg seeking the knife strapped to his ankle, waiting in its leather holster. The thought of sinking the sleek blade into Stephanie, of watching her eyes plead for mercy, had him shaking. Personally he hated violence, but this was survival.

He'd have to silence her. Then he'd go back to the apartment and lay in wait for Luke. One quick stab to the throat and the smartass cop would bother them no more. Zane might even reward him handsomely for removing these two from his life. Bob would take the money and wait awhile, then grab the next shipment and disappear. By the time Zane figured things out, he'd know he'd been outsmarted. He'd be mad, but what could he do? Unlike Stephanie, Bob was far too clever to leave a single clue behind.

Clouds shifted, and in a patch of moonlight, he saw Stephanie quite clearly. Moving closer, his stance confident, Bob reached out, catching her about the waist. Pigeons that had been dozing on the ledge flew off in noisy retreat. Stephanie raised her arm, a piece of wood gripped in a shaky hand. Easily he batted it from her and shoved her toward the edge of the building.

"Let me go," Stephanie yelled. Someone will hear, she prayed. Someone has to.

From behind his glasses, Bob's eyes glowed as he

sensed victory close at hand. He held both her wrists in one hand, his fingers, like steel, pressing into her flesh. No one had ever realized how strong he was, a fact that now worked in his favor. He felt a shiver of pain between his legs, a reminder of her kick.

Stephanie's back was to the low wall that ran around the roof, and Bob pressed his advantage, forcing her over. "Are you scared, Stephanie? Five floors down. Won't be much left of your pretty little body after that fall."

"Luke will find you, Bob. And you forget that my father's a powerful man." The wind whipped her hair about her face, grabbing her words and sending them flying.

Bob laughed. "Your father. He almost wet his pants when we paid him a surprise visit. Some tough guy, all right."

"You were there with Zane?"

"What good's that piece of news going to do you now?" With his free hand, he twisted her face so she had to look down. "You're going over, baby. It's a long way down, but it'll be over fast."

Stephanie pictured her father having to live through her death a second time and felt a rush of adrenaline. Shoving, kicking, punching, she freed herself from his grasp, then set out at a run alongside the parapet. He doesn't have a weapon, she decided, or he'd have used it by now. She had to get away.

But he was too fast for her. At a corner of the low wall, he caught her and shoved her heavily up against the cement edge. Stephanie felt the wind being knocked out of her as she went down on her knees. She looked up in time to see Bob raise his arm, ready to slam a stiffened hand into her neck.

"Hold it right there!" Luke shouted from the other side of the roof as he stepped onto it.

Startled, Bob swiveled, then reacted by grabbing Stephanie and pulling her to her feet.

"Don't move, I said." Luke came closer, walking

slowly so as not to frighten the man into a wild move.

But Bob was beyond reason. He bent to yank Stephanie up, intending to use her as a shield. Suddenly, she went limp and fell to the floor. As Bob struggled to pull her up, a piercing fire exploded in his shoulder and he spun about. With a cry of pain, he stumbled twice, then dropped onto the rooftop.

Luke reached Stephanie just as she scrambled to her feet. "Are you all right?"

She felt light-headed and her hands were trembling. But she was all right now that Luke was there. "Yes. I tried to give you a clear shot by faking a faint."

Several feet away, he saw Bob roll onto his side, clutching the shoulder wound. "It worked." He hugged her to him, his grateful heart pounding as his arms went around her.

Her face was in his neck. "Thank God you got here in time." Now that she was safe, she began to shake.

"Why did you let him in?"

"It was stupid; I realize that now. But I've trusted Bob in the past, and he told me he had evidence against Zane."

Luke rubbed her back. "I hope he does. The bankbook was gone."

She pulled back. "Oh, no. Now what do we do?"

"Don't worry. I have something else in mind." Luke touched her face. "And I'm not letting you out of my sight again." Fiercely, he held her to him.

The pain hit fast and deep, searing his leg. Whirling around, Luke saw Bob Triner propped up on one elbow, a knife glinting in his hand. Blood stained the silvery blade. Pushing Stephanie out of harm's way, he kicked the knife from the man's hand and heard it fly away, then clatter onto the roof.

Luke saw red, literally. Mostly, he was furious with himself for not securing his prisoner. Personal involvement with the victim he was rescuing had clouded his judgment. Raging inside, he straddled Bob and struck him in the face. He wanted to make him pay for having frightened Stephanie. He'd already beaten one of Zane's boys. It would seem he'd have to teach another one a lesson. He swung again, hearing the satisfying crunch of his fist hitting Bob's jaw.

"Luke, don't," Stephanie said, daring to venture closer.

But he was intent on revenge. First his right, then his left pummeled Bob's flesh.

"No, please, no more," Bob whined, raising his hands to ward off further blows.

Frightened that Luke was losing control, Stephanie grabbed his arm. "Stop! Please, Luke. You don't need to solve this with your fists. We can hand him over to the police. He told me enough to put both Zane and him away for a long while. He's not worth it."

Clenched fist raised, Luke sucked in a steadying breath. She was right. None of them were worth it. He wanted his old job back, and this wasn't the way to go about getting it. Rising, he stepped over Bob, his chest heaving. "All right," he told Stephanie.

She let out a trembling sigh of gratitude.

Bob shook his head in a vain effort to clear it. Somewhat wobbly, he got to his feet and touched his puffy lip, then rubbed his sore jaw, mumbling something incoherent.

Luke grabbed his arm. "Where's Zane?"

"I don't know." Bob stood there looking like a defeated rag doll.

From his back pocket, Luke pulled out handcuffs, then led Bob over to a metal post. Slipping the cuffs on one of Bob's wrists, he secured the other end to the post. "You don't want to talk now, that's fine. You might change your mind downtown." He took Stephanie's arm. "Let's go back to the apartment and call the captain."

"You're going to leave me here?" Bob's voice was thin and reedy.

"This way, you won't try to pull some stunt to get away." He watched as Bob yanked on the metal cuffs, but they held securely. "Struggle all you want. You're not going anywhere except the county jail. We'll be back for you as soon as the police arrive."

Swearing inventively, Bob slid down and leaned against the pole.

They found the stairs at the far end and hurried down to the third floor. Leading the way, Luke saw that the door to Pete's apartment was still open. Silently, he went in and checked around. Nothing out of place. Stephanie was already in the apartment so he locked the door behind them and turned to her. Her face was impossibly pale, her eyes huge with lingering fear. He drew her into his arms. "It's almost over, honey."

It would be a long while before she'd forget the look of madness on Bob's face, the icy terror she'd felt when Triner forced her to lean over the edge. She spoke into his shoulder. "I was so frightened. Bob stole the diamonds and let Zane think it was me. There's something wrong with him. His eyes are wild." Her hands at his waist, she clung to Luke as a shudder went through her.

"We'll get the whole story out of Bob soon enough."

Taking a deep breath, Stephanie stepped back. "I'll be all right once this is behind us." She went to the bathroom to clean up while Luke called Police Headquarters. She was just slipping on a fresh blouse when he joined her and held out a glass of brandy.

"Drink this. They'll be here shortly. And they've sent a car to the house to pick up Zane and Chester for questioning." He watched her sip, trying not to let her see the worry on his face. At the house, he'd overheard Zane and Chester say they were on their way here. Why hadn't they arrived?

In the bathroom, he rinsed off his hands, noticing that his knuckles were bruised and swollen again, and this time he had an open cut near one thumb. He'd just barely healed from his encounter with Chester.

Stephanie stared down into the golden liquid, then tipped her head back and finished the rest. She would not think about what had just been, but of what was yet to come. In the bathroom doorway, she glanced at her mirror image and ran a hand through her windblown hair. "First chance I have, I'm dying this back to its natural color. I hate the way I look." She needed to look like herself again, to feel safe and comfortable again.

Drying his hands, Luke turned to stare at her. She was safe. For several frantic seconds there, he'd wondered if he could get a shot off before Bob pushed her off the roof. He never wanted to go through anything like that again. Gently he touched the ends of her hair. "I'd be crazy about you even if you were bald. The color doesn't matter."

"It does to me." She looked up at him, her eyes anxious. "Do you think they'd make an exception at the hospital and let me in to see Dad tonight?"

"We can try. Then we go to my houseboat."

"Mmm, yes." Rising on tiptoe, she sought his mouth. As she let herself drift with the kiss, her nerves slowly relaxed. It really was happening. Soon, she'd be free.

Less than fifteen minutes later, they heard several hard knocks on the door. "Open up. Police."

Luke smiled. The captain loved to bellow. "That's Renwick."

It was late, and the captain was out of uniform. Even so, he was an imposing figure, his years in office showing on his lined face. The ever-present cigar in hand, he walked in, followed by a uniformed policeman and Megs. Renwick nodded to Stephanie, recognizing her from the pictures. "Evening, ma'am."

"Hello, Captain."

"Where is he?" Renwick asked Luke.

"Up on the roof. Stephanie ran up the fire escape to get away from him. He followed her, had her backed to the edge when I arrived. I got off a shot to his shoulder."

"Is he out?"

"Far from it. He was swearing like a sailor when we left him. His wound's only superficial. I handcuffed him to a metal post so we wouldn't have to deal with him down here before you arrived." He held out the key to the handcuffs.

Renwick took it, then turned to Megs and the officer. "Get him and bring him down here."

Megs winked at Luke. She grasped the key and left, the officer following her.

The captain eased himself into the overstuffed chair, swallowing a groan. Damned arthritis was acting up. He set his cigar in a large ashtray and looked over at Luke, who'd moved to the couch. "You said on the phone that you couldn't find the bankbook at Westover's house?"

"No, Zane must have beaten me to it."

Stephanie went over and sat down beside Luke. "We still have the envelope of information I copied. And Bob told me he has the missing diamonds."

That was interesting, but there were still things puzzling Renwick. "Did he say where he had them?"

Stephanie shook her head.

"Give me a few minutes with him, Captain," Luke requested. "I'll find out."

Renwick shook his graying head. "Not that way. He'll talk." His beeper sounded and he got to his feet, looking around for the phone. Quickly, he dialed. "Yeah, Randy, what've you got?" His expression blank, he listened in silence. "All right, get back to Headquarters." The captain frowned. "No one home at Westovers. We'll find them."

Stephanie groaned. "Could you get a warrant and check out the rest of the house?"

Renwick shook his head. "Anything incriminating's out of there by now, moved somewhere else or burned." He ran a tired hand over his face. It had been a long day, and it wasn't over yet.

Luke's voice was unwavering. "We still have our ace in the hole. We can —"

"Captain," Megs called from the doorway, "we've got a problem."

"What is it?" Renwick asked with a frown. If that son-of-a-bitch had escaped, he'd have Luke's hide.

There was regret on her round face as she stepped inside, avoiding Luke's eyes. "The man on the roof handcuffed to the pole is dead. He's been beaten to death."

Luke leaped to his feet. "What?"

"That can't be," Stephanie said, rising also.

"Are you sure?" Renwick asked.

Megs kept her gaze on the captain. "Yes, sir."

The young, uniformed officer appeared in the doorway, his eyes wide. "You want to come up, Captain? The man's face is a bloody mess, his clothes are ripped, his ribs are broken. He must have really pissed somebody off."

"In a minute." He turned to Luke. "Let me see your hands."

Calmly, Luke held out his hands, swollen knuckles and all. One cut was still bleeding slightly. "I only hit him a couple times, I swear it."

"I was there," Stephanie interjected. "He's telling the truth."

Renwick's expression was unreadable. "Was anyone else up on the roof with you?"

"No, just Stephanie and I."

"Then how do you explain it?"

His jaw tight with tension, Luke faced him down. "I was still in the Westover house when Zane and Chester came in. Chester said that Bob Triner had learned Stephanie and I were staying at this apartment and was on his way here. Zane said he didn't like it, that he was going to take care of the matter himself. They left. I rushed out of there and came here, found the apartment empty, the window open. They must have gotten here shortly after. When Stephanie and I left Bob handcuffed up there, they saw their opportunity and killed him. Zane knows I've been in trouble before for using my fists."

Renwick raised a skeptical eyebrow. "You're saying Zane set you up by killing one of his own men?" The

298

captain shook his head. "I don't know. How the hell are we going to prove any of that?"

Luke sat down on the couch. "I don't know."

Stephanie gripped his arm. "*I* was there, Captain. Bob Triner was alive and talking when we left him. Isn't that proof, an eyewitness?"

Renwick stuck his hands in his pants pockets as he studied her. "Mrs. Westover, you're not what we'd call the best witness. You staged your own death to get away from your husband. A judge or a jury might well believe you don't care much for him. Besides, if it turns out you're more than a little fond of Luke Varner, you'd make an even worse witness. They might conclude that you'd lie about Zane to protect Luke, wouldn't you say?"

"But I'm *not* lying," Stephanie insisted.

"I didn't say you were," Renwick assured her. "I'm only stating how a judge and jury are likely to view your actions."

"Do you want me to call for a wagon, Captain?" the uniformed officer asked from the doorway.

"Yeah, and the coroner while you're at it." Renwick paced the small room, his mind in a turmoil as Megs went to the kitchen phone. "Damn, Luke, why'd you have to hit him at all?"

Stephanie indicated Luke's torn pants, the cut on his leg. "Bob came at him with a knife. He attacked."

Renwick turned to Luke. "Before or after you shot him in the shoulder?"

"After."

"What happened to the knife?"

Luke shrugged. "I knocked it out of his hand. It's probably still up there."

The captain narrowed his eyes. "So he was disarmed and wounded. Why'd you hit him?"

Luke ran a weary hand over his face. "He'd had Stephanie at the edge of the roof. He was going to shove her over. When he came at me with the knife, I got so damn mad . . ."

Renwick nodded. "And you did it again. You lost control."

Fear rose like bile in Stephanie's throat. No, Zane couldn't be getting away with all of this. She nervously hugged herself. "This can't be happening. Why don't you find Chester and take a look at his hands? Or even Zane's?"

Luke went to her, slipping his arms around her, sharing her anxiety. "It wouldn't prove anything, honey. No witness can place either of them here at the scene of the crime."

She looked up at him, fighting tears. "But you know they did it. Bob was alive when we left. *He was.*"

He angled her head onto his shoulder. "I know."

They waited uneasily until the coroner arrived and inspected the body, coming down to Captain Renwick to report his findings. A pleasant, balding man, he looked apologetic as he spoke. "It looks like the subject died from repeated blows to the head and upper body. Jaw broken, several ribs, too. Internal ruptures likely. The gunshot wound was minor. A postmortem exam will be more conclusive, of course."

"Thanks, Doctor," Renwick said. "Tell your boys to take him downtown."

Luke walked over to gaze out the window. He felt like hitting something very hard. The blame lay with him. He'd underestimated Zane. He should have brought Bob Triner downstairs while they waited for the captain. Maybe there still would've been problems. Maybe not. Anyone's guess. When a hand touched his shoulder, he turned.

Captain Renwick stood alongside him, a full head shorter, his expression somber. "You know what I have to do, don't you?"

Luke nodded. He knew. He'd been raised on police procedure.

Megs stood and touched his arm, her eyes serious. Luke squeezed her hand, his expression unreadable.

Stephanie went to him, slid her arm around his waist

300

as she turned to look at the captain. "No, please. You can't take him in. He didn't do anything."

"Hang on, honey," Luke said. "It's not over yet."

Renwick flipped open a notebook. "You have the right to remain silent . . ."

The words blurred for Stephanie as she blinked away tears. She looked up and saw two uniformed men carrying a stretcher past the open door. Bob's body in a zippered black bag. She shuddered. The captain droned on, not making sense to her. Nothing made sense.

Her world had collapsed again.

Luke's arraignment would be as soon as possible, probably one day next week, in Recorder's Court downtown, Stephanie learned as she'd watched an unsmiling Luke driven away by Sergeant O'Malley. Captain Renwick stayed with her while she locked up Pete's apartment, then offered to drive her wherever she wished.

"Would you like police protection?" Renwick asked. "I can assign an officer to you, at least for a while. You might sleep better, and so will Luke."

Recalling the image of the houseboat blowing up into a million fragments and knowing what Zane and his men were capable of, Stephanie nodded. "Thank you." She accepted a ride to her father's house, then waited while Renwick radioed for a surveillance car.

On the ride through the dark streets, Stephanie's mind whirled with unanswered questions. "Is he going to be segregated from the other prisoners?" She hated the thought of Luke, who loved open spaces, being locked up at all, but if they put him in with convicted killers . . .

Renwick nodded. "Yeah, he will be. That's normal procedure when an officer of the law is jailed, for his protection."

Stephanie let out a relieved sigh. She knew there were plenty of men in prison who'd be carrying grudges against cops. "There is one other thing. Bob mentioned another shipment is coming in soon, the biggest one yet. Is there anything you can do to set up a watch on Zane?"

"We'll look into it."

His profile was hard and unbending, much like Luke's had been when she'd first met him. "Also, do you know a Matt Lewis?"

Renwick swung onto her father's street. "Yeah. He's a friend of Luke's and his attorney. Did he ask you to contact Matt?"

"Yes, first thing tomorrow morning. He said Matt would know what to do. What do you think Luke meant by that?"

Renwick eased the large Chrysler onto the circular drive of Stephen Sanders's home. "I learned long ago not to try to second-guess Luke Varner."

She met his gaze. "Be honest with me. What do you think Luke's chances are? Can Matt get him out of this mess, especially since he's not guilty."

Renwick shifted into park. "You really care about him, don't you?"

"Yes."

"Luke's a tough bird — and a smart one. I wouldn't count him out just yet. I'll wait here until you're safely inside."

"Thank you, Captain. I appreciate the ride."

"Don't mention it. And Stephanie, don't worry too much. Luke has a way of landing on his feet."

"I hope you're right." She hurried up the walk and rang the bell. It was nearly ten so it took a few minutes for Nettie to come to the door. When she did, she let out a squeal and drew Stephanie into a huge hug.

Stephanie struggled with her emotions as Nettie burst into tears. So much had happened since she'd last been in her father's house. It felt good being back, despite the circumstances. With a final wave to Renwick, she closed the door.

"Oh, Miss Stephanie, it's wonderful seeing you

again." Nettie dabbed at her eyes as she led her to the kitchen.

It was late, and Stephanie hadn't the strength to fight being fussed over. So they ate a little and cried a little together, especially when they talked of Stephen.

"The doctor told me just yesterday that Mr. Sanders is coming along real well," Nettie said when Stephanie headed for bed. "Won't be long and he'll be home with us, for sure."

Stephanie wished she were as certain of it, but once she was back in her old room, she made a mental list of things she had to do in the next two days.

First, she'd call Matt. Next, she'd go to the hospital and see Stephen, then talk with his doctor. Afterward, she'd stop in and have her hair dyed back to blond. Maybe if she looked more like her old self, she'd feel better.

But the uneasiness persisted. After undressing, she wrapped herself in an old robe and went back downstairs. Peering out the front window, she saw the dark unmarked car Renwick had assigned to watch over her. Its presence eased her mind somewhat, but she still went around and checked the alarm system and the door locks. Satisfied finally, she climbed the stairs again.

Turning on the shower, Stephanie wished she had a handle that she could use to turn off her mind. She was afraid, very afraid. She stepped under the spray, fighting to hang on to her control. But it slipped away like the water whirling down the drain. Bracing herself against the tiled wall, she let the tears fall

It had been a frightening day, and she feared there were more such days in store. Luke had seemed so calm as he'd kissed her goodbye, telling her to be careful and to trust him. When she'd asked what he meant by that, he'd refused to say more. She wanted desperately to believe that Matt would win Luke's freedom. But she knew Zane, knew his ruthless ways. What if Luke were to be locked up and Zane were to go unpunished?

303

No! That couldn't happen. She would not think negatively. She would trust in Luke. Closing her eyes, Stephanie whispered the remembered prayers of her childhood as the cleansing water slid down her slender frame.

The Murphy Hall of Justice on Gratiot and St. Antoine is an old building that has had many an accused within its walls, some guilty, some not. On Friday morning at twenty to nine, Stephanie walked along the polished wood floor next to Matt Lewis, her heart pounding.

It had been nearly a week since Luke had been taken from her. She'd thought the delays hideous, one after the next. First, she'd been told the hearing would be Monday, then Wednesday, finally today. She'd nearly gone crazy with worry, especially since she hadn't been allowed to see Luke. Matt had told her it would be best and had advised her to be patient.

She'd also been further unnerved by several calls from Zane. The old Zane, the one who'd courted her so romantically when they'd first met, his voice smooth as silk. He wanted to meet with her, he'd said, to have lunch with her anywhere she named if she was afraid to be alone with him. He wanted a chance to explain.

She'd refused his invitation and finally told him to stop calling. Furious, he'd snarled into the phone that she couldn't avoid him forever, that he'd see her at the hearing. When she'd mentioned their conversation to Matt, he'd smiled and looked pleased.

Matt Lewis was a thinner, younger Perry Mason, she thought, glancing over at his calm features, his brown beard tinged with gray, his conservative tweed jacket and tan slacks. He'd offered her his arm when they'd met outside the Hall of Justice, and she now clung to it, wishing she didn't need the comfort of his support, but knowing she did.

"Now, you remember what we talked about on the

phone, Stephanie?" Matt asked in his deep baritone. "No matter what Zane says, even if he comes right over to you, I don't want you to respond. Just stay calm and unruffled. That will annoy him most. And we want him annoyed. We want him to lose his temper, to show his true colors. Understand?"

"Yes." The very thought of being in the same room with Zane sent a shiver up her spine, but she struggled not to let Matt know. Luke had said to trust Matt, and she did. But that didn't stop her nerves from fluttering.

"I'll be at the front table on the right, with Luke beside me. I'd like you to sit right behind us so, if necessary, we can confer. All right?"

"Yes. But why are they letting Zane be present?"

Matt guided her around the corner toward Recorder's Court. "Because arraignments are open to the public. The prosecuting attorney will be at the table on the left. He'll list the charges, and then it'll be our turn to enter a plea of guilty or not guilty. After that, the judge will set bond."

"You're going to plead Luke as not guilty, aren't you?"

"We may not get that far." Seeing her puzzled frown, he squeezed her hand. "I can't explain any more than that, Stephanie. You're just going to have to trust me." He stopped at the double doors and looked her over. She wore a black shirtwaist dress, simple yet obviously expensive, and her blond hair curled softly around her pale face. "Would you take off your sunglasses, please?"

She did, and Matt smiled as serious blue eyes met his. "You look wonderful. Luke's been locked up six days and nights. He's worried and anxious to see you." Matt rubbed his beard thoughtfully, wondering if he should say more to her. Stephanie Westover was every inch a cool, sophisticated, moneyed woman. He'd spent hours with Luke over the past week and sensed his friend's concern. Right now, they both needed her in Luke's corner. "With you back in your father's house

305

and all, he's probably also concerned about whether you're still there for him."

Her eyes softened, making her look younger. "Where I stay is unimportant. I love Luke, and I'm definitely still there for him." Saying the words aloud seemed to reinforce what she felt.

Satisfied, Matt nodded. "Let's go inside."

Stephanie followed him in, all too aware that her internal butterflies were flitting about. She watched as Matt set his briefcase down on the table and indicated where she was to sit. Sliding onto the bench, she watched him go over and confer with the uniformed officer by the door alongside the judge's bench. Nervously she folded her hands.

In short order, several seats in the public area were taken, and Stephanie wondered who the people were and why they were here. It wasn't until a man in a rumpled jacket, carrying an expensive camera, joined them that she realized they were probably all with the press. She should have guessed, since her drowning accident had been in the papers and the news of her return had leaked to the media. She'd had calls and attempts at interviews, all of which she'd turned down. Feeling their eyes on her, she turned to face the front of the courtroom.

A heavyset man with a thick briefcase entered and moved to the table opposite Matt. Edward Langstrom, the prosecuting attorney, Matt had told her earlier. Langstrom shook hands with Matt, then took his seat.

A uniformed officer approached the bench and turned to face the small crowd, though several more people were entering at the rear. "Court will convene in ten minutes. Silence is requested, and there will be no smoking. Please be seated."

As he walked away, the side door opened and Stephanie's heart leaped into her throat. Luke walked in, wearing prison-issue dark blue pants and shirt. A uniformed police officer escorted him to a chair alongside Matt. Luke's eyes were on Stephanie and he gave her a small smile. Tears sprang to her eyes, and she longed to reach out, to touch him. Instead, she smiled back, letting him see the love in her eyes.

Matt spoke quietly to the policeman, and the man nodded before returning to his post by the door.

The gallery of visitors was buzzing; then the double doors at the rear opened again. The rumble grew louder, and Stephanie stiffened. Someone had whispered his name, and she knew Zane had arrived.

Looking like the successful businessman he pretended to be, Zane walked slowly toward the front, Chester following him. He paused at Stephanie's row, his dark eyes roving over her. She didn't acknowledge his arrival, but stared instead at Luke who'd shifted to watch Zane. Stephanie recognized the alert way Luke held himself, and she hoped he wouldn't do something foolish, worsening his case.

Zane strode forward and stopped at Matt's side. But before either could say a word, the bailiff rose.

"All rise. The Honorable Rupert D. Long presiding." Everyone stood and faced the front while the tall, white-haired judge walked out and sat down at the bench.

"Please be seated," Judge Long said. As the crowd did so, he turned to confer with the bailiff.

Taking advantage of the extra minutes, Matt looked up at Zane who was standing next to him. "What is it you want?"

Zane's gaze narrowed as he stared with hatred at Luke. "I want to see your client punished, Counselor." His voice was low, controlled.

Stephanie clutched her damp hands together as she heard several people behind her murmuring.

Calmly Matt kept himself between Zane and Luke. "We're here to see that justice is done, Mr. Westover."

"Justice?" Zane made an ugly sound. "Luke Varner stole my wife and brutally murdered my attorney and good friend. He deserves to die."

Matt reached out a hand to steady Luke, sensing he

was ready to pounce. "Mr. Westover, your wife left you of her own accord; her divorce action against you is a matter of public record. And I believe that you or your chauffeur killed Bob Triner as well as Marjo Collins."

Zane's color deepened; then he forced himself to relax. He gave Matt a cocky smile. "That's ridiculous. I've never done anything outside the law."

"Gentlemen," Judge Long interrupted, addressing both attorneys, "are you ready to begin?"

"Your Honor," Matt said, "I beg the court's indulgence a moment longer, in the interest of justice."

"Make it brief," Judge Long warned.

"Thank you, Your Honor." Matt turned back to Zane. "You say you've never done anything outside the law, Mr. Westover. You never persuaded and paid a Ralph Mallory, now in Jackson Prison, to serve time for a hit-and-run accident that you committed? You never had someone punch a hole in your wife's brake line, thereby causing her near-fatal accident? You never went to an apartment-house rooftop last Friday and had Bob Triner beaten to death in order to frame Luke Varner? And you never went to see Marjo Collins to get information on your wife, beat her, then held her under water until she drowned?"

"Boss," Chester said, hovering over his employer, "you gonna let him talk to you that way?"

"Shut up," Zane said, obviously struggling to keep his rage under control. "No, Mr. Lewis, I never did any of those things. Check me out. I've never even had a parking ticket."

"Is that right?" Matt turned and nodded toward the uniformed officer waiting by the side entrance.

The man opened the door. A striking brunette wearing a white linen suit walked into the courtroom. Pausing, she took off her sunglasses and looked directly at Zane Westover.

"Marjo!" Stephanie was on her feet, her hands trembling as they flew to her mouth. Behind her, reporters and visitors alike went from stunned silence to noisy disbelief. The cameraman quickly got off several shots before the judge's gavel sounded, demanding order.

Zane's face had gone chalk white as he staggered back several steps. His eyes widened as Marjo slowly came toward him.

"I don't die easily, do I, Zane?" Marjo asked as she stopped near Luke. "Not like Bob Triner."

Chester glanced toward the door, sweat beading on his face as he touched Zane's sleeve. "Boss, we're in trouble here."

Zane swiveled toward him, his eyes blazing.

"Your Honor," Matt said, looking toward Judge Long, "I move to dismiss the charges against my client. The prosecutor, I'm sure, will have no trouble proving Zane Westover's intent to murder Miss Collins. As to the bludgeoning death of Bob Triner by Chester Thomas that is also provable."

Judge Long pounded his gavel hard, trying for order.

Matt moved forward. "I apologize for the theatrics and thank the court for allowing this unorthodox procedure. If those charges aren't enough, sir, last evening the police arrested a Mr. Alex Quentin of Toronto at the Canadian tunnel entrance as he attempted to smuggle a large cache of diamonds into the United States. We were able to persuade Mr. Quentin to identify his partner on this side of the border. He named Zane Westover."

Judge Long banged the gavel again. "Request granted. The court officer will place Zane Westover and Chester Thomas under arrest. I'll see both attorneys in my chambers in fifteen minutes." The judge stood.

"All rise," the bailiff called out.

But the request was unnecessary for no one was still seated. The photographer was having a field day, while several eager reporters rushed out to phone their papers and others stood about scribbling madly. The prosecutor had signaled the uniformed police officer, and together they'd seated Chester and Zane at his table. Matt and Luke shook hands, then turned to watch Marjo and Stephanie embracing, both with tears running down their faces.

"Oh, God, I can't believe it," Stephanie said, her voice thick with emotion.

"Believe it, honey," Marjo said, pulling back to study her friend. "It takes more than a little shove under to kill this tough gal."

Swiping at her eyes, Stephanie reached for Luke who came over and slipped an arm about her. "You knew about this, about Marjo being alive, all along, didn't you?"

He nodded. "Yeah, I did. I arranged with Matt to keep her hidden in his hunting lodge up north. I had a hunch we'd need an ace in the hole, and Marjo was it." He glanced over at Zane, who sat slumped in his chair as the prosecutor talked with him. Chester was being handcuffed by the officer. "And it worked."

Stephanie held tightly to Marjo's hand, reluctant to release her. "But why didn't you tell me?" she asked Luke.

"For your protection and Marjo's. You can't reveal something you don't know."

Matt snapped shut his briefcase. "Luke, why don't you go change clothes while the ladies wait for you downstairs? I've got to meet with the judge. He's been wonderfully cooperative in helping us set this whole thing up. I'll join you right after. I've arranged another surprise for later."

Stephanie hugged Marjo again. "This surprise is going to be hard to top."

"Nevertheless, I think you'll be pleased," Matt said.

"Dad! You're home." Stephanie hurried to Stephen, who was seated in a wheelchair in his study. She threw her arms around him, kissing his forehead. He nodded, his eyes damp but happy.

"He still can't talk much," Luke explained as he led

310

the others in, "but the doctor said he'd recuperate faster at home. He'll have both a physical therapist and a speech therapist coming by, and nursing care. And, of course, Nettie's TLC." Luke shook Stephen's good hand. "Good to see you, Stephen."

Matt walked over and smiled at Stephanie's father. "I think you might like to greet someone else." He beckoned Marjo closer.

"Hello, Stephen," Marjo said, bending down to him.

Stephen struggled with his emotions as his good arm went around her.

"I went to his hospital room last night," Matt explained to Stephanie, "and told him what we had planned for today. He couldn't believe Marjo was alive."

"Neither can I," Stephanie commented. "In my wildest dreams, that was one possibility I hadn't thought of."

Nettie came in then, bringing coffee and a platter of her cakes. Setting the tray down, she served everyone, her lined face cheerful at having her family back again.

Stephanie was too excited to eat. Seated on the couch next to Luke, she took a sip of coffee, then turned to Matt who was busily devouring a frosted cake. "Can you really prove that Chester killed Bob Triner?" She had to know that Luke was truly in the clear.

From the other couch, Megs answered for him. "We found a button on the rooftop the morning after the beating. It was from Zane's custom-made imported suit coat."

"Right," Matt said. "And the prosecutor will subpoena Eula Johnson. It seems that Chester went to her the morning after Bob's death and asked her to tend to some wounds on his hands, telling her he'd gotten into a barroom brawl."

Luke slid an arm around Stephanie, needing the contact. "You see, honey, I called my old partner, Megs, from Florida several times to update her. I needed someone on the force I could trust who knew what was going on."

"I was glad to help," Megs answered. "I want Luke back and working."

Stephanie sent the friendly woman a grateful smile.

Luke went on to explain. "Then she'd call Matt who'd phone Marjo at his cabin so she'd know what was happening. When you told me the story of the hit-and-run and Ralph Mallory, Megs and Matt did some research on the case. Then, when you called him Saturday, Matt drove out to Jackson and questioned Mallory."

"He's running scared," Matt said. "I told him Zane was about to be put away and his payoff money would stop. He wasn't about to stay in prison and not get paid. We called in a stenographer, and he told his story, then signed the confession. So we have Zane on several things."

"Not the least of which is Marjo's near drowning," Stephanie said, turning to her friend who was busily lighting a cigarette. "How did you manage to survive?"

"Damned if I know. He'd all but dislocated my arm trying to get me to tell him where you were. When he shoved me under the water, I thought of two possibilities. Either I'd try to catch him off guard, pull him in with me, and drown him, or I'd hold my breath, go limp, and let him think I'd drowned. The second was easier, so I went with it." She turned to Stephanie. "Remember when I showed you how, when you're floating with your arms up above your head, there's this pocket of air you can tap into?"

Stephanie nodded. "I never did master that. You always could hold your breath longer than anyone."

Marjo puffed out her chest. "Great lungs."

"I'll second that," Matt said with a smile.

"But how'd you get out to Matt's cabin?" Stephanie asked.

"I waited in the pool until I was sure Zane had left. Then I went inside and phoned Luke. He told me to stay put. By the time he got there, I'd damn near finished the scotch, but I'd stopped shaking."

Luke picked up the story. "I decided to enlist Matt's aid, called him, and told him the story. He suggested I take Marjo to his hunting cabin and he'd meet us there. It would keep her safe and give us a real good weapon to use against Zane. I also called Renwick and told him everything. He bought in, told the news media that Marjo had drowned. We wanted Zane to think he was getting away with things — so he'd get careless."

"And he did," Megs added.

"You see, we knew about the smuggling, but we couldn't prove the identity of the guy on the other end. We could have nailed Zane after Marjo's attempted murder, but we wanted the man who was getting the goods in from Africa." Luke allowed himself a smile. "Did I mention how Mr. Q was smuggling this last package?"

Megs laughed. "Yeah, tell them. This is a good one."

"He had his secretary accompany him along with her six-month-old baby. He hid the diamonds in a pile of dirty diapers in a diaper bag, believing the border guards wouldn't want to check something messy. Fooled him, but good."

"Lord, I can't believe he was *that* stupid and careless," Marjo commented.

"He was that desperate," Luke answered. "We had to wait him out, which was why my hearing kept being delayed. We wanted the goods on Zane in that matter before we brought Marjo back to accuse him. A double whammy."

"Here, Mr. Stephen," Nettie said, holding the cup to Stephen's mouth. "You always loved my coffee."

Stephen sipped, then struggled with his words. "Zane here," he finally managed.

"Yes," Nettie said. "Mr. Westover and his attorney were here the afternoon of Mr. Stephen's stroke. He was upset after those two left and told me Mr. Westover had threatened him, then smiled and walked out. Shortly after, the stroke hit."

"Unfortunately," Luke said, "we can't get Zane on that one. While it's true that someone can agitate another to the point of bringing on a stroke or heart attack, it's hard to prove intent. But we have enough on Zane to put him away a long while."

More firmly this time, Stephen nodded.

"One more thing, Stephanie," Matt added. "Luke asked me to check with Charles Hastings, the attorney you hired for your divorce, to determine the status. It seems Charles never reported your so-called death to the courts. The hearing's scheduled in about two weeks. Zane would be a fool to contest it. You should have your freedom soon. Unless, of course, you're requesting a portion of his assets."

"I don't want *anything* that belongs to him. I would like to get my own things back, though if he hasn't thrown them away. My books, some old records, my mother's jewelry."

"I think we can manage to get those for you and your clothes."

Marjo snuffed out her cigarette with quick jabs. "Well, honey," she said to Stephanie, "it looks like you and I just aren't real lucky when it comes to men."

Stephanie squeezed Luke's hand. "For one of us, luck has changed recently."

Watching them, Marjo smiled. "I rather thought so. Are you going to move your things back here, or do you want to bunk in with me for a while?"

"Stephanie's grown fond of living on houseboats," Luke said, his eyes smiling into hers.

"Yes, I have. After Dad gets well — "

Stephen made a sound deep in his throat, and waved with his good hand. "Yes, go," he managed.

Beside him, Nettie nodded. "Miss Stephanie, I'll be here with your father, like I have for thirty years. You come visit him whenever you can, but you need to get on with your life."

Luke had never heard sweeter words. He drew Stephanie closer. "What do you say? You want to go

314

meet my cat?"

She smiled up at him. "Mr. Varner, I'd love nothing better. Think he'll like me?"

"If he's got any taste, he will."

Benjamin was being difficult. Luke decided he was probably punishing him for being left alone so long.

He and Stephanie had come aboard an hour ago, carrying a huge pizza and a can on Benjamin's favorite tuna. Stephanie had cut the fish up for him herself and offered it on her fingertips. He'd sauntered over, sniffed and walked away. Now he sat on his favorite footstool watching the two of them from under partially lowered lids, the food untouched in the kitchen.

"Stubborn, like his master," Stephanie commented.

"Yeah," Luke agreed, drawing her closer to him on the long couch. He was full of pizza and beer and love. He still couldn't quite believe she was here and it was almost over. He could afford to relax, to go slowly, to savor each moment.

Shifting his head, he tilted Stephanie's chin and touched his lips to hers. She responded instantly, avidly. That was one of the things he loved most about her, the lack of pretense, the absence of affectation. She wanted him as much as he wanted her, and she didn't mind showing him.

The kiss was lazy and lingering. He ran his lips down her throat and lower, into the soft vee of her cotton shirt. She was warm and wonderfully fragrant. "How come you smell so good?"

"Compared to what? The fish out there? Your unwashed cat?"

"How do you know Benjamin's unwashed?"

"Because my nose works. That old man who took care of him must live in a sewer. Tomorrow, whether Benjamin likes it or not, it's bath time."

"He's not going to like that."

"Tough. There's a woman on board now and she likes

sweet-smelling things. Benjamin will learn to love cleanliness." She leaned back, her hands staying on Luke's chest. "I hate to think of poor Casey being blown up in Florida."

"Don't think about all that. You have Benjie to fuss over now." Luke grunted as the big cat jumped up on them and began to walk along his legs. "I think he's jealous."

Rolling aside, Stephanie reached out to touch the fur on Benjamin's head. Surprisingly, he let her pet him. "Come on, old boy, there's room for you up here."

"I suppose you're going to spoil him, make him into an old softie."

"Yes, like I've spoiled you."

He took her hand, moving it down low, sighing as her fingers curled around him. "But I haven't gone soft on you."

"Mmm, no you haven't." Angling her head, she met his seeking mouth. She marveled again at how much she enjoyed this man's kisses, this man's touch. She twisted to get nearer, but Benjamin chose that moment to squirm between them. Breaking apart on a laugh, Stephanie slid her hands around the cat.

"Hey, where do you think you're going, fella?" To her further surprise, Benjamin began to purr. Lazily, she ran her fingers along his furry frame, then suddenly sat up. "Hold on a minute here." Shifting the cat into her lap, she examined the body beneath the fur, then turned to Luke with a big grin.

"I have a news bulletin for you, Detective Varner."

Luke eyed her lazily, his hand reaching out to touch her hair. "What's that?"

"Benjamin is pregnant, and very near her time, I'd say."

He frowned. "You're kidding?"

"No." She took his hand. "Here, feel this." She laughed delightedly. "Looks like we'll have a little Casey replacement soon. And we'll need to come up with a new name for the little mother-to-be."

"Well, I'll be damned." He sent the cat a mock scowl. "Benjamin, I told you not to mingle with any strange cats while I was away."

Stephanie set the cat on the floor and turned back to Luke. "Pretty funny. Weren't you the one who said you were better off without females around? It would seem you now have two to contend with."

Luke's arms tightened around her, his body pressing against hers. Pretty funny, all right. He was exactly where he wanted to be, and with the woman he wanted near him. "I'll manage somehow," he said, then lowered his head to kiss her.

PINNACLE BOOKS HAS SOMETHING FOR EVERYONE—

MAGICIANS, EXPLORERS, WITCHES AND CATS

THE HANDYMAN (377-3, $3.95/$4.95)
He is a magician who likes hands. He likes their comfortable shape and weight and size. He likes the portability of the hands once they are severed from the rest of the ponderous body. Detective Lanark must discover who The Handyman is before more handless bodies appear.

PASSAGE TO EDEN (538-5, $4.95/$5.95)
Set in a world of prehistoric beauty, here is the epic story of a courageous seafarer whose wanderings lead him to the ends of the old world—and to the discovery of a new world in the rugged, untamed wilderness of northwestern America.

BLACK BODY (505-9, $5.95/$6.95)
An extraordinary chronicle, this is the diary of a witch, a journal of the secrets of her race kept in return for not being burned for her "sin." It is the story of Alba, that rarest of creatures, a white witch: beautiful and able to walk in the human world undetected.

THE WHITE PUMA (532-6, $4.95/NCR)
The white puma has recognized the men who deprived him of his family. Now, like other predators before him, he has become a man-hater. This story is a fitting tribute to this magnificent animal that stands for all living creatures that have become, through man's carelessness, close to disappearing forever from the face of the earth.